I0748977

Murder in Maverick Bay

Louise Furley

Murder in Maverick Bay

ISBN: 979-8-9953581-0-7 (Paperback)
ISBN: 979-8-9953581-1-4 (eBook)
ISBN: 979-8-9953581-2-1 (Hardcover)

Cover by: Amanda at Pixelmischiefdesign
Photo: Shutterstock

ALSO BY LOUISE FURLEY

Mafia Romance

Distilled Duplicity
His Winnings
Adara
Jozadak

Satan's Brood

Devil's Prince
Devil's Seed

Dutch Military Special Forces

Jungle Treasure
Jancarlo

Medieval

Cini and the Beast
Kultur's Keep
The Butcher Princess

Other titles

Jezábel and the Assassin

Bay's Bet

Solitar

Halo Valley

Jace's Elusive Woman

Isle of Orainn

Neco's Rescue

Anastasia

The Kissing Number

Murder at Red Gem Farm

Murder in Maverick Bay

Blood is Slicker than Water

Capturing Dove

Auction Block

The Poser

Wrath of Wolf

Shawn's Prisoner

Rogan's Desire

Liquid Velvet

Vijay

The Sapphire Bell

This book is dedicated to Bob, my hero.
And to Aaron, you will be forever loved and missed.

Murder In Maverick Bay

Chapter One

Giancomo Montanero raced with his troop, boots pounding dirt, ear-splitting gunfire rata-tatting above and all around them. Bullets pinged off trees flinging fragments like zinging wooden missiles.

Two choppers were in sight. They whirred only a few hundred feet away flattening grass and spinning leaves and dirt in a whirlpooled circle beneath them.

Gian heard rapid gun blasts and screams behind him. He stalled and glanced back. His eyes widened in horror then narrowed in defiance. "Hell no!" he yelled and started to turn.

"You can't help them, Gian!" his best friend Torrand Kristo barked, shoving him forward. "We have the rest to get to safety, bro, we gotta hurry, don't look back!"

But Gian did look back and he saw two of his men crumple to the ground. In seconds their clothes blossomed red with gushes of blood. He could see their mottled bodies shot full of holes, eyes already staring blankly up at the unforgiving heavens. Such a barrage of ammo, their limbs had literally been blown apart.

Gian shouted, "We can't leave them here!" Spraying the area with rapid gunfire to hold the rebels at bay, he ran back to the downed soldiers. He bent and reached for the first man's shoulder-

Torr shoved him again hard, yelling, "Leave them, we have to go, Gian, we have to save the others!"

Wiping sweat from his eyes, Gian nodded then snagged the dog tags off both destroyed necks. Stuffing them in his pocket, he raced after what was left of his team.

Twenty-four pairs of heavy boots thundered over the clumpy grass as they reached the open field, the men ducking gunshots and shrieks of fury from the rebels chasing at their heels. Firepower rained down on the rebels from the choppers forcing the infidels to run for cover into the forest.

Two thick ropes descended from each of the hovering choppers. The ropes had harnesses that were spaced 24-inches apart in increments down the length of the ropes, 6 on one side of the ropes and 6 on the other.

Catching up to his fleeing men and surpassing them, Gian grabbed a rope reeling down from one of the helicopters and helped the first man into a harness. His team was silent but for the panting and grunting as they were clamped into the harnesses and quickly lifted off their feet as the soldiers in the chopper winched up the rope they hung from.

Shouts and screams came from behind them as the insurgents broke from the thick canopy of forest and resumed firing at the chain of defenseless soldiers dangling in the air.

Gian and Torr gave cover, returning fire, forcing the rebels to duck back into the protection of the vine-garbled thicket.

The rebels hurled their outrage from the refuge of the wide leaves, firing their weapons aimlessly hoping to strike the soldiers. As soon as the first 12 men were safely inside a chopper, that bird took flight and was instantly a dot in the sky.

The remaining men attached to the second rope were being frantically hauled up to the waiting chopper. Gian clamped Torr into a harness, then grabbed ahold of the last swinging harness and bellowed up to the pilot "*Go- go- go*!"

The rope rapidly ascended, pulling most of the secured men up and into the chopper. An arm wrapped around the rope and a gun in each hand, as he rose, Torr showered the area with gunfire while Gian wrangled his own harness.

There wasn't time to hook himself into the belt. Gian wrapped one arm around the harness, and swinging wildly, he fired relentlessly into the forest as the soldiers hastily drew up the last long rope with the GIs attached to it like a string of camo-colored pearls.

The helio's ratcheting blades whooshed above, gusting spiraling wind and noise as they circled the machine and suspended men, exacerbating the tension filled chaos in the dusky eve.

Each man was swiftly dragged inside. Gian almost there, hands reached down as they shouted to him to grab ahold.

Below the swirling machine, the insurgents raced out from the concealing woods and fired up at the chopper. Bullets slammed into the metal body near his head and his swinging feet while Gian tried to scramble up the last foot of rope to safety inside.

Taking on fire, the pilot launched the chopper forward into warp speed, flinging Gian from the rope that suddenly whipped from his grip - the gun flew out of his grasp- Soldiers shouted and Gian cursed as several pairs of hands grabbed his flailing arms, catching him just as he went airborne.

Latching on, they snatched him up and he was almost inside when bullets found their target and blasted into his lower body.

Gian bit back screams of agony as his men hauled him roughly inside the speeding chopper.

The last thing Gian saw before he blacked out was Torr's sweaty face shouting down at Gian to not leave him.

Chapter Two

Ten Months Later
Marine Corps Base, Quantico

"You don't have to hang it all up, Sergeant," Colonel Wichek said, watching Gian packing his duffle that was perched on the end of a bunk. "You earned the Silver Star and the Purple Heart, son, it wasn't your fault some men were lost."

The colonel was a poster picture of an older marine, grey buzz cut, heavy brow bone, thick shoulders and hard eyes.

Shoving a stack of folded shirts into the duffle, Gian grunted. "Good men. My men, my team. I was responsible for them. All of them. And they're dead."

"You lost five, Sergeant, but you brought home all the others. It was you that got them through the jungle, it was you that covered them while they escaped into the chopper. You fulfilled the mission. It was you that-"

"Corporal Kristo did it too, Colonel." Gian lifted a pair of boots and shoved them into the bag.

"And he got his stars too." Colonel Wichek sighed. "And," he said, clasping his hands behind his back, "he's giving up his contract as well, accepting an Honorable Discharge, like you. Torrand eats the guilt just like you."

Gian stared at a plaque behind Wichek's head. His eyes were blank, not seeing the eagle with the American flag in its talons. His shoulders flinching, Gian's hooded eyes flit back and forth as if he was reliving the whole horrid event. Watching his men die all over again.

Wichek kept on at him. He raised his voice, speaking louder to pull Gian from the past.

"But, Sergeant, we need extraordinary soldiers like you. America needs exceptional warriors like you two. Not everyone can be the elite, a damned Raider, a Marine Raider. One of the Marine Special Operations Regiment, the MSOR. You aren't a dime a dozen, boy, you're cream of the crop, one in a million, a trillion, you-"

"Enough." Gian sighed. "With all due respect, Colonel, enough. It's done. My plane leaves at 8 tonight."

"Son, listen, don't hang this guilt trip on yourself. Hell, even as young as you were, underage, when you came into service you were already one of the toughest, the coldest, one of the most dangerous men I'd ever met. They say you grew up practically as a toddler in one of the most vicious gangs in Shanghai. Your sheet said your mother disappeared with you and left your brothers with your father back in Maine. He was a-what was he…" his eyes squinted as he tried to recall Gian's history.

"A lobster fisherman."

The colonel chuckled. "Don't hear a lot of those around, right? Anyway," he said, losing the smile, "your mother, I read, had mental illness. She left you on a street corner when you were just a toddler. Supposedly, one day she just forgot you were there and she wandered off-"

"I don't need this happy trip down memory lane, Colonel. My plane-" Gian's phone rang. He fished it out, answered with a clipped, "Montanero."

"Honey GG," a female voice purred into the cell.

Frowning, Gian demanded coldly, "Who is this?"

Annoyance in her voice, the woman responded, "Really? You don't recognize my voice? GG-"

"No. Speak quick, I'm busy. And drop the GG crap."

"Huh," she snorted. "Well, honey, get unbusy. This is Britnee Knoxy. You remember, about 6 months ago you were on a short leave. You recollect that skanky bar in Singapore, the

Sungai Malam; called River Nights in English. You were," she laughed, "trashed. You stumbled in with a few of your Raider buds." She coughed into the phone.

"Listen, Britnee, I'm on my way out-"

"Apparently, a mission had gone boots over ass and some men bit it and you were drowning your sorrows after leaving the hospital. They said you got some kinda star for heroism or some BS, but that you were shot to hell. I got lucky they didn't blow up the important parts, you know what I mean." Garish giggles tumbled through the cell.

"What do you want, Britnee? A two-time pump and jump doesn't entail phone calls."

An angry huff came through the line. "Nice, GG, real nice. Anyway, I'm calling to tell you that you left me a little present."

Gian's eyes shifted to the interested gaze of his colonel. "I didn't leave you crap, Britnee, check with one of your other hundreds of men. I always use a rubber, no matter how drunk I am. You got a disease you-"

"Yeah, well, you passed out and, well, I was feeling amorous and wanted one more jaunt with you before you woke and split. So, I sort of…well…"

Gian felt the heat rising up his neck, the pit of his stomach pinching. "Spit it out, Britnee, get to the damned point."

"Geesh, fine already, still got the patience of a gnat. Okay, big boy. You're gonna be a daddy. I want a marriage certificate, and I want to be taken care of for the rest of my life. Starting right now."

Silence gagged him. His head spun with her words. A child? No way. Never in his plans to have a family. The way his own life had been split a thunder and he was dumped on the mean streets as practically a babe? No effing way.

But he couldn't bring himself to say the word abortion. And he couldn't tell her to take a hike. She was carrying his child. His blood. He couldn't let what happened to him happen to a child of his.

"I want proof. Where are you? And, I don't want you, but I will take the child." He knows some people who would be biting at the bit to help him raise a tile tot.

"Huh. Sure, big boy. The kid stays with me, we're a package deal. Not that I want the snot-ridden brat, but it'll be worth something to you, I wager, to pay my keep as its mum. I am still in Singapore, can't shake the filth of this land from my kitten heels for God's sake."

"Because, you cheated on your husband on your honeymoon and he dumped your whore ass and filed an annulment before he even returned to the States." Why he remembered that tidbit of useless info he didn't know.

She grunted. "He couldn't forgive one or two measly indiscretions for crying out-"

"I don't care about your sordid history, Britnee. Just give me your address." He grabbed a pen off the table by the bed and a napkin and wrote down what she said. Disconnecting, he dropped the phone in his pocket and zipped up the duffle.

"Well, well, son." His hands on his hips the colonel shook his head with the hint of a chuckle. "Sounds like life isn't going to give you a breather."

He followed Gian as he tossed the duffle over his shoulder and headed for the door. "Since I can't talk you into staying in the Raiders, what are your plans after your discharge?"

Gian eyed the older man respectfully. Colonel Wichek was in his fifties. He had a body of iron and a grey crew-cut, piercing blue eyes that studied him under thick grey brows.

"I put feelers out. I have a position offered with a sheriff's office. With my rank and history, after the academy I start as a patrolman then I was told I could study right away and jump grades to detective. We'll see."

"Corporal Kristo going with you?"

A quick nod, he answered, "Yes. Torr was also offered a position. I've had officer as well as military police training so I will make detective quicker, but he will soon catch up. We hope to be partners."

He paused and faced Wichek. "Colonel, I appreciate all you've done for me, for my team. You are a distinguished and honorable man, and it has been my pleasure and honor to have served under you."

They saluted for the last time and Gian headed for his jeep. As he hopped in behind the wheel, he pulled out his phone to change his flight plans.

Chapter Three

A day later, Gian rented a car in Singapore and hunted down Britnee's address.

The neighborhood was in an ugly derelict hood with hookers on one corner, dealers on the other, and meth labs shared with crack dens lining the streets between.

It was a dark and gloomy day, matching his mood. A stomach-churning stench wafted through his open car window, trash bounced sluggishly down the street in the languid humid breeze. Dilapidated buildings with shot-out windows crept along both sides of the filthy pot-holed asphalt.

First thing, he was getting Britnee and his son, or daughter, the hell out of the squalid hovel she was decaying in. No child of his was going to live and be raised like he himself had been. At first, the shock of what Britnee had declared stunned him with disbelief. Then denial. But he'd had time to ruminate on it on the flight over.

Now, pictures of him tossing a ball to a laughing boy, a catcher's mitt on his tiny hand, or teaching a little daughter how to ride a bike had played in his mind. It scared the living hell out of him, yet spawned a hint of- excitement? Joy? The thought of a family of his very own, people he belonged to, his heart defrosted just the slightest.

He barely knew his brothers and father only seeing them periodically while on leave. It had taken them a couple of years to track him down. But they lived in the States, and he…he had no real home. Battle and surviving were his home.

After his mother deserted him on a street corner, before he could starve to death or someone grabbed him off the street and sold him into a life of child prostitution, a gang member thought he'd make a cute mascot for their group and plucked him up. And that was it.

The men in the gang had no use for a child and didn't know what to do with him. Yet they kept him just for fun and someone to mess with. A gopher to fetch for them like a dog. Some just wanted to see how being raised in a gang would affect a youngster.

Brought up by unscrupulous gangbangers that had no idea how to care for a child, if it hadn't been for their various wives and club girls he wouldn't have survived. But even their existence was a precarious revolving door at best.

One of the older gang members called Rabbi had been a teacher so at least he had some schooling. Through online testing Gian managed to obtain his GED.

At 15 he purchased forged documents, joined the Marines, and got the hell out of dodge. Quickly though, he found out that gang hell had only partially prepared him for combat in the jungles, deserts and mountains of foreign countries. Same hell, different locations.

Following the GPS to the address Britnee had given him, he parked the car in front of a ramshackle shack. The front door hung by one hinge; shards of glass littered the brown weeds that grew under the broken windows. Crushed beer cans and cigarette butts were about as plentiful as blades of grass.

"Great," he muttered, making his way to the entrance of the beige dump. Nudging the open door wider with the toe of his boot, Gian stuck his head inside and glanced around.

It was dark, and it smelled. Of everything. Booze, smoke, rotten food, urine, vomit. He peered inside, and his stomach revolted. There was blood. Everywhere. The floor, the walls, and on and around the body lying on the floor by the ratty sofa.

If he hadn't seen a hell of a lot worse things in his stint as a Raider he might have flinched, or balked. But he had. His brain and heart were forged in blood and guts.

The last mission he had been involved with overseas had, in the books, been a success. A nest of terrorists had been slaughtering a village in the mountains between Iran and Turkey. The terrorists had hidden, imbedding themselves into the mountains. Pockets of them had secreted away in forests and caves.

The countries had their own armies, but due to their ghostly lethal reputation, the Raiders were called in to assist. Their specialty was finding needles in haystacks so to speak, cockroaches in dung hills, ferret them out, and quickly dispose of them.

They had been able to suppress the terrorists, but a troop of local rebels five times the amount of soldiers Gian led, and with ten times the firepower had come out of nowhere, an ambush. The intel fed to Gian and his troops had been horrendously inaccurate.

The Raiders weren't sent there to fight the natives, so per their orders they had to flee, leaving behind the bodies of three of their own massacred men at the initial battle impact, and the two more that had been butchered as they made for the choppers. The others made it with only minor wounds. Except for Gian who spent months recovering from the gunfire.

Unfortunately, Gian lost five men in that mission due to the erroneous information. He'd seen limbs blown off and daggers stabbed through eyeballs before it was over.

Men he had known well, lived with, fought beside, joked and teased, lost money with in card games when times were slow. He'd seen pictures of their wives, children, pets, knew their hopes and dreams.

Their faces haunted him. The guilt was overwhelmingly debilitating if he let it creep in. Worse, the idiots that had sent the half-assed intel down the pike received nothing more than a tiny hand slap.

Their CO had insisted the wildness of the country, the rugged brutal land, the unknown rebels were precarious and obscure, and therefore it had been easy to miss some vital aspects and misinterpret the volume of the rebels. Right. Tell that to his dead mates.

Gian had left the Raiders behind and his future was going to be in the town of Maverick Bay in Chicory Landing County, Maine, with a whore to be his wife, and a bundle of his likely born drug-addicted blood to raise. However, it was clear now that those cards had folded.

Britnee lay in her own blood. Glazed eyes open, perpetual sneer still on the lips that had sought his company that night he had been on leave. He had a fuzzy recollection of skinny hips and fake breasts and that glossy sneer.

He'd been so drunk, he hadn't remembered really what she looked like, or her name. She'd just been easy. Had just about leapt into his lap and begged to get it on with him. He'd woken in a dank hotel room, had quickly dressed and stumbled out with a huge hangover.

She'd chased him down after, though, wouldn't take no for an answer. Cried, carried on until he gave in. Unaware she'd drugged his drink, that was the night he evidently impregnated her. She'd wanted someone to take care of her, support her, and she'd used his state of semi-unconsciousness to cement it.

Although drugged, he had still apparently been able to get it up. And now, just as soon as it started, his becoming a father, it was over. The loss became a deep, throbbing, black hole in his heart. The throbbing soon expelled until his heart, which wasn't much to begin with evaporated into an unfeeling splinter of iron.

He stood beside Britnee's prone body. A knife protruded from her swollen abdomen. Her face was bruised, beaten. Her skin had been sliced and diced before the knife ended in her stomach. There was no way to save the baby, it looked like Britnee had been dead for hours.

A sound turned his head. A man sauntered into the room scratching his belly, a can of beer in his dirty hand. He wore a soiled, yellowish tank undershirt, and stained holey jeans. He was barefoot. Britney's blood was splattered over his clothes, caked on his feet, even his face. He halted when he saw Gian.

"Who the hell-"

"You killed her?" Gian asked calmly.

Then man glanced down at the dead body and shrugged. His scratching hand moved from his big belly to between his legs. "What's it to you? What the hell are you doing here? You wanna buy some smack?" he asked with boredom in his voice. He was gangly with a beer gut and stringy greasy hair that hung over his rancid bleary eyes.

"The girl, Britnee, why did you kill her?"

Shrugging one shoulder, he said, "Yeah. Skank whore got herself knocked up. Not even my kid, she said. How am I supposed to make money off her while she's fat as a Thanksgiving turkey? Huh?"

He chugged the beer, wiped his mouth with the back of his hand, belched and rubbed his belly again. "Huh. Coulda used the kid, but hell, woulda taken a couple years anyway before I could put him on the streets and earn some bucks. Until then, he's money outta my pocket, yeah?"

The filthy man grunted. "Called herself Britnee Knoxy, what a joke. Her real moniker is Bethel Knoxville. Thought Bethel was too churchy and Knoxy was like foxy, bigger sell. Girl's a trip, right?"

"You-"

The drug-dealing pimp cut him off. "Said she got some chump on a string. That you?" He sniggered. "Well, too damned bad for you. Or good, depends on how you look at it. Dodged a bullet, boy. Lucky you. Really. Hooker and a diaper pooper?" Sniffing coarsely, he spat on the floor near Britnee's head.

"Who would want that mess? 'Sides it was a boy, coulda made more money with a bitch. Little girls are the hottest commodity doncha know. Now," he said, and thunked the can on a table, "you wanna buy some dope? If not, get the hell out and take that bloody mess with you."

"Thing is, I didn't give a whit about Britnee, chump, but I did care about my child." Gian stomped up to him, and before the man could react, Gian put his hands on either side of his head and twisted.

The man's neck cracked loudly, then he slumped to the raggedy worn rug.

The police will assume it was a drug deal gone back and good riddance to bad rubbish. If the Law comes after Gian, he won't fight the charges. He'll accept the consequences, but he wasn't going to parade himself at the police station in a foreign country.

Gian moved over and stood stoically gazing at Britnee's swollen belly and shook his head. He strode out of the slum, the open door swung loosely hanging by the one hinge making a rusty squeaking sound behind him.

Firing up a cigarette, he toked hard.

Tilting his head back, he blew the smoke straight up and shoved what might have been into the lost recesses of his mind and started for home.

Chapter Four

Seven Years Later

"**O**ne more drink, Gian," Amadeo Montanero said to his brother. "You worked that last case for eight months straight. What'd you get, 3 maybe 4 hours of sleep a night in all that time?"

Gian grunted and picked up his drink.

Shaking his head, Amadeo, Deo to his friends, chuckled. "You knew right from the start it was the singer Carlita's agent, Lindy, who did in Carlita's estranged husband, when the evidence pointed to Carlita."

Gian nodded, tossing back his tumbler of Johnnie Walker Black. "Yeah. Carlita's defense attorney pushed for a new trial claiming shoddy police work. I was tasked with reviewing the case for the appeal."

"And you caught what no one else did."

"Huh." Gian snorted. "A blind man could see through the agent's planted evidence. A tissue with Carlita's lipstick on it found under the body, a button from her dress by the front door, the gun from the singer's own nightstand with her prints on it. Either Carlita was the stupidest, laziest killer in the universe or she was being framed."

Deo took a slurp of his own drink and grinned. "What made you suspect the agent?"

Shrugging, Gian replied, "She'd had a string of affairs with other clients, all female. On the initial interviewing videos of Carlita I watched, Lindy was supposedly there for moral support. However, I saw the fierce way she stared at Carlita. Intense anger. But why? Why would she be so angry at her client?"

"Why indeed," Deo said with a droll chuckle. "Too bad the first detective didn't catch it or even review his own tapes. Or the DA for that matter."

"Yeah. So, I did some research and discovered that Carlita and Lindy had had an affair. Carlita had dropped Lindy and was going back to her husband, Craig. Typical woman scorned. Lindy killed the husband to hurt Carlita, and framed her so she could never take another lover. Well, outside of prison anyway."

"One thing to have a theory, another to find evidence." Deo raised his hand to the bartender and ordered two beers for them to go along with the Johnny Black.

"True that. I pulled tons of videos from around Carlita's neighborhood, and Lindy's car showed up several times on the convenience store camera at the intersection near Carlita's street. Canvassing the neighbors, we garnered doorbell camera footage that showed Lindy sneaking into Carlita's garage. Then we saw Carlita's husband, Craig, come home, pull into the garage and Lindy rush out a few moments later.

"Craig's mother had stopped by ten minutes later to visit and had discovered his body in the garage. The early canvassing dug up nothing as half the neighbors weren't home when our officers went to question them and didn't return calls from the cards the cops left. The detective in charge of the case left it at that. He didn't dig deeper. He felt the evidence was a slam dunk so why waste more time on it?"

"You went several steps further," Deo said, raising his glass in a cheer for well done.

"On the verge of retirement, that detective was lackadaisical with investigating cases. Because of his pure laziness and the DA's sloppy work the defendant was going to spend 25 to life in prison for a crime she didn't commit."

"Which you, of course, decided not to let happen." Deo smirked with a nod and clinked his glass with Gian's.

"Right. I initiated a second more intense canvass and we captured the evidence we needed placing Lindy at the scene. I served a warrant to search her house and found the shoes she'd worn still containing Craig's blood splatter on them. She ultimately confessed at the stack of evidence we were developing."

"Good job, my brother," Deo praised. "It was like one of your first cases while training as a detective that gave you a boost up to move quickly into full detective."

"The original one was my first undercover case. I don't care much for undercover work, you're mostly lying and living a false life. It's never been in my makeup to lie. I have no patience with it. If I or anyone else can't handle the truth then it's pointless and time consuming. It's just easier all around to speak the truth. Someone doesn't like it, they'll get over it. I don't care."

Agreeing with a hefty nod, after draining his glass, Deo said, "Listen, it's been months since you've stopped by the old homestead and visited pa. He follows your cases in the news. You've had some big profile assignments and cleared them all. He's very proud of you. You need to set some time aside to see him, he's not a young guy anymore."

Ignoring his brother's silence, Deo went on, "All us brothers are in Dad's lobster business, hell, bro, who can turn down lobster? We're having a huge clambake with all the fixings; lobster, clams, potato salad, mac and cheese, corn on the cob, burgers, beer, you'll love it. You have to come."

Gian signaled the bartender for two more scotches. He sipped his cold beer while waiting for the harder stuff.

With a short shake of his head, he said in an accent vastly different from his brother's, "It's not that easy, Deo, you know. I didn't grow up here with you all. I was an adult before I realized I had a family. I'm…" he paused, stared at the glass in his hand. "It's awkward. I don't know how to deal…with, around a family. I've never had one."

In fact, it was his friend Torrand who had found the notices on social media of a family searching for a long-lost brother, a son that had disappeared with his mother 17 years ago.

There were pictures of the Montanero family, and Gian looked like the spitting image of his father and brothers. Knowing Gian's background, Torr couldn't ignore the name Montanero so he contacted Amadeo Montanero and provided Gian's DNA to sample.

Amadeo, that is Deo, immediately enacted linking with Gian, eventually hooking their family back together.

It proved futile for Gian to ignore both Torr's and his searching brothers' requests for connection. It was a bit unfulfilling however, as they've never located his mother whom he really doesn't even remember since he was so young when she dumped him. They don't even know if she was still alive.

When Gian left the Marines, he moved to San Diego to begin employment as a police office. After constant pleadings of his family to join them, he finally gave in and transferred to Maine to be near the family he hadn't even remembered having.

For quite a while he kept his distance from his newly discovered family as he achieved a career in law enforcement, but the last year he had allowed them to push themselves into his life.

He hadn't even been four yet when his mother had left with him and traveled from Maine to LA, and then somehow she shacked up with a sailor and he managed to get them to Shanghai before deserting them.

After months of going from shelter to shelter, she had left Gian on that street corner and he ultimately grew up in a gang before entering the military back in the U.S.

He knew his name from a fragmented piece of food stamp application found in his pocket, and learned he was a U.S. citizen, but was in the dark as far as knowing he had any family.

He never would have searched for any anyway. His own mother ditched him, he assumed any family he might have apparently had cared just as little about him too.

His days from as far back as he could remember were pure combat. Fighting was all he'd ever known, from a toddler on the street and on up. Even now as a cop his life was one ongoing battle. But these days he fought wearing a suit and tie.

He thought back to the child, the son, he had been eager to raise, before the fetus was so cold-bloodedly murdered because the child's mother was a greedy whore. He had been ready, excited even to take on the role of father.

It had been snatched from him, the opportunity, and he'd be damned if he would ever put himself, his heart, in that vulnerable position again, to be hurt. He hadn't even met the baby and he'd felt like he'd taken a hatchet to the heart at the loss.

He'd never had anything of his own, he was used to living that way, he was resigned to a lonely life. Sure he had friends, and now brothers and a father and a stepmother he was getting to know, but still, he would always be on the outside, it's just the way he'd learned to be.

Being part of a savage gang and then constant warfare didn't lend to cozy, easy living. But he'd known no other way, it was who he was. It helped make him a good detective. Removing all emotion enabled him to stay objective and unreactive.

"You've always had a family, Gian. We've always been here, waiting for you to come home. It's been a few years since we found you. We're finally making headway on becoming the brotherhood we were robbed of. What you need now is a woman, a steady girl. Stop hittin' and splittin' the broads. There, what about that honey over there? Babe is smoking, burns my eyes just looking at her."

Gian turned to look where his brother indicated. A few feet down the bar, a golden blonde was paying for a take-out order, she held her cell to her ear. He said with a grunt, "Not my type."

Deo's dark eyes rounded. "Not your type? Are you kiddin' me? Long silky curls, curves that go on for days, legs that should have their own zip code and blue eyes like a baby doll's. That girl was made for a man's bed."

"Exactly. Too beautiful, too soft. I prefer brunettes, blondes are too…prissy. And I like a sturdier woman, strong, athletic, rock climbers, surfers, even a bit on the plain side. A girl that can take care of herself, one that I don't have to worry she's going to attract every dog in town and cheat on me left and right."

Britnee had been pretty and blonde, who needed that kind of rubbish? Although Britnee's cheap trashy looks paled considerably beside the woman at the counter.

But Britnee had been hard, tough, that other woman, Gian gave her another once over. Her back was to them now. His gaze lowered from her tiny waist to her butt and heat unexpectedly roiled through his loins.

Britnee's skinny hips could not compete with a behind shaped like a perfect, damned upside-down heart- he looked away. Like he said, too delicately sexy, too soft, not his type.

At least Britnee was tough, took care of herself. Except for her pimp, apparently she wasn't quite tough enough. Whatever. What he didn't need was a permanent woman clinging to his arm, and that babe at the bar was the permanent kind.

"Cheat on you?" Deo snorted. "Since when did you care if a girl left your bed and hopped straight into another's?"

"My point. I don't care. You get a steady girl and then you have to care about that stuff." He glanced at the girl again.

"Hot ones like that think the world revolves around them. They think they snap their fingers and you come running. No thanks. Besides, I don't chase women, they come after me. You see, the plainer the girl, the harder she tries, and she's used to men only wanting one night and moving on. The really hot ones expect you to buy them breakfast the next morning and call them every day. No thanks."

"Bro, I think all those years first in the gang and then the Raiders damaged your idea of a healthy relationship. You only hooked up with barflies, hookers, or combat camp followers. Those weren't real ladies, Gian, you don't know what a real lady is like, and how to treat one."

The four Montanero brothers were almost cookie cutter. They inherited their dark hair and eyes from both parents, but their strapping muscular builds were from their father, Jedediah.

Gian's violent years on the mean streets as a child and then the savage life in special opts combat honed his body to an elite, brutal fighting machine. Harsh events sharpened the angles of his callous face. They etched the hard glitter in his almost ebony eyes, and carved the grim line of his masculine lips.

Those lips curled with distaste. "That's right, I don't. Ladies give me the willies. All soft and delicate," he gave a faux shiver. "Even Jessica. I have to remember not to curse and spit around her, smoke outside."

"Come on, you like Dad's wife. Jessica, Mom to us. Sweet and kind, she's strong but hides her muscles in her spine. She gets things done without being a bully or a bitch. She's the best thing to happen to Dad, and to us. She came along when we were infants and needing a mom.

"You weren't quite 4 when our mother Dyana took you, and lost you. I was only 2, Reece 13 months and Josh just popped out way premature. Dyana didn't even wait for him to get released from the hospital before she took you and split. Dad hired a private detective to find you, but he didn't realize Dyana had eventually taken you as stowaways overseas."

"It's no big deal, Deo."

Deo looked at Gian, his eyes glimmered with sorrow. "I'm sorry you missed out on…" Deo hesitated, "having a mother's love to hold you, guide you, love you. If you grew up with Dad and Jessica you would have learned what love and trust and relationships are about. You-"

"Enough with the head-shrinking, Brother. To be honest, I'm glad I missed all that soft, sweet crap. I didn't need it when I was a kid, the streets looked after me, and I sure as hell don't need it now. A woman has her uses, ah, make that use. They have one use. I can cook for myself, send out my laundry and hire a maid to clean up."

"And you hire for sex too when you want it quick and don't want to bother with the niceties women require. By the way," Deo smirked at his brother and said, "you can't cook for zip, and you forget to drop off your laundry. You're doing good when you have Minnie come in every other week to clean your apartment."

He inclined his head to the blonde he'd been referring to. "Go on, give her a try, a face like a peach rose and a body that can't-"

At that moment the young woman started yelling, "No Nana- no! Stop it! You stay right there, do not move until I get there? Can you hear me?" She paused then shouted, "I said stay there!"

Gian's lip curled wryly. "See what I mean? Expects everyone to do what she says, what *she* wants, self-centered chit. She's giving some chick named Nancy or some guy named Nathan hell. Yeah, probably some love-sodden sap. Give me a plain Jane any day. They whisper around you they want to please you so badly, and don't expect you to be there when the sun rises the next day."

"Gian-"

"I have to go." He drained his glass and set it on the bar. Pulling out his wallet he dropped some bills beside the glass.

"Fine, yeah, whatever." Deo reminded him, "Next Saturday is the clambake. You have to come. You have brothers besides Dad who want to see you. We work hard too, Gian. We may not be cops chasing down thugs on the street but you think pulling in lobster traps and all that goes with it on the high seas in the scorching sun or freezing sleet from before dawn to after dusk is easy? So, no excuses, I'll see you Saturday."

"Geesh, all right, just to get you off my back, I'll put in an appearance." His head lowered, Gian peered over at the young blonde that was going out the door still yelling into her phone.

Her face was red. Gian could only assume it was a tantrum due to petulance or distemper and not from embarrassment of acting like a belligerent shrew.

Not his problem, thank God.

Chapter Five

***"H**ey Josh," Reece Montanero called out to his younger brother as Josh was tossing long rubber gloves and his baseball hat on top of a pile of traps they'd stacked on a wagon on the deck. "I'll shut everything down here and you go grab the truck."

The secured boat still hummed in its slip at the Kifpu Wissei Marina. Painted boldly in broad red letters along the side of the boat was **Seabug** with the g in the shape of a red lobster.

Fingers damp and dirty, Josh swiped his hair back with his wrist, eying the collection of lobster traps sitting in the wagon the marina had for hauling articles to and from people's boats.

"Gonna take more'n two weeks to clean all of those. Can't wait. Be a week of soaking and scraping just to get the weeds and junk off of 'em." He gave his brother a crooked grin then jogged off to the truck.

It was growing dark, near twilight. The briny air stung Reece's nostrils, the brisk wind slapped his exposed arms in the shirt he'd cut the sleeves off and whipped his dark hair. He lifted the last of the lobster traps out of the 87-foot Pilothouse that was tied to the dock.

"Thank goodness we only had to bring in these few dozen stray traps, that we grabbed all the main ones last week," he muttered out loud. "Heaven forbid we drag the deckhands out of Swabby's to help out."

He chuckled to himself. "Yeah, pulling a sailor from a dive bar to haul in just a few traps would be like trying to corral a pack of stray Tomcats that sniffed out a female in heat in an alley."

It was so late, the Kifpu Marina was bereft of sound or activity. A handful of lights glowing mutely through hazy windows here and there showed only a few people were still around. Most likely people that lived aboard their crafts were settled in for the night.

The boats bobbed quietly on the water, even the gulls were nestling down, their constant swooping and cawing silent for the moment. The marina was quiet but the nearby bar, Swabby's Deck, occasionally resounded with music and bouts of laughter when the door opened.

Leaning over the edge of the boat, Reece set the trap near the pile already there. He paused when he heard a clinking sound, along with a weird clicking.

Due to the utter silence the faint noise stood out, sounding like several miniscule tinkling cymbals. It stopped when he did.

His head twitched and he caught a flash of movement behind him. Ignoring the vague distraction, he turned toward the bow-

Bang bang

At the truck, Josh's head popped up. "Was that gunfire?" It also sounded like a faint cry of pain followed the shots. A blur of indistinct color moved, blending into the trees surrounding the parking lot.

His nose wrinkled from a scent that floated on the breeze. No other sound, except a vague tinkling and odd clicking noise could be heard.

He shook his head and opened the door, mumbling, "Fools shooting at street signs or pigeons again. Someone needs to take a belt to those delinquents."

Then he smiled. "Nothing we didn't do when we were teen-"

Bang

Chapter Six

*G*ian disconnected his cell and shoved it in his pocket as he sprinted for his truck.

Flicking the siren on, he slapped the blue light on the roof and raced to the hospital running red lights and stop signs, at one point he drove up on the sidewalk to bypass a jumble of jammed traffic.

His heart pounded in his chest as he came to a screeching halt and slammed the gearshift into park in the hospital lot. Tossing a card with POLICE on it onto the dashboard, he leaped out and ran for the entrance.

At the visitor's desk, breathing hard, he barked, "Montanero, Reece and Josh, where the hell are they?"

The person at Reception drew back, her hand splayed across her chest. "Sir, that kind of aggressive-"

He tore his badge off his belt, shoved it in her face and barked, "Montanero, brothers, gunshot wounds, brought in thirty minutes ago, where the hell are they?"

"Gian," behind him Deo uttered his name. Fear shook through his voice.

Gian hurried to his brother. "How- what's the word? How are they? Are they-"

“Alive, bro, bad, though, they’re bad. Follow me, they’re both in ICU.” Deo clapped his arm and started towards the elevator.

Down the hall, outside a door, Jedediah and Jessica Montanero stood in a clutch. They looked up as Gian and Deo strode towards them.

“Dad, Mom,” Deo huffed, biting back tears. “Gian’s here.”

Jed gave each boy a quick hug and back pat. Jessica kissed Gian’s cheek and clung to Deo unable to stifle her sobs.

“Any word…ah, Jed?” Gian asked his father.

Jed wiped at an eye that was identical to Gian’s own dark ones and frowned. He gently admonished, “Son, about time you called me Dad.”

“Hmm.” Gian nodded without comment.

“They,” Jed sucked in a worried beath and exhaled. Still, the words caught in his throat. “They told us the boys had been...shot. *Shot*, Gian, who, I mean,” his eyes twisted up as tears shivered in them. “Why, who would fire a gun at them? Why?”

“Who could harm those boys?” Jessica cried. “Those sweet boys, they wouldn’t hurt a fly! How could-” she broke into sobs. Jed rolled both arms around her and pulled her in. She shoved her face into his chest, but her body shook with weeping.

Gian rubbed at his own stinging eyeballs. He asked, “What did the doctor tell you about, ah, their conditions?”

Jessica blew her nose into a tissue and replied huskily with tears in her throat, “The doctor has been by twice, he said it’s wait and see at this moment. He told us to stay down the hall in the waiting room and he will send word to us as soon as he can.”

“They let us poke our noses in to see them.” Jed’s voice wavered slightly. “They’re…pale. Tubes and wires and stuff…” He sucked in a shaky breath. Jessica slipped under his arm and wrapped her arm around his waist. Jed settled a shaky arm over her shoulders hugging her to him.

“Let’s go to the waiting room, they will only push us out of the hall, they’ve done it once already,” Jessica suggested, the worry gripping her throat making her words come out tight and whispery.

The group moved slowly down the cream-colored tiles flecked with gold. They entered the waiting room, fortunately there was no one else in there, they could express their fear and grief in private.

Jed and Jessica took seats on the green cushioned chairs, Deo hovered by them, Gian leaned a shoulder near the doorway.

After a few minutes of everyone's tight breaths as they struggled to rein in their anguish, Gian said, "I'll go grab us some coffee and…sandwiches or something."

Jed nodded. "Okay. The cafeteria's on the first floor." They weren't hungry but Gian clearly needed something physical to do to distract himself.

Deo moved and said, "I'll go with-"

"No," Jed said abruptly, patting Jessica's arm as she made a small whimpering sound. "Please, one of you stay with us."

Jed was a big man like his boys, but age added solid mass whereas his sons still carried their youthful leanness. Broad shoulders and strapping musculature ran in the male side of the family.

He still had a thick head of dark wavy hair, and normally twinkly brown eyes that at the moment were swamped with anxiety for his boys.

Jessica, ordinarily a strong spirited woman laid her head on her husband's thick shoulder. Her red hair swam like cotton candy around her head. Generally, her friendly gold-flecked hazel eyes regarded the world with lively warmth but now they swam with tears.

She had met Jed at a church function when the boys were still toddlers. They didn't marry until he had his first wife, Dyana, declared dead after she'd gone missing for seven years.

Jed and Jessica had fallen in love at first sight and Jessica became the only mother the boys ever knew. She raised them as her own but didn't move in until Dyana was legally declared dead.

Jed had never gone so far as having his son Giancomo Antonio declared deceased, he couldn't bear to believe his first born was gone from him for good.

As soon as his other three sons were familiar with the internet he had them rigorously and regularly scour the universe for their missing brother while he built his lobster business.

Practically before they could walk, the boys learned every in and out about lobster fishing. They always thought of themselves as four brothers albeit there was an empty space where the fourth should have been standing.

Half a day went by before the family got word on the injured brothers.

Jed and Jessica had chosen the moment to head to the restrooms just before a doctor came around to discuss the young men's chances of recovery.

The doctor approached Gian and Deo. After introductions, he told them that Josh was very slowly coming around, it was too early to see how he would mend and if any long-term injuries could incur or be permanent. Reece was in an induced coma. They were talking about life support.

Gian couldn't look at his white-faced brother, Deo. A fist gripped his heart so tightly he could barely draw a breath. This was why he didn't do relationships if he could avoid it. The pain, the fear, his stomach clenched.

Apparently there still was a tiny fragment of his heart still beating. And not an altogether pleasant feeling. He should have run far and wide and denied that he was any sibling of the Montanero brothers when they had come searching for him, then he wouldn't have to suffer this mental agony and dread now.

When Gian's best friend and partner Torrand Kristo had connected with the Montaneros, they'd asked Gian to meet and do a match.

With Torr pressing at him from the inside as well, Gian had reluctantly agreed. The second he saw them he knew they were related.

The four boys could be quadruplets; looking like identical thumbprints they resembled each other so closely. Gian could hardly deny it when he looked into four, plus his father's, mirrored reflections.

Once the affirmed results came in, his old man Jedediah, and brothers Deo, Reece and Josh declared Gian was one of them. When that happened, they refused to let him go and forced him to learn to accept his place in their family.

Gian, ambivalent, not knowing what being part of family was like, balked. They pressed. Pursued. Cajoled. Begged. Stalked, until he gave in, moved from San Diego to Maine and acquiesced to family visits, holidays and other events as he slowly waded into the welcoming family.

He was getting used to the one-armed man hugs they foisted on him. Not to mention his step-mother, Jessica's full body hugs and kisses on the cheek.

A mask shoved up his head pushing back salt and pepper hair, the doctor looked from one brother to the other.

Dread was written all over Amadeo Montanero's pale face, but Gian's was a stone mask.

Gian asked, "You kept the bullets of course?"

The physician actually felt a frisson of fear zipper up his spine at the man's formidable eyes. Sweat broke out over Doctor Hamilton Hill's forehead.

He'd hate to meet this fierce guy in a dark alley. The nurse told him he was a detective with a foul mouth. The doctor felt bad for the felons that pissed him off.

Standing stiffly, his voice stern, he answered, "Of course. One of your CSIs took them. They were…" he paused, not the thing family members wanted to hear, but Montanero was a detective, he'll find out anyway. "The bullets were large. The men were lucky they hadn't incurred more damage than they did."

Deo's face paled further.

Without blinking, Gian said to the doctor, "Their effects? Wallets, watches?"

Slightly affronted, Hill replied, "Yes, they were bagged and tagged, also gone with the CSIs. Not our first rodeo, son."

Gian muttered, "So not a robbery. Can we see Josh?"

Hill hesitated, but clearly the detective wasn't going to be easily put off. "Uh, yes, sure. He should be coming around. He lost a lot of blood, he's weak as an infant. Gentlemen, you must be," he glanced at Gian then Deo, "gentle. Quiet. I'll give you only a few moments, he needs his rest. Follow me."

He turned and the brothers followed his blue clad solid figure as he hustled down the hall. He had removed the blue booties and dropped the gloves in the hazard bin, he still wore the blue scrubs.

Josh had been settled into a room that held two beds. The other bed was empty, they were hopefully holding it for Reece, if he survived the night in the ICU.

Josh lay still, intravenous tubes attached to his hand, an oximeter clamped to his forefinger, a blood pressure cuff wrapped around his arm, and oxygen was attached to his nose. Machines beeped and ticked and whirred along the wall behind him.

Gian and Deo entered the room quietly and moved carefully to the bed. Standing beside it, they stared down at their youngest brother clinging to life.

"He's made it this far, gentlemen," the doctor said softly behind them. "The next couple of days will tell. But he pulled through the surgery so that signals a good chance of hopefully full recovery. He's awake, you have only a few moments," he reminded them then shuffled silently to stand near the door.

Slightly leaning over his injured brother, Deo whispered, "Josh, bro, it's Deo, and…" he glanced at Gian, "Giancomo is here too."

Josh made no movement, no response. Deo and Gian shared a concerned look.

Deo tried again but with levity, "Can you hear me, Josh? You always said my voice could hurt a blackboard's ears."

Josh's lashes fluttered on his pallid cheeks. His eyes opened slowly, a wince of pain crimped his young face. Under swollen, slit lids, he peered first at Deo then to Gian.

Gian said softly, his voice gravelly from emotion, "Can you talk, Josh? Did you see who shot you?"

His lashes flapped for a moment, Josh licked his dry lips, it looked like it was difficult for him to swallow, to even breathe.

"Here." Deo picked up a cup of water off the table beside the bed. Gian slid an arm around Josh's back lifting him slightly while Deo held the cup to Josh's lips. Josh gratefully took a few sips before Gian gently settled him back against the pillows.

"Josh," Gian said again, "did you see who did this?"

"Come on, Gian, give him a break, he's just come out of surgery," Deo chastised his brother.

Gian replied gruffly, "I know. I want to get the prick who did this before he harms another person." *And make him pay.* "I need a name or description."

He turned his attention from Deo, second oldest after Gian, to their youngest brother. "Josh, what did you see? Do you know who did this?"

Josh blinked at his brother for a moment, then swallowed hard. With an imperceptible shake of his head, his voice a bare rasp, he croaked, "No. Came from behind. I was opening the," he paused, sucked in a painful breath, "truck door. Reece stayed with the boat-"

His eyes suddenly burned with alarm, he bleated weakly, "Reece? Is Reece okay? I heard shots before- before I heard another retort and felt a sting in my back. Was- was it Reece? Oh my God, Deo-" He turned fearful eyes to his brother.

"Shh," Deo patted his arm. "Reece is here, uh, at the hospital."

Gulping with pain, Josh rasped, "Oh thank God, he's okay." His chest collapsed as air sieved wheezing out in his relief.

"All right, that's enough, he needs his rest." Doctor Hill stepped up. He gave Gian and Deo a look regarding them letting their injured brother believe his brother Reece was fine and waiting in the visitor's room.

"Okay," Deo said to the doctor. To Josh, he smiled and said gently, "Dad and Mom are here. You have to nap a little before they'll let you see them. We'll be right outside."

"Josh," Gian persevered. "Did you hear anything before the gunshots? See another car, hear voices? Accents?"

"I said that is enough, Detective," the doctor told him. He had his arms out as if about to shoo them out of the room.

"Josh-" Gian tried again.

"Out. Now, or I'll call security," Hill threatened.

His mouth nicked in at the side, Gian nodded and started to turn away when Josh made a sound. He turned back. "What, Josh, what do you remember?"

Gasping, Josh's chest rose as he inhaled deeply, lines of pain streaked around his eyes. "A- a jingle. I heard a…some jingling, may- maybe clanking, or-or clinking? And, uh, clicking. Something clicking."

Gian paused. "Like car keys? Or like change being shuffled in a pocket? Bells on a boat ringing?"

"Detective-"

Josh weakly spoke over the doctor, "No, no. Not like that. Not…sure. Sleepy… heard…laughter…" His eyes drifted closed, his head turned slightly, his breathing slowed.

"Male? Female laughter? Josh," Gian said urgently, "what did you hear?"

Josh mumbled, "Citrus… orange blossoms," his eyes crunched hard. "Round red… apples? No," he muttered with a wince, "not apples."

Gian looked to Deo who stared back blankly. "Are there orchards near the marina?"

"Not, sure…" Deo's lips pursed. "Certainly not oranges in Maine. But apples? Don't know."

"Citrus? Maybe perfume? Could it be a lady's perfume you smelled, Josh?" Gian asked.

Josh's nose wrinkled, his eyes stayed closed, he murmured faintly, "N- no, not feminine…not flowery perfume…can't remember…apples…" He sighed and fell silent.

Gian waited.

Josh blinked hard a few times as he thought back. "Ah, splatch of color, molasses, ah, those cookies at- at Chrissmas," he slurred.

"Josh-"

"That's it." Hill ushered the two brothers out.

The three men stood outside the door. Frowning at the doctor, Gian ordered, "I don't want him told about Reece until we're sure he's…out of the woods."

Hill considered his words, then nodded. "All right. But if his brother doesn't survi-"

"No," Gian said sharply. "You tell him nothing other than what we, his family advise you to tell him. Am I clear?"

Taken slightly aback, Hill said, "You don't have to be so militant, Detective. I assure you, my only concern is for your brothers. Both of them. I will make sure none of the staff reveals any information without your permission."

"Thank you," Deo interjected quickly before Gian said anything else to insult the doctor. "I guess the clambake is on hold," he muttered to his brother.

As Gian turned around, Deo said, "Where are you going?"

Over his shoulder as he strode down the hall, Gian replied, "I'm going to go find the bastard that shot our brothers."

Chapter Seven

Several days later Gian and Torr met with their lieutenant.

Lieutenant Huxley McKay was not happy. He stood behind his desk leaning his block body over with his catcher's mitt sized palms on the desk. The straw-colored hair spiked above matching brows.

"Montanero," Hux glared at Gian then Torr and back to Gian. "I got reports you canvassed the Kifpu Wissei Marina along with the detectives I assigned to the shooting cases."

He leaned over further, blocky shoulders bunched, eyes narrowed, he spoke with emphasis, "And that was after I strictly forbade you from being involved. The victims are your brothers, it's a conflict. You know damned well you can't be part of the investigation."

McKay snapped at Torr, "And you either, being his best friend." His angry eyes flit from one suited man to the other.

Gian stood glaring back. "We are not suspects, LT," he growled, insulted at Hux's insinuation.

Looking slightly abashed, his wheat-colored brows hopping over light blue eyes, McKay responded, "Your brothers out of the way, your dad getting on in years, he's semi-retired, you are in line to inherit the business."

"Yeah," Gian snorted. "I really want to quit my job as a detective and take on the back breaking chore of a lobster business."

He narrowed a dark eye at his lieutenant. “I already have a job, if you recall, one that you are tying my hands behind my back to work at.”

McKay wriggled his heavy shoulders and lifted his square jaw. “Yeah, well, it’s a very fruitful business according to reports Conny Vinci brought me. Quite lucrative, your dad’s made a helluva success out of hunting the red bugs. His bankroll is thick, and that house and property he owns tell their own story.”

Gian’s spine straightened. “Are you serious, LT? You really think that I would off my own kin to take on those red-clawed monsters?” He scoffed with a snort. “Sure.” His mouth twisted in scorn. “And anything you get from that slug-eyed, media whore, Cornelius Vinci-”

Cutting him off with a coarse huff, McKay said, “Nonetheless, it’s a conflict of interest no matter how you look at it. Stay away, hands off, that’s an order. And,” he bowed his head to look up at Gian from under his thick brow, “Vinci’s just doing his job. Quit pickin’ at him. You fellas need to work together. You’re professionals, detectives of the highest caliber. Both of-”

“Yeah,” Gian sneered. “I’d like to put a caliber in his big fat behind.”

“Watch it, Detective,” McKay warned, his brow lowering.

“I meant that cute man-bun he sports.” Gian grinned at Torr’s mutual chuckle. “The spriggly goatee and man-bun, that’s real professional.”

McKay crossed his arms. “He keeps that appearance to fit in better with the younger locals, so they’ll open up to him more easily.”

“Ha, right. Rather to shine in metrosexual display and show up pretty on camera is more like it. Probably gets facials and manicures and polish on his toes and all that crap too. I bet he carries a manpurse to keep his lip balm in.”

McKay sighed wearily, scrubbing a hand down the front of his face. “Whatever. That’s his business. You two just keep your noses out of the investigation. End of story.”

Torr glanced at Gian then said to the lieutenant, "LT, if it were your brothers, your kin, seriously, would you just step aside?"

McKay's head swung in his direction; he eyeballed him hard. His wheat-colored buzz cut appeared to stand up at attention like most people did when McKay barked. His white and olive-green uniform was pressed so harshly it screamed in protest.

"We aren't talking about me, Kristo, we are talking about *my* orders. My orders are all that matter here. Now-"

Gian cut him off, "Lieutenant, your *detectives* didn't bother questioning the people that were on the boats. They only questioned the employees and people wandering the marina at that moment. You know boat people can be either exceptionally private or extremely outgoing."

Disregarding McKay's pinched lips and glowering glare, Gian said, "Your staff needs to go knock on cabin doors, make phone calls, check who was visiting that day, the night before. Check with charters, guests, captains and crews. What boats had come and gone. One of your witnesses could be out at sea and halfway to Nova Scotia right now."

"Montanero-"

Gian went on, "We checked. There is an apple orchard within three miles of the marina. My brother said he saw or smelled apples. The perp could be a migrant worker; he could have had the smell of apples on his clothes or hands."

He glanced around the room, slapping his broad hands on his lean hips, shoving the bottom of his suitcoat back. He practically tapped a dress boot in taut annoyance as he carried on.

"Someone needs to check the orchard out, the employees, the migrants, the customers. There was nothing in the interview reports that I read that indicated any of that has been attempted."

Beside his relentless friend, Torrand Kristo dragged thick fingers through the trimmed sides of his dark hair. The longer top had ruffled furrows from his strong fingertips raking through it.

He wore his long-sleeved, button-down brown shirt tucked into dark blue slacks, a red tie dangled between the dark suit lapels, a large detective's shield glinted from his belt.

Torr crossed thick arms and planted his boots shoulder width apart. He stood in stolid solidarity with his brother in law enforcement as well as comrades in arms. During combat they had pulled each other's bacon out of the fire on too many occasions to count.

Torr always had Gian's six, and vice versa, and that would never change. If Gian was hell bent on relentlessly pursuing his brothers' shootings and standing up to their LT, Torr was at his back or by his side, ride or die.

"And don't forget that pub next door. Chap Swabinski's place, Swabby's Deck. It was jumping that time of night. People constantly toing and froing," Torr submitted. "Could be a gluttony of witnesses there alone. I understand the deckhands from the Seabug hang out there."

"Are you done?" The anger intensifying, deepened McKay's voice. He leaned over further, his neck burgeoned into a deep puce. A blast of dark red popped over his blunt nose, his square jaw jutted out in fury at his orders being disobeyed.

"No, I'm not," Gian replied calmly. "The jingle. Josh said he heard a light clanking or jingling or tinkling. I've searched the area for anything of that kind of sound, recorded a couple of ship bells ringing, a wind chime on a boat, that's all."

The lieutenant shoved his cuff up and looked pointedly at his watch.

Gian didn't bat an. Continuing his rant, he said, "Because of your restrictions I can't go onboard and question people myself, so you need to get your *assignments* rolling on that BS. I want everyone at that marina; staff, boat owners and their guests, visitors, truck drivers, suppliers, merchants, I want everyone's records pulled to start with."

McKay opened his mouth, Gian charged on. "I want whomever in the Maverick Bay area has form, ah, criminal history, pulled in and questioned. And bakeries. Josh mentioned he smelled molasses. Or saw it. A customer could have been chowing a freshly baked gingerbread cookie shortly before the shootings."

Torr added, "We did a cross to see if there were any prior shootings at that marina, or another marina, or in that area in a fifty-mile circumference. Came up with a few muggings and bar fights and a car-jacking but no gunfire."

The red rolled up McKay's neck and over his face to his forehead and then out to his square ears. "You too, Kristo? Who the hell do you two think you are telling me how to do my job?"

"When you aren't doing it, someone has to," Gian snapped with a cold edge to his hard voice. "Yeah, those are my brothers. You tell your people to step it up or I stay onboard." He grimaced. "Pun intended."

McKay stomped out from behind his desk and moved to a few steps from Gian. "I don't even know what the hell you are doing here. From what I understand, the largest hauling of lobster is to climax at the big wingding festival in the next few months."

"Yes, and? Your point is?"

"Your father's company is down two people. Rough weather is reported on the horizon, don't you need to be filling in at home? I offered you a leave of absence to help your da, not keep your nose in this case."

Gian's lips flattened. "Speaking of, I want criminal histories run on my father's ship-hands too. Lobster fishing is tough work, takes tough people to work it. I know Kopper Komer has a record for petit thefts, and Skitty Hawkins has had DUIs up the wazoo. Look into the rest of them."

He barely took a breath before charging on, "I want checks on any trouble between my brothers and the crew, the lobster merchants, love triangles, even the people involved with the purchasing of seafood for the upcoming festival. Check any gambling debts owed, prior brawls, a retailer unhappy with his product."

Shoving his finger in Gian's face, McKay sputtered furiously, "You son of a-"

Gian didn't flinch, back up or shut up. "So far, the rest of the crew have been holding things together with my father's business. But you'll be pleased to know I cleaned lobster traps this last weekend."

He held up a hand and grimaced at it. "My blisters have blisters." Which was saying a lot as his hands were normally calloused. "I'll be keeping in touch, LT," Gian said, and turned and stalked out.

Pinning his lips together, Torr nodded to the lieutenant and followed Gian, leaving Hux McKay standing with his mouth open and his face blindingly lobster red in fury.

Hissing furious burbles behind grit teeth, McKay struggled to keep his invectives in. Gian and Torr were top-notch, the elite of the badges at Chicory Landing County Sheriff's Office.

He couldn't fire them, it would leave a gigantic deficit in operations. Gian had the highest closing of cases, Torr second. Team the two men up together and they were preternaturally undefeatable.

McKay owed it to the citizens of Chicory County and the tourists of the town of Maverick Bay to keep them on the force. "Damn those sons'a bitches," he cursed another blue streak as he stood in fist-clenched impotence then snatched up his phone.

Gian paused near his desk to grab an extra pen. Torr took the opportunity to hit the men's room.

"Ah, the prodigal son has whipped up the fires under our LT, eh, JoCo? Can hear his outraged roars from out here."

The snide voice squeezed egregious fingers tightly around the back of Gian's neck, raising the hairs on it. Without looking up, he growled, "Mind your own effin' business, Corny." He swallowed a grin at the peeved inhale he heard at his mock.

"It's Conny you hopped up hothead," Cornelius Vinci reminded him. Detective Vinci kept the frown off his handsome face, plastering the lopsided smile in place that the ladies dropped their panties over.

He smoothed tendrils of hair that escaped his man-bun back with his palms and ran the backs of his fingers under his goatee. Beside him, his partner, Simon Nucacher, snickered.

"Sure, got it, Cornball, why do I keep forgetting that?" Gian shot the detective a fake grin.

"Listen here, JoCo-," Vinci countered, under the mustache his mouth turned viciously down. He narrowed his eyes at Gian. "You keep stickin' your nose in where it's been told to step back and the LT will chop it right off along with your balls."

"Yeah," Simon chimed in. "You can barely investigate a hole in your pocket much less an aggravated shooting. Leave the detecting to us pro's."

Gian's glower shot to Simon. "You need to check the score cards, Nutcracker. Torr and I bag the most cases all the way to court convictions, double that of you and Cornball."

Vinci stepped in front of Gian, his face apoplectic with bulging eyes and snarling teeth. Jabbing his finger in Gian's face, he ground out, "Ain't true, bro, we close as many-"

"That's Nucacher," Simon shouted at the same time, "not Nutcracker, told you a million times. I'm gonna file a complaint with HR you-"

"Come on, bro," Torr interrupted the beginnings of a verbal brawl which could only end in them all getting sanctions. "Leave the tots to their sandbox, we've got work to do. Real work that results in real, successful, convictions and closed cases." He clapped Gian's arm, motioning towards the door with his head.

Gian couldn't believe he had allowed himself once again to get drawn into verbal sparring with the two nimwits. Vinci with his man-bun and Simon the nutcracker with his blow of slicked back, straightened black licorice hair, dark chocolate skin and charcoal eyes. What a pair. What's he care? His and Torr's records speak for themselves. They were the prime detectives of the unit.

"Yeah," Gian grumbled, letting Torr lead him out of the room.

Chapter Eight

A couple of weeks later, Gian and Torr headed for downtown. Reece was going to be released in a few days but he has a long recovery ahead of him. He took a bullet to his spine which had led to blood clots and other fun issues like trouble walking.

He had nothing to offer on the shooting. He'd been taken completely by surprise as his attention was fully on unloading and shutting down the Seabug.

Josh had taken a bullet to his leg, chipping off bone and breaking his femur, and a second bullet sliced a piece of his kidney, so with the addition of an angry infection he was fighting, he was out for a while as well.

His testimony of what he'd seen and heard was just as sparse. Nothing but splotches of red apples and molasses, woody scent of orange and faint tinkling and odd clicking. All of which floated like an LSD hallucinogen around the fog in his brain of what happened that night.

Now the family business was looking grim as two of their team were down for the count and the biggest haul of the season was coming due.

McKay was right, Gian had to pitch in. He spent the last weeks learning the trade, and yes, it was tough work, brawn work, but nothing he couldn't handle, he'd lived a rough life for a long time. Torr was assigned other cases.

"Damn town is in full lobster swing," Torr noted, looking around at the boisterous village.

"Yeah," Gian agreed. "Lobster festival, party of the year they tell me."

The two detectives surveyed their surroundings. Signs hung everywhere, in shop windows and tacked to trees advertising the Lobster Festival at the end of next month would be the grandest of events.

Cutouts of vivid red Lobsters grinned down at shoppers, and multi-colored flags on poles whipped in the wind.

Chicory Landing was a cliché of the picturesque coastal village. Cottages and McMansions dotted the seaside along with amusement parks, waterslides, rustic restaurants. It teemed with artists and galleries. People exhibited their work on streets, canvasses were perched on sidewalks and attached to wrought iron fences.

The town was chock full of cheerful residents enjoying food and swimming and festive merriment. In the last of the full lobster season before winter assaulted with its snow and icy chill, the town burgeoned with visitors.

Lobstermen fish year-round but in the milder months they can yield within two or three miles from shore. In the harsh winter they have to travel forty or fifty miles or more from home.

Many Lobstermen pull up their traps for the winter due to the dangers of high turbulent seas, icy decks and freezing weather. Subsequently they have to make hay while the sun was still shining and the weather was cooperative.

The hauls will be less over the blustery winter, therefore they need the big money they'd gain during the festival. The town's coffers get much of their year's enormous fill from the nationwide attendance.

"Boys," a cheery voice greeted the detectives.

Gian and Torr turned to see their mayor, Gregory 'Gator' O'Grady standing there with a grin on his plump jolly face. "Mayor," they hailed in unison.

"I've never seen such commotion, Mayor," Torr remarked, glancing around, marveling at the lively activity. People promenaded gaily up and down the walks of the shops, visiting and carrying colorful bags filled with purchases.

Between stores were glimpses of sparkling beige sand and brilliant blue water. The ocean breeze sliding through was growing stiffly cool and salty even though the strong sun still warmed the land.

"Yeah, yeah." Mayor O'Grady nodded joyfully. "Busiest time, most important time of the year for me!"

"Important?" Gian asked, "How's that?"

"Ah, votin' for mayor, son, at the end of the festival. I mean, I have nothing to worry about of course," a tiny wrinkle creased his shiny forehead negating his comment.

"But," he explained at the detectives' questioning looks, "the success of the festival kind of denotes, you know, the choosing of the mayor. If the festival is a failure, then the standing official looks lacking, like he can't keep his town solvent. Well, most prefer it floating rich like the yachts on the high seas.

"The festival brings in big, big revenue, boys. People come from all around the country to revel in it, and if it fails, the town fails, and then as the one in charge," he took a deep breath, his belly expanded, "well, then I fail."

"Surely an entire town and election doesn't hang on buckets of spiny red lobsters, Mayor?" Gian said with wry disbelief.

Wiping a pudgy hand across his sweat-beaded forehead, Gator O'Grady nodded. "Well, yes'um, crazy as it sounds, it does. Tradition, son, long held tradition signifies who carries on as mayor. You see, a poor festival indicates a poor town and a poor leader, ergo," he shrugged a plump shoulder, his palms up. A frown pushed the happy smile from his friendly face.

"Gator!" A woman was hurrying towards the men. She wore a blue flowery dress that belled to her knees with a white belt and white collar. Her blonde hair was in a face-curving, wavy bob and she carried a white purse that matched her high-heeled sandals.

She gleefully flaunted white in the off-season. It was only a week or so after Labor Day but fundamental fashionistas would decry her choice of wearing white in autumn.

"Darling," the mayor said, and held his hand out to grasp his wife's hand. Her pretty face was rosy, freckles peeked out from under the makeup she'd used to try to hide her Doris Day speckles.

Drawing her to him, Gator tucked her hand under his arm. The jaunty smile back on his face, he introduced her, "You know my wife, Nectar, boys?"

"No, pleasure to meet you, ma'am." Torr bowed slightly to Nectar O'Grady.

Gian inclined his head briefly, murmured, "Pleasure."

The two men didn't dare catch each other's eye at Mrs. O'Grady's unusual name.

"Hi boys, how are you Mounties doing covering crime today?" Nectar greeted them with a friendly, gay smile. She was perfect as a seaside village mayor's wife. Hometown spun but chic, just as if old timey Doris Day stepped out from the movies.

Charming with guileless smiles and perky friendliness, she portrayed genuine warmth that made people feel immediately at ease.

Gator gave his wife a tender frown of correction. "Sweetie, Mounties are in Canada. In Maine you know they're troopers."

"We're detectives, ma'am," Torr offered with a polite grin.

Nectar giggled her apology and started chatting about other local events. Gian and Torr politely listened.

She gushed on about, "You couldn't miss the Big Moose Rodeo, or the Breeze Jazz Fest, our Miss Maple Syrup Pageant was glorious. We can't forget about the Clam Chowder and Hazelnut Fairs with so many varieties of pies and cookies."

Gator added while licking his chops and rubbing his belly, "I'm partial to the variety of rich homemade cakes and that invigorating apple cider that everyone gets just the teeniest tiniest buzz from! Of course they were all enjoyed the last few months past, but the townfolk do so love their festivals!"

Gian listened with half an ear as his gaze wandered the celebratory hubbub on the streets. It was moving into fall. In the evenings the air was becoming brisk with a slight chill. The wind sharp at night eases to a crisp breeze during the sunny days.

Yet people still donned bathing suits with light coverups as they scurried through the public access paths to the beach.

He could see colorful umbrellas popped up all over the sand like frilly mushrooms.

His gaze passed a hotdog and lemonade stand, then a lunch truck oozing with interesting smells of grilled cheesesteak sandwiches and sauteed shrimp with sausages and onion rings. Next to them was an ice cream vendor.

Gian's eyes traveled over a souvenir stand then stopped at the steps of the courthouse. Busy people traipsed up and down the steep steps to the brick building.

But what caught his eye was the woman that was standing beside an old, pale yellow Volkswagen convertible parked at a meter.

Long blonde curls flapped in the wind, the skirt of her saffron sundress flounced around legs that he couldn't pull his eyes from. He recognized her.

It was the woman from that day at the pub. The one who had been shouting into the phone. The blonde his brother had been urging him to go after.

A man was grasping her arm, and she was trying gracefully to dislodge his grip without causing a scene. He appeared angry, she appeared unnerved. Gian's feet were moving before his brain was aware.

"Please, Lawford, let me go, I don't have the time. I told you we are not-"

The man, a foot taller than the woman snarled as he squeezed her arm, "And I said make the time. You want the bank to take that damned farm? You will do as I say. Now, come with me-"

"She said let go," Gian growled as he approached the pair.

The man shot him an annoyed look, the woman's was aggrieved.

The man remarked rudely, "Bug off, mister, mind your own business." He turned back to the woman. "Now, Nicolle Kelly, not gonna stand out on the street arguing with you."

Tipping his head towards her, he smiled, his voice softened slightly. "Come on, sweetheart, you know you can't handle it, it's too big a job for a little girl like you. I can help you keep afloat, you just have to let me-"

"Let her go," Gian ordered, moving in front of the man, he pulled back his suit coat to display the badge on his belt.

Personally, he'd rather settle things with his fists, but his lieutenant told him after the last time that he had to wait until he was attacked first before retaliating with brute force.

He glanced quickly at the woman. Her cheeks were scarlet. Mortification was written all over her beautiful face.

You see, he told himself, not his type. She clearly couldn't take care of herself, she needed a man to watch over her. His father's wife Jessica would call him sexist but that didn't alter the truth. Gorgeous, delicate females like this one would always have brutish aggressive men chasing them down.

They required a male's dominance to shove another male's unwanted attention off them. He noted there was no ring on her finger to help ward off the bullies. Her only jewelry with the light sundress was a slim gold watch and small gold hoops in her ears.

The man looked down at the badge and scowled. Reluctantly, he released her slender wrist.

Immediately she rubbed the red ring around her wrist and stepped out of his reach. Embarrassment flooding her face with more color, without looking him in the eye, she mumbled to Gian, "Um, I…" and she turned and quickly opened the door to the yellow VW.

The men watched the skirt flutter and rise exposing a shapely leg as she climbed inside. Within seconds the car disappeared around the bend in the street.

"That was none of your business, Officer," the man ground at Gian. Moussed dark hair loosened from the wind flopped over one eye.

"Treatment of the citizens of Chicory Landing is my business, mister…" Gian narrowed his eyes at the handsome man who glared back at him.

The man also wore a suit. He tugged the cuffs of his starched white shirt down and then the dark jacket sleeves over his wrists. A Rolex flashed before being covered by a cuff. Gold cufflinks winked at each other. Wriggling his shoulders before pushing them back and puffing out his chest, he told Gian, "I am Lawford Raines, Officer."

"That's Detective, Detective Giancomo Montanero. I can spell it for you if you wanna file a complaint."

Lawford sniffed, lifted his head and glared at Gian with a haughty eye. Lawford was tall but Gian had a few inches on him. He didn't respond to Gian's words.

He started to turn away when Gian said, "You work at the bank?" He nodded to the huge Northeast American Fiduciary Bank on the corner that he was headed for.

Another haughty sniff and Lawford replied, "Yes. I am the manager. Now, I must return-"

"What was your business with the woman? You said something about keeping her afloat?"

Lawford glowered at Gian with undisguised irritation. "See here, Detective, it's none of your-"

"I asked you a question, Raines. I can follow you inside and ask it again in there in a really loud voice. Or if you prefer, since you were causing a disturbance on the open street, I can invite you downtown to the station to answer my questions. What will it be?"

Lawford's eyes rounded in trepidation, his mouth dropped open. His head swiveled as he quickly glanced around to ensure no one was privy to this…humiliation. "Really, Officer, accosting a gentleman on the street like he was nothing but a- a hoodlum!"

Gian calmly crossed his arms over his broad chest. Disregarding the man's flustered expression, he said, "Not gonna ask you again, Raines, here quietly, inside the bank loudly, or down at the station with lots of attention. Media attention. Journalists hang out around the station all the time looking for stories to showcase on their news shows."

Lawford's lips slammed shut. Then he scowled. "Fine." Tugging at his cuffs again, he brushed an invisible piece of lint off his sleeve and said, "Miss Nicolle Kelly had been summoned to her family's farm for her assistance. She was, ah, I understand away at college, when her grandpappy," he paused and sucked in a harsh breath.

"Her grandfather, Tane Kelly, fell ill, and then her me-maw, that is," he coughed, "her grandmother also took a spill and broke her leg. Or was it her arm?" He rolled his eyes and smoothed the sides of his wavy hair with his palms.

"Whatever, they have a farm out the southern skirts and a small grocery. They sell fresh milk, eggs, cheese, vegetables and some baked goods. The housekeeper up and left them with only a couple of servants, and two of the farmhands also had to leave for some family sickness or whatnot."

Gian tucked his hands in his trouser pockets and nodded for the man to continue. He could relate to the 'being summoned to assist with the family business.'

Clearing his throat, Lawford tugged at the knot on his tie then smoothed it with his fingers before looking around again.

Keeping his voice low, he explained, "Well, with no one else to carry on, they brought Nikki in to help. Well," he said with a chuckle, "a slip of a skirt, how much can she do?"

"She's a woman, not an invalid," Gian interjected.

"Sure. Anyway, with her grandpa and the hands down, things have fallen behind, the harvest, the milking of the cows and such. Then there's the running of the household, well, hells bells, girl can't do it all. I'm sure they must be losing money hand over fist. I," he coughed again and his gaze shifted away from Gian.

"You what?"

His eyes moved back to Gian then canted off to the side of his broad shoulder. "I offered to help her with a loan to keep things going until circumstances level out."

"Why did she refuse the loan?" Gian asked, because apparently that was what the dispute between them was about.

His eyes snapping angrily to Gian, Lawford responded, "Well, I can't just hand the girl money for nothing, now can I? It's not like I asked for a lot, just a fuc- uh, freaking date. I asked her for one simple date in exchange for...well, a month's reprieve on the mortgage. And, well, you can see, the little chippie wouldn't give me the time of day." He turned and glared down the street where Nikki had disappeared.

"Anyway, she'll come around, she'll have to," he said with determination. Straightening his jacket, he looked back to Gian and declared, "And the price will be higher then, for making me work for it."

Lawford's bottom lip pushed up. "That enough to satisfy your nosey curiosity, Officer?"

Gian didn't respond or act as if he was placated and ready to move on.

Lawford squinted a warning blue eye at Gian and said, "Just for the record, the girl is mine. Don't you entertain any ideas of taking her for yourself. She was a hard widget to nail down to begin with, now's my shot and I don't need a damn foreigner," because he'd noted Gian had an accent that wasn't local, or even American, "sticking his fingers or anything else in my pie. Got it?" He pivoted and stomped off in the direction of the bank.

Gian muttered at his retreating back, "No worries, governor, last thing I need or want is that pretty fluff of soft trouble." He saw Torr waving at him and he strode up the walk to rejoin his partner.

The mayor and his wife also gave jaunty waves as they traveled back down the avenue to join the excited throng eager for the festival celebration to get on.

Chapter Nine

With a bottle of beer in his hand, Gian clipped around the side of the house to smoke.

Jessica strictly outlawed smoking at her parties. She didn't allow vaping either because of the youngsters present.

The clambake was going gangbusters. Running laughing children trampled acres of green lawn. Local villagers mingled gaily and ate robustly.

The patio abounding with happy hungry guests watched Jed Montanero and friends wielding huge grills that were smoking and steaming, proliferating the air with vibrant aromas.

Spicy and smoky mixed with briny, it was like being at San Francisco's Fisherman's Wharf on the 4th of July.

Gian wanted a cigarette and he also wanted to avoid Coco Gentry. She had gone to school with Gian's brothers, and slept with all of them. Gian was the next notch on her bedpost. She was the most relentless pursuer, but she vied with her sister Poppy for Gian's attention, as well as Jessica's choice of wife for him, Hollyann Ontario.

A redhead, Poppy, a brunette, Coco, and a blonde, Hollyann- a veritable trifecta was tenaciously intent on boxing him in. Coco was arrowing closest- as soon as her head turned when a child squealed near her, Gian slipped around the corner of the house.

There were others, he hadn't managed to recall their names. He felt like a rooster who'd been shoved into the henhouse and the door slammed and locked behind him.

His brothers recovering from their wounds sprawled like slain knights on lawn chairs, cocktails in hand, girls on both sides of them coddling the poor things.

While Josh and Reece basked in the female attention, they aimed smirks of amusement at their brother trying to fend off the hornettes of Chicory Landing.

The brothers had been advised against drinking and meds, but as both were still immobile, needing canes to even stand upright, they claimed the liquid pain killers were necessary.

Gian had only managed a couple of puffs before someone spoke, making him sigh. Busted.

"Giancomo, I declare," Jessica pronounced as she skirted the corner catching him mid-suck.

Gian leaned his back against the house, bent a knee and propped his foot on the wall. He blew out a flume of smoke and took a drab of beer. "Hey, Jessica," he said politely without looking at her.

She moseyed up to him moving her hands from her slightly plump hips to fold across her pink blouse. In her mid-fifties, Jessica was a softly pretty woman, a tad shorter than average height, she only came up to her husband's wide shoulders.

Dressed in white capris and sneaks, her billowy red hair was tied back in a flouncy ponytail. The hazel eyes brimmed with sparkly laughter even as she scolded her husband's long lost now found son.

"Gian," she admonished, coming closer, "cancer sticks. You know better, why do you-"

He leaned his head against the wall and took another puff, letting the smoke seep into his lungs, turning so it drifted out and away opposite from where she stood when he exhaled.

A sigh ruffled out, she smiled pensively. "I'm sorry, Gian, totally not my business. But," her voice sad, she said, "I sort of understand. Your father told me about your formative years spent on the streets, in a gang, and in deep, furtive combat. There wasn't much for you to, oh, I don't know, hold, have, meditate with."

Groaning silently, he took a draught of beer, tossed the cigarette on the stone path near the house and ground it out with the toe of his boot. At the lifting of Jessica's brow, he grunted then bent and picked up the stub and tucked it in his jacket pocket then braced his back and foot back on the wall.

He wore black jeans, boots, black thermal, and dark brown leather jacket. The rest of the guests might be running about in shorts and T's, but it was really growing damned cold.

He had been used to a steamy jungle climate and then warm, dry San Diego. Moving to Maine had been a helluva culture shock. Freezing shock.

Yet, the land was stunning with bright blue skies, deep sapphire ocean and lakes, green summers and colorful falls. He embraced winter sports, skiing, snowmobiling, snowboarding and ice hockey. He even tried ice fishing. It was okay. Once in a blue moon.

Jessica positioned herself in front of him and smiled warmly. "Gian, honey, I don't mean to scold you. Obviously, you are free to do anything you wish. I only want to see you happy. You know Hollyann's family owns Blossoms Up, that lovely florist shop over on Hoover Drive. She's pretty and she sings in the choir, you-"

He dropped his foot, his hands fell to his hips. Trying to keep the aggravation out of his deep voice, he said coolly, "Jessica, I don't need a mother. I don't need a matchmaker. I don't need a woman."

With an exhale of lament at her unhappy expression, he said, "Listen, I like you, Jessica. You're the best thing that could have happened to my dad and my brothers, I should know, they repeat it like a broken record. You're a really nice lady and I don't want to hurt your feelings but-"

"I know, I know," she interrupted him with a smile and nodding. "You've been alone a long time and dependent on no one but yourself. Having a family suddenly dropped on you would shake anyone up. Even if it's been a couple of years now, although you did live a distance away, we only saw you intermittently. We're all thrilled you chose to move here."

She touched his arm with a gentle squeeze. "Like I said, I only want to see you happy, it makes your dad happy and that makes me happy. Truly, I would love to see you settle down with a good woman and kids. They would give you purpose." Her hazel eyes widened ardently as she studied his hard face, she added, "And fulfillment and contentment."

Lowering his head, he gave her a crooked smile that didn't reach his eyes. "I have purpose with my job. I have friends and brothers who I really care about, Jessica. I have you and Dad, I'm pretty content right now. What I don't need is a ball and chain and a drooling babbling posse of miniature money pits." He disregarded the pang of loss that he still felt over his baby that Britnee had been carrying.

Her red brows knit, Jessica shook her head. "When you find the one, Gian, the arrow through your heart, you won't think ball and chain, you'll think safety, support, an easing of your heart even as your breath quickens at the sight of her."

She pushed at a few wisps of loose red curls caught in her eyelashes and tilted her head looking up at him.

At his look of skepticism, she said gently, "You'll see. But," she sighed and said with an acceding grin, "I guess Coco and Poppy, and maybe even Hollyann aren't the right ones for you. They're too…" she cocked a brow and studied him closely. "Yes, they're too forward. You're one of those alpha types my girlfriends ramble on about. You like to do the chasing, the catching, the conquering."

A burst of laughter ripped from Gian, he arched forward and wiped an eye. "Oh yeah? You make me sound like a barbarian warrior ready to bop a woman over the head with my club then drag her off to my cave by her hair."

She laughed with him. "Well, not quite. That would be a caveman. You're just…a man who is still finding his way in a new world. Come." Jessica had learned from Jed that much of Gian's early police work was undercover with some of the most dangerous drug dealers and smugglers in San Diego and LA.

His life certainly hadn't gentled after he left the military. He was not used to being around genteel people. He'd learn, she supposed. Hopefully. She linked his arm and said, "Come back to the party."

He let her lead him back around to the patio. As they emerged from the side of the house, his brother Deo spotted them and jogged over.

"Ma," he said to Jessica, "you told me there would be that hummingbird cake I like here." Jessica had promised if he showed, she would make sure his favorite cake, the one he always asked for on his birthday, the three-layers of banana, pineapple and spice with cream cheese frosting would be present.

Jessica's brows drew down. "Oh dear. I asked Lolly Kelly at Shamrock Farm to provide the cake. She's been down with injuries and illness, but she assured me she would have one sent for the party." She fished her phone out of her pocket. "Let me call her."

"I can go pick it up, Mom," Deo offered. He was talking to Jessica but he was eying a young woman chatting with a group of people near the pool. She had a long brunette ponytail that flit coyly with her head movements. In tight jeans and a crop-top, she periodically peeped over her shoulder at Deo with a shy smile.

Today turned out to be too cold to swim. Instead of people splashing in the pool, floating flamingoes and white swan blowups sauntered around the water. Some of the children threw other pool toys at them.

"Shamrock Farm?" Gian asked. "The last name of the owner is Kelly?"

Jessica nodded with a, "Hmm. Tane and Lolly Kelly own the farm. They have livestock, chickens, vegetable gardens and such. Lolly's a heck of a baker. She only has time for special occasions though, so busy with the farm. They export their products throughout the state but also keep a supply at their store for the locals."

Watching Deo watching the cute brunette, Gian offered, "I'll go get the cake."

"Oh, no, Gian-" Jessica shook her head.

"I need a break anyway, Jessica. Text me the address I'll put it in the GPS." He bent and kissed Jessica on the cheek. "I'll be right back." A half-smirk at Deo, he said, "Good luck, you owe me."

Chapter Ten

The farm looked generations old with modernized updates. At the foot of the long driveway, three wooden beams made a square Western arch over the drive.

Across the top of the arch Gian noted a sign with SHAMROCK FARM written in green on it that was embraced with bunches of green clovers.

The tarred drive led up to the main house that sat a distance off the road. It was a large, two-story grey stone with white shutters and trim.

A white, two-beamed fence encircled part of the brown barns and the weathered, dark red stables looming further in the back.

In the pasture, another fence, this one was three beams made of oak, corralled half a dozen horses, their long necks bent as they peacefully chewed the tall swaying grass, the occasional swishing tail chasing off flies.

Over to a far side, Gian could just make out the gardens. Stakes with the last of the summer's cucumbers climbing them, and posts of season's end tomato plants were bright green and red splotches in the distance.

He pulled up to the small grocery store that was only thirty feet or so in from the main road.

There were no other cars at the store. The driveway swirled around the back of the house where Gian could see another huge building, he assumed were the garages containing the residents' cars.

He parked and climbed out, gazing around the farmstead as he sauntered up to the store. Doves cooed above him in the stately oaks. It was otherwise surprisingly quiet for a working farm.

Gian could just hear a strain of music playing somewhere. He had expected the rumbling of farm tractors or maybe cows lowing in the meadows but it was as if the place was deserted.

Opening a screen door, he stepped inside and the smell of fresh vegetables assailed him along with the musky scent of wood from the planked walls. Several tidy rows of vegetables in bins lined down the middle.

Along the inside walls there were refrigerated eggs and cheese, and canned goods in clean shiny jars were neatly displayed on shelves beside them. The store was vacant.

A handwritten sign on the counter read: Please phone or text # for service. A phone number was listed on the sign.

Used to dealing with every kind of criminal lowlife that slinked across the land on its evil belly, Gian was aghast that the Kellys were so trusting. Especially that vain entitled bitch who he had hoped was here. His offer to come and get the cake wasn't entirely altruistic.

But then, he wasn't sure why he wanted to see the woman from the incident near the courthouse. Maybe to see the queen bee, or rather a princess in her element, in her castle on a throne disdainfully tossing out orders to every poor slob that came within her royal presence. Gian shook his head. He was an idiot.

There was even a cash register on the counter a child could easily carry out. He dialed the number on the sign but only voicemail came on. He left a message that he was in the shop to pick up a cake for Jessica Montanero. Then he placed a text message stating the same. He wandered around the shop while he waited.

After several minutes of nonresponse to his messages, annoyed, Gian tramped outside and glanced around. There was no sign of human life. Then, a bursting flock of birds squawked and ruffled with loud flapping of wings sprang from behind a stable. Gian started for that area.

As he passed the stable, he heard grunting and groaning. Afraid he was about to happen upon lovers in heat in a haystack, he slowed.

But it wasn't a lusting couple rolling in the hay he saw, it was the peachy rose princess struggling to push a wheelbarrow. She wasn't making much headway, the single front wheel dug in and refused to roll over the clumpy grass.

The wheel caught a rock and the cart suddenly toppled and large stones rolled out onto the ground. A cry of weary despair came from the woman as she fought to straighten the heavy wheelbarrow and then knelt beside it. She lifted one heavy stone after another straining to get them back inside the wagon.

"What the hell, woman," Gian growled, as he stomped to her. He nudged her aside and lifted the remaining stones and dumped them two and three at a time in the cart.

The woman tumbled backwards swiping blonde hair out of her eyes. "Hey! What are you doing?" She squawked again when he grasped her arm and lifted her to her feet.

Then he placed his hands on the handles of the barrel and said, "Which way?"

She blinked at him. Sweat poured down her temples, her shiny hair had been tied back but much of it floated around her shoulders and stuck to her damp face.

The sun dappled over light freckles making her look like a teenager. Her white t-shirt was soaked as were the jeans that were caked with mud and torn at one knee. He could see a trickle of blood in the tear.

"Which way?" she parroted.

Gian struggled to keep his eyes on her flushed face and not on the soaked T. It was so clinging and transparent, including the pink bra underneath, she might as well be naked. "Yeah. Where were you taking this shit?"

"I've got it," she announced, trying to push his hands off the handles.

"Yeah, sure you do." His scathing gaze raked down her feminine form. "It'll take you a year to go a few feet. Just tell me where this needs to go."

"I-" she started to argue then broke off. He was right. Pressing a hand to her lower back she pointed and said wearily, "Behind the second barn. Hoot said I needed the stones to prop up the broken fence."

He started pushing the cart, the wheel rumbled and squeaked over uneven grass. He wheeled it easily as if pushing a basket of feathers. The woman hurried after him. When she caught up, he said, "Hoot?"

Nodding, she shoved hair back off her sweaty face. "Yes. Hoot Jones. He's one of the hands here."

"Hmm." Gian made a sound with a grimace. "And where is this Hoot now?"

She stumbled over a rock, he threw his hand out and steadied her then kept pushing the cart. "Oh, he, uh, the guys, they're on a- a break."

He glanced at her then ahead. "Yeah? And what the hell are you doing out here?"

Her eyes on the ground lest she trip again, she told him, "Well, the cows got out of the broken fence this morning. It's imperative it gets fixed. There's so much to do, we're down some of the help. It's all hands-on deck, so to speak." She was breathless trying to keep up with him.

"How can it get fixed if the farmhands are on a break?" He was annoyed. No, he was pissed. He came to get a cake and had to stop his mission to help this useless girl.

Just as he thought, he let his gaze surreptitiously slide over her. As feminine and soft as a butterfly, her arrogant snotty attitude hidden under that swirl of golden hair and pearly skin that was rapidly becoming sunburned. And tired. The girl looked about on her last legs. Shapely, slender legs- he snapped his attention back forward.

"Oh, well." Her breathing came shallow and rapid, she replied, "I don't really know. I haven't seen much of them lately, but heavens, the work, it's-" she sucked in a deep breath, exhaled hard, "endless."

"Who's supposed to be running that store up there?" he asked, and slowed his stride.

As they passed a garage, Gian noticed a man inside in overalls bent over the engine of an old tractor. He muttered curses and lifted a wrench off the side of the tractor then stuck his head and the wrench inside the engine.

The music Gian had heard when he arrived was coming from a radio propped on the rung of a ladder.

Grateful, although winded, she replied, "That would be me. I'm sorry, did you-" she slipped her phone out and it lit up with his messages. "Oh, dear, mister, ah, I'm sorry. I didn't hear it ring or buzz. Probably couldn't hear it over my groaning and huffing," she said with wry, tired humor.

"Oh here," she pointed, telling him, "this is where I need the rocks."

Gian stopped the wheelbarrow and stepped over to where she indicated the broken fence. He squatted and examined the pillars lying on the ground. "Honey," he said with slight condescension, "the fence isn't broken. The pillars just need to be pounded more deeply into the ground and the beams reset."

The woman reached into the cart and picked up a stone with both hands. "I know. I tried to do it, see," she indicated a sledgehammer in the grass. "I just couldn't..." her shoulders rose in an embarrassed shrug. "Well, I couldn't do it, so Hoot said just prop them up with rocks."

Gian couldn't wait to meet this Hoot fellow who sent out a delicate, useless female to do a man's job. Chauvinist thought be damned it was true. Hell, the hammer was almost as big as she was. It was doubtful she could lift it, much less keep the pillar up while trying to pound it into the hard ground. If he wasn't so pissed he'd be laughing at the ludicrousness of it.

"Anyway," she said, "what do you need at the store? I'll fetch it and bring it to you at your car, then I'll get back and finish this."

He looked at her. Fortunately, the hard mask he called his face didn't show her how ridiculous she sounded. He trod over, straightened the pillar in its hole then retrieved the hammer and swung it a half-dozen times before he was satisfied the pillar wasn't coming out. Then he did the second and third ones.

When they were planted secure, he lifted the beams and strung them back through the holes in the pillars. Smacking his hands on his pants to clean off the dirt, he turned to her and wiped his sleeve across his forehead.

"There. Done. Come and get me my cake." He started to turn to head back to the store.

"What? No, wait, I mean thank you, but I have to put these stones back now or Hoot will-"

He snatched up her arm and ushered her ungainly across the rumpled grass muttering, "Hoot can come get his own damned rocks."

Gian ignored her protests all the way back to the store. He opened the screen door and pushed her inside then followed her in.

Red spots lit on her high round cheeks. Infuriated, she exclaimed, "How dare you manhandle me like that! You have no right to-"

"Okay, you're right. I shouldn't have put my hands on you," he said calmly, peering down at her, privately amused at her expression of ire. "I'm not known for my patience, and watching some poor girl try to shove around a bunch of rocks for a totally unnecessary task burned my ass."

"Oh, well," she sputtered, backing down at the apology she hadn't expected. "I, um, well, thank you, anyway, for your help. You are right, it would have taken me ages to accomplish what you did in minutes and I have so many other chores to get to. So, you've been of great assistance." She wiped at the perspiration dotting her forehead.

"Now, what would you like to purchase? It will of course be on the house as a thank you for your aid." She futilely tried to push her hair back into what used to be a braid.

To Gian, she looked like a pretty fluttering bird that had been suddenly unbranched and trying to get her wings under control and resettle. He had a surprising urge to grin. He had to regroup his thoughts. Pretty, graceful birds were not what he had any interest in.

Clearing his throat, he firmed his expression and said, "A cake. My…stepmother, Jessica Montanero ordered some kind of…" there it was again, another bird reference. "I don't know, it's some kind of a bird cake or something."

That brought such delicious laughter and twinkling in her sky-blue eyes Gian felt sharp tingles way down below. And he did not like it. The scowl on his face made her take a step back.

"Oh, um, I didn't mean to laugh at you, at your description. The cake Mrs. Montanero ordered is called a hummingbird cake."

The scowl firmed, he nodded. Sure, leave it to his brother to ask for such a sissy sounding cake. "That sounds like it. Mrs. Kelly was to have delivered it," he said with accusation in his tone.

Her face tinged redder under the sunburn. "I'm sorry. We've had some help issues and things have gotten, well, behind."

His brows arched. "Are you saying the cake hasn't even been made?"

Quickly she shook her head and said, "No, no, it's done. I finished it late last, well, early this morning. I just," her shoulders slumped with exhaustion.

"Well," she said feebly with her palms raised, "I'm sure delivering it is on the list of tasks for me to do, but I just haven't gotten to all of them yet. I'll go retrieve it for you right away. Wait here, it's up at the house." She tried to smile at him with reassurance but it came out wobbly.

She turned and started for the door and was startled when he reached around her and pushed it open, then held it for her to pass through. "Sir?" she asked in question over her shoulder.

"I'll go with you. I could use a drink of water."

"Oh, but I can get that for you here. I'll-"

"I'm on a schedule," he said, nudging her slightly with his torso out the door, the screen door slammed behind them.

"But it would only take a second. You don't need to come up to the house." She protested but he kept moving in the direction of the house so she traipsed after him with huffs of exasperation.

At the house, she ran around him and up the steps. Her muddy shoes tapped on the wooden floor of the verandah, his heavier stride followed right at her heels. The front door stood open and she hurried inside, he entered behind her.

The farmhouse was huge and modern but retained the old-world rustic, homey appeal. The central rooms were large and were entered through by wide archways instead of doors.

As they trod on polished wooden planked flooring, she muttered, "Should have come in through the mudroom off the kitchen, now I'm going to have to clean and polish the floor all over again."

Indeed, a trail of their muddy footprints followed them through the living room with the thick cushioned chairs and sofa done in shades of blue and red, with wood trimmed archways and scattered throw-rugs.

A stone fireplace anchored a wall with bookcases on either side of it. Grand windows let in bright light, family portraits hung beside antique landscapes on the buttercream walls.

They tracked down the hallway to a den. There were voices coming from the den.

She paused in the doorway and announced, "Um, everybody, I've fixed the fence." She shot a glance of apology at Gian for stealing credit for his work.

Continuing on to whomever was in the room, she said, "I've got to get that hummingbird cake and then I can get back to the hay baling. After that I can finish cleaning the kitchen before I tackle the bathrooms."

She sent someone a remorseful smile. "Auntie Jacalyn, I don't think I can get to your laundry today. I'm sorry, there's just not enough hours in the day."

A haughty voice uttered from the den, "Sorry? Miss, was I sorry when I took you in on holidays when your parents had their accident? Was I too busy to have the domestics feed you?"

The voice rose to a curt pitch. "Was I too selfish to provide you with your cousin Portia's very expensive cast offs when you grew out of your own clothes? Hmm? I rather think not. I think you were well taken care of. You are the height of laziness!" She took a very loud aggrieved breath before marching on.

"I've always said your parents would be appalled at your lack of breeding, now I have to add indolent to the list of your character flaws! All we ask is a *little* assistance in return whilst our home, *Manoir sur la Colline* is being repaired. Your poor departed parents would roll over in their graves at your rank ungratefulness."

The voice annoyed Gian's ears. The woman had pretentiously named her home House on the Hill in French. And worse, she pronounced it in a deplorable French accent. And that annoyed him too.

Yeah, he'd been feeling an abundance of annoyance lately, sometimes he missed the cussing and brawling of his days in the wild jungles. At least that had been honest hostility and blokes fighting with fists and curses instead of whining and tedious simpering over bullshit.

"Right on, Mama," a priggish voice joined in, a younger female's. "She's so unthankful, the plain pigeon. I mean we're guests, and since Grandma Lolly can't take care of us, you'd think Nikki could help out a little, am I right?"

"Now now, ladies," an older male's cultured voice intervened. "The girl does work hard. I'm sure if she puts a little more elbow grease into it she can get all her chores done in a reasonable timeframe, by oh, say, midnight?"

A harrumph of a snort sounded. A younger male remarked, "Geez you guys lay a lot on Nikki. You need to give her a break."

"Ah," the older woman replied, "are you offering to help her? You can start on the bathrooms." There was silence, then a smug, "I didn't think so."

The young male said without much assurance, "Well, I can help her by bringing in the firewood and getting the fireplaces lit and going. The remaining maid set a casserole for us in the oven before she left, I can set the table."

A third female voice chirped, "Don't forget, Nikki, the maid only made the casserole, you need to prepare the rest of the fixings. None of us can boil water for Pete's sake, you must feed us at least. You want us to starve? The potatoes won't peel themselves, and I need those cookies for my book club. We're family, you need to treat us better. So, you get supper going before you go taking care of that hay. The baling will take too long and we'll starve long before then!"

The elder woman rejoined, "Don't forget Grandma Lolly's bandage needs changing and she needs her tea. And, Grandpa

Tane needs his medicine, and Lolly said he needs something soft, like eggs for dinner. Only you, Nikki, make them the way he likes."

Bright pink lit Nikki's cheeks, she kept her mortified face forward not sparing a glance at Gian. "I- I'll get the cake and-and- start dinner then-" She blinked rapidly, clearly tired and embarrassed at being called out for being ungrateful, lazy and homely in front of a stranger. She started to pass by the den, but Gian stopped.

Nikki had to move aside as he used his body again to maneuver her so he could see inside.

Shades of freaking Cinder-effing-rella. Gian wondered, had he fallen into a pit of viperous wicked step-sisters and ugly stepmother?

In the large room, several people were lounging around on comfortable furniture that was plaid in color, with black and yellow plaid drapes bordering mullioned windows.

He noticed the white brick fireplace at the side wall, the couch and chairs were set semi-circle in front of it. A drink sat on tables within each of the occupants' reach, and a platter of pastries was set on a glass coffee table between the furniture.

"Oh my, whom do we have here?" A young woman pushed herself from a cushy plaid chair to approach Gian. Shoulder-length brown hair jostled across the tops of her shoulders. She tossed it back as she thrust her breasts up.

"Hi." She held her hand out and said, "I'm Lanira, and you are?" Brown eyes swept his frame and heated as they moved over his muscular body. A long mouth lifted at the corners in a coy Joker's smirk indicating she liked what she saw.

She appeared around thirty, and Gian wondered where she got off calling Nikki a plain pigeon. Lanira was average in everything; height, weight, looks. Her face was too long to keep her from being beautiful, that and the snobbish curl to her very long mouth, and the startling lascivious crook of it.

Gian moved to just inside the room, then stepped to the side to avoid her hand as well as to let Nikki enter the room.

"Uh, Auntie Jacalyn, this is, um…" Nikki turned fretfully to him, her brows inverted in question.

The woman she called Aunt Jacalyn who looked older than Jessica even with the heavy makeup slathered on her sallow face, said, "I believe you are Jessica Montanero's stepson. Giancomo. *Detective* Giancomo Montanero. There's been talk all over town about you. You're the hot topic of every salon and café. Jessica has been surveying all her friends' eligible daughters to start a queue for you."

Gian's eyes slid to Jacalyn. Brunette as well, she was a much older model of her daughter Lanira.

The three females had dark brown hair and various hues of brown eyes. The older male who was likely Jacalyn's husband, and the younger male had light brown hair and blue eyes. Gian nodded to the older man. His light brown hair was actually mostly white.

The man coughed and shoved to his feet. He wore a navy blazer with gold buttons over a white turtleneck and pressed trousers.

Made Gian think of the moneyed kind who hung at country clubs playing golf or yachting, swizzling cocktails, and chasing every tail in a skirt. His thinning hair was combed neatly to the side. The flaccid sides of his mouth shook as he hurried over to Gian with his hand out.

Gian shook it.

"Yes, ah, Detective John, ah, komo is it? Ah, I am Warren Canfield. This is my wife, Jacalyn," he said with a short cough and a huff, introducing them. "The taller girl is our eldest, Lanira, and Portia," he indicated a shorter version of Lanira, "is a year or so older than Nicolle."

Motioning to the young teenaged male, he told Gian, "Our son, Mason is the youngest. Oh," he said as an afterthought seeing Nikki's face pink with embarrassment, "but of course you know Jackie's brother's daughter, Nicolle. That is, we call her Nikki."

Jacalyn moved towards Gian blatantly studying his face and figure. She said, "The word is you grew up apart from your family. Your mother, it's said, took you when you were young and then dumped you while you were practically still in diapers in some foreign country where you were sold into a gang."

Ignoring the darkening of Gian's skin, she carried on with interest although she looked down her rather long nose at him as she rattled on. "They say you ended up in some elite killer opts or some such before-"

"Jackie!" Warren blurted, horrified at her rendition of Gian's private life. "We don't take to gossip here!" At least not to their faces.

He pressed his palms down the sides of his jacket to wipe the perspiration that was excreting from his discomfiture. His expression screamed '*what the hell is this policeman doing in our den*?' But he was too mannered, and intimidated, to voice his question.

Jacalyn was attired as her husband, as if she'd just left *the club*. She wore a dark blue dress that draped to her knees with mid-heeled pumps. Her hair was styled in wide short curls that brushed just below her ears. Pearls adorned her neck, ears, and one wrist.

"Oh Warren, get off it. It's not gossip if it's true. It is true, isn't it young man?"

"Hey." Her youngest daughter slipped over to join them. More shyly but with the same lascivious gleam as Lanira's in her amber eyes, she cocked her head in a coquettish manner. She minced, "I'm Portia, pleasure to meet you, um, John-komo?"

"No darling," her mother corrected her. "It sounds like John but it's Gian, the J sound is a bit softer, more like Shawn with a harder J instead of an S."

"Well, Gian," Portia offered, shifting closer to him, "won't you join us for a cocktail? Nikki will make you whatever you'd like."

"Thanks, but I've come for the cake for Jessica's clambake. I understand it's ready. Nicolle, you were going to retrieve it?" Urgency to get away from the despicable people made his accent heavier and his voice growly. The two cousins practically purred in response.

Nikki jumped. "Oh, yes, of course, please come with me, I'll get your-"

"Yes, numbskull," Lanira sneered at her cousin, "give him his cake so you can get on with our dinner." She glanced at her mother with a frown. "Why is it we decided not to attend the Montaneros' clambake? Everyone in town is supposed to be there."

Through pursed lips, her mother told her, "Because dear, we Canfields do not run around with heathens in Daisy-Duke shorts gnawing on chicken wings, spitting tabaccy and sucking down domestic ales."

She inclined her head to Nikki, with a haughty smile. "Now dear, please hurry along. We will entertain Mr. Montanero whilst you're away."

Her face tinted pink, Nikki's eyes lowered to the floor as she started to turn around to do as her aunt bade.

Gian moved to block her retreat. Taking her arm, he said, "I'm sorry, but Miss Nicolle will be coming with me, she will be unable to complete any of those…chores you have planned for her."

The women gasped, Warren frowned, the boy, Mason grinned.

Jacalyn rose to her feet, her head lifted with queenly dignity. "Why on earth would she be going with you when she has work here to do?"

"I-" Nikki opened her mouth to speak but Gian cut her off.

"She agreed to deliver a cake to my stepmother's party, and that is what she will do. You all will have to fend for yourselves. You ready?" he asked a stunned Nikki.

"But," Nikki protested, jerking her arm away from his grasp. "You're here now, you can take the cake with you."

He turned to face her. Looming over her, he used his height and breadth to intimidate warriors in the field, she was but a declawed kitten beneath his harsh perusal. "Am I not correct in stating that you had agreed to deliver the cake?"

Her lips flapped open and closed. "But- but, it's unnecessary as you are here-"

"I see. So you don't keep your word. Understood. I will report this back to my stepmother who will assuredly advise her friends to not avail themselves of a business that does not keep its word, fails to fulfill its contracts. Well," he let out a heavy sigh and nodded to Warren and Jacalyn, said, "I'll be on my way-"

"No, wait!" Nikki moved to now block his exit. "I- I will follow you in my car. If you just give me the address, it will save time in looking it up."

"I don't think so, Miss Kelly. You've inconvenienced me enough. You either come with me and follow through on your contract, or, well, as I said…"

"Hey," the boy interjected. "I can drive it over. I'm practicing for my learner's permit when I'm eligible. Get me a chance to get the heck out of here and take Granddad's Lincoln for a spin. I heard a funky noise the other day, I can get up under the hood and check it out." He had the dreamy look of a boy in love with cars on his face when his mother spoke over him.

"You will do no such thing, Mason! First of all, you are not old enough to drive. And second, you are not a laborer. Working on autos is way beneath your station. A Canfield does not get his hands dirty!" Jacalyn remonstrated him.

The boy's crestfallen face crumpled further.

"You ready to complete your contract?" Gian calmly said to Nikki.

"But this is ridiculous!" Jacalyn insisted. "It's not a contract, it was simply an order. You can't expect her to abandon us in our hour of need just to go with you to-"

"I'll go!" Lanira announced.

"No, me! I'll go with you!" Portia pushed her sister aside.

"You heifer, I'm going with him!" Lanira pushed her back.

Portia shoved her, shouting, "No! Me!"

"Girls, girls," Warren begged wearily, getting between his hellcat daughters. He said to Gian, "Now, son, I'm sure we can work something out to your desires and allow Nikki to stay here where she is needed. I mean, you can carry a simple cake by yourself, can't you?"

Muttering, "What the hell did I fall into? Freaking Cinderella-ville," Gian rolled his arm around Nikki's shoulders and turned her towards the door then he faced back to the room.

He said to the others, "How about I tell you how it's going to be. You," he nodded to Jacalyn, "you can see to the elderly folks' needs while you do your own damned laundry. You," he said to Warren, "can retrieve the firewood and get the fireplaces going."

Ignoring their gasps, he looked at Lanira and told her, "Time you learned to cook. Make dinner and prepare your own damned cookies. You," he said to Portia, "can start on cleaning a bathroom and then the living room floor needs re-mopping."

As if they weren't all gawking at him with looks of aghast, he continued, "Then you can help your sister. It's likely the hamfisted pair of you will make a terror out of the kitchen and I don't want to hear what kind of mess you leave for your cousin Nicolle to come home to and be expected to clean up."

He slit such a mean eye at the girls they both took a step back.

"Uh," Mason gulped, asked, "what should I do, sir?" He was in his early teens, but Gian had held a gun and charged into street-gang battle when he was half the lad's age.

Gian eyed him up and down. Mason wore a cashmere sweater over a long-sleeved shirt and tweed trousers that likely his mother had bought him. Loafers with tassels were on his sockless feet.

"You," Gian told him, "can change the phone number on the sign in the store to ring you when there's a customer. Then you can go put on jeans and a sweatshirt and help the mechanic work on the tractor in the garage."

Mason's eyes lit up. Fist punching the air, he crowed with glee, "All right!"

"No, you will not-" Jacalyn shut her mouth as her son raced out the door to follow Gian's, not her orders. Furious red streaks blared on her square cheeks as she regarded the interloper. "How dare you!"

When Gian kept moving, she yelled louder. Ignoring her, he hustled Nicolle quickly down the hall out of ear range.

Chapter Eleven

Gian kept his hand on Nikki's lower back until they reached the kitchen. Neither said a word.

Nikki moved to the commercial refrigerator and opened the door. She pulled out a huge round Tupperware with an attached handle.

Moving to the white-tiled island in the center of the kitchen she set the Tupperware down. Her back to him, she said, "See, it's all ready. There will of course be no charge, you can go ahead and take it-"

"No," he said from the doorway.

She turned around. He stood with boots planted hard on the ground, his arms crossed over a very bulky chest.

"But mister, you-"

"It's Gian. Nicolle, we are not going over this again. I'll wait here while you shower and change your clothes."

Her brows rose. "Shower? Change my clothes? Why? As soon as I return, I'll have to go right back out and finish the chores that need-"

"You are changing because you are not coming to my parents' house looking like you just won a wet T-shirt contest." His gaze lowered to her chest. The shirt was still wet, still transparent. He watched her look down then heat blazed across her face.

Her hands went first to her hot cheeks then her arms folded to cover her chest. "Oh my God, why didn't you say something?" Her voice came out in a high squeak.

Because I was enjoying the view, he thought to himself, but said to her, "Because I'm in a hurry. I mentioned that before."

Her face beet red, she scowled at him. "Then if you're in such a hurry just take the darn cake and go! There is certainly no need for the both of us to go."

"I'll wait for you in the living room. I would wait in my truck but I fear if I leave you alone with those people they'll stuff you in a closet and hide you until I leave."

Shaking her head, she bit back a smile. "You're insane. My family wouldn't do such a thing." The stifled smile diminished to doubt. His comment was absurd, yet…

Gian didn't share her smile. He was a cop. One look and he could tell this *family* of hers had not one iota of her best interests at heart.

He felt like Cinderella's fairy godfather for cripes sake because apparently she had no one looking out for her and she was too much of a bleedin' simpleton to do it herself. One of those beauty no brains chicks, the epitome of the dumb blonde bimbo.

"Get a move on, I've wasted enough time here."

"Really, you make no sense. If I shower and change, the time that will take will-"

"Just do it."

She stood blinking at him, appalled at his bullying. But, she saw the determined lift of his strong jaw, and the Kellys' company couldn't afford to get a black eye from him blabbing all over town that they renege on their sales deals. With a laborious sigh, she swept past him.

As she headed down the hall for the stairs to her room, he said, "Put on something picnicky, something nice, not slutty."

And she almost turned right back with a fierce retort. However, she knew he was not going to back down. The sooner she did what he asked- no ordered- the sooner she could return and get her work done.

She would never admit to herself she was actually looking forward to a break, even an enforced one. And a neighborhood clambake sounded like a divine escape.

Gian didn't head straight for the living room. He went out the back door of the mud room that exited towards the barns.

Tromping over grass that needed mowing, he made his way to the bunkhouse. When he reached it, he could see a variety of cars and trucks parked along the side. He didn't knock, just pushed the screen door open and stepped inside.

The door wafted a few times before it slammed behind him. By that time, he'd already taken in the room and was swiftly moving through it.

It was a long T shape. One end was lined with bunks with bathrooms and private lockers at the far back. A large square room was in the middle which was where the hands hung out when not working. At the other end a kitchen area with a small farm table were situated.

In the center section, two card tables were set up with straight-backed chairs placed at them. Several easy chairs sat in front of a huge flat-screen TV. Three sofas were placed along the wall, and across from the TV was the requisite fireplace.

Several men were hunched over a card table playing poker. Two men snoozed on sofas. Closest to the door, a man sat in a wooden chair. He tipped back on the two back legs and leaned his shoulders against the wall, he was reading a girlie magazine. Gian could see the naked girl on the cover from the doorway.

First thing Gian did was stomp over to the man in the tipped chair and swung his foot out kicking the raised legs up- the chair and the man instantly toppled. The man let out a yelp before crashing.

Then Gian moved to the poker-playing group and swept his forearm across the table scattering cards, money, drinks, ashtrays, and plates that contained remnants of chips and sandwiches. Everything went flying.

"Hey!" the men bellowed. Three of the four farmhands jumped to their feet.

Gian marched over to a sofa and thumped a sleeping man on the side of his head. The man woke with a spluttered curse.

Before Gian could get to the other sofa, the man reclining on it was already getting to his feet. He backed away from Gian with his hands up to ward him off. "Whoa, bro, back off," he exclaimed, his drowsy eyes rounding with confused fear.

"What the freakin' hell?" the man still sitting at the card table barked.

"Which one of you lazy bastards is Hoot?" Gian demanded. Eyes darted around but no one said anything.

Gian drew his fists up and repeated, "Not gonna ask again, gonna knock heads." Eyes flew to the single man still sitting at the card table. Gian turned to look at him.

The man let out a huff and pushed his chair back then stood up with a glower. "I'm James Hooten Jones, what's it to you? Who the hell do you think you are coming in here like some goddamned gangster and attackin' us?"

Gian stared at the man with the weathered, pock-marked face. He appeared to be in his forties, hadn't shaved for a day or so, his lanky hair could use a comb and a wash, he pushed a toothpick in his mouth back and forth.

With angular features, his deeply tanned skin was woven with creases around his dark eyes and thin mouth. Jones' knobby fingers clamped on lean hips. He wore dusty jeans and a flannel shirt. He held his ground when Gian crossed the room to him.

His boots clomping on the floor adding to the scuffmarks already littered on the planks, Gian ignored the other men who all backed away from the pair.

Gian's skin was dark with fury but he spoke coolly, "I came across a young woman in the pasture trying to maneuver a wheelbarrow filled with rocks. She said you told her to prop the fallen pillars up with them to fix the fence. Besides it being the stupidest jerry-rigging I've ever seen in my life, why the hell would you have her do that?"

While Gian spoke, the side of Hoot's lip nicked up, the toothpick shifted insolently to the other side of his mouth and Gian heard the men around them snickering. His eyes narrowed at them and they quieted.

Gian said, "Is there a joke I'm missing here?" The laughter started again, louder, and Hoot's thin lips broke out in a snide grin exposing cracked yellow teeth.

"You gonna let me in on the joke?" Gian asked Hoot.

Hoot glanced around at the other men who were all cackling and then back to Gian. He shrugged. "Sure. Yeah, it was a joke. Lanira and Portia Canfield paid me fifty bucks to pull one over on the little sweetheart. She's a college girl, didn't grow up here, knows nuttin' 'bout farmin'. They thought it would be funny to see how far the girl would go before she collapsed from exhaustion. I mean, we were watchin' her out the window and when the gales of laughter struck us, we had to give up and stop watchin' or we'd split a royal gut, ya know?"

"Yeah, how gullible can a broad be?" One of the hands bent over laughing. Between guffaws, he spurted, "A beauty, trying so hard to please her uppity family who keep telling her she owes them," he nudged the man beside him grinning.

"I'm gonna check out how hard she'll try to please me. I plan on finding out how sweet she is on the inside; you get my drift?" The farm crew roared with laughter.

Gian's mouth hardened as he looked around at the hysterical men. "Hmm, yes, real funny." He said to Hoot, "I hear the Kellys are down some hands and the farm is falling behind in work that needs to be done."

Hoot nodded in agreement, said around the toothpick, "Tru dat, boy."

Gian retorted, "Then why in the hell are you guys sitting around here playing games and letting things fall apart?"

Hoot sent his friends a wink then replied with another shrug, "Hell, boy, the old man is down and can't crack the whip. The old lady is out too so there's no one to be in charge. The prissy couple stayin' there with the useless daughters wouldn't deign to lift a manicured finger to work the likes of a farm. Why should we work if we don't have to?"

Gian wished he wasn't a cop, just for two minutes. It was all he could do to keep his fists to himself and not pound the yellow teeth into the man's stomach. "You idiots, if the farm goes under you all are out a job."

"Not a big deal man." Hoot shrugged with a glance at his cohorts. "Jobs like this around here are dime a' dozen. We already got bankrolled two months ahead. So we get a little paid vacation for a bit, what's it to you?"

Gian who had worked his ass off since he was a tot saw red. He'd seen other orphaned children literally starve to death on the streets. Most had to turn to crime or prostitution to keep bread in their mouths.

And to sit back and watch the Kelly family lose their home, their livelihood through unmitigated laziness and selfishness, before he realized it, his hands were clutching Jones' collar. He lifted him off the floor and slammed him into a wall. The toothpick fell out of Hoot's open mouth.

The other men froze, then two moved forward- Gian snarled at them, "Stay back or you're next." They froze.

Gian shoved his face in Hoot's letting his rage show through burning dark eyes and grit teeth. His deep voice gravelly with his accent, he said, "I am only going to say this once. You," he glanced around, "all of you, are going to get off your useless duffs now, right now, and get to work."

His face inches from Hoot's, he went on, "You're getting paid for cripe's sake to do your jobs, not sit around and freaking knit. And, you will not let that girl step one foot on the grounds to do one scintilla of farm work. Get it straight," he squeezed his fist in Hoot's collar cutting off half his air.

The man's feet twitched as he hung, but he was too afraid to kick out at Gian.

"What the hell are you, man, her- her enforcer? Her freakin' boyfriend?" one of the men queried from a safe distance.

Gian didn't look at him. He said to Hoot, "I am the man that says the girl does not lift an egg from under a hen, toss feed to a chicken, rake a strand of hay, swing a hammer, touch a lawnmower, carry a bucket, milk a cow, climb a ladder, paint an inch of wood. Nothing, nada, zilch. She reaches for a shovel, you take it from her. You don't tell her why, she doesn't hear about our conversation." He was so enraged, Gian felt steam rolling out from his ears.

"If I find out you assholes didn't do one hint of your jobs, or you let that little girl harvest an ear of corn, I'll be back and finish what I started." *And I'll leave my badge at home.*

Hoot's blood-shot eyes reared back at Gian. Breathing stale booze into his face, he stuttered, "W- who the hell do you think you are to tell us what to-"

Gian pulled Hoot's head back and slammed it against the wall. "I am Giancomo Montanero and I am telling you that you will do as I say or I'll be back and I'll be putting your dentist to work. And the hospital. Make me really mad and it'll be the morgue that comes calling."

"He's bluffing," a man blurted, stomping forward. "He can't threaten us-" He froze when Gian swung his unearthly gaze to him.

"Am I bluffing?" Gian glared at the man then back to Hoot. "Go ahead, try me."

"Who the hell do you-"

"By the way," Gian said, "I have friends from a world that just knowing them would make your balls shrivel to dust. If anything were to ever happen to me or my family or friends, or Nicolle Kelly, you will be begging them to let you die." His eyes narrowed to dark slits, he sneered, "Am I clear? Any questions?"

His eyes crossing from the head slam, Hoot shook his head, blinked hard, muttered through his crooked yellow teeth, "No."

Gian looked around at the others. "What about the rest of you? Do we need to each have a little talk?"

A collective shaking of heads moved in the room.

Gian went on, "Do I need to tell you what will happen if one of you even thinks of laying a finger on that girl? If her bitch cousins pay you to hurt her, touch her, try to bang her, I won't beat *them* to a bloody pulp because they are women." He looked unwavering at each of them through eyes slit hard.

The men all took a few steps away, stuffed their hands in their pockets, hung their heads and shook them, mumbling, "No, sir, nope, gotcha."

Gian gave Hoot a hard shake then opened his hands and the man tumbled to his feet, then his knees gave out and he dumped on his ass on the floor.

Without another word, slapping the screened door open with his palm, Gian strode out of the bunkhouse, the door wafted a few times before it slammed shut behind him. Fuming, he stalked across the lawn to the house.

Stomping inside, he reached the living room just as Nikki was coming down the doublewide staircase. He almost stumbled.

She wore a pale-yellow sundress with tiny white flowers on it and capped sleeves, along with heeled sandals and was pulling a short, waist-length sweater on over the top.

Gian swallowed the sudden glitch in his throat. Reminding himself he does not do soft and pretty, no, he prefers sturdy women a shade on the plain side. She'd already peeled open a protective side he didn't even know he possessed.

It made his mind boggle and he couldn't get a handle on what he was thinking, feeling. He stepped up to her, keeping his eyes off her legs, and her hips, and her breasts, he said to her shoulder, "You ready?"

She halted at his voice, she hadn't seen him come in. "Oh, yes, no, I mean I need to get the cake."

She hurried down the hall, wet ringlets flopping on her back, and returned in seconds carrying the large round Tupperware. Gian took it from her when they reached the door.

He held the door open for her to go out, and they crossed the verandah, down the steps and to his truck. She felt like he was rushing her, but bit back the protest because she thought she was forgetting something.

Opening the passenger door, he said, "Hop in."

Nikki stood, her lips pulled in, in consternation. "Listen, really, it makes no sense for both of us to drive out to your mom's house. I'll need to return home so it will be best if I follow you in my car if you insist-" she started back to the house to get her car keys but he grabbed her arm.

"I said I was in a hurry, just get in the truck and quit wasting my time." He about lifted her by her arm and pushed her inside and onto the seat. "Buckle up," he said, and stood waiting for her to do it.

With a huff of vexation, Nikki buckled the seatbelt, and he set the cake on her lap and shut the door. Then he trod around the front of the truck and climbed in behind the wheel.

She sat staring at him like he was completely insane.

Neither said a word until they had traveled a few miles, then Gian asked, “Why in God’s name do you let them treat you like that? Like some kind of brainless slave?” He didn’t hide the derision in his voice.

He thought she was just plain dumb to let herself get used like she was. He shot a glance at her and his stomach clenched. She lowered her head but not before he caught a glimmer of a tear.

Before he could say another word, she lifted her head, sucked in a deep breath and told him, “I was six when my parents were killed in a boating accident. They were with some other couples and the driver, well, I understand all of them had been drinking. It was dark when they were returning, he didn’t see the jetty until it was too late.”

His head turned briefly to her. Feeling like a heel, he murmured, “I’m sorry.”

She bumped one shoulder. “Thanks, it was a long time ago. We were living in Amsterdam, they had just entered me into a boarding school. Daddy was a data architect and mama was a pilot.”

“Busy people,” Gian noted.

“Yeah, very. Mama was a floater. Her home base changed often and randomly, and Daddy worked 16-hour days. They thought it would be better for me, more stable if I was in the same school instead of bouncing around and getting nannies or tutors. I was unplanned, a…an accident.”

Her shoulders rose sheepishly. “They didn’t plan on having children, at least not then, and they didn’t have the time for me. When they…passed, they had little in their bank accounts. They liked to work hard and play hard. I was lucky that Daddy’s insurance paid for the rest of my education through college, but that was it.”

“You stayed in the boarding school?” His brow furrowed as he glanced quickly at her then back to the road.

She nodded. “Yes, everyone thought it was the…easiest, it would be for the best.”

A snort erupted as he shook his head. "Easiest for whom? You have a family, why didn't they take you in? I mean, you were an orphan for God's sake."

Nikki turned her head to look out the side window; she didn't want him to see her tears brimming. She sniffed them back. "I guess Grandma Lolly and Auntie Jacalyn thought just leave everything status quo. It was what my parents had planned…so…"

He snorted again. "Nice. What was that crap then that they were on about? That your evil stepmother Jacalyn gave you food and donated your wicked stepsisters' clothes to you?"

Not smiling at his ugly quip, he was too close to the truth, she looked down at the cake on her lap.

"She's my aunt, not my stepmother, they are my cousins, and I am not Cinderella. Out of the kindness of their hearts they let me come and visit on holidays when the school was closed and everyone had to leave."

Gian glanced at her then quickly looked away.

"In those earlier days, Nana and Gramps were too busy at the farm to have a young child stay there permanently. Aunt Jacalyn and Uncle Warren only built their mansion here a few years ago, until then they had resided in Newport, and they were busy, um… too."

She had never been too clear on what they did other than raise their children with nannies and servants so she left it at that. Aunt Jacalyn never worked and Warren Canfield came from old money.

"Uh huh. They *let* you visit on holidays. How generous of them. So, why are you here now, and why are you allowing them to work you like a dog?"

Staring back out the side window, she answered, "At least I had family to stay with on the holidays, Mister, um, Monta- ah, and, well, the insurance was a paid plan for my education and my room and board, but it didn't pay for clothes or anything else. Gram and Auntie Jacalyn put me up when I came home, and my aunt gave me clothes that Portia grew out of."

"So? It was the least they could do, feed and clothe their orphaned granddaughter and niece." The snide sarcasm wasn't the least bit curbed.

Her head twisted and she gave him a mild glare. "They didn't *have* to do anything."

When he looked at her, she turned back to face the window. "My grandparents are well off now, but in the early days they worked around the clock. Gram sent me money when she had extra, yet most of the time the money they made had to be reinstituted back into the farm."

"But-"

"Anyway, several months or so ago Gram fell off a ladder and broke one of her arms and gouged up the other pretty badly, and Grandpa Tane became ill. A few farmhands and two maids left, so my grandparents needed help in a hurry. Hence, my aunt brought me home to help out in the house and with the farm."

"So why are those freeloaders living here?"

Nicolle rolled her eyes at his insult to her family. She patiently explained, "As I said, Aunt Jacalyn and Uncle Warren don't live at the farmhouse. They have their own place a few miles away. There were some bad storms that caused a lot of damage. Shingles on the roof ripped off causing massive flooding and then mold leached in. The home needs a lot of repairs so they are staying at Gram and Gramp's until their house is habitable again."

"Hmm," he grunted. "Your grandparents are out of commission, that doesn't explain why you are slaving away and doing everything. Cooking, cleaning, doing their laundry for heaven's sake, girl, put your damned foot down."

Nikki cried angrily, "You don't understand! I owe them! They didn't have to be kind on the holidays. I was on a student visa in Amsterdam but not allowed a work permit when I came of age. Granddad and Gram sent me pocket money, what they could afford while I was away at school. They took care of me the best they were able to. As I said, the farm went through some rough patches for a few years so money was scarce.

"I am grateful for what they've done for me. I don't want to stir the waters when Granddad is so sick and Nana needs help. She's a little hard of hearing to begin with when she doesn't wear her hearing aid. I always have to yell into the phone. I- I can't let the household fall apart, or stand back and watch the farm go under without doing all I can to help.

"We're short help on the farm too. Lanira told me Hoot was in charge while Gramps was out of commission and that I needed to assist there as well. I just," her chest collapsed with a burdened sigh. "Just, let it be. I've told you too much. It's really none of your business."

Gian had to hold his tongue. She was incredibly gullible. The family and the farmhands were outrageously abusing and using her and she was too naïve to see it, and too selfless to not pitch in and do all she could to help them.

Too bad she couldn't see her aunt, uncle and cousins were not helpless and could fend for themselves, and she didn't owe them shit. They'd laid a huge guilt trip on her. A couple of lousy holidays and some cast-offs for the poor lonely child and they acted like they'd given her a kingdom.

He wanted to set her straight, but seeing that little sharp chin of her raised defiantly he knew his words would bounce right off her pretty head. Woman needs a keeper. His lips bunched, it wasn't going to be him, so he needed to do what everyone was telling him, mind his own business.

Sure. How does a soldier warrior stand with his hands in his pockets and watch a bank manager accost a defenseless female on the street while said banker offers his help if she sleeps with him?

Lawford Raines hadn't said that specifically but he intimated strongly enough that was his plan.

And, how was Gian to look the other way while indolent farmhands gave her dangerous work that was too hard for her to accomplish, and, was he to keep his mouth shut while her loving family worked her to death like a dog?

Yes. Absolutely. MYOB. Of course, that doesn't explain why he was driving to his dad's house with her sitting in the passenger seat of his Ram 2500.

Chapter Twelve

They were silent for the rest of the way to his family's home. When Gian pulled up in the driveway and parked, he said, "Wait for me to come around for you."

He opened the door and took the cake from her and set it on the floor at her feet. "Swing your legs around," he told her, "but don't get out of the truck," and he opened a rear door.

Puzzled, Nikki did as he said. For all she knew she was stepping down into a nest of snakes or a mud pile or something.

Slamming the door, he came back and stood in front of her. He set a medic kit on the hood of the car, then took out antiseptic and bandages.

"What-"

Tucking the bandages in his shirt pocket, he crouched in front of her and opened the antiseptic then held a cotton ball over the top and poured some liquid onto the ball. "You didn't notice the gash on your knee?" he asked, while dabbing at the cut.

"Ow- hey, I- hey that hurts," she complained trying to draw her knee up and away from him.

He grasped her calf to hold her still. "These sorts of things usually do." He patted the cut, holding her leg tightly when she squirmed. "It's deep enough to still bleed. I can't believe you weren't feeling the pain."

Scowling down at the top of his head, she said, "I did. I put a bandage on it; it must have fallen off. You were in such a hurry, I, well it distracted me from the pain. I just wanted to get you out of the house before my family- anyway, I can do that. Just give me the bandages." She held her hand out, which he ignored.

When he was satisfied the bleeding had stopped, he pressed the bandage over the cut and secured it. Slipping his hands around her waist, he lifted her from the high seat and set her on her feet like she was a child. Tossing the kit on the seat, he grabbed the cake and shut the door. "This way," he said and lightly grasped her upper arm.

Nikki was about to complain about his treating her like a child, but the stinging pain in her knee had subsided from the antiseptic he'd put on it, so she kept quiet and allowed him to propel her up the driveway.

Surrounded by a few acres of neatly mown lawn, the house was brick, not institutional red brick but had more variegated colors in them like green and pastel blues and pinks and yellows. Hunter green shutters trimmed the many windows.

Gian guided Nikki through the front door painted lacquer black. He brought her through the foyer done in blue and white tile and led her down a hall where voices flowed from.

The kitchen was huge and bright with reds and yellows, and filled with numerous women that were chattering. The air was crisp, but bright sunshine shone through the large window framed in yellow and white ruffled curtains.

A side door was open to the outside and more voices filtered from it. The patio could be seen through the doorway.

"Gian!" Jessica saw him and dropped the tomato she was chopping for a salad. A huge bowl of greens and veggies sat before her on the butcher block island.

Wiping her hands on the apron tied around her waist she hurried to him. "You were gone quite a while I was afraid you weren't coming back." She stood on her toes and kissed him on the cheek.

He didn't blush but he looked like he had to fight it. "Yeah. Here's the cake, where do you want it?"

Motioning with a flip of her hand, Jessica told him, "You can set it right there on the counter." The counter was crammed with food, dishes, condiments, the party was a big and busy event. Smiling at Nikki, she said, “Now, who have you brought with you? A date?” She sounded thrilled that Gian had brought a young woman to the clambake.

“Shit, no, Jess,” the tips of his ears darkened, then he quickly explained before she could correct his profanity. “This is Miss Nicolle Kelly. Lolly Kelly’s granddaughter. She’s helping out at the farm. She baked the cake and helped me bring it.”

Jessica glanced from Gian to Nikki, a red brow arched. “Helped you bring it? Does it weigh that much?” She looked to the Tupperware on the counter. “Looks big, but I think you could have handled it on your own.” Her voice held mirth.

“Mrs. Montanero,” Nikki said, “I must apologize for my lack of attention to your order. I prepared the cake but, well, time just got away from me. I, well, I forgot to bring it over. Mr. Montanero,” she nodded to Gian without looking at him, “sort of insisted I come with him with the cake to, uh, offer my apologies in person.”

“Oh?” Jessica’s gaze swung to Gian, the brow raised higher, a twinkle danced in her hazel eye.

“Don’t read anything into it, Jess,” Gian told her. “There was…” he glanced at Nikki, her cheeks stained pink. “I’ll explain later. Right now, I need a beer and she needs some lobster. She could use a little meat on her bones.”

At Nikki’s affronted gasp, Gian said, “Come on, we-”

“Honey!” Jessica cried out. “She’s hurt.” Indeed, the blood had started again leaking through the bandage.

Embarrassed, Nikki grabbed a paper towel off the counter and pressed it to the cut. “It’s nothing really. Mrs. Montanero, if I could just use your phone to call a taxi-”

“A taxi?” Her mouth falling open, Jessica looked to Gian.

His eyes were on the blood running down Nikki’s leg. “She just needs a thicker bandage. I have a kit out in the truck.”

“Nonsense,” Jessica said firmly. “Come with me, dear, let me take care of it.”

Shaking her head, mortified, because all the people in the kitchen had stopped what they were doing and were staring at her with curiosity. "No, please, if I can borrow your phone, I didn't bring my purse. He rushed me, I forgot-"

"Of course, dear." Jessica took her arm and gently ushered her across the kitchen to a door. "Let's get you fixed up, get a cold drink and some food in you, you look a bit pale." She gave Gian a wink over her shoulder as she escorted Nikki to one of the many bathrooms.

It only took a few minutes and they returned to the kitchen. Nikki had thought for sure the bossy bully would have been long gone. But no, he was standing by the sink washing his hands. A brunette was gabbing in his ear. A tall, voluptuous, pretty brunette.

Nikki's stomach quelled. She was so confused. Giancomo continuously glared at her like he didn't like her, but then he ordered her family to do her chores and insisted she come to this party with him.

At first she thought he was trying to punish her for not delivering the cake. But then, he seemed to settle down and was almost…kind to her. Nikki had entertained the thought that perhaps he…was interested in her? How wrong she was, he has a girlfriend.

But now, observing that beautiful woman hanging all over him, Nikki gave herself a mental slap. Of course, he was angry with Nikki for falling down on her job and he was punishing her by making her take time out of her busy day to come with him. He was trying to humiliate her.

Well, she had enough humiliation thank you very much.

Besides, big, buff, cold, harsh men were certainly not her type. That is if she was inclined to date, or even had the time, she would be more interested in a more refined man like Lawford Raines. Well, not him either, he was a cad. Just… she shook her head.

"Mrs. Montanero," she said to Jessica. "I appreciate you helping me. I must be going now. I have so much work to do at the farm. Can I borrow your phone?"

At the sink, Gian dried his hands and set the towel on the counter. Turning around, he lifted a brow at Nikki. "And how do you plan on paying the taxi?"

Nikki frowned at him. Her eyes narrowed with puzzled accusation. "You hurried me, you- you deliberately made me forget my purse. Why? Are you trying to force me to stay here? You've made your point that I fell down on the job. I have apologized, and now I really must return to the farm, there are many people depending on me. You can be satisfied that I'll have to work late into the night to catch up now. Perhaps one of your guests is leaving and can give me a ride?"

The voluptuous woman sidled over and slipped her hand through Gian's arm. "Chuck Larame is between women right now, Gian, I'm sure he'd be more than happy to take care of your little lady friend." Her gaze rolled insolently up and down Nikki's figure attired in the sundress and tiny sweater. Her attention stalled on the bandage on her knee and she snorted. "What are you, five?"

Nikki's eyes rounded, appalled at the rude woman.

"Hey, is that my cake?" Deo strode in through the back door, a grin decorating his handsome face. He beelined for the round Tupperware on the counter. Grabbing a paper plate off a stack, he lifted the lid which was already unlatched, and his tongue poking out the corner of his mouth he set the lid on the counter then squawked, "Hey!"

Everyone looked to see what he made him bark. Deo turned his attention to glare at his brother. "There's a damned slice missing from my cake!"

Gian shrugged. "Not your cake. It's Jessica's for the party. I'm part of the party." He had been washing his hands because he'd cut a slice and hadn't bothered with a fork or a plate. He'd eaten the slice using his hand.

He moved to Nikki. "Come on, I promised you some lobster, and I need a beer to wash that cake down. You're right," he said to Deo, "it's a damn good cake."

A scowl creased the pretty brunette's face. "Gian honey, where are you going? I thought we'd-"

As if the woman hadn't spoken to him, his hand on her back, ignoring Nikki's protests, Gian ushered her out the door to the bustling patio.

"Really, Mr. Montanero-" Nikki blustered at his high-handedness.

Keeping them moving, Gian said, "My father is Mr. Montanero. I've answered to Sergeant, Detective or Gian for the last few years."

"But- your girlfriend, for heaven's sake, she's going to be so angry-"

Keeping them moving, he led them to the long buffet table laid out to the hilt. The table groaned with burgers, hot dogs, steaming clams, corn on the cob, a variety of salads, chips, desserts and on and on.

"Grab what sides you want then we'll go over to the grills and get the lobster," Gian said as he handed her a plate.

She wanted to fight him, but her stomach was growling. And he was correct, she was thin. Since leaving college and working so hard the past few months, she either worked through meals not having time to eat, or the hard work was shredding pounds off her. Already on the slim side she really couldn't afford such weight loss.

In seconds she was piling potato salad, corn on the cob, and macaroni salad on her plate. Glancing over at Gian's piled high plate, she said, "You aren't going to have room for the lobster."

He cocked his head with a brief smile at her. "I'll manage. What do you want to drink? There's soda, beer, wine, iced tea," he looked across the patio and saw someone had set up a makeshift bar. "There's also hard stuff if you want a real drink."

Nikki needed her wits about her. She really wasn't sure why she was there, and when and how she would return to the farm. If she had to, as a last resort she could call and ask-beg one of her relatives to come and fetch her. "Iced tea sounds refreshing," she answered.

"Tea it is." He brought her to a table containing buckets of iced sodas and carafes of water and iced tea. "Sweetened?" he asked, his gaze sliding down her figure.

Before she could respond he set his plate down and grasped the pitcher of tea that had a yellow dot on it indicating it had sugar in it and poured her a glass. He handed it to her then plucked a can of beer from a bucket and tucked it in his jacket pocket.

Next, they moved to a grill. "Hey, ah, Father," Gian greeted the man who was wearing an apron that said, 'No kisses, this cook only takes cold hard cash.'

Jed smiled at his son. "Gian, damn son, glad you could make it." His greeting was warm, clearly he loved his firstborn. His gaze slid to Nikki and his brows arched. His eyes darted to Gian. "And who is this lovely young lady?" His expression held the same matchmaking interest his wife's had when she was introduced to Nikki.

"This is Nicolle Kelly. Nicolle, this is my father, Jedediah Montanero."

Still unsure of her presence at the party, Nikki's cheeks suffused a slight pink. She said with an awkward smile, "Um, nice to meet you, sir. Please call me Nikki."

His eyes flicking from Gian to Nikki, Jed grinned. "Call me Jed, hon. I've tried for years to get my boy here to call me Dad. The least you can do is call me by my given name." His smile broadened. "So," he said, "how long have you two been seeing each other?" He wore a Hawaiian t-shirt and khakis under the apron.

Her mouth gaped, she said awkwardly, "Oh, but we're not dating-"

Gian's attention was on Nikki's face flooded with pink. "Nicolle is the granddaughter of the people who own the Shamrock Farm. She brought the bird cake Deo requested."

Nikki turned to Gian with a giggle. "It's called a hummingbird cake."

Jed chuckled but Gian still stared at Nikki.

Jed gave her a broad smile and said, "I know the Shamrock Farm of course, been here for generations, same as us. When they inherited the farm, it had practically fallen into ruin from ancestral mishandling. Tane and Lolly Kelly, good people, worked their fingers to the bone to make it pay for itself and earn a good profit."

Nodding with a smile, with a pointed look at Gian, Nikki commented, “That’s my grandparents. Very hard workers. Honest, upstanding people.”

Sharing her smile, Jed turned to Gian and went on, “Had some obnoxious lazy relatives mooched off them for a long time until they got their own place. I vaguely recall a young girl, grandchild or whatnot visiting a few times over the years. A pretty little poppet. You were living overseas with your parents?”

Gian made a snorting sound. Nikki gave him a side-eye and smiled back at Jed. “Yes. My parents passed when I was around six. I stayed away at school after that, coming here only infrequently for visits.”

“So, you’re here visiting your grandparents? I bet that’s a special treat for them,” Jed said as he lifted a whole albeit small lobster off the huge grill and plopped it on Nikki’s plate then did the same to Gian.

“Don’t forget to grab some clams and a pot of melted butter, Deo’s supposed to be manning the steamer.” Jed motioned to a huge iron pot on an electric griddle a dozen feet away that had vapor gushing out from under a tin lid.

Deo was actually standing a few yards away from the steamer chatting with the pretty pony-tailed brunette in the jeans and crop top.

Jed shook his head with a wry smile. “Yeah. Anyway, Gian, go help yourselves. Jessica and I will join you in a few and get to know a bit about you, Nicolle.”

“Oh, but you don’t need to-”

Gian grasped her elbow and nodded to his father. “We’ll be over at one of the picnic tables, Jed- uh, Father. See you in a few.” He rolled his eyes at his dad’s grin as he wriggled his bushy brows at his son while darting his eyes at Nikki and back at Gian.

As soon as they found a seat, Gian glanced up and noticed Detectives Cornelius Vinci and Simon Nucacher were present. The pair, standing near the pool each held a beer, they were speaking with two men, who to Gian appeared to be identical.

Nucacher also held a briefcase in his free hand.

Vinci smirked at Gian and crooked a finger at him to join them.

"Ah, if you'll excuse me for a moment, Nicolle, we're still investigating my brothers' shootings, I see some officers I need to speak with. Will you be okay on your own for a few moments?"

Nikki craned her neck up at the tall man, her lip tugged in at a corner.

She picked up a lobster fork and said, "Contrary to your popular belief, Detective, I am not quite so helpless and brainless that I can't fend for myself. Especially at a clambake. Please," she picked up a claw cracker with the other and waved the tiny fork at him, "carry on with your duties, don't worry your pretty little head about me."

The corners of his mouth twitched up. Gian stared down at her for a beat, then nodded. "I'll be right over there if you need me." As he turned on his heel, he heard, "Don't worry, I won't need you. I am not the timid little loris you think I am."

"Coulda fooled me," he mumbled as he trod across the green grass. He stuffed a hand in his pocket to retrieve his phone. He typed 'loris' into the search icon.

A photo of a shy, small furry animal with enormous eyes and tiny fingers popped up. Chuckling, he stuck his phone back in his pocket. "Check it out later," he promised himself as his boots thumped along the patio where the detectives were huddled.

"Hey Nicolle, mind if I join you? I just must get off my feet for a second." Without waiting for Nikki's response, Jessica slid onto the wooden bench beside her and plopped a lemonade down on the table.

"Where's Gian going?" Jessica asked as she watched her stepson stride across the manicured grass.

"He said he was going to go talk to someone," Nikki said, slipping a hunk of lobster into a cup of melted butter. "He said he'd be right back."

"Huh," Jessica snorted. "Not likely. Those are two of the detectives from his station, and the way Conny Vinci is glowering at him, Gian is about to begin grilling them. And if I know him, issuing orders too. You might as well sit back and enjoy the great food."

She smiled with friendly eyes at Nikki. "I'll keep you company and fill you in on all the fun village gossip."

Chapter Thirteen

As he reached them, Gian gave a slight nod to olive-toned Detective Cornelius Vinci then to the darker-skinned male with him, Detective Simon Nucacher. "Gentlemen," he greeted brusquely.

"Surprised to see you here, JoCo, *rebelde*, thought you considered yourself above your lobster-trolling family." Conny Vinci grinned mockingly while as usual Simon snickered beside him.

The blue eyeballs of the two red-haired men they had been speaking with bounced back and forth between the three detectives then between themselves.

"Apparently my folks hung an 'All Welcome' sign out front. I don't think they meant 'All scurrying little rodents,'" Gian said coolly. "But then, who knew you two could read?"

Conny's brows daggered down. "Listen you freakin' maverick," he shot back, "you ass-"

"Who're your *friends*?" Gian asked with slight sarcasm insinuating Conny couldn't possibly have friends.

Conny's mouth pushed out and he huffed. "Yeah. Uh," he gestured to the two men. "These are the mayor's boys, twins Chip and Oreo O'Grady."

Gian's brows jumped at the names. "Those are rather…unique uh, nicknames? Are those actually your real-"

Before Gian could finish, rolling his eyes with a sigh, apparently he'd had to answer this question his entire life, the man Conny indicated was Chip said, “Yes. My mom’s favorite cookies. Chocolate Chip and the renowned Oreos.”

He shared a look with his twin. Both men appeared around 30 with the average height of about 5’10”. They shared abundant reddish-brown curls and amply spotted faces and arms.

The only difference seemed that Oreo was bespeckled along with his freckles where Chip chose contacts to correct his near-sightedness. Oreo’s fingers were also adored with numerous rings whereupon Chip wore only a wedding band.

Gian was starting to realize the coastal fishing village had apparently been settled by copious Irish clans as many of the residents had ginger hair.

“I see,” Gian said. “Noting the names of Nectar and the mayor’s nickname of Gator, I can understand Nectar making your childhoods quite teasable with your…unusual names.”

“Oh, no,” Oreo said. “Nectar is our stepmom. Our natural mother, Tuppence named us. She’s remarried, and is now Mrs. Tuppence Mills.”

“Yeah,” Chip added, “she ran off on our dad when we were two. Said we were too much of a terrible-twos handful and split for easier pastures. Mr. Mills was 50 when she snatched him up 28 years ago. His children were grown and he didn’t want any more. He was worth buckets and mama dropped us like a pair of red-hot potatoes and jumped on the calmer, greener, *richer* grass.”

“No great loss,” Oreo sniffed, twitching his glasses back up his nose. “Nectar is a great stepmom. We’d do anything for her, right, Chips?”

“You bet, we-”

Gian spoke over Chip. He turned to Conny Vinci. “Anyway, Corny, you and Nutcracker got a minute? I’d like to chat about the case.”

He directed his gaze to the briefcase Simon Nucacher clutched. “You brought information for me as I requested?”

Conny’s lips pulled in but he let the name-calling taunt go. “Yeah. We can understand you staying interested as it was your brothers.” He turned to the O’Grady twins. “Catch ya for some brews later at Swabby’s Deck?”

The twins set a time to meet, then with a curt "So long, bros," they left to grab some platefuls of food.

Gian watched the pair sort of swagger, at least they tried, to the grill. "Well, there's two Jokers the Deck won't miss. What do they do for work?" He looked to Simon.

Simon shrugged. "Oreo works at the salon with Nectar, runs the front desk, does the books, probably mostly only sweeps up. They aren't the swiftest duo. As twins, I think they share the one brain."

He and Conny elbowed each other with a snigger.

Gian was thinking the same thing about the two detectives. "And Chip?" he asked Simon.

Simon gave another shoulder shrug. "Not sure what he does. I think he works in his dad's office like helping him with mayor stuff. Due to the election coming up I believe he said something about working on flyers. I guess he can handle hammering flyers of his father's ongoing candidacy on trees.

"Surprisingly, the dude is married. He and Bambi Bodine were high school sweethearts. She has that old 80's look. You know, big teased yellow hair with thick eyeliner and lashes, think Cyndi Lauper. Hope their kids, when they pop 'em out look like her, and not the carrot-tops of their father. At least their hair is more brownish-yellowish-orange than real carroty, huh?"

"Bambi's not too bad looking. Surprised the ol' Chipper pulled that one off, eh?" Conny snickered.

Gian asked Simon, "Is Bambi Bodine seriously her real name? This town has the oddest named residents."

Simon laughed. "This coming from a guy name Giancomo? It's Bambi O'Grady now. Anyway, I think it's short for Bernadine or something."

Conny added, "Bernadine Bodine? If it were me, I'd change it too."

"Okay Cornelius." Rolling his eyes, Gian swung his attention from Simon to Vinci. "Tell me what you got so far, Cornball."

Vinci rotated his shoulders as if to roll off the mock. He'd instigated it with the JoCo moniker. The name shame game was pretty childish but he had started it. He pawed his goatee as his olive-toned cheeks darkened slightly.

He said, "Well, actually, we've been kind of busy with some other cases and haven't really had a chance to make much headway. We stopped by here to question your brothers. Find out who they pissed off enough to make someone take pot shots at them."

Gian's gaze was withering. "Uh huh. Great. Hardly pot shots, Cornball, if the assailant had been closer both of my brothers would be dead."

He swallowed down the furious retort that bubbled up his throat at the pair's lack of movement on his brothers' attempted murders.

"Their accounts are on record on the probable cause reports. Try reading them to get a grasp before jumping on them. They're here recuperating, proceed cautiously with them."

Conny narrowed his eyes at him. "We thought they might have remembered something else by now. You think you can do better, Mr. G-Man?" His urge to denigrate overcame his sense of adulthood. "Where would you start?"

Gian tucked his fingertips in his pockets. He wore black jeans, boots and a black thermal. "I treat my cases like a jigsaw puzzle. Start in the corners, then the borders, then hit the center."

Conny and Simon blinked at him. "Huh?" Simon uttered.

"You make a picture, boys, fill in all the pieces, the spaces, connect them," Gian told them.

At their still puzzled gazes, Gian explained, "See if my dad had any rivals for the business. Any fights he or my brothers were involved in. Did my brothers owe anyone any money? Any angry husbands or boyfriends out there they might have cuckold. Any scorned girlfriends for that matter.

"Check into any disgruntled crew, maybe someone recently fired. Do a better canvass for witnesses than you did the first time around. I gave Lieutenant McKay a list of people he should have you guys looking into."

"We talked to the witnesses," Conny protested. "It was late and dark, not too many people around."

"Like I told the LT," Gian said, "check the bar. People are always going in and out of it and walking around. People making out in the dark alley. Also, get a broader roster of anyone around the marina, coming and going for the entire day; merchants, charters, including those who had already sailed away. And," he kept going, ignoring Conny's frown and mouth opening to say something. "Check out the crime scene in person."

"CSI covered it, for crud's sake," Conny reminded him.

Reaching an arm up, Gian scratched the back of his head, ruffling the short hair. "I know, but even the best sometimes miss something. A good, thorough detective should always review the crime scene in person if possible."

"Why retread what others-"

"I read the ballistic report," Gian continued. "Garfield said the bullets were Winchester Dual Bonds. He thinks it's likely the gun used was either a 44 Magnum or a Ruger .454 Casull. He's centering his mind more on the Casull."

"That's one I've never heard of," Simon remarked.

"People call the revolver a hand cannon. It's used for hunting large and dangerous animals, think bear and wildcats. Check out who are registered gun owners as well as folks with hunting licenses."

His brothers had been damned lucky with a weapon that powerful that they had survived the shootings. Fortunately, they had been far enough away from the shooter and that helped lessen the damage.

"Hells bells, G-man," Conny protested. "That's got to be hundreds, maybe thousands of people!"

"Yeah, so you should get started right away. Be thankful this is a small town, could be a lot worse."

As Gian spoke, Simon had set his briefcase on the ground and pulled out a small notebook and was now writing notes. Both he and Conny wore white dress shirts and slacks. They'd left their ties and suit jackets in the car. It was a clambake after all.

"Anything else, O' Supreme Cream of all Detectives?" Conny asked snidely.

"Yeah," Gian said. "What's with the *rebelde* comment?"

At Conny's arched brows, Gian informed him, "Oh yes, I speak Spanish, it means rebel. By the way," he ignored Conny's attempt at a response. "I thought your family was Hispanic, yet isn't Vinci Italian?"

"My mother was Italian, her last name was Vinci, probably originally DaVinci. My name was Cornelius Vinci-Pizarro. When my folks split my mom dropped the Pizarro. She was hateful, wanted all traces of my old man gone. Legally changed our names to Vinci. Satisfied with my heritage, JoCo, not that it's any of your business."

"Don't really care, cornball, I was just giving your sidekick time to finish his notes. So," he tilted his head, stretching his neck. "You can follow up, but I'm going to go ahead and do all the shit I just advised you to do because I know I'll be more thorough."

"But the LT told you to butt out!" Conny sputtered.

Simon looked up from his notes.

The edge of his mouth nicked in, Gian regarded Conny as if he were an annoying bumblebee. "How about if you miss something really important and blow the case? How's the LT gonna take that?"

Conny protested, "You can't just-"

"Don't worry, I'll keep you abreast of my investigating and you can take credit for anything that comes up useful."

Crossing his arms over his chest, brows arched, Conny said sarcastically, "Don't you have to go a'lobstering with your dad? I heard your crew has come down with the flu. The rumor is some chick with a cold slept with half of your boys and those fellas infected the rest. With your brothers down and now the rest of the deckhands out, the Seabug is screwed."

Conny didn't hide his glee at the Montaneros' bad luck and the likelihood that Gian would have to help out to keep them afloat during the last of the season.

Simon added his two cents, "If your dad doesn't supply the lobsters as planned for the festival not only your family is screwed, but Mayor O'Grady goes down too. I've heard Nectar O'Grady can be a bit of a shrew behind that Doris Day big-toothed smile and sweet freckles. I wouldn't want her on my bad side." He elbowed Conny and they snickered.

"How about you worry about your life and I'll take care of my own?" Gian's frigid expression clammed the two detectives up.

Gian's temper and legendary harsh treatment of both felons and people he deemed useless or morons was well known.

Simon picked up the briefcase and handed it to Gian. Sheepishly, he said, "Here. There's a list of all the boat owners at the Kifpu Wissei Marina and crew that we could find records of."

Taking the case, Gian said, "That's all you got?"

"No. there's a bit more. The merchants that sold produce and liquor and whatnot to the clubhouse and restaurant on the pier. Of course, it's all on computer and a drive too." His lips pulled in then pushed out.

"Only interesting fact I found was that the name Kifpu Wissei is Native American, uh, specifically Mi'kmaq. Kifpu is eagle and wissei is nest; ergo, Eagle's Nest Marina. The regulars just call it the Kifpu."

At Gian's blank stare, he cleared his throat and muttered, "That's, uh, all we've got so far."

Gian gave the briefcase a dirty look considering the scant information they'd come up with so far. He opened the case and glanced inside before snapping it back closed.

He said to Vinci and Nucacher, "I'll check this out. You get the rest of the information I mentioned, and we'll meet tomorrow at one in my office."

Conny raked his fingers through his dark hair clumsily dismantling half his man-bun. "Well, heck, that's not much time. We can't be expected to-"

"You should have already had all that, Corny. See you tomorrow. Be prompt." Gian spun on his heel and strode away leaving the two disgruntled detectives standing with their mouths open in chagrin, as usual.

When he reached the table, he'd left Nicolle sitting at, he slowed his step. She was not there. Jessica smiled up at him, her lips were wrapped around the straw poking out of her lemonade.

Gian took the seat he had abandoned and picked up a lobster claw. “Where’s Nicolle?” He scanned the area searching for a spot of yellow sundress.

Jessica’s smiled widened. “She said she had been pondering on your visit to her home and some of the things you’d said to her.”

Her forehead furrowed at Gian’s likely rudeness to the young woman. “She said something about a light going off and she needed to make some changes. So she left.”

Gian’s dark brows shot up. “Left? She has no car and no money for a taxi. How the hell did she-”

Jessica swiped a potato chip off Gian’s plate and munched it. “You thought you had her trapped and tied to you? Ha. Girl isn’t as empty-headed as you think.”

At Gian’s scowl she smiled and told him, “Sun Li from Nectar O’Grady’s beauty shop, the Beautella Salon stopped by to say hi to me. She and Nikki shared a few words and when Nikki mentioned she’d like to leave but had no transpo, Sun said she was headed out that way and would be happy to give her a lift. So, there you go. Are you disappointed not to be able to spend more time with Nikki? She is a lovely girl, so pretty and sweet.”

“Huh.” Gian grunted. “I see pretty every day.” His attention roved over to where Coco and Poppy Gentry were strutting around in barely there bikinis even though it was a coolish day.

His gaze moved on to where Hollyann Ontario was staring across the patio at him with big, wanton inviting eyes. He blinked, trying to hide his disdain and looked back to Jessica.

Jessica sighed, then snatched another chip. “Yes, but Nikki has substance. She’s more than a pretty face. She has big plans in mind. I think once you get to know her-”

“I don’t want to get to know her. If I want to get laid I have plenty of hens in the pen that I don’t have to ‘get to know’.”

“Oh Gian, that’s so vulgar. You need to work on that sexist mind of yours,” Jessica admonished him gently. She knew if she really started on him, he’d just get up and leave.

“Too old to change my spots, Jess. The only thing I care about right now is getting a killer, or killers off the street.”

He certainly didn't want to delve too deeply into why, when Jessica had said he was disappointed that Nicolle had left he literally felt a pang in his gut.

While talking with the two detectives, in the back of his mind he had been thinking about the ride home with Nicolle. What about it, he couldn't actually figure out. It was just a sort of…anticipation fermenting in the hollows of his brain.

He shook off the thoughts. "I gotta go." He stood up with his plate in his hand.

Bending down, he kissed Jessica on the cheek. He was starting to do that automatically these days.

He wasn't sure whether it was just a new habit from doing it, because she had been so insistent about it since she first met him, or whether he was starting to…like it.

Chapter Fourteen

At exactly one o'clock the next day, Cornelius Vinci and Simon Nucacher stepped into Gian's office.

All the detectives had small offices allotted to them but Gian's was slightly larger and he had a window so most meetings he conducted with staff, as well as outsiders, were in there.

He'd acquired a round table and chairs and when the detectives arrived, he motioned for them to sit at the table.

Both men carried files. They arrived at the meeting promptly, not because Gian had ordered it, but because their lieutenant, Huxley McKay had reprimanded them.

He warned them all to play nice, and he didn't want to hear about another verbal brawl betwixt any of them or he'd start transferring people out to one of the satellite offices.

That meant holing up in one of three satellite locations that were all pretty much little more than forest ranger lookout towers in the deep woods. Suits and tasseled loafers wouldn't fare so well amongst the weeds, mud and furry animals with big teeth, and, God forbid, Conny had thought with a shiver, *reptiles*.

Gian dragged a chair out and flopped down. He had his own file and pulled a pen out of his suitcoat pocket. "All right, let's go. What'd you get?"

Conny sucked in a deep breath and exhaled it with a loud woosh. He opened one of his files. "Okay." He lifted a sheet filled with typed names. "Here's the list of registered gun owners. There are 568 names. Damned hunting town."

His sigh groaned out. "No Magnum 44's or Casulls. We have uniforms checking into every one of the owners. Doesn't tell us though, when people bought weapons privately or inherited them."

Gian nodded. "Uh huh. Go on."

"I have the list of all staff at the marina and restaurant as well as known merchants. I've had Admin personnel run criminal histories. Nothing too major popped, no murders or real violent offenses so far. They've only gone through about a third of them to date. I will update you if anyone of interest hits." Simon handed several sheets of papers to Gian. Gian set them on top of the gun owners list.

"Now," Simon went on, pointing to the paper he'd handed Gian. "What caught my interest was there were only two fisherman who at the time of the shooting lived aboard their boats in their slips at the marina year-round. All others either sailed off on their adventures around the world or had local houses or hotels to go to."

Gian nodded again, but remained silent. He folded his big hands together and set them on top of the papers, his broad shoulders hunched as he leaned over slightly.

"So," Simon continued. "One of them, old geezer, name's," he glanced at his notes. "Koh Boone. Refused to speak with the uniform I sent out to question if he saw anything. He's lived on his boat at the Kifpu Marina for over 10 years. He isn't around much though, travels a lot for the fishing.

"The boat looks to be about 100 years old. Peeling paint, rusted poles, worn and torn netting. Barge stinks of rotting fish guts and gull poop." He stuck his tongue out under a curled lip as he read further.

"Boat's name is Fishnet Stalkings. Figures. Perv. Cantankerous old cretin, keeps to himself. According to others at the marina he's rude and very unfriendly. We didn't get anything out of him as a witness, but maybe he took offense at your brothers.

"Because they're young, maybe played loud music or just annoyed him in some fashion. Could have just had it and came out blasting at them. Could be why he's uncooperative, has something to hide. There're no weapons registered under his name, doesn't mean he doesn't have any."

"Okay. See if you can scavenge up a warrant for his boat to search for a gun." Gian leaned back in his chair and propped his hands behind his head, elbows sticking out to the sides.

Frozen straightened hair slicked off the back of his head not moving as he shook his head, "There's no probable cause for a warrant," Simon said. "We can't just go-"

"Find something. Drinking in public, lewd and lascivious, maybe he stared too hard at the young girls in their bikinis. Check out trash around his boat. That kind of guy likely litters. Find something with his name on it, use that for the warrant. Suspicion of smuggling or drug dealing. Perhaps he's been seen talking with that guy, that known cartel guy, Michel."

"Jon Michel of the Mexican cartel? Wow, that's a helluva stretch, G-man." Conny shook his head. "That other stuff is pretty light for a warrant, bro."

"Use your imagination, just get on that boat, legally, check it out. Come up with a witness who was suspicious the guy was smuggling something. Drugs, whatever. Plenty of drunks or druggies will tell you what they think you want to hear."

Simon offered, "I think I saw something with the same address, wait a sec." He rifled through his notes. "Yeah, here," he tapped a dark brown knuckle on the paper. "The old goat has a roommate, or whatdoyacallit, shipmate? Some old fishing buddy that had been down on his luck a couple years back. Clyde Collins. But," he peered down at the writing.

"According to my guy who tried to interview Boone, Collins is out of town. Um," he ran a finger along the words typed there. "Supposedly in Miami. No one really knows too much about him. We'll check it out." He clicked his pen open and jotted down a note.

"Oh, and," Simon said, looking up at Gian, "neither live-aboard boater has an alibi that we can determine. Boone of course offered nothing, just ran my boys off, and the other liveaboard fella that resides at the marina just said he was home alone on his boat, sleeping or watching TV, didn't recall hearing anything. He couldn't really remember the night, so he said. Basically told the officers to bug off and leave him be."

"All right. What else?" Gian hurried them along with a wave of his hand.

"Okay. That other seafarer is," Simon checked his notes and tapped the paper. "Tex Coltrane from, you guessed it, Texas. This is the interesting part. He's a lobster fisherman like your dad. The word I got from the canvass of other boat owners is that he's always been jealous of your father. The Seabug is twice the size of his boat the Red Claw, and hauls triple what the Red Claw pulls in, including financially.

"Plus, your dad hired away a couple of Coltrane's best deckhands. Lotta animosity there, I'd say. You see, if your dad is out of commission due to your brothers getting clipped, Coltrane will pull in the full lobster haul and not only earn the big bucks, but he'll win the title at the biggest lobster fest in the country, make that the world! And the mayor will be in his pocket."

"It always comes down to money," Simon winked a licorice eye at Conny.

"Yeah, that and love. Murder is almost always about love or money," Conny smirked at him.

"Sometimes both," Simon shot back with a grin.

"But, could also be payback for a perceived wrong." Conny shrugged, setting his palms on his paperwork in front of him.

Simon frowned. "You're right. There are a lot of reasons someone can come up with to do away with a person. In fact, it could be-"

"Enough. Please." His lips pulling in with the information he was hearing, Gian jotted down more notes. "I'll hit the marina and check Coltrane out. I'll talk with Boone too."

Simon chuckled. "Good luck with that."

His head tilted back, Gian gazed at him under lowered lids. Simon's mouth pursed and he sat up straight.

Gian said, "Just work on that warrant and email it to me when you get it. I'll be on Boone's boat waiting for it."

Clearing his throat, "Anyhoo," Conny said, to cut the tension. "We found out your brother Josh had recently dumped his girlfriend, a Miss Kaleigh Duncan." He laughed and glanced at Simon. "Apparently Josh was none too pleased to discover Miss Duncan already had a boyfriend she forgot to mention."

"Who's the guy?" Gian needed to get more involved with his brothers' lives, this was news to him.

Conny reviewed his paperwork then said, "Axle Kallen. I have calls into both Kaleigh and Axle. Will check their alibis asap." He handed Gian a copy of what he just reported.

"Good." Gian nodded, his head down, he scanned the notes. Then he looked up at Conny, his brows rose, asking for more.

"Ah," Conny pinched his nose as he thumbed through the paperwork now scattered around on the table in front of him. He lifted one of the papers.

"Okay, so, per the event report of your brother Reece, the interrogating officer asked if he'd had any problems with anyone recently. Reece told him he had been in a poker game oh, about three weeks ago and he won a lot of money and some of the guys weren't too happy. Yesterday at your pop's barbeque I reviewed this with Reece."

"Clambake," Gian said, not looking up.

"Huh?" Conny's brown brows inverted.

"Nothing. Go on. What did Reece tell you?"

Conny cut a glance at Simon whose dark head was down reading his reports.

"Yeah," Conny said, continuing. "Reece confirmed the only instances that he could recall of anyone being angry with him in the past say 6 months or so were the displeased men at the game. Reece won a bundle and he was much younger than the other players. They hadn't expected him to wipe their faces and take all their money so they kicked up quite a fuss."

Simon set his paperwork down and put his attention on Conny.

"Do we have their names?" Gian asked Conny.

Conny picked up a paper and read out loud, "Let's see. Uh, Frenchie Chad, he owns that fancy French Restaurant, Bon Savoureux, pardon my French, I flunked it in fourth grade twice. Anyhoo, according to Solange Lavigne in Compliance it translates to good tasting or savory. Not that I care, it's way outta my price range. I think French cooking is all snooty with rich sauces and weird food like chapon."

"Chapon?" Simon's black brows inverted.

Conny let out a snort. "Solange says it's really capon. It's a castrated rooster. It-"

"Conny," Gian bit back a groan. "Stay on freakin' task, please." Damn he hated the station rules that he couldn't curse.

Smirking at Gian, Conny coughed out a laugh. "Okay. A little TMI, eh? That Frenchie guy is a regular at the weekly Monday night poker game when his restaurant is closed. They play at different locations but most often at Liam Kuno's club at the marina."

Gian jotted down a note and nodded for Conny to continue.

"Okay, number two at the table was Lawford Raines. He's branch manager of the Northeast American Bank down there on Main Street."

Gian's head popped up. "That name is familiar." He thought for a second, then remembered the name of the goon in the 3-piece suit who had been accosting Nicolle Kelly that day near the courthouse. "I thought you said the men were all much older than Reece."

Conny pulled reading glasses out of his pocket and slipped them over his nose then squinted at the paper. "Well, three of them are. Frenchie Chad is 55, Liam Kuno is part owner of the country club at the Kifpu Marina, he's 62, and," he scrolled down the paper.

"Redford Damon is 57, he owns that big butcher chop shop on the corner of Sycamore and Pine. It's a few blocks from Frenchie's place."

"How old is Lawford Raines?"

"Hmm," Conny ran his finer down the paper. "He's 42."

Nicolle was in her early twenties. Gian muttered, "Dirty old man."

"What?"

"Nothing. Anyone else at the game?"

Conny blinked like a nerdy sparrow through the lenses. He glanced back down. "No. Yes. Kenneth Vaughn was the bartender at the game. Huge guy, looks more like an NFL Tackle or a bouncer than a refined bartender. Dark complexioned, braids down his skull, hands the size of box trucks.

"Anyway, the group played in the back party room of Liam's country club. There was a girl who brought them food too. We spoke to both Vaughn and the server," he had to refer to his notes.

"Lila Nelson. They both were very reticent to talk, of course. Staff with blabby lips don't get to stay around long, and earnings at the Club are big cake. But after much pressing, they both admitted the four men were quite heated when Reece, young and a newcomer walked off with the pot. Liam Kuno and Redford Damon cursed him. Frenchie apparently swore in French while shaking his fist, but Lawford Raines allegedly said he'd kill Reece for cheating them."

Gian kept his face impassive, a poker face as it were, but a pulse beat wickedly at his temple. He was livid. Idiots calling his brother a cheat. Reece had played poker since he was practically in diapers according to Deo. The brothers hated playing with him because he always walked away from the game with his pockets bulging.

When they were kids it was pebbles and marbles, later it was cold cash. Tired of losing their allowances, Deo and Josh refused to play with him. But according to Deo, Reece was honest as the day was new. He was just a great player and a really good reader of faces and tells.

"Hey," Simon said gleefully. "We got the butcher, the banker and- and the candlestick maker. Well, maybe not the candlestick mak-"

"It's the butcher the *baker* and the candlestick maker you asshat," Conny informed him, removing his glasses he set them on his file.

"Okay, fine, but the baker can translate to the restaurant owner as in chef or cook," Simon said helpfully. "You see, they were all in on it! Like in the Orient Express."

Conny rolled his eyes at his partner. "Sure. Four men tried to commit murder because of a nursery rhyme. It all makes so much sense now."

"Shut up," Gian said flatly, giving Simon a look that said he clearly questioned his IQ. "Anything else besides the trolls and fairies?"

Simon smirked then sobered at Gian's stony glare. Coughing into his hand, he replied, "All I have left is, your dad fired two deckhands over the past year. One he caught red-handed stealing, that was Brandon Cook. But Cook has been in the pen for the last four months for other crimes. And the other was Jason Landry. He fired Landry for pure laziness."

"The word was that he was a bad egg all the way around," Conny said.

"Yeah," Simon agreed. "He was always late and wasn't worth a nickel when he was there. Usually hung over or spaced out on weed. I don't think he could have strung two thoughts together to plan the murders, and he was too lazy to even do it. Plus, if he had that great of a gun, if it was a Magnum or Callus, he would have pawned it. Guy was always borrowing money to pay his rent. His crappy car was repossessed last week, for the second time."

"I agree. I know both men and they were both useless as nipples on a crocodile." Conny smiled at Gian. He said hastily at Gian's cold expression, "Uh, yeah, if Reece and Josh had been robbed then we would look more closely at those two. Well, not Brandon, he was in lockup at the time of the shootings."

Gian started to say something but Conny jumped in, "I'll check on Jason Landry's alibi."

The three detectives grew silent.

Then, Conny said carefully, "We uh, checked into your dad."

Gian's eyes swung up at him and narrowed.

"No worries," Conny added quickly. "Comes up clean as a whistle all the way around. People speak highly of him. No complaints from merchants or other people at the marina other than Tex Coltrane. And Tex has no issue with your father as a man or fisherman."

"That's not what I hear," Gian told him.

"He's just pissed Jed Montanero has a better boat and is basically twice the lobsterman Tex is. Your dad's bills are all paid and on time, there's no angry merchant with his hand out coming after him."

Gian slammed his palm on the table making both Conny and Simon jump. "Well, if that's all, I'm gonna head over to have a chat with Coltrane and Boone."

"Huh," Simon snorted. "Good luck with that, bro," he repeated his chant from earlier. "Coltrane's an asshole and Boone's a cranky reclusive dick. Coltrane probably won't even talk to you as you're Jedediah Montanero's son." He glanced at Gian with a smirk then looked back to Conny.

"And Boone will hate you because you're a person and a cop. That said, he doesn't discriminate, he hates everyone. I heard he only took in that roommate 'cause the guy was free labor."

"Wait," Conny slipped his glasses back on as he read one of his forms. "Funny little note; the poker playing group are all friends of Mayor Gregory 'Gator' O'Grady." He raised his head to peer at Gian then back down to his notes.

"Apparently, according to Vaughn, the bartender, Gator is usually at the table as well. I guess I can check into why he wasn't that night Reece played. But, hell, he's the mayor for Pete's sake, he'd hardly be out and about shooting at village folks."

"Yeah," Simon snorted a laugh. "Besides, the guy looks and acts like a Santa at Christmas. Portly, balding and pink cheeked. Guy's just a big cherub."

Conny grinned at him. "From what I've seen, dude can hardly get out of his own way. Gator and Nectar for God's sake, with Chip and Oreo, the family is a food joke on legs." He and Simon laughed together.

His eyes on his notes, Gian said, "Just for the record, I want his alibi for the night of the shootings."

Simon's brown eyes winged up and his lips pushed out. "You can hardly think, Gian, that the mayor, old fuddy duddy pudgy Gator O'Grady tried to kill your brothers?" He choked a laugh out. "Come on, that's ludicrous. It's plain-"

"And," Gian continued, "find out who else was running for mayor. They might just be eliminating the competition through the lobster festival."

“Huh,” Conny grunted, frowning at his notes. He ran his finger down a few pages while muttering. Then he started jabbing his fingers at his iPad.

The frown lines deepened between his brows. Lips pressing together, then sucking in and pushing back out in huffs, he scrubbed a few fingers through his scalp in exasperation.

He groaned. “I can’t believe we didn’t think of that. Crap. Bugger be damned.” Jotting a note, he scowled at his iPad before slamming the cover closed.

Gian abruptly stood up, indicating for the pair to leave.

Chapter Fifteen

Gian jumped in his Ram and headed for the highway that would take him to the marina. He drove through the heart of the fishing village passing seaside homes most sporting aquatic decorations like resin turtles on their garages and lobster traps as flower pots on their lawns.

He took the exit that led to the crooked and curved road that wound along the coast of Maverick Bay to the Kifpu Wissei Marina.

It was a scenic ride as the trees had turned in partial autumn color. In the last few weeks sprays of brilliant red and yellow had burst along the streets and up the mountains. Late blooming asters struck like purple popups dotting grassy banks along the way.

Soon, the huge white structure of the two-story marina came into view. The Dutch-gable roof was black and overhung most of the building offering shade in the hot summer and protection for guests entering the building when it rained. Hundreds of boats seesawed on the sparkling blue water behind the marina and restaurant.

Gian parked the Ram and pulled out his phone. He looked at his notes to locate where the Red Claw and the Fishnet Stalkings were docked. Tex Coltrane's boat, the Red Claw was closest at slip 18 in port 5.

Gian's boots clomped noisily along the metal dock as he made his way from one ramp to the next. The layout over the water was one giant grid of metal walkways with the boats lightly bouncing, tethered in their slips, bumpers protecting the vessels as they rocked against piers.

Further out, those live-aboard people that either didn't want to dock or couldn't afford the slip fees, paid a little less to hook up out in the open water to a mooring buoy.

Then they would motor a dinghy in to the land when they wanted to go to their homes, or use the laundry facilities at the marina or visit the restaurant, shop, bar or club house, or just go about sightseeing if they were visiting the area.

From the records report Conny had given him, it appeared the majority of the boats were docked there full time. The owners had permanent residences in and around Chicory Landing County.

Coltrane's boat was white with an enormous red lobster claw painted on the side.

"Yeah," Gian murmured. "Nowhere as big or as nice as Dad's." The boat was tidy with fresh paint and polished wood but was half the size of Jed Montanero's Seabug.

He trod up the dock, his footsteps panging on metal announcing his arrival. He stopped near the bow of the boat.

"**Tex Coltrane**, **police**," he said in a loud curt voice. He waited a moment, then when there was no activity, he said louder, "Tex Coltrane, come out or I will come aboard to conduct a wellness check."

He waited, and observed the Red Claw rocking heavier in the water indicating someone was moving on it.

In seconds, a large man with a spring of grey hair stomped out of the cabin. "Ta hell you want, boy?" He scowled at Gian.

Thick, bushy grey brows lowered over his brown eyes as he studied Gian, determining his honesty or if he was a threat, or someone selling crap. Soliciting wasn't allowed at the marina but that never stopped people from doing it.

Gian tugged his ID from his pocket and held it up. His badge hung from a lanyard around his neck. The gold glinted against the black shirt he wore under his dark blue suit coat and dark blue tie.

"Detective Giancomo Montanero." He mumbled his last name hoping the fisherman wouldn't catch on that he was related to Jed Montanero. He'd clam up for sure if he knew.

"I'd like to ask you a few questions. Mind if I come aboard?" He put one foot on the deck of the boat.

Tex glared at Gian's boot on his deck. He appeared to ponder the request, then grunted and stepped back. "Come on. Ain't gonna give me no peace until I spat with ya ah'm sure." He had a Texan twang of an accent.

He looked like he'd be more comfortable atop a galloping stallion roping cattle in dusty pastures than on a lobster boat in frigid waters in northern Maine.

"Thanks." Gian was grateful for the past week he'd spent on his father's boat as he was able to easily keep his balance on the slightly rocking vessel.

Tex flopped down on a bench seat and nodded to one that was kitty corner to his. "Take a load off, boy, and spit out your bizness, quick. Ah'ma busy guy."

The Texan was many brawny inches over 6 feet with a beer gut. A well chewed cigar hung out the side of his mouth. A bushy grey mustache looked in danger of dangling onto the cigar and maybe catching fire. Good thing the cigar wasn't lit.

Gian sat down on the cushioned bench and tucked his ID back in his pocket. "I'm investigating the attempted murders of Reece and Josh Montanero on the night of the 10th of September. Can you tell me where you were from between 8 and 8:30 that night?"

Tex settled his bulk back against the side of the boat, the cushion squeaked with his big body's movements. He wore a denim shirt with a white t-shirt under it and very worn jeans that sagged under his belly. As he shifted positions, a large belt buckle of a pair of silver bullhorns showed until his gut covered it again. He shook his head in annoyance.

"Them boys, they ain't dead, so who cares who took potshots at 'em? Prolly out horsing around, more'n likely drunk and on that maryjane shit. High with their friends and shootin' it up, eh?"

"They ended up in the hospital with severe bullet wounds. Don't you want to know if there's some crazy fool out there shooting at boat owners here? Could have been you." Gian let that sink in for a second. Of course his implication could go either way, whether Coltrane could have been the victim or the perpetrator.

"Now, we'd like to eliminate as many people as possible as suspects, and that includes folks on boats docked here. So, I ask you, to eliminate you from the pack, can you tell me where you were during that time on that night? And, if you were home, I need you to tell me if you can recall if anyone may have seen you between 8 and 8:30."

Coltrane let out a hurumph. "How'm I supposed to recall that? I don't remember what I had for lunch today, boy."

As if he hadn't said anything, Gian continued, "And, also, if you were home, did you see or hear anything of note like unusual cars or people or activities, or gunshots?"

Tex's lower lip pushed out, he pulled on it with his fingers, managing to not dislodge the old cigar clamped between his teeth. His darkly tanned forehead screwed up as he thought about the question.

"Yeah, alright. Don't need you flatfoots comin' around hasslin' me. I heard about the shootings. That night I met up with some pals down at that country western bar on Chokecherry Lane near the dogleg. Therefore, I didn't see anyone or anything goin' on here."

"I need the name of the bar and the names and numbers of your friends, and precisely what hours you were there."

Tex leaned forward, his angry face steeping in furious red. "Listen here, boy-"

"That's Detective, Mr. Coltrane. You want me to stay here all day and hang around then don't answer my questions. I get paid overtime. I don't mind sitting here in the warm sunlight and doing nothing." Gian sat back, set his arm along the rim of the boat and crossed an ankle over the opposite leg's knee.

He turned his head as if to enjoy the sparkling blue water. He let his attention settle on an immense private yacht that glistened bright white in the sun as it slowly chugged by further out in the deeper channel.

Blustering, his jowly cheeks jiggling, Tex huffed a furious breath, then took his phone out from his jean's pocket. He scrolled through it. "Yeah, bar's called Hoofin' and Calfin' and my pals, well, easier you give me your number and I'll text 'em to ya." He looked up at Gian, his lip curled in a snarl. "I got there aroun' seven and stayed until, ah, at least one in the a.m."

"So, you lied to the police when you told them you were home that night sleeping or watching TV and heard nothing."

Coltrane's face darkened, his eyes shifted down. Tanned cheeks puffed out, he blew air from pinched lips.

Running a beefy finger under his nose rubbing the grey stache, scowling, he gritted out, "Ah, well, didn't want to get involved. Not the cops' bizness where I am and what I'm doing." Plucking at the t-shirt under the denim, he stretched his neck and looked away from Gian.

"Catch a bit of a jail term for obstructing and lying to law enforcement." Gian paused, letting it sink in. "We expect full honesty and disclosure from here on out. Because," he leaned forward towards Coltrane and squinted an eye at him.

"I catch you or hear word you lied again or misled or withheld information I won't hesitate to lock you the hell up and impound your boat for cause." Not that he could, but it sounded like a nice threat.

His head tilted back, eyes slit at the Texan with intimidation, Gian nodded sharply once, letting the threat settle in.

Gian gave him his number, and with more huffing and puffing, Tex stabbed at the phone's keys with one huge sausage of a finger as he very slowly transferred his friends' names and info.

"The longer this takes, the longer I hang around," Gian warned the man.

Coltrane hemmed and hawed a second, then reluctantly said, "Okay, okay. I was with a filly, uh, woman, later that night. I was pretty lit, can't tell you when I left my friends and went to her place. I mean the exact times. Didn't get home until the next day. So I wasn't here to see nobody, or hear nothin'."

"Okay. I need her info too, to verify."

Haggering out a beleaguered sigh, Tex scratched his chest while thumbing through his phone. “Name’s Ingrid. I’d like to hook up with her again. Not only’s got a decent rack, honey makes a mean cornbread with shrimp and grits.”

“Good for her,” Gian said derisively.

“No, good for me. So, I’d appreciate it if you don’t make it look like I’m some kind of a maniac serial killer. Okay?” One grey brow arched over a brown eye. He plucked the cigar out from between his lips, stuck it between two thick fingers then shoved his phone back in his pocket.

“Thanks for your cooperation, it is appreciated.” Gian said.

“Does that mean you flatfoots will leave me the hell alone now?”

“If your alibi checks out, Mr. Coltrane, then you will be crossed off our list of suspects.” Gian stood up. “Thanks for your time and cooperation,” he said politely.

He trod over to the side of the boat then easily stepped over onto the dock. He was a few feet away when Tex called out to him.

“Didn’t catch your name, boy- uh, Detective.” Tex moved to the side of the boat where Gian had exited.

Gian glanced over his shoulder, and said clearly, “Montanero, Giancomo Montanero.”

It took a few beats before Coltrane sputtered then cursed, then yelled, “You bastard! Yer that asshole’s boy! Yer his kin! He steals my bread and butter, he seduces my deckhands away, he-”

Gian waved off behind his head and kept walking.

He was on another side of the dock grid searching for Koh Boone’s boat and he could still hear Tex yelling and cursing.

Chapter Sixteen

Gian spotted the Fishnet Stalkings in slip 143. Raking a hand through his hair, he muttered, "Guy has to be some kind of tool to name his boat that."

There wasn't much left of the white lettering of the boat's name because that along with the rest of the dingy green boat now more of a gutter grey was peeling and it listed on the port side.

The railings were heavily rusted, the wood deck hadn't been polished in forever, and where there was sea deck flooring it was grimy and scraped up.

Gian stood beside the boat and called out like he did at Coltrane's. He called out several times, but the boat just rocked lazily. There seemed to be no sign of life.

He pulled out his phone and called Simon Nucacher. "You get that warrant on Koh Boone?"

Simon sounded pleased with himself as he replied, "Yep. Turns out, we asked around at the Swabby Deck bar and apparently Boone was bragging all over the place how he saw something the night of the shootings but had no plans to go to the pigs, his words, and that he was looking to make some money out of it."

"What did he say he saw?"

"Well, he hinted that he had seen a car in the vicinity that was parked well off behind trees and bushes, not in the driveway or parking lot, but like it was hiding. And he knew whose it was."

Gian shifted the phone to his other ear as he peered around the boat. "Could have been anyone coming to the restaurant or bar, or going for a boat ride, or grabbing some private sex time."

"Yeah, but the way the witnesses tell it, Boone claimed he just happened to mention to the car owner that he'd seen it that night and, well, the person denied being there and became highly agitated. Boone took that as guilt, and the more he pushed it the more disturbed the person grew, and the more Boone thought he could make some cake off it."

"Blackmail."

"Yep."

"Did the witnesses say who Boone thought the owner of the car was?"

"Nope. And zero description of the car either. It's a no go until we find Boone."

"So," Gian tried to stuff his impatience, "you got a warrant for Boone's boat? And, does he have a car?"

"Sure thing, G-man," Simon replied smugly. "Got the warrant." Gian could hear him pat his pocket over the phone.

"Guy was also witnessed dealing crack at the bar by two barflies."

"Email the warrant to me. And, a car?"

"Uh," Simon took a breath. "Lemme look it up." It took a few moments. While he looked for his information, Gian climbed aboard the boat.

Simon said, "Drives an old Ford pickup. Dark blue 1996." He added vaguely as he was apparently reading something, "I'll get the truck added to the warrant."

Then, his voice rose in excitement. "And, get this, the best part is that Boone also bragged that he wasn't worried about anyone gunning for him because he has a big bad weapon of his own. Considering there's no gun registered in his name, that and the alleged blackmail and the suspicion of crack solidified the warrant."

"Thanks." Gian hung up, and as he glanced around the deck, he could see through the window of the bridge that it was empty.

The bench seats around the boat were torn and stained, trash covered half the deck. He made his way to the cabin. He tried the knob, the door was locked, but it was so flimsy he gave it a shove and it pushed open with a whining creak.

Inside was as bad as outside. Pizza boxes, Chinese takeout containers, beer bottles, coffee mugs with spoiled milk floating in them, full ashtrays, the place was a floating smorgasbord of takeout and garbage. No wonder the guy was cranky, his diet sucked.

Cupboards in the galley hung on single hinges. A deck of cards was on the kitchen table, the cards sprawled out as if a game of gin had been played by two players.

Gian shuffled through the trash to the main berth. He stuck his head in. A tiny messy bed took up the space. Clothes hung out of drawers and scattered on the bed and floor. He rifled through the few drawers that were there and the miniature closet but found no weapon.

He moved to the front of the boat where it narrows to a point designating the bed, the V-berth. A single mattress was stuffed in the compartment. More clothes were strewn over the rumpled bedding. Gian noticed they were a size large, where the clothes on the bigger berth were 2XL. Two different men occupied the cabin. So there truly was a roommate somewhere.

Wandering around, Gian stuck his head in cabinets and closets but found very little. No gun or drugs, and nothing indicating an address where the roommate could be. When he had searched the entire vessel, Gian climbed off the musty boat and took a deep breath of clean, fresh, ocean air.

He took out his phone and called Conny Vinci and told him to have a crime scene team come and do a workup on the boat. He might have missed something. Maybe a note about the person he was possibly blackmailing. Nothing wrong with hoping.

Traipsing down the end of the grid of slips, his boots made clanging sounds on the metal. The breeze off the bay wisped through his short hair and ruffled his clothes. Tiny fish zigzagged just below the surface of the deep blue water.

He paused here and there, but there wasn't another person out and about. Finally, his feet hit ground.

Hesitating near a towering oak tree, he twisted to face the parking lot debating where to start his search for Boone's truck, just in case the guy was around somewhere. He could be at the main building doing his laundry, eating a burger in the restaurant or at Swabby's swilling beer.

"Yah, you'd be looking for Clyde Collins."

Gian had hunkered down in the deepest, darkest, most dangerous jungles in the world, a deep voice coming from behind him didn't give his heart a jump.

He turned slowly. The person had to have been deliberately stealthy or Gian would have heard, felt or sensed his approach. He should have been watching his six, he chastened himself for not keeping a wary eye out for his safe perimeter.

Gian's stance appeared relaxed and innocuous, but a trained eye could tell his body was in full preparation to fend off a surprise attack.

"And that would be?" he asked the man who had spoken to him.

The man was tall with a medium build and a weathered yet oddly boyish face. He didn't appear quite homeless, but close. His clothes hung on his angular body, a dirty ballcap draped over hazel eyes that appeared dodgy and cunning at the same time.

"Ayuh, Koh Boone's vessel mate. Your next step, I presume?"

The man gave off a creepy vibe. His expression implacable, Gian asked, "And you are?" And the guy was wrong. Gian's next step had been to check the parking lot for Boone's truck.

The man inclined his head in a slight bow. One side of his lips under scruff curved up. "Ayuh, of course. Paul Roosevelt Schmitt at your service. Ol' Schmittsy can always recognize a Five-O, ay."

Gian's brothers had gentled most of their Maine accent, his father still held a stronger bit of it. But this guy had generations deep in his voice. "What do you know about Clyde Collins?"

Schmitt's smile was lopsided, he tilted his head and peered out at Gian from under the grubby cap. "Yah, Boone hisself is a lunkhead, a cunnard the man. But-"

At Gian's quizzical grimace, Schmitt chuckled and said, "You're not from these parts, ay? Cunnard means, ah, crazy. Yah, Boone was a bedbug all right. But Clyde, he's kind of an unknown, but I'm pretty sure he's not flatlander. Though a tad tatty even fer a seafarin' fella."

Tucking his hands in his trouser pockets, Gian asked, "Do you know where I can find either of them?"

Schmitt stretched his neck. Twisting his head back and forth, he rubbed the back of his neck then pushed the cap back slightly off his forehead. Springy brown hair feathered out.

"Boone, nah. Clyde, he has kin or a girl or sometin' down in I think the Cape Cod area. He's probably there as I haven't seen him for a few days."

"Hmm, I heard he was in Miami."

Schmitt's mouth quirked in a smile. "Yah, twas really the Keys. Key West for some bonefish and red snappah. Heard he has a half-brother with a fishing chahtah had invited him down for a spell. Probly spends most days downin' shots at Sloppy Joe's. But that was months ago. Clyde's been back helping Boone with the lobstah fishing. Although," Schmitt scratched his head through the ballcap.

He pointed out, "They aren't too good at it, never seen any kinda big haul taken down to the markets. They just go out on the open water for days, sometimes weeks and come back with one or two lobstah cages and that's it. They suck at lobsterin' and fishin', need another line of work I say."

"Uh huh. So, you don't know where I can find Clyde now?"

Shaking his head, Schmitt replied, "Nah. Marina grapevine said Boone was acting all wicked cunnard, more than usual and I think it spooked Clyde, so Clyde is probly holed up with anothah fishing buddy until Boone settles back down."

Great. "All right then, what about Boone? You have any idea where he might be found?"

"No sah. Drives an old beater pickup, dark blue Ford. I think it's in the lot, but haven't seen hide nor hair of the man for a day or so past."

Reeling in his patience, Gian grit through his teeth, "Then why the hell did you even mention Clyde or talk to me at all if you had nothing to offer?"

His sly grin revealed surprisingly white even teeth. Schmitt might come across as creepy and homeless looking, but Gian would bet dollars to donuts the man made up the façade. For what reason, who knows? Trying to get some freebies maybe?

"Wellah, just wanted to be paht of the investigation, don't ya know? It's wicked boring as hell around here and I could tell you was a copper, written all over that stoic face and confident swagger. Figured you had a bit of a pissah of action going, ay? Figured you're looking into those boys that were shot."

"Where were you that night? Did you see or hear anything of note to offer?"

Schmitt grinned again because apparently he could see he was annoying Gian. And he was getting a kick out of it. He shook his head. "More'n likely just a bunch of crazies running around waving guns everywhere for no reason other than to raise hell. Probly hit those boys by accident just screwin' around." He paused then spit off to the right.

"Nope." Schmitt answered the question, "I was visiting my poor ol' ma who is in a home, called, ah, Golden Haven. Clear across the other side of Maverick Bay. Here, wait," he clapped his pockets until he pulled out a rumpled piece of paper. You got a pen? I'll give you names and numbers you can confirm."

Gian could feel fire burning out of his dark eyes. If he could incinerate the annoying creeper with a blink, he would.

He let out a rough exhale. Sliding a card out of his pocket and a pen, he handed them to Schmitt. "If you hear about or see Collins or Boone, or hear or see anything that can be of *value* to me, please call."

"You betcha, glad I could be of help, sah!" Paul Schmitt smirked ear-to-ear knowing he was getting Gian's goat and loving it. He took a minute and wrote down the name of the home and his and his mother's name and handed the paper to Gian. "There ya go, son, lemme know anything else you need. I live to serve the Five-O."

Turning swiftly on his heel, Gian strode away and to the vast parking lot. It took him ten minutes to locate Boone's Ford pickup. It was locked. At that moment he realized Schmitt had kept his pen, dammit. And he likely did it on purpose.

Grunting a loud aggravated breath, he peered inside the truck. It was a trash heap like the boat. Gian slid his phone out and swiped it, punching in Cornelius Vinci's contact number.

"Yeah?" Conny answered.

"When the crime scene techs get here, have them go to the parking lot, east side, near the back. I found Boone's truck. Tell them to do a search of it."

"Sure thing, G-man."

Great, now Cornball was calling him that too. Oh well, it's better than Jo-Co or whatever else he normally spouted. Gian spent another few minutes looking around the perimeter of the parking lot concentrating on where he'd found Boone's truck. He saw when the CSIs arrived and they headed to the docks to scour Boone's boat.

He was about to pack it in and go check out the rest of the marina or bar, when he noticed part of the grass directly behind where Boone had parked his truck was smashed down. His head down, Gian walked over to the flattened grass. The cellophane to a pack of cigarettes glinted in the light near the grassy area.

Gian automatically patted his own breast pocket for his pack of smokes then remembered he had tossed them. He was trying to quit.

There were more smushed grassy footprints, Gian followed them. The grass led to a wooded section. His eyes scanned up and down and back and forth as he pushed through foliage. He was in around ten feet when he could smell it. Then he saw a person lying in the weeds and grass under thick shade of the dense trees.

He could be sleeping, but with his face planted into the ground and limbs at odd angles, it was evident the male was deceased. Dark red fluid that covered half the upper torso and had pooled over some dried colorless leaves, a few still maintaining their bright autumn colors.

The blood was darker than the scarlet leaves, dulling some of their brilliance. Buzzing flies and other insects roving over the body added to the sickening ambience.

Growling, "Bloody hell," he quickly snagged his phone out and hit Conny's number again. As he waited for the detective to answer, Gian knelt carefully beside the body and checked for a pulse.

As he expected, there was none and the body was stone cold. More unidentifiable bugs were munching away and busily buzzing as they zipped up and down and around it.

Gian gingerly tilted the face up. The part that still existed matched the DMV photo they had of the 58-year-old Koh Boone.

He stepped back to preserve the crime scene from his footprints or DNA from any falling hairs or epithelials, sloughed skin cells, dropping onto it and took out his cell.

Conny answered the call, "Yo, G-man, working on it."

"Grab more CSIs and meet me at the back of the parking lot, east side where the truck is. I found Boone."

"He tell you anything worthwhile?"

"He won't be telling anyone anything ever again."

Conny was silent as he absorbed what Gian was inferring.

Then, "Oh bloody hell."

"My words exactly. Hurry."

In 15 minutes, Conny's white Chevy SUV with blue lights flashing came tearing around the lot, he came to a screeching halt near where Gian waited. He hopped out and waved at two other vehicles that had followed him.

The first unit of crime scene techs were already combing over the truck.

"Watch where you're stepping," Gian warned with his arm out. "Need that bagged." He pointed to the cellophane wrapper on the ground. "CSIs are going to need my footprints to rule me out of any print evidence leading to and around the body."

"Sure it's Boone?" Conny tried to peer into the thick woods.

"Yeah, but they'll test him anyway to make a positive ID." Gian watched the tech teams put up barrier tape and marker cones to preserve the area, and remove evidence collection kits from their vehicles as they made their way to where Gian and Conny were standing.

"What's it look like? Gunshot?" Conny asked. He was rocking back and forth on his feet, clearly he wanted to march into the woods and see the body himself.

Gian nodded grimly. “Yeah, head shot. Large bullet, half his head is gone.”

Stuffing his hands in his pockets, Conny’s shoulders rolled with a shiver. He crossed his arms and spread his legs for a firmer stance as he observed the crime scene activity. He muttered, “Gonna be a long night, huh?”

“Yeah.”

Chapter Seventeen

Boone's body was taken away and the forensic scientists wrapped up their initial investigation. There would be a more thorough search tomorrow when the natural light was better.

Gian went home, drank a beer, microwaved a frozen dinner and sacked out.

The next day he went to the station and reviewed all the evidence they had so far on his brothers' shootings and now Koh Boone's murder.

After several hours, he sat back and rubbed his eyes. He was feeling grungy, dirty, as if Boone's worms were slithering along his skin. The shower last night and this morning did nothing to refresh him.

He craved…well, he combed his fingers through his hair. What did he crave? His eyes shifted to his door as a female officer strode by.

A woman? Did he desire some sexual relief to cleanse his mind of the darkness he had to deal with on a daily basis? A picture of soft blue eyes and blonde curls floated into his mind. A wave of purity and sweetness swam over him, bringing warmth and an odd feeling of well-being. Well, not completely.

His brain's visual moved from Nicolle Kelly's pretty face and kind smile to her body. He had tried not to stare at her figure the day he brought her to his father's house, but, hell, he was a red-blooded male and the girl was a total fox. Seriously hot.

She wasn't elaborate in her enhancements, no giant breasts or the bus-sized butts that were in vogue these days. No, her curves were clearly there, yet soft and feminine.

Gian realized, although to each his own tastes, he actually really did prefer the soft and feminine to the highly athletic body builders and boxers a lot of women were turning themselves into.

Kickboxing and weightlifting were fine for some, but for him, if he wanted a hard muscular body he'd be into men. And he was not. Yeah, he had told himself that he liked the pudgy plain Janes, but that was because he didn't want to put in a huge effort to get laid.

And sure, he'd told his brother he preferred plain, tougher, more solid women that can kayak and mountain climb, but at the time he was trying to get his own and Deo's minds off Nicolle.

He sighed and closed his laptop. Yeah, what he really wanted to see, and feel, and yes, have sex with, was a pretty, delicate, blonde with the biggest crystal blue eyes he'd ever seen. Just the thought of her made his lower body turn hard and his brain grow mushy.

Gian had the overwhelming urge to see Nicolle Kelly. He wanted to immerse himself in her pure freshness and girlie femininity. He hated to admit it, but he had quite enjoyed talking with her that day, and the little bit of sparring they'd done. As much as he kept telling himself otherwise, she was no dummy, and she'd made him laugh.

He blinked hard and shook his head. What the hell was the matter with him? He had no interest in that flighty blonde. No, he did not. How the heck had she wormed her frilly little way into his mind?

He snorted. She snuck in through his pants, that's how. But, he thought, he should, as a law enforcement officer check up on her and see if ol' Hoot what's his name was not tricking her into doing more of his work.

It was really his duty to follow through and make sure everyone at the Shamrock Farm was pulling their weight and honestly earning their pay. Right, it was his job to ensure no fraud was being committed, like farmhands taking pay for work they were not doing.

Convincing himself that was the reason he was heading off to Shamrock Farm, he shut off his light and trod down the hall.

Passing the bullpen, he nodded at a few staff hard at work and made his way out to his truck. And, yeah, all blonde fluff and no brains, the girl at Shamrock needed a watchman. Not him of course, no way. Not as a man, but as a cop it was only right that he keeps an eye on the good citizens of Chicory Landing. Right. He kept telling himself that all the way to Shamrock Farm.

Passing under the green, clover covered beamed entrance to the farmstead, Gian parked his truck and paced to the front door of the sizeable house. It took a few moments before the door was answered to his knock.

A woman wearing a black uniform-styled pantsuit with white collar, cuffs and rounded apron opened one of the two, huge front doors. She gave him a quizzical brow arch. "How can I help you, sir?" She was a slim fortyish with her maple- colored hair neatly pinned back and dark, probing eyes.

Gian pushed the front of his suitcoat back and showed the gold badge he'd removed from the lanyard and hooked to his belt. "Detective Montanero. I'd like to speak with Nicolle Kelly."

The quizzical look widened to surprise. "Oh! Is the young miss in trouble? I can't believe-" She cut her words off. Well-trained, she knew her place was not to question anything regarding a household member.

"No, not at all. I'd just like a moment with her. Is she home?" He knew she was, he'd seen her old, pale yellow VW convertible parked near the garage.

Her gaze on his badge, the maid said, "Yes. She is out back in the gazebo with her grandmother Mrs. Kelly and, um, a guest."

Gian's brows hopped at the word *guest*. Was that asshole Lawford Raines here pressing his suit? That was fine if he was, there were questions Gian could ask him regarding his brothers' shootings, and Raines' antagonistic remark about killing Reece for winning the card game.

If the questions made Raines look shady in Nicolle's eyes, well, Gian shrugged, too bad.

"If you could show me where they are?" Gian made it sound like a question, but it came across as an order.

Her head jerked back, the housekeeper blinked at him. The Kellys were highly respected residents of Chicory Landing, and the police never darkened their door.

"Um, ah, well, of course. I will show you to the gazebo, sir. We can go around the outside of the main house to the back lawns, it'll be quicker than passing through the entire house. Please follow me."

She closed the door and stepped down the few steps and started for the paved walk that rounded the house. The pavers were wide, flat connected stones of different shades of glossy grey.

Gian strode a few inches behind as he walked with her to the rear yard. At the back were pretty gardens. A few tenacious pink roses clung to wilting stems, beneath the bushes lay confetti splotches of pink petals. A few dozen yards back set a white gazebo with columns and a railing that circled it.

Inside the pergola was a white, wrought iron bistro table and chair set. Three women sat at the table.

Gian could see what appeared to him to be a fancy tea setup as well as a three-tiered rounded thing with food on it. His stomach rumbled. His eyes flit from the food to the women.

A woman in her 70's was daintily sipping from a rose-flowered decorated China cup. He assumed that was Nicolle's grandmother, Lolly Kelly. She wore white and light yellow slacks and a white tunic. An iridescent butterfly pin was attached to the lapel of the tunic.

Her white hair curled upon her shoulders with two matching butterflies adorning either side of her head. Her one arm was encased in a cast. She was facing out towards Gian and the housekeeper.

Of course, he recognized Nicolle. She was sitting to the side of her grandmother. She was wearing white jeans and a soft pink top. Her hair was pinned up at the sides with small pink bows. She didn't see Gian approaching.

The third woman, clearly not Lawford Raines, he also recognized, was none other than his stepmother, Jessica Montanero. Astonishment blazed in his eyes. What the hell was she doing here?

Oh, right, he thought, it was a small village. The residents pretty much knew each other, and Jessica was familiar with the Kellys. She had ordered the bird cake from them.

Gian and the housekeeper reached the gazebo. Mrs. Kelly's head tipped to the side and her eyes narrowed, not in an unfriendly way, but in a curious study of why a policeman was in her back yard.

At her bemused glance, Nicolle and Jessica turned their heads to the pair approaching them. Nicolle's eyes widened in confusion and dismay. Jessica smiled broadly at him.

"Mrs. Kelly, this police officer would like a word with Miss Nicolle," the maid announced. At her words, the dismay on Nikki's face turned to apprehension.

Lolly Kelly set her cup down and put her hand on the table to stand up as she greeted Gian. "I believe that's Detective Montanero, not officer, Maureen," she corrected kindly. "Please, um, Giancomo I believe it is? Join us."

"Don't get up," Gian said quickly as the elderly lady appeared awkward and unsteady with her broken arm in a cast as she tried to rise. He moved rapidly up the few steps to where the ladies were seated.

Instantly the aroma of savory chocolate along with the pungency of mayonnaise and spicy Dijon assailed his senses. He couldn't help it, his eyes lurched to the tiered stand. It was loaded with eclairs and tiny cakes and cookies as well as small, crustless finger sandwiches and other rich looking edibles.

He wasn't big on cucumber sandwiches, but right now he could devour the two that were perched amongst the sweets and other delights on the trays.

A mischievous light twinkled in Lolly Kelly's blue eyes. "Maureen, please bring another cup and plate with settings for the detective."

Before Gian could decline, not that he planned to, the maid nodded and scurried off to do the elderly lady's bidding. "Have a seat, Detective," Lolly gestured to a fourth chair at the table.

"Ah," Gian felt somewhat awkward. The women were all dressed so femininely and sipping their tea so delicately perched upon dainty looking chairs, albeit they were wrought iron. He felt like a brute beast that had stumbled upon a Victorian ladies' tea party in a lush English garden.

He glanced askance at the elegant chair, but decided it could sustain his weight. He pulled it out and carefully lowered himself onto it.

"Gian, honey, what are you doing here?" Jessica asked him with a happy smile. She loathed the distance her stepson kept between himself and his family. He was coming around finally though, after numerous enforced hugs and sincere affection and constant invitations to visit. Her red brows drew down in sudden concern. "Is something wrong? The boys? Your dad?"

"No, no," Gian said right away. "Everything is fine. I just, ah," his eyes danced over the tiered food trays.

Lolly chuckled lightly. "You growing boys, here," she lifted a small plate of turkey and cheese sandwiches, the crusts trimmed off. "Start with these. No need to stand on ceremony and wait for your own plate. Dig in, son," she encouraged as he stared doubtfully yet hungrily at the sandwiches. Dijon mustard oozed out the sides from under the smoked turkey.

"Well, ah, okay." Gian snatched up a sandwich and chomped right into it. He chewed and swallowed quickly then set the half-eaten sandwich down. A stack of flowered paper napkins sat nearby, he snagged a couple, wiping his mouth and fingers.

Although small, the sandwich was gourmet with thick smoked turkey, melted camembert, lettuce, tomato, sauteed shitake mushrooms, even caramelized onions and a spicy Dijon.

"Wow." His eyes closed, Gian couldn't hold back the moan of elation that oozed out with the mustard. "That's amazing," he murmured while stuffing the second half in his mouth. Chewing vigorously, he didn't see the women were all smiling indulgently at him.

Nicolle's smile held apprehension along with indulgence.

Lolly glanced at her granddaughter then smiled at Gian as he picked up another sandwich. "So, Detective, Giancomo if I may, what brings you by?"

Brioche plumping one side of his mouth, Gian wiped at the corner of his lip. He looked towards Nikki then swallowed. "Please call me Gian. When I was here the other day, Mrs. Kelly," he nodded in deference to the woman of the house.

"I noticed your household, as well as the farmland was in, well," he licked his lips. "I've heard you are quite shorthanded in both areas, and I thought I'd stop by to see if you need any, well, I can garner up some assistance perhaps? I know a few guys who could offer some volunteer work." His gaze stayed on Nikki. Her eyes turned down as her cheeks heated.

Lolly's eyes volleyed from Gian to Nikki. "Darling, is this about those rumors that we were hitting the skids?" She turned an ear to her granddaughter, a miniscule hearing aid nestled inside glittered faintly when her hair moved.

Nikki rolled her eyes. "No, Nana, I mean yes," she glared at Gian. "Mr. Montanero happened to come by at a particularly, ah, unfortunate moment. I was, um," her lips bunched in embarrassment.

"It happened to be when he came for the cake and I, well, I was out in the field trying to fix the fence, and Aunt Jacalyn was sort of going on about the chores not getting done. And, well," the color darkened in her cheeks, she peered at Gian then quickly away. "Well, apparently he-"

"The hands were abusing your granddaughter as in tricking her into doing their work, and your lazy kin were foisting their responsibilities onto her as well. She, Nicolle," he nodded in Nikki's direction, ignoring the ire that flashed from her blue eyes at him.

"Was shouldering a heavy bulk and burden of work. I understood the farm was falling on hard times, the help fleeing the ship so to speak, and the shortness of farmhands." He kept his stern gaze on Lolly as he spoke.

"I may have said a few unsavory words to your daughter, ah, Jacalyn I believe her name is, about handling their own shit, apologies," damn, he had to remember refined ladies didn't like cursing. Jessica was always on him about it. A matter of respect, she'd scolded. He sent her a short look of remorse.

"Oh," Lolly sat back with a shake of her head and a smile. "I don't know how all those rumors got started! I think a disgruntled servant that we reasonably fired started it. Listen," she leaned forward with warm eyes and a kind smile.

"We are doing just fine. More than fine actually. I had no idea what was going on here. You see," she turned her smile to Jessica and then Nicolle.

"After my accident, I was out of it for a few days, and my husband, Tane, he was quite ill for a spell and, well, unfortunately, integrity amongst family and staff around these parts doesn't seem to be all that, well, great." Her smile dipped into a frown. Then she reached over and patted Nikki's hand.

"Once I was on the mend, the servants I've known for a long time and have fantastic loyalty, came to me and told me a bit of what was going on."

Her other hand flattened on her chest, as her head shook back in forth in perturbance. The silvery-white hair in a tufted-out bob swung across her shoulders, the butterflies at the sides appeared to dance.

She wasn't what Gian had expected. She was hardly frail, and the word 'elderly' didn't fit her at all. She was energetic, dressed chicly with smooth makeup and a stolid posture. Her blue eyes were clear as bluebells in the summer sun and her smile was bright, lovely and genuine.

Unaware of Gian's internal assessment of her, Lolly continued, "It was all blown out of proportion. Two maids up and left. One ran off to get married and her fella lives in Kentucky, and the other graduated college and is onto her career. That did make us a bit short handed at first."

Her brows slanted down as her expression grew angry. "Unfortunately, simultaneously, the farmhands were taking advantage of Tane not being around cracking the whip. Well, I'll tell you," her lips tightened and her chin pressed up, "we have plenty of income. I've hired two new house staff already, and Tane is up on his feet and he has been out to the ranch-hands' cabin and he lowered the boom."

Peripherally, Gian could see Nicolle nodding her head as her grandmother spoke.

Lolly said with satisfaction, “Cleaned them all out and hired on all new hands and a solid foreman with excellent references.” Her head moved side-to-side with the disgust apparent on her soft face. She turned sad eyes to her granddaughter.

Chapter Eighteen

Gian picked up another sandwich and dug in.

The maid arrived with a fresh pot of tea and a plate that was no longer necessary as Gian planned on finishing off the rest of the turkey and then some.

The servant set a large mug down in front of him and poured tea into it and then refilled the ladies' cups.

"Please, sir, cream and sugar if you desire are on the table." Maureen permitted a tiny giggle to leave her lips. "I didn't think you could comfortably manage one of the delicate China cups so I brought you a mug." She looked pointedly at his big hands and the small tea cups with the very small fingerholes.

"That was thoughtful, thank you." Gian offered her up a fleeting smile. He was still working on learning the skill of smiling. In his life smiles had been extremely rare.

"Thank you, Maureen." Lolly turned back to Gian. "Nikki's young cousin Mason told us what my family has been up to. I in turn had a conversation with my daughter and her husband and their daughters. They know they will pitch in and take care of their own responsibilities and necessities or they can go stay in a hotel." She harrumphed and took a quick sip of tea.

"Then, Tane and I, and your lovely stepmother Jessica here," she smiled at the silent redhead who smiled fondly back at her. "We had a conversation with Nikki and discussed what she wants to do. Jessica," she nodded at Gian's stepmother.

"Jessica came over to also discuss Nikki's future." She raised her grey brows at Jessica and inclined her head to her to take over.

"Yes," Jessica said, and gently touched Nikki's arm. Jessica's red hair was loose around her shoulders. Freckles speckled on her cheeks and nose from the sun she had been enjoying the past week.

She told Gian, "I had the opportunity to speak with Nikki at the clambake while you were doing police work. She had been studying culinary arts in college but left to come home to help out, and now that she's here, she doesn't really want to go back to Europe and finish her studies."

"Yes," Lolly leaned forward with excitement shining out of her blue eyes. "Nikki explained to us what she'd like to do, and Jessica offered to help her out with a loan, which," she said swiftly with a glance at Nikki, "we, Tane and I, have offered to just give her the money she needs, because the truth of it is, contrary to rumors, that we are quite well off. But the stubborn child," she gave Nikki an affectionate smile, "insists on a legal loan. Which we are more than happy to supply."

She lifted an éclair on its doily when she saw Gian's eyes keep flitting to it and set it on his plate. "Detective, please don't be shy. You're a growing boy, eat as much as you'd like."

Gian nodded his thanks and picked up the éclair. He said to Nikki, "What is it you want to do? I mean a girl can only shop so much." He shoved half the éclair in his mouth and smothered a groan of rapture.

Her mouth dropped open and eyes flew up. Nikki spurted, "Oh! Are you a headless frog, or just a- a sexist troglodyte?"

Gian gulped down the savory cream and chocolate and licked his fingers. "Probably both." He took another bite of the éclair and his eyes rolled heavenward.

Jessica frowned at him. "Gian, women do more than just shop, you know. This is the 21st century. You-"

"Anyway," Lolly spoke up. "Nikki does have a couple of years of culinary studies under her belt. She loves to cook, she would like to make a living at it."

Gian twisted his head to regard Nikki's angry face. "So, get a job in a restaurant. There are millions of them. Why would you need to borrow money to be a cook?"

Nikki's mouth tightened, her blue eyes smoldered. "Listen you thick-headed neanderth-"

"No, no, Detective." Again, Lolly stepped in with a smile to Nikki then to Gian. "She would like to open her own, um, tea shop."

He had a great poker-face, but still Gian's brows jumped up. "What the hell? How can you make any money selling pots of tea? Sounds a bit, well, absurd."

He finished the éclair and went for a macadamia nut cookie, but his eyes still roamed the tray. They stopped at the creamy quiche-looking thing. His tongue swept out of its own volition.

"Darling," Jessica said calmly. "Nikki prepared everything on this table. From scratch. You haven't even tried the white chocolate lavender scones with lemon curd, or the honey tea cakes, or the buttercream crab puffs. I daresay after eating this gloriously prepared food you will loathe to eat any other restaurant food again."

Gian's gaze moved from the quiche thing to Nikki who was scowling at him. "Yeah, but tea? That's so… plain. Bland."

Nikki's eyes fell to his empty mug and she smirked. "Oh? Did you not enjoy your ambrosia tea?"

At his blank look, she said, "There are tons of different amazing tasting teas. There's sweet leaf and dancing leaf, floating leaf, dreamy leaf, souchong, white peony, chocolate lavender, chai. On and on."

Her head tilted at him. "Would you care for some more? This is my own recipe, a special blend I put together with herbs and spices. I use all local grown herbs for now." One blonde brow arched in question as she reached for the tea pot.

Gian cleared his throat, his glaze slipped over to the pot she held. He looked down at his mug, it was indeed empty. Damn, the brew had tasted so good it slid down like sap on a maple tree.

He hadn't even needed sugar or cream, and he normally was not a tea drinker. Tasted like sewage to him, but this stuff… "Sure." He moved his mug closer to her reach. He waited until she was done pouring.

"You think you could make a go of this- this," his hand motioned to the three-tiered stand still chock full of delicious looking and smelling delights.

"I mean, yeah, what I've tried is incredible, and the tea, well," he shrugged. "Not a tea guy but it was damned tasty." He muttered thanks to Nikki for the refill and gulped half of it.

The three women watched him as he reached for an interesting looking tart and set it on his plate. He gobbled down the rest of the éclair and picked up the fork Maureen had provided for him.

After a taste of the tart, and stifling his moan of luscious relish, he said to Nikki, "So, what all is involved in you setting this whole…shebang up?"

"I don't want to bore you with the de-"

"Well," Jessica jumped in. "We procure the loan, search for the perfect location and building, retrieve the necessary permits and get things moving from there. She already has a name picked out."

Chewing on the tart, Gian cut another piece with his fork. "Oh yeah? What is it?"

Nikki blushed, her eyes beamed. "Lavender Sips. You know," one shoulder bumped up shyly. "Like sipping lavender tea, it's my favorite, another special blend I concocted. I have zillions of ideas I want to try. I love cooking and really think I can make a go of it."

"You have had the schooling," Gian noted as he chomped.

She agreed with a sigh. "Yes, I have put in long hours in school labs, as well as working as a free intern in restaurants as a cook and a few months shadowing a manager. I'm not afraid nor unaware of the hard work involved." She took a breath.

"I've studied how the business side of a small restaurant works. The developing, accounting, loans, OSHA's rules and regs, bulk food purchasing, reviewing and researching the demographics of the best area suited to my shop, and on and on."

She glanced at Lolly. Was she rambling too long? Lolly gave her a smile and nod to continue.

"Well, I'd like to provide Wi-Fi access for people who want to work or do school studies while sipping tea and enjoying scones, as well as having a sort of library around the sides and back for people to relax and read while eating and drinking. The middle area would be for people visiting with friends or family like a regular restaurant.

"I want to develop an entire…oh, atmosphere of refinement with food and drink and relaxation. It would hopefully be an experience people would like to do at least once a week. Then, once we're up and rolling I'd like to look into growing my own tea leaves."

Gian asked with surprise, "You want grow your own tea?"

She nodded emphatically. "Oh yes. I have also studied tea cultivation. The soil preparation, fertility management, climate requirements for optimal tea grown, bugs and fungus prominent in tea fields, the selecting and sourcing-" her cheeks pinked.

"My apologies." Her eyes darted around the table as her shoulders rose and fell. "I get excited about it all and tend to run off at the mouth with all my ideas. I try not to be a big bore about it. I guess farming is in my genes, huh?" Her half-grin to her grandmother was sheepish.

Then she narrowed a serious blue eye at Gian, her mouth firmed with resolution. She said, "This is not a frivolous silly pipe dream. I plan to make a sizzling success of the business. I've thought about it forever. I've studied and plotted and planned and spoken with experts. It'll be tough in Maine to grow tea but it can be done. Along with most of the herbs I will be using."

"We have plenty of land here for her to use," Lolly said. "It will be interesting and exciting to see how it works. Something entirely new and exotic to watch flourish. Plus, we have good help now that can assist her with the digging and planting and so on."

Nikki sat back in her wrought iron chair and clasped her hands together setting them on the table. Both Jessica and her grandmother gave her smiles of pride and encouragement.

Gian was quiet for so long the women thought they had lost his attention.

Then he pointed the fork at Nikki while he spoke. "I think I know a person who can help you locate the perfect place for this, tea shop. I recall seeing a couple of locations with For Sales signs up."

"Oh? Where?" Lolly asked excitedly.

"I'll show Nicolle where they are tomorrow. What time shall I pick you up?" He polished off the tart and was reaching for a cucumber cream cheese sandwich.

All three women gawked at him.

Jessica and Lolly grinned at each other. Lolly gave Jessica a wink and a nod, while Nikki just stared at him with her mouth hanging open.

Chapter Nineteen

*T*he next morning, Gian drove through a fast-food restaurant and bought two egg and bacon on croissants with a side of hash brown tots and a large black coffee.

He barely tasted the sandwiches, the memory of Nicolle Kelly's food made everything else taste like cardboard.

The girl could cook, and if her enthusiasm and determination were anything to go by, he had little doubt that she could definitely make her tea shop a success. He had a few ideas where he could show her some good sites for her shop.

But first, he needed to get a killer off the quaint streets of Chicory Landing.

He decided he needed a more rounded picture of his father's business. He was almost 100% sure the attempted killings of his brothers and the murder of Koh Boone had something to do with the lobster fishing or the marina, that they weren't just random attacks.

The mystery is actually why his brothers were shot. Boone's murder is clearly explained. He saw the murderer, or at least their car and could therefore ID them, and he shot off his mouth about it while simultaneously attempting to blackmail the killer(s).

The fact that his brothers were put out of commission and it sounded like someone, a woman, deliberately spread a flu or some other dire disease amongst the deckhands. Yeah, someone was trying to knock his father out of the largest event to hit the northeast quadrant.

Was it all about the money the festival was supposed to bring in, especially to his father who had planned on supplying the main part of the event, the lobsters as well as crabs, or could it be about knocking Gator O'Grady out of the mayorship?

And if it was that, who would that benefit the most? Was it about the power of the mayor's superior place in the community?

The mayor had the majority say in things like rezoning and approval of new building structures both commercial and residential. Perhaps someone wanted control of the construction and planned to deluge Chicory Landing with condos along the beloved lakefront of Maverick Bay.

He couldn't believe his easy-going brothers had enraged someone bad enough that they were targeted for death.

No, it was more likely about the money or power. Was someone trying to get Jed Montanero as potentially the largest earner out of the festival picture? Which leads back to the money motive. These thoughts jounced around Gian's brain as he headed to his father's house.

Gian parked his Ram in the driveway behind Jessica's light blue Tahoe and strode up the stoned pathway that led around to the side door to the mud room and into kitchen. The kitchen door was open; the screen door was still intact. In a month it will be replaced with the storm door. He curled his hand around his eyes and peered through the screen.

His father was sitting at the large kitchen table that overlooked the back yard with the patio and pool. Jed Montanero was pouring maple syrup over a stack of blueberry pancakes, and as collateral damage fat sausage links got a dosing of syrup as well.

A glass of orange juice next to a mug of steaming coffee sat in front of the flapjacks. He looked up as Gian knocked lightly on the door frame while entering the kitchen.

The room done in cheery reds and bright yellows beckoned Gian to grab a mug and fill it with aromatic dark rich coffee. He pulled out a chair and sat down across from his dad.

"Jessy made a load of cakes, son, they're warming in the oven, go on and snag yourself a bunch," Jed offered with a wave of his knife that dripped butter on the red and yellow tablecloth.

"Ate on the way here, thanks." Gian sipped his hot brew. Nonetheless, he snagged one of Jed's plump sausages and gobbled it in two bites, then wiped off the drop of syrup that slipped off the sausage onto his chin.

"Not that you need a reason as you are always welcome here, Gian, this is your home too," Jed said, "but I assume you have a reason for stopping by this morning. As soon as I'm done here, I'll be at the boat. There's a lot of preparation to get started for the big set off."

"I'm sure you have a long list of things that need doing."

Jed grinned at him. "You're welcome to come along and get more lobster lessons. We have tons of lobster traps and nets that need cleaning and repairing." He winked at Gian and stuffed a forkful of pancakes slathered in butter and syrup into his eager mouth.

"As much as I'd love to hop aboard and get to scrubbing, sewing, scraping and hammering," Gian's dry tone indicated the opposite. "I'm still investigating the shootings, and now I have a murderer to catch."

"Ayhuh," Jed nodded, chewing away. "Heard about old Boone buying it. You think it's tied into Reece and Josh's shootings?"

"Undoubtedly," Gian replied. "We looked into a girl Josh had dumped because she already had a boyfriend, however both the girl and boyfriend have tight alibis. We're checking on a poker group Reece played with and beat the pants off, heard there were some hard feelings involved."

He sipped his coffee while watching a robin in the back yard trying to tug a worm out of a hole.

"Yuh, your brother is a tremendously good poker player. Practically undefeated."

Gian nodded grimly. "Unfortunately, the players' alibis look pretty airtight as well. Frenchie Chad, who runs the Bon Savoureux, had a hundred witnesses in food staff as well as customers during the time of the shootings."

Jed cut a big piece of sausage and popped it in his mouth. His nose wrinkled. "Tried that Frenchie place once, talk about pretentious. A hundred bucks for a teensy morsel of duck breast with a single long chive laid across the top to make it look pretty, and a bottle of red wine I can get for twenty dollars at the grocery and Chad charges $155 for it."

"I heard it's very expensive."

"It is that. Your ma, ah, Jessy is ten times the cook that Frenchie is. Simple and flavorful, and enough to make your belly feel comfortably full without costing a week's wages, eh? What else you got?"

"Hmm," Gian set his mug down and rubbed his chin thoughtfully. "Then there's Liam Kuno, who owns the country club at the Marina, same thing. A bunch of witnesses say it was a busy night and Kuno would have been missed if he was gone even to the restroom for a minute. Redford Damon, the butcher, he was in Atlantic City on some gambling excursion with his wife and niece."

"That lets them out of the picture."

"Yep. And the last player, Lawford Raines is on some kind of pickle ball team and they had a tournament. All went out for beer and wings after."

"Maybe it was just a random drive-by kind of thing," Jed suggested while pouring more syrup on his cakes.

"Don't you worry about your sugar intake, diabetes? Cholesterol?" Gian nodded at the butter and syrup Jed kept steadily adding to his fluffy pancakes.

The side of his mouth bulging like a chipmunk's, Jed shook his head and washed his food down with a slug of orange juice. "Nope. Work it off, son. Lobsterin' is long hard work. Need to keep my strength and energy up, eh?" He set the glass down and picked up his fork.

His eyes on the forkful of cakes his father was stabbing, Gian said, "I'm pretty sure the murder attempts and Boone buying it is tied into you or your boat. We've checked into Kopper Komer and Skitty Hawkins, those two hands you fired, and Jason Landry the nickel-dime thief. They all have solid alibis."

"Hey, Gian, bro, good to see you." Gian's brother Amadeo trod into the kitchen making straight for the coffee pot. Filling a mug, he set it on the table and settled onto a chair.

"Deo," Gian greeted.

"Running thoughts by Dad, huh?" Deo smiled.

"Yeah, sort of," Gian replied. "Helps to sift through things in my head. Easier than having screwy ideas tripping around from Corny Vinci and his sidekick Nutcracker."

Jed and Deo chuckled.

Deo got up and piled a plate full of pancakes from the oven. He ignored his father's frown as he snatched the syrup from his hand.

Sitting back down, Deo asked, "What about Tex Coltrane? He's always been a rival of Dad's. No where's near the fisherman Dad is, but it never stopped his grousing and whining about the Seabug's huge hauls compared to the Red Claw's. He sees Dad as his competition for the big lobster fest coming up."

Deo laughed shortly. "Not that he has a chance of competing against us. Even with us being so shorthanded."

"Speaking of," Jed said, keeping his eyes trained on the crystal flute the amber syrup poured from. "We're going to definitely need your help on the boat, Gian, and," he sighed heavily, "that won't even be enough. Our entire crew has come down with some kind of flu bug or something."

His brows rose, Gian cocked his head at his father, his gaze on his brother. "I heard that the entire crew is sick."

Nodding, Jed wiped his mouth with a napkin then balled it up and dropped it on his now empty plate. "Seems one of the guys brought some girlie or other on board late Saturday night. Against the rules they know, but did it anyway."

"Horndogs," Deo mumbled around a mouthful of blueberry pancake.

"Yeah. Anyway, Deo and I went to Ted Jacobs' house when he and the others didn't show up yesterday. He was in bed. Face as red as a beet, hackin' and coughin' and sneezing."

"Totally gross," Deo cut a hunk of sausage. "Basket overflowing with snotty tissues and crap. End table laden with pills, cough medicine and such. Disgusting." He chomped on the pork link.

Jed nodded and wrapped his big hands around his mug. “Yeah. Apparently, the dipsticks knew the chick was sick. A couple tried to fend her off, but she kind of pushed her way on board. And, well, you know how men are, drunk men. They aren’t exactly discerning.”

“So I’ve heard,” Gian said with a smile.

“Yeah. I guess the bunch of ‘em all took their turns, and the next couple days after, lo and behold, my whole damn crew is fu- uh, mucked.” He glanced around quickly for any sign of Jessica the profanity police.

Gian set his elbows on the table, folded his hands together and rested his chin on his fists. “That sounds…odd.”

Jed shrugged. “Nah, boys, booze, broads,” he glanced quickly at the door for his disapproving wife. “They don’t think with their brains, they let their pants do the deciding. Dicks don’t care about colds. They only care about,” he looked around and shrugged again.

“Uh huh. Still…” Gian pictured a sick woman pushing her way on board a boat of drunken males and deliberately having sex with them. “Dad, it was done on purpose. She got the crew sick on purpose. This whole thing clearly has something to do with your boat, the Seabug. Someone is trying to keep you from going out to sea.”

Jed shoved his mug away and his lips pushed out ruefully. “But why would some girl want to keep me from fishing?”

“Not some girl,” Deo said, he got his brother’s point. “Someone else, bigger up pulling the strings. Someone hired the shooters, or they did it themselves-”

“And killed Koh Boone when they heard he could ID the suspicious car that was half hidden in the woods,” Gian said. “I need to find his shipmate.”

“Hey,” Jed spoke up. “You might want to check on that cartel guy, ah, what’s his name?” He scratched his head. “Um,” he looked to Deo for help.

Deo snapped his fingers. “Yeah, Jon Michel. He tried to hit you up a few times to smuggle some dope or other.”

"What?" Gian's head jolted to his father. "What's that about? Smuggling? Why the hell didn't you say something to me? That crap needs to be shut down immediately!"

Jed held his hands up. "Yeah, yeah, calm down. The guy never came right out and tried to set up a deal, he just hinted around about whether I wanted to make some extra dough bringing in drugs or guns or some such."

"Dad," Gian blurted. "Come on. We could have set up a sting, shut down an entire smuggling ring or whatnot."

Shaking his head, Jed said, "No, like I said, he only hinted very vaguely. And, you think I'd want to endanger my family, my sons, my deckhands in that kind of deadly sting? Who knows how deep, how high up the chain Michel is?"

"Well, maybe-"

"What if you only caught and took out the middle people and more gangsters at the top decided on revenge? No." Jed shook his head more adamantly. "Didn't want to step one toe into that quagmire. I could lose my livelihood, the Seabug, my children, put Jessica in danger, no sir." He waggled a finger at Gian.

Gian stared at him for a moment, then his shoulders lowered. "Okay, you're right. Still, I would have liked a head's up on that. We could have been watching them more closely." He sat back and wiped at his eyes then raked a hand through his hair.

The men were quiet for a spell, each deep in his own thoughts. Gian asked Deo, "You talk any with Josh about that night? About those scents he said he smelled, or colors he saw? Orange and molasses or something?"

Deo's lips pulled in. He bumped one shoulder. "We've gone back and forth, even took a small trip to the store. He's still recuperating, has to use canes to walk. Tried some perfumes, and drove by that apple orchard down from the marina. But he said nothing smelled familiar."

"It's probably not something we're ever going to be able to figure out," Gian said. "It's too…obscure. Not enough specific to grab onto."

"We even tried the Country Garden Nursery. Checked out wind chimes for the tinkling sound he heard, and some flowers, but no go. None of the bakeries close to the marina sell any kind of gingersnap or gingerbread type cookies. We'll keep trying."

Gian frowned at his brother. "I didn't ask you to do police work, Deo, that's my job. I don't want you guys putting yourselves in danger. I just asked you to keep on him about what he remembered."

Deo returned his brother's frown and then gave him a lopsided grin. "Really, Gian, a trip around orchards, flower shops, bakeries and perfume stores is hardly painting targets on our backs."

"Well, I don't want you guys talking to people. You don't know if you're speaking to a suspect or not."

"We didn't question anyone. The condition Josh is in we hardly were even on our feet for very long. Don't worry, I'm not reckless or a fool, well," he ducked his head with a smile at his father's snort. "At least in this sort of thing. Besides, I would never put our youngest brother in danger. Give me some credit, ay?"

Gian stared evenly at Deo for a few seconds then nodded sharply. Setting his palms on the table he pushed his chair back. "You're right. Thanks for trying what you guys did, I appreciate the help and effort. Just, be careful, don't ask anyone any questions."

He dipped his head to his father. "I have to get going. Tell Jessica and the boys I said hey. I'll try to check back later." He stood up.

Gian started for the door then stopped. He turned around. "Dad, do you know a guy, might be homeless, hangs around the marina name of Paul Schmitt?"

Jed stood up and chuckled. "Yeah, freak. Gives the girls the creeps. But I think he's harmless. He's just really nosy. Kind of pops up here and there, sneaking people's drinks off their tables when they hit the head or not looking. Steals their smokes too. Never stole money or any complaints of his molesting the girls. I toss him a lobster roll and chips occasionally. Why do you ask?"

"He…like you said, appears nosy. Asked me about the investigation. He looks like a bum, but I think there's a lot more going on with him. Doesn't act like an addict or like he has any kind of mental health issues. His eyes are clear, alert and intelligent. He's hiding something. Told me to look for Koh Boone's roommate, Clyde Collins. Thinks Boone might have told him about the car he saw."

"I hear Clyde's okay folk," Jed said. "He's quiet, pleasant, doesn't hesitate to lend a hand to anyone who needs it. I think…" His forehead wrinkled, he set a few fingers on his upper lip and tapped them. "There's a dorm house at the far end of Maverick Bay I gave him a ride to one day. You could check there for word of him."

"Thanks, Dad. Can you text me that info?"

"Of course. Take care son, stop by later if you can. Jessy's got pot roast in the oven slow cooking and that pretty little lady, Nikki Kelly sent her home the other day with an apple pie that'd make you cry it's so damned good."

Gian left the house and jumped in his Ram. It was around the time he said he'd pick up Nicolle.

"Yeah," he muttered as he hung a right onto the main street. He could understand how those deckhand idiots felt when that woman, even though sick, freely offered herself, was even pushy about it.

She showed clear intent to deliberately infect the crew making them unable to work, and therefore debilitating Jed's lobster business.

But Gian had his own desire for a woman. His pants were growing tight just at the thought of laying eyes on soft curls and shiny blue eyes.

Truth be told, he'd be happy just to have her sitting beside him in his truck.

Chapter Twenty

Gian drove under the Shamrock Farm archway and up the pebbled drive. The stones crunched under his tires as he made his way to the front of the house. A smile touched his lips. Nicolle was standing outside waiting for him.

The smile wavered. Either she didn't want anyone to know she was going somewhere with him, or she hated to have anyone waiting on her, or she was eager to see him.

He hoped for the third but it was more likely the middle option. At least that was better than the first. He pulled right up to her and shut the truck off. Before she could blink, he was out of the vehicle and around to the passenger side.

"Hey, you ready?" he asked, stopping a foot in front of her. Close enough to see the different shades of blue striations in her eyes, but outside of her personal space.

Her eyes lowered shyly then rose in uncertainty to his. "Are you sure about this?" The way her forehead wrinkled Gian could tell she hadn't really believed he was truly going to show up.

"Of course I'm sure. Do I seem the kind of guy who offers a plan and then doesn't follow through?" One dark brow curved up, his head tilted to the side as he regarded her coolly. The question was rhetorical.

He looked down at the top of her curly blonde hair. The soft breeze pushed the loose strands around and the sun painted golden highlights along the curving tresses.

Her blonde brows screwed up in confusion. “But I don’t understand. Why? You’re a busy man with crimes to solve, and-and you don’t even like me. I don’t-”

Gian planted his boots firmly on the gravel and crossed his arms, he crooked his neck to make eye contact with her. “I never said I didn’t like you, Nicolle. I…”

Nikki crossed her arms, mirroring his posture. “I’m right. You don’t like me. You think I’m weak and gullible, stupid, and well, Lawford told me you thought women like me were high maintenance, that we order people around to slave for us. That I’m not anywhere your type, that you like, oh, bigger, stronger, more- more sturdy women. He, well he said you thought I was too soft, too delicate for you.”

Gian thought back. He did say those things, but he wasn’t talking to Raines. He had been in a bar, talking to Deo, his brother if he recalled. Yes, Deo had pointed out the beautiful blonde and they discussed her, and Gian’s antipathy towards her type, and the fact that he preferred plainer, tougher kinds of women. Great.

It seems Lawford Raines must have been in the pub and eavesdropped on their conversation. Figures, a snake in the grass to be sure. And that was disparaging to snakes. He liked snakes in general. They tended to mind their own business and slithered away when humans came around. Yeah, he placed snakes a step above Lawford Raines.

“So,” Nikki, said, “I just don’t get why we, you, are here.” Her face was wreathed in bewilderment. “I’m thinking you have some kind of agenda. I don’t see what part I have in whatever it is.”

Letting out a long breath, Gian dragged strong fingers through his short hair in his own perplexity. “I, well, to be honest with you, yeah, you aren’t normally my…type. But, trust me, Nicolle,” he uncrossed his arms and set his hands on his lean hips. “I have no agenda. I just…” He shrugged broad shoulders and allowed a brief smile to lift his harsh mouth.

“I find myself thinking of you. It’s never happened to me before, thinking about a woman, a particular woman, or anyone for that matter. I’ve been on my own a long time and I don’t especially desire to have any, ah interest, in an individual.”

He rifled his hand through his hair again making the short dark tufts stand up. “I admit my incredulity, and, well, unwelcome interest in you have me dumbfounded.”

Her eyes widened, blonde lashes slapped up against arched brows of affront. “Well! Then, this is certainly easily remedied.” She stepped back with a glower, waving at his truck.

“Please, hop in and be on your way. We’ll just pretend this never happened, and when we cross each other’s paths in the future we’ll just nod politely and carry on. No need to really acknowledge one another.” She started to turn towards the house, Gian shot a hand out and caught her arm.

Her words made his heart cringe, and the idea of climbing in his truck and driving off alone made his stomach plummet, a feeling of…he checked his gut. He couldn’t put a name on what he was feeling, but he didn’t like it.

“No, Nicolle, please. I’m not really too good with words, I’ve blundered.”

“It’s okay,” her voice was soft with a hint of kindness. “You’re off the hook. I won’t be angry with you if we run into each other. Don’t worry, I’m fine.” She petted the hand that still held her arm. She pulled to free it, to no avail. Gian had an iron grip.

“No, listen. Let’s,” Gian glanced off over the verdant lawn sprinkled with fallen autumn colors, a few spiraled in the breeze. “Let me start over.”

He cocked his head to the side and pushed a smile out. “I would truly like to spend the next couple of hours with you as we’d planned. I have several locations for your tea shop I’d like to show you and I think you will love at least one of them.”

She tugged her arm but again he didn’t release it. It was like he was afraid if he let go she’d fly off out of his reach, forever. His fingers wrapped more tightly around her slender arm.

Nikki said, “It’s okay, really, Detective Montanero. My feelings aren’t hurt. You don’t need to-”

He gently pulled her to his truck and opened the passenger door. “Just get in and let’s see where the day brings us, all right?” He nodded to the truck. “Let’s start over, okay? Clean slate.”

“But I-”

"It's a high step, let me help you." Gian ignored her protests and practically lifted her up and into the truck. He closed the door in her shocked face and trod around to climb into the driver's side.

Starting the engine, he turned around in the curved driveway and while she was still sputtering objections, he drove the truck under the archway of the Shamrock Farm and to the highway.

They drove in silence for around twenty minutes as Gian maneuvered through the village. He pulled up in front of the first location he had chosen to show her. It was a small shop in a strip mall along one of the main streets.

He helped her down from the truck and said, "I have the keycode from a relator for these empty stores." He put the code into the lockbox and removed the key from inside. He unlocked the door and swung it open.

The empty store was in worse shape than he had been led to believe. The walls had large holes in them, the floor needed a lot of sanding and waxing or a new carpet. Everything was filthy, the kitchen area was pure grime, and the appliances were old and rusted.

Gian put a hand to Nikki's back and quickly ushered her back out the door.

At the truck, as he helped her in, he said, "Sorry about that. The agent drew a totally different picture of what to expect. I knew these places were empty and checked with the real estate agent for prices within your range you gave me, as well as availability before I set this up. He was a bit misleading. I hope the next spot is better."

"It's fine," Nikki said as he climbed in the driver's side. "I'm used to hard work. I can clean it mostly myself. May take a while but it's doable."

"Yeah, no. It's in great disrepair. The ceiling was so sunken down I was afraid it'd collapse on us. It needs a new roof, plumbing, total rewiring. It would cost a fortune to repair and those are things you couldn't do yourself. Let's check the next one."

"Okay." She smiled broadly at him. "It's exciting to just be doing this. Checking out locations for my shop. It makes my dream seem so much closer, tangible. Even if none of them don't work out, I so appreciate you taking the time and effort you've put in for me. Thank you so much, Detective."

He grunted. "It was, well, I enjoyed it. And, can you drop the Detective? I thought we were…friends now?" He glanced quickly at her then back to the road.

White teeth gleamed at him in a happy smile. "Friends. I'd like that."

Gian didn't look at her, but his mouth slightly bent up at the corners. The tips of his ears turned red.

Unfortunately, the next shop spot was worse than the first. They were in and out in 5 minutes.

Parking in front of the third site, Gian gave her a lopsided smile. "Third's the charm? This was the one I was thinking about yesterday when you talked about your tearoom idea. Ready? Cross our fingers?"

"Okay!" Nikki grinned and opened her door. He hurried around to help her down the high step.

She stood in front of him and clasped his thick wrists. "Really, Gian, it's fine if it doesn't work out. It's the thought and effort that count. Physically doing something concrete towards my plan, my dream, as well as imagining how I can remodel these places into what I'm picturing, is exhilarating. I…" her cheeks pinked with a blush.

"I've enjoyed the day." The blush and smile geared towards him expressed that part of her enjoyment was the time spent with him.

Gian squeezed her hands but didn't return the benevolent words. "Okay. Got your fingers crossed?" He lowered his head to her with a positive nod and was rewarded with her sweet smile.

The outside of the shop was antique cute. Big windows with a striped awning over the front door bordered in curlicued, black wrought iron. It held that bit of classy whimsy Nicolle had alluded to in her description of her ideal shop.

Holding his breath, he put the code into the lockbox and opened the door. He let her step in first. He heard her swift intake of breath. *Uh oh.* Gian followed her inside.

"Oh, Gian," she gushed in a hushed voice. "It's perfect. Better than perfect. It's…amazing." Nikki took small steps as she moved further inside and turned in a circle to take the whole place in. "It's exactly what I dreamed of, pictured in my mind."

The building was in a line of stores along one of the main streets but it took up a corner. It had large windows in front and also along one side. With the big windows the natural light enhanced the place.

There was a center area with dozens of round tables gathered throughout. Along two walls were booths with seats in a lilac shade of vinyl, and silver-speckled white tables. A loft with more seating overlooked the central area.

Nikki strolled along, her shoes tapping on the hardwood floor that she was envisioning polishing up to their former brilliant gleam.

To one side near the back, she paused. "Here is where I'd put some types of coffee tables and small divans for lounging for people doing work or studies."

Further back, she stopped again. "And here," her voice lifted with glee, she motioned with her arm. "This is where I can put up bookshelves and make a sort of library. I'm picturing like a Barnes and Nobles where there are alcoves and such for people to peruse and sit down while thumbing through a book and sipping on a beverage and nibbling on a cream and strawberry biscuit."

Gian traipsed behind her. His shoulders relaxed, his gut had settled. She was such a joyous butterfly, flitting and dancing about looking here and there with such delight and excited planning.

He felt his mouth soften into a genuine smile. He pictured himself here on weekends and evenings helping her put up shelves, polish woodwork, getting the shop into shape. He realized it made him feel…happy?

Yes, strangely, the idea of helping her build her dream made him *feel*…yes, it truly made him feel. Making her happy made him feel happy. He'd been numb most of his life, because that's all he knew. His family was breaking up the ice around his heart, and Nicolle was warming that ice up and melting it.

He shook his head. What the hell was happening to him? He needed to go out and get hammered with his friends and pick up an easy lay, he needed to- his stomach gripped in pain at the thought of hitting the sheets with anyone else who wasn't Nicolle Kelly. He was so screwed.

"Here," he said, handing her a pad and pen. "Write down your thoughts, ideas. We can take some photos, so as soon as you put an offer in we can start specific planning. Both the location and condition of the building are fantastic, this place has not been on the market for long. There are a lot restaurants around here, but nothing like what you're planning. You can use the pictures to decide on decorations, paint, curtains or whatnot."

"Oh, Gian!" she exclaimed, clapping her hands together. "I can't wait to get started!"

He grinned. Her enthusiasm was so contagious. "What do you need to do first?"

Her lips pursed as she continued scanning the facility. "I've already been to the bank with Nana to facilitate a loan, so that's in the works. I need the name of the real estate agent to put in my offer. I'll have to take a long hard look at everything to see what I can use, get rid of what I can't, and purchase what I need. The kitchen appears fine, but can use some updating and of course huge cleaning."

Gian glanced at his watch. "I need to get on. Let's grab a quick bite before I take you home and get back to work. There's a restaurant a few blocks away that has good barbecue and wraps I think you'll like. Okay?"

Her blue eyes blazed with delight up at him, her smile was dazzling. "Whatever you say, whatever you want, Gian, I'm game. Thank you so, so very much for this. Helping me make my dream come true. It would have taken me some time to get to this point to check out locations and set up with an agent to lease, or buy." She tucked her phone in her purse.

"You've put the jump on getting it all rolling. And, I don't know if I would have ever found this shop without you! Look," she grasped his hand and pulled him to a side glass door.

"There's an area out back, a courtyard, that I think I can turn into outdoor seating. I can make it like Nana's place, like an

English garden. It will be lovely, brilliant flowers and greenery and patio type tables with those colorful umbrellas."

He gave her an indulgent smile. "You do have a lot of ideas. Workable, pleasant ideas. Come on, let's go. The sooner we get lunch and get you home the sooner you can get started."

"Oh," Nikki said with excitement. "I just remembered, my best friend at University, Bobby Brown, is planning on moving here. She's an artist, quite a spectacular one actually, and successful. Her work is displayed in galleries all over the world."

"Yeah?" Gian smiled at her enthusiasm for everything. Especially her tea shop and her affection for her friend.

"She is thinking about opening her own gallery here in Chicory under her real first name of Barbara. But she's more a Bobbly to me than a Barbara. Anyway, it would showcase mostly her own work with a smattering of other artists she'd like to help give a leg up in the art world."

"That sounds great, Nicolle." His forehead wrinkled in thought. "You know, there's another space for lease right on the same street here. Perhaps she might be interested in it? I didn't show it to you because it's quite a bit pricier than what you were looking for."

She turned to him, her eyes sparkling and lips curved up in happiness. "Oh, that would be marvelous! I miss her so much! With her amazing singing voice she's lead in her church choir and, Gian, Bobby is just the funniest girl. She used to tell these stories and quips that always had us rolling in the aisles holding our stomachs from laughter!"

"She sounds like a fun friend."

"Definitely. And," Nikki grinned with a pretend frown, "on top of talent and a great personality, it's so not fair that she's also pretty well put together."

His brows wiggled with a leer. "Ah, your friend is hot, huh?"

Nikki nodded. "Oh yes. Thick, rich chocolate hair, a movie star's face with a Victoria Secret's figure. Girl's got it all. Hmm," she pretended to frown again. "On second thought, maybe I don't want that exquisite competition so close to me."

Gian was peering down the street, he turned back to her. "Oh, the green bug of jealousy, eh?"

She laughed and slapped him lightly on the arm. “No. She’s just too grand of a person to not like. She’s a doll, really. I can’t wait for her to come here. Can you imagine, our dreams of my tea shop and her art gallery side-by-side?”

She clapped her hands together in glee. “I can’t wait for things to unfold!”

He smiled with affection down at her joyful face. “Yeah, Nicolle, me too.”

Chapter Twenty-one

After a short yet very pleasant lunch, Gian dropped Nicolle back home and was on his way to the station when he got a call. "Torr?" he answered, it was his friend and normally his partner, Torrand Kristo.

"Now, don't panic, he's okay-"

"Who? Dad? What-"

"Calm down, G, I said he's fine. It's Josh. He's at the Elizabeth Mary Medical Center. I thought you should see him before we call Jed."

"I'm on my way. I'm ten minutes from Dark Water." The phone to his ear, Gian yanked the wheel and spun in the opposite direction of the station and to the hospital on Dark Water Circle.

"What happened?" he barked brusquely into his cell. The tight gruffness abrading his voice expressed his fear for his brother.

"Well, he gave me a brief account when they brought him in. I happened to be at the hospital."

"What were you doing at the hospital?"

"We had picked up a suspect wanted on RICO charges and the fool had a heart attack. Anyway, Josh, he should have known better, the doctor had told him he had several months of rehab before he should really be up and about. But, for some stupid reason, he went to see if he could help out a little on the Seabug, but your father and Deo had taken it out to gas it up."

"That idiot! What the hell was he thinking?"

Gian heard Torr's hair brushing his phone as he nodded in concurrence. "Wasn't using his brain for sure. He said he was feeling light headed so he went into the Swabby's Deck tavern for a soda and sat down at the bar. That's when, well, he thought he smelled that smell, you know, what he had described the night he and Reece were shot."

Torr paused, then said, "I guess he wandered around a little sniffing. Then he got really tired and went to sit in his car where he was going to call you. When, hell, someone took a potshot at him. Bullet took out the back side window. He called 911 and when they showed up Josh looked so sickly they brought him to the hospital."

"Did he see anyone? A car? Witnesses?" Gian fired off questions as he entered the hospital complex.

"I saw them bring him in so I went into the room with him. We spoke while the doc checked him out. Basically, no. He said he heard the bullet crash into the window and the window splinter, glass flying, the startling loud noises and all."

"Damn," Gian sputtered a ream of curses.

"He said he instantly ducked and dialed 911. Then when he poked his head up, a crowd had gathered. The retrieved bullet is in process and I have Conny Vinci and Simon Nucacher canvassing the witnesses. So far we've got nada."

"Great. As we already know there're no surveillance cameras at or near Swabby's." Gian parked in the first open spot he came to and jogged to the entrance.

"I'm here. What floor?" He didn't bother stopping at the visitor desk to check in, just dashed right on past holding up his badge to the guard.

Torr gave him the room info and was standing outside the room when Gian came rushing up. Torr held a hand up. "Slow down, pard, he's okay, just tired. The adrenalin of it all has worn off and he's almost asleep. Go steady. I'll call Jed now."

"All right, thanks, Torr." Gian sucked in a deep calming breath and pushed the door open. Inside were two beds. His brother was reclining on the one nearest the door. A nurse was beside him quietly checking his vitals. He looked pale but otherwise unharmed.

"Josh," Gian murmured as he neared the bed.

One of his brother's eyes cracked open. He peered a bleary brown eye at Gian. "Hey, bro. I'm okay." He cleared his throat and tried to sit up straighter. "Listen, don't call dad, all right? Torr was gonna call him and I convinced him to call you instead."

The nurse gave Josh's shoulders a gentle push back against the pillows. "No, stay as you are, hon."

Gian's mouth quirked as he gazed down at his little brother. He didn't like the worried feeling in his gut at seeing him for the second time on his back in a hospital. His words came out with heavy sarcasm.

"Sure, kid, you're in the hospital and we're not telling Dad or Jessica. Right." He snarled at Josh, "What the hell were you thinking? You were told to stay off your damned feet, stop doing your own investigating, and what do you do? Go spying around? Alone no less! Geesh, Josh, if you had half a brain-"

"Sir, if you're going to raise your voice you're going to have to leave." The nurse scowled at him and set a protective hand on Josh's shoulder. She was probably in her forties with a serious mien which turned caring and gentle when she smiled at Josh and gave his shoulder a maternal pat.

Josh smirked at his brother.

Gian rolled his eyes. "Yeah, we'll see what happens when Dad gets here."

Josh's eyes widened in alarm. "No, Gian, see, as soon as I arrived at the marina I realized it was stupid of me to be out of bed. I was weary and dizzy. Dad would have killed me if he'd been there. I headed to Swabby's for a soda to get my strength back up before going home. That's where," his face scrunched up as he recalled stopping in the bar.

Gian pulled a small notebook from his inside jacket pocket. He was wearing a black shirt and black jeans with a black leather jacket. He wasn't working while he had taken Nicolle around so he was still dressed in casual clothes.

Clicking a pen, now that he could see his brother really was okay, Gian was all business. "Start from the beginning," he ordered.

Josh glanced at the nurse who smoothed the hair off his forehead with a small murmur of comfort. He smiled up at her then turned to his frowning brother.

"Okay, yeah. So, I went into Swabby's for a soda. I was sitting at the bar, totally wacked. All I wanted to do was crawl home and climb in bed. Then," his lips bunched, nose crinkled and brows drew down as he thought back.

"I smelled it. That scent the night Reece and I were shot. It was the same, apples, orange-like, and- and now I recall there was a woody kind of smell too."

"Like perfume or cologne, aftershave maybe? Could it be one of those air freshener things, or one of those things they hang in a car for scent?" Gian asked while jotting down Josh's words.

"Ahh," Josh looked up trying to remember the scent. "I…I don't know. I pushed off the stool, thought I'd roam around and sniff it out, but then, hell, I got so dizzy. I probably was standing out like a big clumsy sore thumb. I was so sick and weak I just stumbled to my car. Thought I'd call you and have you come and check it out. That's all. Crazy, huh?"

Gian asked, "Do you recall who was around in the pub? Including staff?"

Josh closed his eyes to picture how things were when he was sitting at the bar. "Ah, it was actually pretty busy. Tons of customers roaming around. Staff, was, um, that barmaid, Suzette behind the bar. Um, and that guy, the tall gangly blond who serves the tables was around. There were only a few deckhands I recognized from the Boundsea boat crew.

"The Boundsea had been having water in their engine so it was in port getting maintenance, that's why they were there. That's all I can remember noticing." He opened his eyes, they were red and goopy looking.

Gian made his notes. "Anyone else? Think hard, it could be important."

"Oh," Josh sighed then drew in a heavy breath. "Wait." He blinked hard a few times.

"I think there was a poker game going on in one of the back rooms. The guys Reece played with, you know, that French restaurant owner and the butcher guy down the street. I saw one or two of them hit the john. Might have been some other people hanging around watching them play."

"Good." Gian nodded as he wrote. "That's real good, Josh." They talked for a few more minutes but Josh couldn't come up with anything else.

There was a commotion at the door and Jed burst in with Jessica and Deo right behind him. Deo caught Gian's eyes.

"He's fine," Gian reassured them. "I have to go." He moved to Josh's bedside.

The nurse stepped back so the family could get close to Josh.

"I'll check in with you later. This time, stay in bed, okay, Detective?" Gian smiled at Josh's weak grin.

Torr was waiting for him outside the room. "Hey, G, I've got something else. Let's walk down together." They took the stairs to the lobby.

Gian waited until they reached the ground floor before asking, "Okay, what's up?"

"Well," Torr nodded his head to the left. They stepped over to a coffee stand. Torr ordered a latte and Gian declined anything.

"Early this morning, before the heart attack guy, I interviewed this girl," he stirred his latte then sipped. "She's Chinese, Wén Chen. She's a massage therapist at this beauty salon, Beautella."

"That's Nectar O'Grady's place, right?"

Torr nodded. "Yeah. She and this other employee, ah, what was it, oh yes, Sun Li got into a physical fight in the parking lot."

"So? Two girls fighting over customers or boyfriends or whatever. Why were you there, you're a detective, not a uniform."

Torr shrugged one shoulder. "Station was short-staffed. Big car chase after a store robbery. All men on deck to the chase scene. Anyway, the claim at the salon was about a customer who was a guy who both girls wanted to work on *and* date. Big hair-pulling, biting, scratching, bodice-ripping fight. Wish I'da been there." He grinned making ogling eyes.

At Gian's rolling eyes, Torr held his palms up. "Come on, cat fight? We don't all have ice in our veins like you, bro.

Anyway, I showed up after the smoke had cleared. Couple of male customers and one well-muscled gay employee dragged them apart."

"Okay, so I'm sure there's a moral to this story, Torr." Gian tried to move him along.

Torr sobered. "Not sure if it means anything or not, but when I was there a customer came in and sat in a chair."

"Torr-"

"It's who the customer was. It was none other than Jon Michel. You've been suspicious of him running a Mexican cartel for a while. I've noticed every time his name comes up your ears prick."

Gian gave a slight nod of agreeance. "Sure. I know he's up to something, why else would he be in this basically quaint fishing village? We've managed to keep the drug trafficking in Chicory Landing County minimal. I don't see why else he'd be here unless it's smuggling of some sort. I've had feelers out, but so far nothing he has done has generated anything suspicious enough to get my fingers into."

He checked his phone then said, "So why did it strike you as noteworthy that Michel was getting a haircut?"

"Well," Torr replied, "in the time that I was there taking notes, I observed that after an employee washed his hair, Nectar O'Grady the owner of the shop herself came out from her office in the back. She spoke to Jon Michel while she combed his hair. Occasionally she hovered around him with a pair of scissors but I noticed she never actually cut any of his hair."

Torr's grin returned at Gian's lowering brows. "Uh huh. What do you think that's all about?"

Gian pondered for a minute. "Hmm, could mean a myriad of things. Maybe he just wanted his hair washed. Or, he was scoping out the joint for a cover for possible money laundering or drug dealing, or he might just have the hots for Nectar. How was their behavior towards one another? Besides, isn't he like 20 years younger than her?"

"Not the first guy who likes a cougar."

"I've researched him, Torr. His criminal history could toilet paper a street full of trees on Halloween, although there are no major adjudications. Nectar isn't his usual type. From the meagre reports I've read, he is normally surrounded by hot, beautiful, *young* women. He has a ton of AKA's. He's also known as Juan Miguel, JJ Migs, Joaquim Micales as well as others."

"So, what do you think?"

"I think you need a haircut."

Torr smirked. He primped his short hair. "Yeah, I believe it's getting a little long at the collar."

"Give it a day for the dust to settle so it looks less suspicious. I'll have Cornball pull all the criminal histories of everyone working at Beautella see if anything pops. Oh," he pulled out a small torn piece of paper from his pocket.

"Simon Nucacher called and said that the cellophane cigarette wrapper I found had Boone's prints on it. I was hoping for a lead on the possible suspect."

"You're hoping the bad guy or guys are stupid enough to leave their prints all over the place?" Torr said with a snort.

"Yeah, well, most criminals are block heads or they wouldn't risk their freedom thieving and murdering. Meanwhile, I'll get our forensic accountants started on looking into Beautella's finances."

"I thought you weren't inclined to think Gator O'Grady was on our bad guy's suspect list."

Gian headed for the door. "Everyone is on our list including the King of England. I'm interested in who the O'Gradys' bedfellows are. Someone may be using them as unknowing puppets."

"Okay. I'm going to put a tail on Jon Michel, see who he hangs out with. I'll catch up with you later for debriefing."

"Oh, Torr," Gian said over his shoulder causing Torrand to pause with a brow arched. "My ears don't prick." He smiled at Torr's laughter as he went to his truck.

Chapter Twenty-two

A few days later Gian and Torrand met at Pan's Pub to discuss the cases. The pub owner was a fan of the Greek mythological creature Pan. The god of the wild, the iconic deity of shepherds and peasant music, and the nymphs' faithful cohort.

Many images of Pan, the half-goat Satyr played on the walls of the green and blue pub. The nymphs, bountiful and beautiful and naked, frolicked in the green forests and bathed in the shimmering blue lakes.

The bartender set two frosty, fresh tapped beers with an inch of foam in front of the detectives. They each took a healthy swig before Torrand spoke.

"I got a haircut at the Beautella Salon yesterday." Torr fingered the barely there length of the back of his shorn hair. "Not that I needed it," his bottom lip pushed out in loss of the few cut strands. "But," he shrugged and took a hefty glug of his brew and sighed happily as he swallowed. "I have no problem taking one for the team."

Gian side-eyed Tor's new haircut. "They took off about an eighth of an inch. It will grow back. *Crybaby*," he muttered under his breath.

"Anyway, anything of interest happen while you were snoop-trimming?" By habit, he patted his breast pocket for his smokes, before remembering with irritation he was trying to quit. Bugger.

One side of Torr's mouth snicked up. "Not really. The girls were all hesitant to talk about Nectar or Jon Michel. And that's probably because he was there. So much for the tail I put on him. They lost him the other day five minutes after they started to follow him."

Gian's brows rose. "Oh yeah? Did you speak with him?"

Torr drew his fingers down the side of his stein making streaks through the frost on the glass. "Briefly. It was just like the first time I was there. One of the staff washed his hair then Nectar appeared and just combed it with a bit of blow drying. No cutting or moussing or anything else. Just a comb through."

"Sounds a bit suspicious. Go all the way to the salon and take the time to only have them wash and brush your hair."

"Yeah," Torr nodded. His head rotated to watch two young women as they entered the tavern giggling and nudging each other. His eyes narrowed when they bellied up to the bar, ordered cocktails and the bartender served them. He turned his attention back to Gian.

"So, ah, nothing untoward happened. Michel and Nectar did a lot of whispering and gesturing. They seemed close but not lover-like close. Of course they might have just been being careful. After all, she is married. I was sitting near the front desk. As Michel checked out, I tried to start a friendly chat with him. It was difficult with tons of people swarming around. Asked him if he liked the salon, naturally he said yes. I mean it would appear odd to disparage a barbershop then keep going there."

"Hmm." Gian sipped his beer. "I don't know, I hear women complain all day about their hairdos and stylists but they keep going back. It's looking pretty good that Michel and Nectar are up to something."

Torr's lips bunched as he nodded. "I can't imagine it would be about lobstering and your dad's boat, the boys' shootings or whatever. What interest could Jon Michel have in any of that? Or Nectar for that matter. She wouldn't have an iron in the fire to get your dad out of business."

"Maybe he just likes her as a woman. To each his own taste," Gian said.

"I still find that hard to believe," Torr replied. "According to what Gator said, if the lobster haul fails then the festival bombs and he in turn fails as mayor. Their livelihood goes to ground. Don't know any woman who would want that." His phone buzzed in his pocket. He slid it partially out, glanced at it then shoved it back in.

One shoulder lifting in a partial shrug, Gian said, "I'm thinking it's more like money laundering. Salons are famous like laundromats and strip clubs for easy money laundering facilities. We need more info and recon on them both, and the salon."

"I don't mind returning," Torr told him with a grin. "They give a fantastic neck and head massage."

"You returning right away is too suspicious. I could use a trim, though."

"Oh sure," Torr's pretend protest came with a smirk. "I find a place that gives a good rubbing and you want it for your own, you thief."

Gian's lips twitched, but he said soberly, "Anyway, we've interviewed everyone in the vicinity of my brothers' shooting cases, including all the witnesses. The card playing group, girls Josh and Reece had been seeing and their ex-boyfriends, everyone at the marina, all the merchants, staff and boaters they could come up with. Everyone has an alibi, even those with any records. We've pulled CCTV at the marina."

"More? I thought we've looked at all of it."

"We have. But I now have Conny and Simon reviewing the tapes surrounding Boone's truck and his murder scene. They're going to check all the cars coming and going, and anyone that was near the truck or the spot where I found Boone. His truck and body were located way at the rear of the parking lot, in the darkest area where there are normally few cars. It's a huge, tedious job."

"What's your next step?"

"I think it's time we pull this Jon Michel guy in and work on him."

In his mind, Gian scrolled through all of the info they had been able to glean so far. "I also suggested Simon Nucacher do a deep dive on the other mayoral candidates. Check their financials, see who they're in bed with, figuratively and literally.

He'll have officers look into loans, outstanding debts, anyone living beyond their means, see if any of their friends are fishy."

"That makes sense." Torr nodded as he added to his own notes. "They can't be too amazing as Gator O'Grady has won by landslides for the last 12 years. In Chicory County there are no limits on how often a person can be elected to mayor. I don't think I'm even familiar with who is running."

"You probably wouldn't be. They are all basically not very well-known nonentities. There are two other men and two women," Gian told him.

His dark brows hopping up with a bit of interest, Torr asked, "Who are they? Maybe I'll recognize their names from our records checks."

Gian swiped his phone on and looked for the file on the case. "Ah, let's see. There's Dureen McMillan. She's a fifty-five-year-old homemaker with a family of five. Her husband is in insurance." He scrolled down.

"Then, there's Adam Abbott, 39, married with two kids and owns a marine repair business. Does pretty well from the initial quick glance at his financials, and the nautical aspect fits right into the marina and lobster festival deal. Let's see, number three is Perla Chanterelle, a former model," he grinned at Torr's head snapping towards him and brows wriggling lasciviously.

"Uh huh, down boy. She's in her forties and has an upscale boutique in the Apple Blossom mall, and judging by her photo and weight gain her modeling days are way behind her."

"Okay," Torr chuckled. "You convinced me. Next?"

"Last is James P. Jensen. He's 56, lives with his fiancé Ethan Strang and lists himself as an entrepreneur, but there wasn't much in the way of any specific industries. It's indicated that he subsists on old family wealth. Simon will check out the boyfriend Ethan as well, but at first glance he also appears to come from a monied background."

"The rich get richer as they say."

Gian gave him a side-eye. "I don't see what that-"

Torr shrugged and shook his head. "Whatever. Never heard of any of them."

"Like I said, nonentities."

"What about political affiliations?" Torr questioned.

Gian swirled his beer before taking a big sip. "I think they all denote independent or NPA, No Party Affiliation. They're carefully unaligned with Democrats or Republicans so as not to piss off either group."

"That kind of sucks. You don't know what their platforms are then."

"I know. This way they can flip and flop according to how the wind is blowing. Most of their promises are lower taxes, better health insurance, you know, the basics."

"Seems cowardly to not directly align yourself with your true beliefs," Torr grumbled.

"Of course. They are politicians, Torr," Gian reminded him. "Besides, the mayor can't exactly levy taxes. The city council has that power."

"But he can influence them, and he has the choice to break a tie when the council can't make a decision about something."

"I don't think he can affect insurance costs either."

"I think," Gian explained, "that those candidates are just trying to defeat O'Grady with everything they can come up with whether it's factual or not."

"There you go, politicians."

They finished their drinks and paid their bill. Torr started for the door, Gian approached the two young giggling girls. One was blonde, the other brunette.

Very gently, Gian said with a friendly smile, "Those look like delicious drinks. Can I ask what they are?"

The girls giggled thinking he was trying to hit on them. The blonde raised a shoulder coyly, flapped her lashes at him and answered, "I have 'sex on the beach' and Misty is drinking an 'orgasm'." They burst into laughter.

Gian tried not to roll his eyes. Didn't those drinks go out of fashion about 20 years ago? "Uh huh. Are they strong tasting? Aren't you worried about getting too smashed and becoming vulnerable? The streets can be dangerous."

The brunette's cheeks puffed out. They were red, her skin was blotchy and her eyes were watering. "No! We are very experienced drinkers," she spouted overly loud, then quickly sucked on her straw and immediately broke into coughing hacks.

The blonde smacked her on the back a few times while she laughed at her friend. “She’s a lightweight,” the blonde said with affection. “*I* can hold my liquor!” she announced proudly.

Gian nonchalantly pulled out his badge and said, “Show me your ID’s.”

Their mouths dropped open and eyes rounded. “But, but we don’t uh-” the blonde spluttered.

“Now,” Gian commanded quietly.

They paused and looked balefully at each other, then started rifling through their purses. They produced their driver’s licenses. They were both 17.

Gian was surprised. “I thought you had fake ID’s.”

“He never asked,” the brunette offered bleakly.

Gian reached over and took their drinks. He photographed their licenses with his phone then called the bartender over.

The bartender had been watching from the end of the bar. He tossed his cleaning rag on the counter then turned around and *ran* for the back of the pub.

Torr was waiting outside the back kitchen door. He grabbed him as he emerged and threw him face first against the brick wall.

After cuffing the bartender, he read him his rights, then helped him into the back seat of his truck. He grinned and waved off to Gian as Gian drove past.

Gian had two very unhappy teenagers in the back of his truck.

They were unhappy because he was taking them home to their parents.

Chapter Twenty-three

Gian decided to bring Jon Michel in for questioning. Torr would do the inquiries as Gian has the conflict of interest being related to two of the victims.

Actually, they were both told to back off of the investigation due to the conflict, but Gian didn't feel the inquiry was going as quickly or being conducted as in depth as it should be.

They were his brothers and he would be damned if Conny Vinci or any of the others dropped the ball due to incompetence, haste or just plain disinterest. Or having too many other cases to work on thereby spreading themselves too thin and not giving the Montanero shootings the full attention they deserve.

Jon Michel was a handsome, fairly fit though husky man in his early forties. His dark espresso hair was combed straight back and stayed plastered to his head. His gaze shifted back and forth warily as Torr escorted him to an interview room.

Inside the miniscule space, Torr gestured for Michel to sit in one of the two plastic chairs that were at a small square table.

After introducing himself as Detective Torrand Kristo, with a practiced, polite, earnest smile that made him look honest and maybe a tad green, Torr plopped down in the other chair. He set a file down on the table.

He wanted to keep Michel off balance. The guy was probably expecting to be treated rudely and roughly by a snide dick of a detective, but Torr had a different approach planned.

"Well, thanks for coming in, Mr. Mitchell," Torr said with another big smile. Nodding cheerfully at the alleged cartel boss, Torr lowered his head to his file. He opened it and read the first page while deliberately moving his lips silently to appear a tad slow.

Although Michel said arrogantly, "Yeah, sure. What's this about? I am quite busy. I'm a businessman, I have a ton of work I need to get to," he sat back in the chair like he had all day and puffed his chest out with an air of self-importance.

He crossed one leg over the other and laid a forearm relaxed along the table. Not hiding his derision, his nose in the air, Michel sniffed and said with a curled lip, "It's pronounced Meeshell, not Mitchell. It is *French*."

"Hmm. So that's the accent I couldn't place," Torr announced, pleased with himself. "You're French!"

This caused a doubletake shake of Michel's head and an eye roll with a groan. Clearly, he has a Hispanic accent, but the double error of mispronouncing his name and misidentifying his accent made Torr look brainless. Which was his plan.

To tell the lies from the facts, Torr started asking baseline questions to learn Michel's body language and determine when Michel was just thinking up an answer that likely wasn't truthful, rather than trying to remember something that actually happened.

Torr started his questions. "Are you a permanent residence here in Chicory County?"

Michel shook his head, then replied. "I heard it was a picturesque village with lots of fishing and boating, so I decided to mix a bit of business with pleasure. I'm renting a cottage on Maverick Bay for an indeterminate period of time."

"Are you married, with a handful of little mini-me's running around?" Torr grinned in male camaraderie. Of course he was already well versed in Jon Michel's life, personal, criminal, and as much of his business that they could find out, which was sadly not very much.

There were loads of rumors he was head of a Mexican cartel and into smuggling anything and everything, from guns to drugs to women. But nothing had ever been substantiated and no serious convictions ever sustained, just a lot of arrests and dismissals on his NCIC report.

Michel stroked a palm over his slicked back hair and smiled. "No. Sorry to say, Cupid has so far failed to shoot me with his bow and arrow," he added with a short laugh.

Squinting deliberately at him, Torr snapped his fingers with an, "Oh." Then said as if he just realized, "I know, didn't I see you the other day at the Beautella Salon?"

The other man froze imperceptibly. After a beat, he replied, "Oh, ah, I guess I was there the other day. I, well, felt a bit dusty from the day's, um, tasks, and thought I'd just drop in for a quick wash."

"You go there often?"

"Ah, well, I was in the neighborhood, you know, and, just thought I'd try it out. No big deal." He was controlling his expression, schooling it into a blank slate.

Torr noted Michel was no longer glancing to the left as if he was truly remembering something. His eyes were now flitting rapidly to the right. But he brought them back levelly to Torr.

Torr smoothed a genial innocuous smile onto his face and asked, "So, Mr. *Mee*shell, you like to fish? Do you have a boat?"

Michel's head gave a faint tic at the question. "What? No. I haven't been out fishing for a while. I was going to rent a boat at some point. But," he lifted his palms up in the air, "busy, busy, busy you know."

"So, you don't go lobstering?"

Jon Michel looked surprised at the question. "Huh? I've scuba-dived in the Keys and the Bahamas during mini lobster season but I haven't gone anywhere here. Water's too damned cold, bro. Listen, I don't see what any of this-"

"Can you tell me where you were on Saturday evening the second week of September between 8 and 8:30?"

Michel blinked wordlessly several times, then he leaned forward, anger and confusion sparking in his eyes. "Who the hell remembers that? What are you getting at, Detective? I don't-"

Torr gave him his innocent green smile again. "No worries, Mr. Michel, just standard questions we're asking everyone in town. There was an incident that night. We need to eliminate as many people as possible as suspects so we can narrow in on the true perpetrator. So," he paused, sat back as if enjoying a long chat with an old friend. "Can you recall where you were? It wasn't that long ago. Maybe check your day planner?"

The side of his mouth tweaked in, Michel laughed sardonically. "Day planner? What is this, the 90's?" He leaned back relaxed again at Torr's look of embarrassment.

"Ah well," Torr stammered. "I haven't been a detective for that long. I guess my inexperience is showing."

"Fresh out of college, eh, mi amigo?" He laughed again to take the meanness out of his tone. He held a hand up as Torr's face grew red and his lips popped up and down in discomfiture. "Sorry kid, I mean Detective. You don't look *that* young. Kind of a late bloomer?"

"Yeah. So," Torr pulled the file closer and took out a pen. Clicking the pen, he set the point on a paper in the file prepared to write. "Can you remember where you were that night?"

Michel pressed his shoulders against the back of his chair as if grounding himself. "What happened on that night? What am I being suspected of? I have a right to know why I'm here." An edge of caution and suspicion deepened his voice as he answered the question with a question.

Torr held both hands up and smiled while shaking his head. "No, no, you aren't being suspected of anything, sir. There was a shooting at the Kifpu Wissei Marina around 8:30 on September 12th. Two young men were critically injured but did survive. We are trying to eliminate folks that are members of the marina or frequent the restaurant and bar there."

"That has to be hundreds, thousands even. How did my name get involved?" Michel asked, "What's this got to do with me?"

"Like I said," Torr reassured him, "during an investigation people tend to throw names out and we are obligated to check them out. I suppose because of your, ah, criminal history someone hurled your name into the ring. Again, we don't actually suspect you, in fact, at present time we don't have anyone under our microscope." He sounded embarrassed and bleak at this pronouncement.

Torr glanced around then leaned in and said in a hushed conspiratorial voice, "Tell you the truth, the way this thing is dragging out with zero leads, I'm pretty sure it's going to be tossed into the cold case file and forgotten. That's why they sicced me on it. You know, the newbie gets the deadwood."

Michel drummed his fingers on the table but didn't say anything.

"So," Torr sighed dramatically, "here I am, bashing my head against the wall trying to figure out a dead-end case. I'm sure it was just a bunch of punks running around blowing off steam. Probably didn't even realize they'd hit someone. Screwballs. But boys will be boys and all that, am I right?"

The corner of Jon Michel's lip curled up, he nodded in disgust. "Damned coppers, making mountains out of molehills," he groused. "No offense, son."

Even though Michel wasn't all that much older than him, Torr grinned. "None taken. So, speaking of your criminal history…"

Michel's torso jerked forward in annoyance. His cheeks reddened. "I've never been convicted of any major crime. The other stuff is just misunderstandings. That's all. Some eager beaver copper trying to do me in because he wants to make a name for himself or whatnot. Assholes." He flopped back with an angry grunt.

Torr surreptitiously watched the man's eyes darting like crazy to the right. Hmm, he thought to himself, lies, lies, lies. "So, as I was saying, we aren't looking at you, sir, but I need to cross names off my list so it looks like I'm doing my job. Right?" He gave Michel his boyish grin again.

Jon Michel studied him for a moment before answering. His eyes scrolled up and to the left as he thought back. "Saturday, let me see…" He clicked his fingers with a grin.

"I remember. I was in my favorite cigar bar, Midnight Smoke from 5 until eightish. There were at least, let me think, at least 20 to 30 other people there. Customers as well as staff. Give 'em a call. There will be plenty who will remember me, not counting the huge tab I paid.

"From there I stopped in to visit a girl I see occasionally for, well," he winked, "you know. Now, is that all, will that satisfy your boss' curiosity?" He smiled at Torr like a benevolent uncle. Too bad there were switchblades behind his innocuous pupils.

He provided contact info for Midnight Smoke and some of the staff, a couple of friends that he had smoked and chatted with, and the girl he visited.

It wasn't really a good alibi. The woman would likely verify he was there, but the timing would have to be carefully studied. Like, how long was the drive from Midnight Smoke to the marina to the girl's place.

He could have stopped at the marina on the way to her home, quickly fired off a few rounds at the Montaneros, hopped in his car and sped away.

How long would it all actually take? There would be no way to completely confirm every minute of his time, from leaving a busy establishment, to chatting with a couple of friends outside, to the drive to her home.

The guy could easily manipulate his time as needed. There could have been a traffic jam on Oak Drive, the girl was sleeping and took a while to answer the door, a million explanations could be offered for where he was and what he was doing during the time of the shootings.

It was going to be a bit of luck with tedious detailing to nail down exactly where Michel was at every moment. Unfortunately, there was too much room to pinpoint any part of his whereabouts.

His eyes lowered to the paper he was writing on, Torr asked abruptly, "What is your actual business?"

Michel's brows quirked, his lips bunched. His leg dropped.

Torr had been recording his mental observations of Michel's body language, particularly when it indicated deception to establish a baseline.

When he had answered Torr's questions with a verifiable truthful answer such as his address or age, Michel's glance was to the left. Now it sliced sharply to the right again, his lids shuttered down, and his leg started jumping.

When he didn't respond, Torr looked up at him with a benign smile, and waited. Silence often was his best tool.

"I, ah, am in the importing and exporting enterprises," Michel replied, then offered his own smile. Except his was made with stiff unmoving lips and scant eye contact.

Torr wrote down his response then he said with a nonthreatening grin, "So, can you give me a little example of what that is? Like, what exactly is the merchandise and what countries are involved?"

Clearing his throat, "Yeah, yeah, sure, sure," Michel shifted several times in his seat. He paused for so long Torr almost started speaking.

Michel coughed into his hand then told Torr, "We purchase estate sales of jewelry, fine dinnerware, furniture, um, high-end art and antiquities and the like from, well, pretty much anywhere. We distribute, well, resell the goods at things like auctions and exclusive shops where upscale merch will bring in top dollar."

With a huff, he sat back in his chair and looked at Torr, this time with a smug smile. Michel assumed Torr was not the sharpest knife in the block and would be satisfied with his account of his 'trade'.

"Are Mexico and the U.S. on your client lists?"

"Um hmm," was Michel's noncommittal nonanswer.

Torr let it go. Michel wasn't going to give anything important away. Torr would, though, be interested in what the IRS has to say. "Well, let me ask you, have you heard any gossip or rumors regarding the shootings?

"Or, on that night, perhaps as you were driving near the marina on your way to," he glanced down at the info Michel had provided of his whereabouts. "Nona Suarez's home. Did you hear the gunshots, or see anyone or anything that could possibly be involved in the incidents?"

"Nope," Michel answered shortly.

"Hmm," Torr nodded, once again reviewing his notes. "Do you know a Koh Boone?"

His lower lip protruding as he ran the name through his head, Michel replied, "Nope. Can't say that I do." He set his palms on the chair arms and went to stand up. "Well, if that's all, I'll be heading out-"

Torr asked suddenly, "What do you have against the Montaneros?"

Michel plunked back down with a scowl. "Don't know no Montererons. Now-" he made to stand up again.

"Montanero," Torr corrected him. Quick change of subject, he asked, "Are you and Nectar O'Grady romantically or otherwise involved? Business partners perhaps?"

His mouth dropping open, Michel's eyes expanded in innocence at the detective. "I uh, no um, we, of course not, she's a married woman!"

This time he did get to his feet giving Torr a dirty look.

"Listen chico, my personal and business life are none of your business. If you have any more questions for me, you can call my attorney. If you need his name and number, text me, *niño*." He tacked on the insult before shoving his way huffing and puffing out the door.

"Well," Torr sat back smiling. "That went well. Person who has nothing to hide doesn't get upset over simple questions about their occupation. I think he doth protest too much."

He gathered up his files and recorder, mumbling to himself, "Unfortunately, that isn't evidence that will work in court."

Pulling out his phone, Torr called Gian to tell him the interview was basically a waste of time. However, he might have ruffled some feathers and who knows, person feels guilty or trapped he might do or say something incriminating. We can only hope.

He left the room feeling a bit more cheerful.

Chapter Twenty-four

"Not unexpected, we didn't anticipate getting too much out of him, anyway," Gian said to Torr on his phone as he was making his way to his truck. "Guy is as shady as a tree and slick as ice on a hill."

"It was a pretty useless meeting, a waste of time. I didn't learn anything we already didn't know." Torr's beleaguered sigh bounced through the air waves.

"I don't know whether we made a mistake or not, making Michel aware that he's on our radar." Gian climbed in and took off down the street.

"Yeah," Torr's huff weighed heavy like a hot air balloon with rocks in it. "So, where are you off to?"

Gian spun the steering wheel as he rounded one of the winding curves that the town of Maverick Bay was made up of. Roads were built to go along or around lakes and rivers and mountains so it was constantly coiling and snaking, rolling and curving like a slow-moving roller coaster.

There were very few straight roads in Chicory Landing County.

"I want to go check out the scene at the marina where my brothers were shot."

"Crime scene techs were all over that site like ants on ice cream. Why are you going over it again?"

Gian braked slightly as he saw a deer standing by the road. They could be unpredictable, like all wild animals, *and humans*, and you never knew if they were going to leap away disappearing into the forest or bound right in your path.

Surprisingly, the critter just stood there complacently watching the traffic go by. Furry dude was lucky it wasn't hunting season yet.

Gian's phone was in a holder attached to the dash. He replied to Torr, "I don't know. I feel like we aren't getting anywhere on this case, at all. So, when I feel like that, I always go back to the beginning and start over. I like to immerse myself in the scene and, I don't know, I kind of like 'feel it out'. I hope something will hit me while I'm submersed in it. Crime scenes talk to you, you just have to be patient, open your eyes and ears and listen to them."

Torr laughed. "Sure, like the murderer will show up with the weapon and turn himself over to you and confess without compunction?"

Gian joined him with a shaggy chuckle. "You never know, mi amigo."

Torr barked another laugh. "No, please, I've had enough Spanish for the week, thank you. Jon Michel started calling me friend as in amigo and changed it to little boy. Niño. Guy just wanted to keep me in my place."

"Lummox."

"Yeah." Swallowing his chagrin, Torr said, "All right. I've got some other interviews lined up. I have some marina staff as well as a couple of the weekly poker players stopping by for a more thorough interrogation. I mean interview. You've got Conny diving into all of the mayoral candidates' lives. So far, no flags waving there I heard."

"Yeah. I told him I want Koh Boone's boat taken apart, and I mean *a*-part. I want the entire thing dismantled and the hull completely opened and scoured, including every inch inside and out of the engine area, toilet and plumbing systems, etc."

There was a beat of silence. "Come again? *You* searched the Fishnet Stalkings yourself and then the crime scene techs did I'm sure a thorough job. What could you all have missed?"

"I had a conversation with a bum who hangs out at the marina. Need to look into him also. A real character by the name of Paul Schmitt."

His teeth came together in a grimace as he recalled the conversation with Schmitt. Annoying man.

"However, Schmitt made a comment that he never noticed Koh Boone or any of his crew hauling lobster or fish, shrimp, whatever off his boat and to the fish markets and restaurants. For a guy supposedly angry at my father for being a better lobsterman, it sounded like he was zero competition as it was. Something fishy is going on, pun intended."

Torr said, "Yeah, that doesn't quite compute, does it?"

"Makes my 'little grey cells' wriggle," Gian replied.

"Your what?"

"You know, Hercule Poirot."

"Who?"

"Never mind."

"Uh, okey doke. I'll check in with you later and see if our murderer drops in your lap."

"Yeah, later, bro." Gian disconnected. He was beyond the wooded area and nearing the center of town. He drove past the strip mall where Beautella was housed.

As he passed by, he caught sight of Nicolle Kelly's little yellow beetle in the parking lot. He considered stopping and just saying hi…why not? They had a date set for Saturday, but he wanted to see her, even if only for a moment. He could check on the progress of her tea shop.

He parked and walked up to the pink and lavender building. Wow, he thought as he opened the door and stepped in. It was really girlie with ribbons and lacey stuff, and perfumey with all the copious scents from shampoos and such.

He glanced around and spotted Nicolle speaking to a stylist that appeared to be just finishing trimming her hair. As he passed the front area, Nectar O'Grady came swanning out from a back doorway.

Nectar blinked and narrowed her eyes when she saw Gian, as if realizing she recognized him, but couldn't remember from where. He was wearing a suit and seemed out of place.

It looked like she was going to walk up to him and converse for a minute but then another staff member called her over to speak to a customer in a chair who had big silver things sticking out all around her head. Can you pick up radio signals with those things? Contact from aliens?

Gian decided it would be more polite to wait until Nicolle was done before approaching her. He wandered over to study the bottles and jars of items for sale on display shelves.

Ten minutes later he noticed Nicolle handing her stylist some cash with a smile of thanks. The salon was quite large with many people milling about doing different things. Paying the cashier, going in and out of the restroom, people sweeping, male and female stylists moving back and forth and around as they mixed potions or washed hair.

Just as Gian was nearing Nicolle, he spotted of all people, Jon Michel.

Michel was standing not even a foot away from her. They weren't looking at each other, he was speaking with an employee with a neon shock of pink hair sticking up in all directions, with so many piercings her face bedazzled like a sparking diamond and gold encrusted ring.

Jon Michel was dressed casually in a brown bomber jacket and jeans. Although he usually acted dodgy in Gian's opinion, somehow the depiction of 'thug' didn't radiate off the guy. He appeared confident, as if he was trying a little too hard to come across shifty.

When Gian said, "Nicolle," she and Jon Michel both turned towards him. Nicolle's expression was a warm broad, yet uncertain smile.

Michel's face expressed…alarm? His eyes went wide and he paled. He was looking beyond Gian.

Gian turned to see what alarmed him. Probably the neon pink's face glowed too brightly with all the gold and metal and temporarily blinded him as she turned and walked away from him.

Then Gian saw the gun pointing out of a doorway. He didn't have time to inhale much less grab Nicolle and dive for cover before a shot rang out!

Fortunately, or very shockingly- Jon Michel tackled both Nicolle and Gian, slamming all three of them to the ground.

People shrieked and screamed and stampeded for the door, crashing into each other as at least 30 people tried to get out the single door at the same time. Women in capes with their hair in all different setups- half cut, half dyed, half wet streaked out, shoving and bursting through the door in hysterical chaos.

Catching his breath, Gian rolled off of Nicolle where he had managed to shift at the last moment and land on top of her, using his body to cover her while buffering her head and back from the tiled floor with his hands.

Glancing around in all directions for the shooter or shooters, Gian spared a quick glimpse at Nicolle to insure she hadn't been hit.

His gaze darted from her to back around, surveilling the room. The area was totally empty, not a soul in sight. The shooter likely ran out the door blending in with the rest of the panicked crowd.

Gian asked tersely, "Are you okay, Nicolle? You're not hurt, are you?" He could hear her rapid shallow breaths as she struggled to climb to her feet.

"No," Gian gave her a gentle push back to the floor. "Stay down until I give you the all clear." He yanked his phone out and called for backup.

He shot a quick look to Jon Michel who was also breathing loud and rapidly. The man appeared astonished, yet not as shocked as he should be, almost as if he was used to shootouts happening suddenly around him. He acted so quickly, it was as if it had been muscle memory that launched him into action.

"Bro," Gian said quietly, "thanks man." He gave the guy a narrowed glare. It was odd, the man now appeared to look more like, well, a cop, than a gangster. He came across as shaken yet calm. *What the heck*?

Just as Gian was about to race to the back of the building to search for the perpetrator, he saw a gun in Michel's hand and the man's jaw and eyes were rigid with fortitude as he crouched and peeked over the small display wall they had landed behind.

He set his fingers near the large black hole that hadn't been there before. He was judging the bullet hole but not getting near enough to touch the evidence.

"Whoa, Michel," Gian warned, his own weapon raised in his hand. "Put the gun down," he ordered.

His eyes lashing in all directions, Jon Michel snapped his gaze back to Gian and looked down at the detective's gun aimed at his belly.

One last quick scan of the area and Michel reached over and set his weapon on a small table beside him. He raised his hands up and said coolly, "It's all right, Detective, I'm on the job. I'm gonna reach in my pocket and get my creds. Okay?"

His jaw set hard, Gian jerked his head in consent. "Slowly."

Gingerly holding his jacket open with one hand, Michel reached inside with the other and showed Gian his shield.

Gian leaned in to read it.

Three big letters stood out, **F.B.I.**

Brows arched, Gian took a picture of it and said, "Special Agent John Michael, you have a lot of explaining to do."

Chapter Twenty-five

When the backup deputies arrived, Gian gave them instructions to interview all of the people that were waiting outside the salon, and also to canvass the area for other witnesses. He instructed them to secure the perimeter and search to see if the perp was hiding in the vicinity.

When he was a younger cop on the beat, he'd once found an offender hiding in nearby bushes who had tried to rip off a car share driver. The fool was looking at his phone and the light shone through the leaves. He might as well have had a spotlight shining on him. Dope on dope.

Gian scanned the locale but didn't see Nectar O'Grady. He told a cop to go find her. Had she split out of guilt, or fear?

Next, he directed one of the officers to obtain any CCTV in and around the salon, then he saw Nicolle to her car after ensuring that she was not too shaken to drive and that she hadn't incurred any injuries from her crash to the floor.

He briefly questioned her, but she hadn't seen the shooter or the gun sticking out of the door. Gian did all this while keeping Jon Michel beside him. He didn't want to chance the man making a disappearing act. He confiscated Michel's gun for the moment.

As soon as he had given out orders, Gian brought Michel to headquarters. After verifying with Central FBI that Michel was in fact an agent, Gian skipped the tiny interrogation rooms and brought him directly to his office. He gestured to the round table near the window.

"Have a seat, Mr. Michel, Michael, or whatever your name is." He set Michel's gun on the table.

With a wry smirk, Michel flopped onto a chair and retrieved his weapon. He slid it into the holster at his back, hiding it once again under the bomber jacket.

After he set down a legal pad of paper and a pen on the table, Gian asked Michel, "Get you a coffee, soda, water?"

"Nah, I'm good," Michel replied with a tight smile. "Let's just get this rolling."

Gian picked up the pen and clicked it open. He also took out a small recorder and pushed the power on then slid it across the table between them. Michel eyed the recorder but didn't object.

"So," Gian said, "let's start with your real name, since Michel is French but you sport a Hispanic accent which has vanished by the way in the last hour or so."

Michel's brows rose with his small smile. "Oops," he said. "Musta been the action blew my accent right outta my mouth."

"Yeah. Name, then get on with what the hell you're really doing in Chicory."

"Okay," Michel set his forearms on the table, clasped his hands and leaned forward slightly. "Real name is John Michael. Born and raised in Greenville, South Carolina. Try erasing a southern accent and adopting a Hispanic one. But," he sighed, "you get used to stuff like that in my job."

Gian sat silently waiting for him to continue.

"You're good, brother, I'll give you that," Michel said with slight admiration. "All right, what do you know about fentanyl?"

Gian's mouth pursed, he absently tapped the pen on the paper. "It's a synthetic opioid 100 times stronger than heroin and morphine and lethal as hell. Heard about K-9's getting it on their paws and dying. Kills couple thousand people a year, comes from China, a devastating epidemic we're struggling to eradicate. What is this crap to you?" He sat back with his arms relaxed, head tilted slightly in curiosity.

Michel mirrored him, sitting back and letting out a heavy sigh. "All true. Except last year the garbage took out 80,000 people."

Gian's brow furrowed along with his low whistle.

Michel went on, "So, the stuff comes from China, well the separate chemical components do. Then they're transferred to other countries such as Mexico, and surprisingly Canada to labs where the elements are combined together along with some additives, then disbursed to other countries including of course the U.S."

"Why are they shipped as raw ingredients from China then put together in labs elsewhere? Why not just send the lot of it?"

"Because you only need a tiny fraction of fentanyl to ship then the quantity gets combined and becomes much larger. It's easier to smuggle tiny separate elements. Easier to hide it from authorities."

Gian nodded. "So, you're in Chicory because…?"

Michel explained, "After the ingredients are shipped out, they go to these so-called superlabs where the fentanyl is mixed into its final product. The largest labs are in Mexico. We, the FBI, have been surveilling the trafficking from Mexico to the U.S. and one of our leads was tracked right here to Maine. Chicory is just one small area we traced it to. All the seafaring business with fishing and cruise ships and the like are perfect covers for smuggling."

"Uh huh, so who were you following here in Chicory?"

Michel's confident mug fell. "That's the problem, no one. We don't have anyone on our radar. We only knew that recently, past year or so, the fentanyl epidemic exploded suddenly around this neck of the woods."

"Yeah," Gian agreed. "We've seen the uptick in arrests and deaths locally. Unfortunately, we don't have the resources to really delve into investigating the source or sources of it. We put Band-Aids on by arresting as many offenders as we can. Of course, at least half go into drug court diversion programs and eventually their charges are dropped by the DA or State Attorneys through a nolle prosequi disposition to keep their records clean.

"Normally we'd follow the perps up the chain, who each dealer gets their stuff from and so on until we get to the main traffickers. So far we haven't been able to catch any leads. They either really don't know who is one step above them or they are paid too well or are too scared to point fingers."

"Yeah," the agent said, "addicts and dealers are the worst to pin the truth with."

"They'd rather do jail time than risk getting their throats slit in the dark of the night. Plus, with the judges releasing them to drug court, knowing their charges will be dropped, they don't have to make any deals with us."

"Exactly," Michel agreed. "Sadly, we don't have enough to obtain warrants for boats. We think the stuff is being shipped in, not trucked or flown in."

"How does Nectar O'Grady's salon enter into it?"

Michel's brow hitched with surprise then he smiled. "Yeah, you are good."

"My people are good," Gian corrected.

Michel wiped his upper lip then removed his cap and ran his fingers through his hair. Stuffing the cap in his back pocket, he said, "I centered in on the salon because we had an influx of ODs from people that were found or arrested in and around that whole strip mall. Since it's a bit of a cash business, it does fall under suspicion, but then so do the laundromat, the restaurants and the cash-checking store."

"You cozied up to Nectar O'Grady to spy or what?"

Michel grinned then twisted his lips. "Kind of. I didn't think she was actually involved, I mean the town mayor's wife and all, but I thought if I could make friends with her and some of the staff working there that I could gather intel through them."

"Makes sense. Sounds like a good plan."

"I was also cozying up to Nectar, letting it slip that I was oh, morally ambiguous and that I might have a lot of cash I needed to clean, and a lot of that money could go her way. Her hands might be clean with the drugs, but she and Gator do hang amongst the rich and the illustrious."

"Any nibbles?"

Pinching his nose, Michel responded with a small shrug, "Maybe. At first, she acted all uptight and law abiding, but I've been working on her. Lately she's been asking more and more questions about my…enterprises. This whole latest shooting episode adds a funky layer to the entire thing."

"And that's what you were doing there today? Trying to reel her in?"

"Yep. Trust me, I was as surprised as you when I saw the gun. Totally unexpected. However, it does tell me I'm getting close. Question is, who were they shooting at? Me? You? Someone else? Nectar? Front desk girl? That woman you're hot for?"

Gian smiled at that.

"Until we look at the CCTV, if there is any, we can't be sure who was the target. And if we don't know who the target was, it'll be tough to establish who the shooter was. Unless we're lucky enough that the shooter was caught on the CCTV."

"We haven't been lucky so far, so I wouldn't hold my breath," Gian said.

Michel sighed. "Yeah, I know."

The door suddenly opened, and a grinning, blushing young woman peeked in. Tangerine colored hair swished across her shoulders. Seeing Gian and Michel at the table she moved inside. She carried two bottles of water.

"Um," she sent Michel a flirty smile, her cheeks pinked brighter. "You fellas looked a little…thirsty." She held the bottles up with one quirked tangerine brow in question. And invitation. Her heated gaze spearing Michel, she ran her pink tongue around matching tangerine lips.

"Lolita," Gian frowned at the admin assistant attired in a lime green sweater and skirt outfit so tight he feared for her ability to draw a breath. "Set them on the table and go." What did she think this was, The Dating Game?

Michel smirked at him and grinned at the girl. Right behind her, another young woman entered.

"What is this, Grand Central-"

Michel got to his feet. "It's okay, Montanero," he said, beckoning to the second female to come closer.

The woman was a stunner. Blonde hair pulled back in a tight twist, she had bright cocoa eyes and under the suit appeared a well-built woman. Gian's gaze swung back and forth between her and Michel.

Lolita stood awkwardly staring at the blonde, whom Michel clearly knew.

"Special Agent Veronica Cleaver," Michel introduced. "Detective Giancomo Montanero. I sent her a text. Have a seat, Vern." He pulled out a chair.

With a thin smile of her full lips, the agent sat on the proffered chair.

"Michel, what the hell-"

John Michael cut him off. "You may go," he said, motioning towards the door to the tangerine.

Lolita gave him a mulish look, then spun on her heel and flounced out.

"Special agent with the FBI?" Gian inquired of Cleaver.

"DEA," Michel answered for her. "She and I are collaborating on this operation. She has been undercover as a customer of the Beautella Salon, the laundromat and the check cashing store at the strip mall. Along with a few other places of interest around town."

He said to Agent Cleaver, "I'm catching the detective up to speed. My cover, at least with him is blown."

"Pleasure," Cleaver said to Gian with a kind smile.

Michel told her about the incident at the salon. She had heard part of it on the news on the way to the station.

"Anyway, Vern," Michel nodded to her, then said to Gian, "I was explaining about the superlabs and our mission here."

Gian's eyes swerved from Cleaver to Michel. "Right, Special Agent John Michael."

"That's SAC, Detective. Special Agent in Charge," Michel said with a grin.

"Okay SAC John Michael, carry on," Gian said with a short smile.

With a nod to Gian, Michael said, "Now, what the traffickers have been doing is making what they call 'master boxes.' You see, around 4 million packages per day are sent from China to the U.S. and other countries via Amazon, FedEx, UPS, all sorts of delivery transports. Because there are so many, for Customs agents and other authorities to actually search each and every box would be almost impossible.

"It would take forever for that process to occur, hence many tariffs and taxes and things like that are lifted or exempt for these types of goods because collecting tariffs on imports that are real cheap would cost way more than the revenue acquired. It's called the *de minimis* rule.

"Of course, the smugglers use this to their advantage. So, they put the separate chemicals into very small boxes, then they put those boxes into larger boxes, and then those into real big boxes."

Agent Veronica added, "It's kind of like those Russian nesting dolls, you know, start with a tiny one and put it in a larger one and on and on."

Gian clasped his hands on the table and nodded as Michel continued.

"Many of these real big boxes are sent 'accidentally' to warehouses and fulfillment centers claiming mislabeled addresses. Then, they're picked up under the guise of being delivered to the proper addresses when they're really being transported to covert labs to complete assembly."

"Huh," Gian grunted.

"Yeah," Michel said. "We think some of these boxes have been shipped here on boats, except they have the finished product in them. Anyway, at this juncture, it appears neither of us is making any headway with our missions, your brothers' shootings and our drug smugglers."

"How come you didn't check in with our PD when you guys started here? We could have all been working together." A shade of accusation filtered into Gian's tone.

Michel, or John Michael as was his true name, leaned back in his chair. One shoulder bumped, his lips pulled in sheepishly.

"Ah, we were suspicious of everyone, especially anyone with vessels capable of being engaged in the smuggling. Your dad makes a pretty penny and has a big boat.

"We didn't know if he was involved. In fact," his eyes flicked away from Gian for a second. "I did try to work him, you know, at first. Tried to feel him out if he was interested in smuggling some minor stuff, like small amounts of guns, maybe a little cocaine."

The side of Gian's mouth tugged up, he crossed his arms over his chest and propped an ankle on a knee. "Yeah, he told me about that. Not your name or any details, but he alluded to having been hit up to possibly be interested." He tapped his fingers on his arms. "How'd that work out for you? Found a stone wall, eh?"

A sharp laugh and Michael nodded. "Pretty much told me to shove it, but carefully. I think he was concerned of any backlash hitting his family. We did a thorough background search on him and of course his financials."

"Everything was 100% accounted for and above board, right?" Gian shot him a dry smile.

His head bobbing up and down in agreement, Michael replied, "Oh yes. Man is so squeaky clean he practically glows." The three shared a mild chuckle.

"Do you think your smugglers have anything to do with my brothers' shootings?"

"Unfortunately, no clue. Could be, maybe not. Might be unrelated incidences."

Gian pondered everything for a moment. "I wonder if my brothers saw something, you know, with regards to the smuggling and didn't realize at the time what it was?"

Slanting his head, John Michael scraped his fingertips above his mouth in contemplation. "I assume you've questioned them until their ears bled about what they saw before and during the shootings? If anything suspicious had occurred, anyone shifty hanging around, anything that made them wonder, 'What are they doing? What is going on'?"

His laugh caustic, Gian smiled grimly. "Upside down and backwards. Went over their movements and anything visually that might have seemed…off. Heard anything that didn't make sense at the time. Saw someone or someones who didn't quite fit in, belong. Strangers among the locals."

"That's tough because there's such a mix of people that go to marinas."

"Yes. Marinas can be tight knit communities, especially in small towns like Maverick Bay. But the larger encompassing Chicory County pulls in plenty of visitors from all around the world. So, noticing a stranger, unless they were really way out there or acting extremely odd or suspicious, wouldn't likely happen. If anyone like that caught their notice, believe me, those two would have heralded it all over just for the attention of it. What's your next step?"

"Ahh," Michael sighed deeply then looked to Veronica Cleaver. "We got nothing. Back to the drawing board."

"We did have another shooting today, Agent, involving both of us. I can't think that was a coincidence."

"Cops don't believe in coincidences," Veronica stated with a shrewd smile.

Both men bobbed their heads in concurrence.

His brow wrinkling slightly, Gian asked John Michael, "So what was the deal with the French name Jon Michel?"

Sharing a smile with Veronica, Michael chuckled lightly, replying, "Well, I set up my background to appear as a member or leader of a Mexican cartel in hopes someone would come to me with offers of joining in with the trafficking. The criminal and personal histories were plants of course, including my fake mom at the old folks' home."

"Yeah," Gian grimaced. "We checked it out and it cleared. Good plotting of false info."

"We're the FBI, we can do anything," John Michael grinned at him.

"I started with Juan Miguel, but then I decided it was just too hokey. So, I went with the French connotation along with the Hispanic accent to make it appear I was trying to hide something. I stuck with variations of John Michael so I could more easily remember the fake name."

"Deliberately made yourself look suspicious with an obviously phony name," Gian said with respect in his voice.

"Either that or he was schizophrenic," Veronica laughed and lightly punched Michael in the arm.

He grinned. "Just wanted to make myself seem approachable to bad guys. Hasn't worked so far." His shoulders slumped slightly.

After a few minutes of reflective silence, Gian set his palms on the table as if readying to stand up. "All right. I have people digging into the salon attack. CCTV, witness reports, financials, a deeper dive into Nectar O'Grady's background. We did Gator O'Grady's when the shootings first occurred due to the big lobster fest thing and all, but he's pretty buttoned up and transparent. Been under the spotlight for years, something would have popped by now."

"We were checking into O'Grady as well. As I said, suspicion surrounding the salon. Mayor doesn't pay all that much but they have a huge house and ho-de-do cars. However, all his banking and such passed scrutiny. We were unable to find out how he and the wife live so high on the hog whilst not bringing in the bacon." Michael smiled at his own terrible pun.

Gian said, "We are still investigating her and their unaccounted for income. Whenever anyone is brave enough to bring it up to Nectar, she claims ancestral inheritance. She's not from around here and she apparently didn't obtain an SS number until she married Gator. It seems she hadn't needed to work the earlier part of her life. Again, perhaps family money. We haven't been able to track anything so far without actual warrants."

"I'll have my people research her. She didn't hatch at age 30," Michael said.

Gian stood up. "Okay, I'm going to check a few things out. What are your next moves?"

John Michael looked to Veronica who inclined her pretty head to him in deference. "Hopefully my cover, other than with you, hasn't been completely blown. We'll carry on undercover and keep digging."

"What about some more support, resources from your own teams?" Gian asked.

"Our SAC above me felt it would be better for me to keep a low profile. I'm on my own. And Vern here," he motioned to her, "is in the same boat. Our leaders thought having groups of us here hanging around with the locals would draw more attention."

"Now that we are aware of you, you will have our resources available to you too," Gian offered.

Michael turned slightly, flashing a glance to Veronica. "That's kind of you to offer, but, at this juncture, we don't know who the bad guys are," he held a hand up as Gian started to object.

"No offense to your police here, but corruption within police departments is not unheard of. It's better we go on as we have been. We would appreciate it if you didn't advertise who we are and what we're doing here. You understand?" There was a hint of apology in his voice.

Gian's lips pursed ruefully then he nodded. "Of course."

SAC John Michael and Special Agent Veronica Cleaver stood up.

"I'll take you both out the back way to preserve your anonymity. I should have thought of that on the way in."

They exchanged deets and Gian led them out the door and to a back staircase.

Chapter Twenty-six

G*ian*, Torr, Conny Vinci, Simon Nucacher and numerous others spent several days reviewing the video cams found in the Beautella Salon. In the large bullpen, or the 'floor' many bodies sat at computers for hours looking for, well, they'd know when they found it.

Chatter resonated throughout the room as people discussed things they saw of interest or questioned. They also chatted about their personal lives, who was hooking up with whom, football games and other things people who have worked together for a long time yak about.

"Hey," Conny Vinci called over to Gian. "Check this out."

Gian looked up from his computer then got up and went to Conny's desk. Torr and Simon traipsed over as well. The three men peered at Conny's monitor.

"What are we looking for?" Simon asked, his face scrunching as he studied the video.

"Just watch, see if you notice anything…off," Conny said. The screen depicted the shooting event that transpired in the salon from their CCTV cameras. People were milling about, staff worked on customers, customers preened in mirrors, one person bustled around with an automatic suction sweeper.

"There we are," Gian pointed at Nicolle, FBI agent John Michael and himself way off to the side near the display shelves.

Nectar O'Grady was standing relatively in the center of the shop speaking with one of the stylists. Then-

The shot rang out, and people started ducking and screaming and running. Off to the side, Gian saw John Michael shove Nicolle and him to the floor and landed beside them.

"So," Torr commented, his brow wrinkled over eyes glazing from so much computer viewing. "We've seen this a hundred times. What's new?"

Conny pushed rewind and they watched the event unfold again. "Just watch." The four pairs of eyeballs studied the activity again.

Gian squinted as his head raised suddenly. "Yeah, I see," he mumbled. "Son of a gun."

"What?" Simon spluttered, still not seeing it.

"Everyone looked shocked, confused and terrified," Gian explained, "except her." He pointed at the screen. Conny Vinci nodded emphatically, sitting back with a smug smile. The group leaned in closer, eyes narrowed, pin-pointing to what he gestured to.

As soon as the gunshot reverberated through the room, folks ducked, screamed and ran for the front door. Everyone except Nectar O'Grady. It was several beats before she registered shock on her face. She raced for the door along with everyone else, but she didn't look the least bit shocked or terrified.

"She's almost…smiling," Torr said, shaking his head with confounded disbelief.

"Yeppers," Conny's grin practically swaggered.

"Proves she's not the shooter," a hint of puzzlement entered Simon's observation.

Gian said, "That's right, but she knows who is."

"Gonna be tough to prove," Torr submitted. "Need more than a non-shocked expression for the DA to proceed."

A deputy came over to the group. "Sir," she said, holding out a piece of paper to Gian. "This just came in."

"What is it?" he asked her as he took it and quickly scanned the paper. "Hmm," he murmured thoughtfully.

"Gian?" Torr asked, peering over his shoulder.

Gian told them, "Report on the bullet found at the salon. It's a Winchester Dual Bond, same as the ones that hit my brothers." The group took this new information in.

Simon's phone rang, he stepped aside to answer it.

"So, as we thought, it's all connected. Still, doesn't answer why or who," Torr said.

"No, but-"

Simon spoke up as he was still staring at his phone, "Just got a report from the crime scene people that took Koh Boone's boat apart. You ain't gonna believe it." All eyes turned to him.

"Spill it," Gian ordered impatiently.

"Pretty sure they found the gun. A Ruger .454 Casull. One of the types we thought it might be," Simon responded with a victorious fist pump.

Gian's eyes narrowed and he plunked his hands on his hips. "Where did they find it?" he asked, his words coming out harshly with disbelief.

"Uh, lemme see," Simon scrolled through his phone. "Says in the toilet tank."

Gian's head shook back and forth. "No way. I looked in there, CSI looked in there. Hey, Rob," he called to one of the officers studying video on his computer. The deputy looked up with brows arched.

"You get the cams from Koh Boone's boat, the latest ones after we found his body?"

The deputy typed a few words on his keyboard then leaned in to read what came up. "Um, yeah, Sergeant Lydia Carlson was just going over them. She sent me a text to view them, said it was vital."

Rob paused, then smacked his forehead with an exclamation. "Oh yeah, check this out!"

The group left Conny's desk and hurried to Rob's, they all bent over to see.

The video showed two masked men sneaking onto the Fishnet Stalkings under the cover of the dark night. One held a bag in his bare hand. The only noticeable difference between the two was one of the males was wearing glasses.

They disappeared for a few moments on the boat then returned and almost tripped in their haste to get off and away.

“Who does that look like to you?” Gian asked the group.

“You can’t tell,” Simon answered him. “They’re wearing masks.”

Torr gave him a dry look. “Look at them, Nucacher, really look at them.”

Simon shook his head, annoyed that he couldn’t tell what he was supposed to see.

Rolling his eyes, with a not quite subtle patronizing undertone, Torr informed him, “The hair, the freckled hands, the height, weight, build, they look identical.”

A line formed between Simon’s eyes in perplexity. “How are we supposed-”

“The O’Grady twins, duh,” Conny pretended to slap the side of Simon’s head.

“Hey,” Simon complained while ducking the whack. “How am I supposed to know that? They’re wearing masks, plenty of people here in town with red hair and same height and weight. Geesh, you can’t tell. It’s not like I know those guys or anything.”

Conny’s eyelids wavered up and down in exasperation. “Come on, Simon, we’ve done nothing but study the O’Gradys from the start of this because of the mayor and the whole lobster business. Are you blind or just-”

“Okay,” Gian cut him off. Back to Rob, he asked, “Has the gun gone to prints yet?”

Rob turned his attention back to his screen and scrolled around. “No prints on it, but they’re still taking it apart for other analysis. Even though clearly one of the guys wasn’t wearing gloves there were no new prints pulled from the boat. The gun was wrapped in a cloth and then in a bag so some DNA may have been preserved.”

Gian said to Conny, “What about Nectar O’Grady’s financials? They in yet?”

Conny trod back to his computer and clicked for a minute. He looked up with a smile. “Oh yeah baby. She’s made large deposits over the last year, with money without corresponding receipts. She claimed with the IRS, that they did home visits and brought in a lot of cash through on site and home visits. Credit cards are charging that extra percentage now so people are paying in cash more.

"She also said they sold a lot of product, you know like shampoo and stuff, again without many matching receipts. She advised again that they were cash sales. And, get this, she said she wins big, a lot and often at the casinos and also through poker games amongst friends."

He bent his head closer to the monitor. "She's covered her tracks so far with the IRS, but it really looks like she's moving some big money somewhere."

"I want her brought in, now," Gian commanded as he started for the door.

"Where are you going?" Torr called out.

"Back to the crime scene."

Chapter Twenty-seven

*G*ian parked his truck at the marina near where analysts had ascertained the shooter had hidden in the copse of trees when they had fired at his brothers.

The exact area where the shooter stood hadn't been completely isolated. The direction of the trajectory was a broad estimation judging velocity and direction of the bullets. Plus, both men were shot in different places, although it was established that the shooter fired at the pair from around the same location.

Gian remembered Josh had said at the time of the first shots, the ones that hit Reece were followed by a faint howl of pain. He trod over to where the Seabug was docked in its slip and headed to the thicket of trees that surrounded two-quarters of the marina parking lot.

His boots crushed dead leaves and dry twigs as he tromped over the tall grass. He could hear music drifting over from the bar, Swabby's Deck, next to the marina.

Occasionally bursts of laughter bounced from the door when it opened as patrons entered and exited. Multicolored fairy lights twinkled from the bar and marina giving a holiday and party feel to the late day.

Normally Gian loved hanging at the marina. The undulating water, fish jumping, friendly happy people sailing the world sharing their wild adventures. Unfortunately, this whole investigation was dropping a pall on his normal enjoyment of visiting the marina.

The sun was lowering in the sky. He pulled a flashlight from his pocket he'd grabbed from the truck and shone it all around as he walked the area.

He moved the torch across the grass and up and down tree trunks as he trod along. It was getting quite chilly, he should have brought a jacket, but he persevered on.

An hour later, the sun had almost set and his teeth were starting to chatter. He hated giving up, he just knew the land had something to tell him.

"A few more minutes left of sun, then I'll have to come back and try again tomorrow," he muttered to himself as he kept walking and shining the light.

He was just about to pack it in, when, "What..." he squinted at where his torch lit on a tree. It was only in a few feet from the lot but tall bushes surrounded the tree.

Gian noticed there were still some footprints in wetter, slightly muddy areas where the CSIs had tramped around. He moved to the tree and put the flashlight close to the bark.

Gian was 6'4", there was a mark down around where his chin was. He moved the light closer still. "Yeah," he said softly, thinking out loud, "an inward rounded impression, and..." he stuck his face inches from the bark.

The tree was a paper birch. It had a white-ish soft bark.

"Parallel dark splatter stains separated by several inches, maybe blood? Those Winchester Dual Bonds are slugs like a bullet within a bullet. A powerful weapon. I'm guessing that possibly the gun hit the shooter during recoil and slammed his head into the tree spraying his blood past both sides of his face onto the bark."

Not that it would show up that great, but dark blood against a light background was more detectable than if it was against a darker oak or maple. If it was blood, it was no longer a vivid glossy red but was now a mottled brown. It looked like plain old tree sap.

Whatever it was, Gian took a picture of the stains on the tree trunk. He also took photos of the rounded indentation into the soft tree bark.

Then he happened to look down. Something glinting in the last slender ray of sunlight caught his eye.

Pulling a small case out of his inside pocket, he bent and using a pair of tweezers, he picked up the object that was mostly concealed by a blade of grass. Took him a minute of studying the tiny thing before he realized what it was.

"Why, I'll be damned, it's a nail. A fingernail." It was a fake nail with some kind of sparkly jewel decoration on it. He whipped a folded baggie out of the case and dropped the nail inside and tucked the case and baggie back into his pocket.

Gian didn't touch anything, no need to contaminate any evidence. He called the supervisor of the crime scene techs.

She picked up on the third ring.

"Yo, Valerie Proffer," he said when she answered.

She was the lead Crime Scene Analyst, CSA. She had a mind like a steel trap. Tucked inside that big brain was a truckload of knowledge and an extraordinary skillset.

Val Proffer never ever forgot a thing; not a statistic, not a person, not a chemical makeup. A superlative scientist, the woman was known for her brilliance.

They kept pulling her out of the field to teach because she was so gifted intellectually, and she loved people and they loved her. But when she wasn't out there, the field work suffered, didn't measure up to par.

She was the best CSA in the field as well as the labs, collecting and analyzing. And with her energizer bunny dynamism, rookies couldn't keep up with her.

He knew her well. Another attractive redhead one of the guys had tried to set him up with. She was gorgeous, but he didn't want to get serious with anyone so it was better to avoid temptation, especially on the job.

"It's Giancomo Montanero. I need your crew to head back out to the marina at daybreak. Yes, the Kifpu Wissei. Tell them to bring metal detectors and their entire kits, blood and tissue gathering and testing. Make sure you're with them. I want the expert there this time."

"Sure thing, Kemo Sabe," Valerie said to him with a laugh. He pictured her saluting with a grin. A great sense of humor was also one of her many attributes. "Anything for you."

"You must not have been assigned to examine the scene where the shooter stood when they fired at my brothers, huh Val?"

She paused, then said, "I didn't know you had ESP, Detective. How did you know that?"

"Because evidence was overlooked. Sloppy work, Val, not your style. You never would have missed what I just found."

"Well, now I am very curious to see what plunder you've stumbled across. Can't wait to see it!"

"I'll drop my find off at the lab per chain of command before I go home. I'll meet you and your people here at dawn. All right?"

Listen," a serious note entered her voice, "give those bad guys hell for me, yeah? But always keep your head down and watch your six."

Now he let out a light laugh, "I will do that. I'll meet you and your crew here, thanks, Val."

"Super," she replied. "Get a good night sleep. Later."

As he hung up, something else lying in the now smushed grass caught his eye. Crouching, he took out the tweezers and picked up the shiny object. "A shell casing. Now that's interesting." He slipped it into another baggie and tucked it into his pocket.

Feeling like he was on a treasure hunt, Gian directed the flashlight back on the ground and slowly moved it back and forth to see if anything else was lurking there.

He moved his foot out slightly and brushed it over the grass. He knew chances of him finding anything else would be- "Oh yeah," he uttered and crouched down.

Carefully, he set his hand on the top of the grass and very gently swished the blades aside and something glittered in his light. Back with the tweezers, he held clipped the object and held it up in the torch and examined it.

"Appears to be a fragment of clear glass. Could be from a beer bottle or something totally meaningless, but," he slid it into a baggie and stowed it in his pocket.

Gian couldn't believe the half-assed lousy job the crime scene techs had done. They must have been in a big hurry to get home. Someone, like Val Proffer, needed to get after them and whip them into shape.

Chapter Twenty-eight

*S*eeing Nicolle Kelly's name come up, Gian answered his phone.

"Hey, Nicolle, good to hear from you." Warmth and a speck of joyful excitement invaded his greeting, and his belly. Two things that were normally unheard of for him.

Her voice came across with a shade of shyness to it. "Hi Gian, how are you doing?"

He smiled into the phone. "Good, great, working around the clock."

"Oh, yes, I'm sorry, I know you're busy! I um-"

Gian chuckled, something he was doing a lot more of lately.

"Not too busy to hear from you, Nicolle."

She didn't seem like the type of woman who called men out of the blue that she didn't know that well for no reason. "Is everything okay?"

"Yes, yes, I'm sorry to bother you at work, Gian, but uh, well, something came to me, my mind, I mean. I've been running the day of the salon shooting around in my head, and I heard from Pat Hooper, who's in my yoga class. Her and her daughter Rhonda both work at the station, 911 dispatch. Do you know them?"

"Not personally, but I've heard of them. They're both very highly thought of."

"Yes, they are. They made Rhonda a supervisor because of her incredible due diligence and innovative aptitude, and Pat makes employee of the quarter so often she should get her own title. She's so sweet and loving, everyone thinks of her as a cherished sister. Anyway," Nicolle sounded hesitant. She took a breath, he heard her exhale.

"Well, everyone is talking about the shooting, and Pat enjoys a good gossip, um, nothing ever malicious, just fun or fascinating things that come up. Not that you're interested in gossip, um-" she petered off in embarrassment.

Gian laughed without impatience. "It's okay, Nicolle, what has you stirred up?"

"I'm sorry. It's just, well, Pat said you all were looking for Nectar O'Grady, the owner of Beautella, and, well, I recall that her son Chip was in the shop that day. I know it was Chip because his brother Oreo wears glasses, otherwise they are identical. Except Oreo also wears a lot of rings. He thinks he's a fashion plate."

Gian mumbled an, "Uh huh," so she'd know he was listening.

"They constantly click obnoxiously together, like someone endlessly clicking a pen, you know? I assumed Chip was just visiting his mother because Oreo works at the salon, although he wasn't there that day."

She took a breath and went on quickly. "What struck me as odd, when I thought over the horrible um, incident, was that I never saw him speaking to anyone, Chip I mean, including his mother."

"That's not overly odd."

"I know. But it's weird. Why would he be there then? He just sort of appeared near the back room for like only a minute before the shooting, and then, I'm not positive, but I'm pretty sure, he wasn't outside when the police showed up. I would have thought he would stick around to answer questions, or at least make sure his mom was all right."

Gian pondered her words. "You're sure it was Chip? They are identical. It might have been Oreo just not wearing his glasses at that moment at work. Maybe had on contacts?"

"No, I've never seen him without his glasses. He works with his dad, the mayor so he's out and about Maverick Bay all the time, he's also on some TV ads with his father. And, Chip wasn't wearing any rings, except his wedding band. Besides," she paused, "he wears this god-awful cologne." There was an 'ick' in her voice. Gian could almost hear her nose wrinkling.

He felt his brain twitch. "Cologne? What does it smell like?"

"Um, let me think. It doesn't really smell that bad. I think it's because he drowns himself in it that makes it so offensive. It's called Z'rain Noir Essence. It's a citrusy, woody fragrance for men. My cousin Lanira's ex wore it until she made him switch. She's allergic to cedar and it has cedar, apple and orange blossom extracts."

Gian was quiet for so long Nicolle feared he was bored, fell asleep, or just thought she was too stupid for words.

"Gian? I'm sorry, I shouldn't have bothered you with this silly nonsense. You're so busy, and I thought, well, never mind, I shouldn't-"

"No, no Nicolle. On the contrary, you have really offered some very good information. Excellent information as a matter of fact." He thought for a second. "This ex guy, what's his name?"

"Oh, he can't be involved. He works for the American Embassy in Istanbul. He's been there for three years now. His name is John Demirel and his family is Turkish. He just got married a year ago and has a 2-month-old baby girl."

Not too much of a chance this Demirel is their guy. He'll have him checked out anyway. "Listen Nicolle, I need to follow up on this right away. Can I buzz you back later?"

She sounded relieved. "Sure, of course Gian. I'll be at the farm. Gram and I are teaching Lanira and Portia how to bake cookies so Gram doesn't get stuck making them for all their clubs. Wine club, women's club, tennis club, yacht club on and on."

Gian laughed out loud. "Better make sure to keep the fire extinguisher handy. And I wouldn't try any of those cookies they're making if I were you. Accidentally drop one on your foot and you're liable to break a toe."

Nikki's laugh was cute and engaging, made Gian's smile reach his ears.

"Okay, I've got to go. Later, Nicolle." At her 'bye' he hung up and called his brother.

"Josh, I need to come by and see you and Reece. How are you feeling?" Gian spoke to his brother.

A soft groan came through before Josh replied, "Okay. Pretty much. I mean, I get sore and tired after only walking a few feet. Reece is still fairly immobile. Us like this and all of the crew out with what they thought was the flu."

"Flu isn't all that unusual, Josh."

"Normally it isn't. But come to find out this is a particularly virulent form of Respiratory Syncytial Virus (RSV)."

"Say what?"

Josh explained what he'd learned. "People, more so infants and others with weakened immune systems can spread the virus for 4 weeks or more even after the symptoms resolve. Half the guys who seemed to have been recovering were getting vile symptoms all over again, like a rebound thing."

"Sounds wicked."

"It's horrendous. Dad's gonna be so screwed, Gian. We just don't know what we're gonna do about the damned lobster fest."

"Don't worry about that now, Josh. We'll find some help, somehow."

Gian wasn't so sure about that, as all the boats lined up for the lobster festival haul were full up with crews. There weren't any able-bodied people left available to help out on the Seabug.

He didn't know how only Deo, their dad and Gian alone were going to manage it. They normally had 12 to 15 or more hands during the big scores. Besides the lobsters they also pulled in crabs, tuna, halibut and bass.

"Anyway, I need to come by and show you guys something, get your input. Are you up for it?"

Josh sounded a little more cheerful. "Oh yeah, sure! We are so bored with TV and video games we could scream."

"You could try reading, learning to crochet or take an online class, paint, learn a new language, you know. There's more to life than just television, movies and games."

Josh laughed. "Sure. Anyway, what can we do for you? Is it about the investigation?"

"Yes. I'll be there in an hour, maybe two." Gian hung up. He called Torr and told him what he needed then he drove to the station.

After downloading information he'd asked Torr to obtain on a flash drive, he took off for his father's house.

Once inside and after greeting Jed and Jessica, Gian sat down on the couch and set Jed's laptop on the coffee table. He inserted the flash drive and powered the computer on. Then he asked both Josh and Reece to join him on the couch.

Sitting down, Reece wriggled his butt on the cushion and nudged Gian with his elbow. "How's this for brotherly love, eh? Soon we'll be wrestling and throwing a football around." He grinned at both of his brothers. Josh sat beside Reece.

Gian gave a fake snicker, "Ha ha." Then his mouth thinned with seriousness as he pointed to the monitor.

He said, "All right, I'm going to show you some film of a couple of people. I want you to look at them, and try to think back to when you were shot." He heard a gasp from the doorway.

Gian glanced over and saw Jed and Jessica standing there, Jessica had her hand over her mouth.

"Son, the boys both have nightmares still. Do you think this is wise?" Jed asked his oldest son.

"If it wasn't important, Fath- uh, Dad, I wouldn't put them through it." Gian adjusted the screen so both brothers could see it.

Jed and Jessica silently took seats in the cozy chairs nearby. The room, thanks to Jessica, was done in different shades of comfy blues with white and yellow accents. Pretty landscapes on the walls and family photos perched on end tables added to the homey feel.

Although Nicolle's family seemed to think they needed to have the fireplaces going at all times, for the ambience no doubt, the Montaneros didn't feel it was cold enough yet to light a fire in the white brick fireplace.

Gian typed a few words, then hit return. "Okay, guys, just watch for a moment before you say anything." Both young men leaned in a touch, their expressions earnest, eyes narrowed on the monitor.

All three viewed the video that went on for ten minutes. Reece's forehead was wrinkled in concentration, and confusion. "What are we looking for exactly?" he asked.

"Just watch, let your eyes flow over the video, and open your ears. Don't try to force anything, just let it sift over you, okay?" Gian recommended.

When the video ended, Gian hit replay.

The third time around, Josh sat up straight, his eyes blinking rapidly, lips pulled in tight. "Yes, yes, yes, I get it," he said urgently, his hands clenched in fists.

Reece looked at him, his lids lowered slightly befuddled. "It's the O'Grady twins. I don't understand. Why are you showing us them?"

In fact, the video was a compilation of several films that showed the O'Gradys during commercials and events such as fundraising for the mayor, election forums, Oreo working at the salon, Chip working with his father, a couple of parties and other affairs, charity events.

Lastly, there was an auction where a grinning Oreo was on stage with other men for sale to raise money for the local shelter for at risk teens.

Gian had Torr and a few others cull together everything they could find on the O'Grady twins.

Josh announced, "Oh yeah, putting those pictures and sounds together with films of the brothers, yes, it brings it all together. Wow, Gian, just…wow." Everyone was staring at Josh as if he was delirious.

"Tell me, Josh, what do you see, and hear? In your mind, what do you smell?" Gian spoke quietly, slowly, encouragingly.

Josh waited a minute, then took a long, deep breath. Expelling it, he rifled his hand through his thick dark mane, and smiled musingly. He glanced at everyone around the room then centered on Gian.

"It was a confused jumble in my brain for a while. Now, I can see it, I can put it together. The red, I thought was apples. In fact, it was one of their helmets. Shiny and red, like a fresh macintosh." He paused for a moment.

"Take your time, Josh," Gian told him.

"I remember now, I think I heard a car and then a motorcycle that came in right after it that night. The molasses, yeah, it wasn't a scent, it was hair color. One must have worn a helmet and the other didn't. The dudes have that reddish-yellowish-brownish hair."

Everyone in the room except Gian gave Josh a skeptical look. Josh shrugged. "I know it sounds way farfetched, but seriously, it's what comes to my mind when I picture the twins' hair color. Molasses. I thought that when I saw them at a party a while back."

"It's because you're always thinking of food," Jed commented with an affectionate wink.

"I remember wondering, kind of jokingly," Josh smirked at his father, "if their hair smelled like it looked. Screwy, I admit, but true. Probably something was baking in the oven at the party that contributed to that crazy thought like gingerbread cookies or something."

His shoulders hunched, straining to grasp what Josh got, Reece's lashes rippled as he listened to his brother. He turned back to the laptop and leaned forward with his elbows on his knees, his hunched shoulders rising up to his ears as he studied the screen, hard.

Josh's voice rose with excitement. "Yes, there was a smell, orange blossoms and, I think, uh, woody, like cedar, and wait, yeah, there actually was also a scent of crisp apples. I didn't think of perfume because it wasn't feminine floral."

"But like cologne, maybe?" Gian prompted him.

Josh grinned at Gian. "Yeah, totally. Cologne. I was thinking a little bit about that when I tried to chase the scent down at the bar the day I ended back up at the hospital."

"Won't do that again, will you?" Jessica said with a twinkle in her hazel eyes. She had left the room and returned with a tray of drinks.

"We went back to Swabby's," Gian said, "and interviewed everyone that we could determine was there that day you played detective, including the poker players in the back. It was confirmed that none of the players left the building, and as far as we could glean, no one else admitted they had or that anyone had noticed anyone else leaving either. Therefore, whoever shot at you either slid past undetected, going out the back possibly, or was outside already. We hit a dead end on surveillance film of the area as well."

Gian didn't take his eyes off the laptop even when Jessica handed him a soda. "Thanks, Jess," he took it absently as he continued watching the videos of the O'Grady twins.

"Okay," Gian said, "so it's appearing that it wasn't just a car that Koh Boone claimed he saw the night you guys were shot. More than one person was present during the crime, the shooter or shooters came by motorcycle *and* vehicle."

Jed smiled at Jessica as she also handed him a soda. Then his brow furrowed in question.

Mirroring Reece, he leaned forward with his elbows on his knees. Holding the soda in one hand, he asked, "If one was on a bike and the other in the car it would make sense that you only saw one helmet. Right?"

"Might have been more than two people present," Gian said.

"I'm thinking that that could be," Reece said. "I recall maybe hearing voic*es*, multiple, like more than one or two. I remember a giggle, I think."

"Yeah, me too." Josh nodded in concurrence with his brother's observations.

Jed asked, "You think maybe that's why Koh Boone was killed? Because he was stirring the pot by running his mouth around town that he saw the car of the shooters that night?"

Gian shook his glass loosening the ice cubes in it before he took a sip. His lips bunched as he considered the idea.

He said to his father, "That may have provoked the people he was working with or for, or whatever to come after him to shut him up. They may have been concerned that as he was jawing in the bars, he'd get drunk and become careless with things he said.

"Even if he was fabricating the part about what he saw, the car, I think he was just vying for attention, trying to look important and it backfired on him. We're also considering he might have been attempting to blackmail someone."

Jed reached over and patted Jessica's knee as she sat in the chair beside him. They'd been married for 20 years and yet they still acted like teenagers deeply in love, constantly playing touchy-feely.

He asked Gian, “What about that fella you have that BOLO out on, you know, Boone’s partner? Any word on him yet? You think he’s the one that popped Boone?”

Their touchy-feely and clearly lust-filled starry eyes with each other used to gross Gian out and make him super uncomfortable because he’d grown up with zero affection and it was unfamiliar to him.

However, since spending time with Nicolle Kelly, he was starting to understand, and desire that closeness with a woman, mentally and physically.

He blinked and shook his head to dispel images of the soft beauty. Now was not the time to indulge in wanton thoughts of her. Saturday night was coming up soon.

He smiled the images away and said, “It may well have been Clyde Collins who killed Boone. We won’t know until we catch him. Unfortunately yes, so far, he’s still on the loose. But then again he might be dead, murdered as well, which is why we can’t find him-”

Reece broke in, jubilation dancing with his words, “The jingling! I know what that was! Bracelets!”

Josh’s head swung at his brother. “You’re right! The tinkling I thought was real soft chimes were actually bracelets jingling together! And the clicking,” he shot his brother a sly gaze.

“Those damn rings!” Reece shouted.

“Oreo!” Josh yelled with a high-five to Reece. “I remember at a function we attended he was there, those freaking rings clacked and clicked non-stop. Like a nervous tick. I wanted to hammer his hand to the table!”

They were all quiet for only a few seconds when Josh snapped his fingers in glee.

“And the stink! Yes, I recognize it now that I’ve smelled it a few times. It was in Swabby’s Deck that day you just mentioned, how I foolishly went to the marina and was too weak to stand.” He gave Jessica a sheepish side-eye.

"I ended up in Swabby's Deck to get a coke hoping it would help my fatigue and I was positive I smelled that scent. Chip O'Grady had to have been there."

"It's likely, I think that he had been there, inside, and as he was leaving, he saw you arrive and waited outside for you to leave so he could ambush you," Gian said. "That would explain his cologne being inside but you didn't see him. Plus, the witnesses all claimed no one had left since you came in."

Reece frowned. "But I don't recall ever seeing either of them wearing bracelets. Do you?"

Josh thought for a minute, then shook his head. "No. Neither one."

Jessica spoke up, "What about Bambi, Chip's wife? I'm thinking about whenever she was with the family doing promotions for the mayor, I recall she always had tons of bracelets on her arms. I wondered how she wore them all the time and if she took them off when she slept or showered. They would annoy the heck out of me if I wore all those bangles."

The men all smiled at Jessica who beamed back at them.

"Do you know where she works? What she does?" Gian inquired of the redhead.

Her eyes flit up as she thought. Her tongue tsked, then she smiled. "I remember, she works at that used car lot. Ramage's Reruns, down on Lantern Lane, you know, by the lighthouse. Remember Jed, we went there a few times with Reece when we bought his last car."

Jed cocked his head with one bent brow. "Can't say I ever noticed the girl. We were there to look at cars." He said to his sons, "Bracelets jingling and rings clicking wouldn't really make a lot of noise. How could you have heard them that night?"

Josh replied, "It was late, not a lot of activity around and, with the woods behind them, and the water in front which amplifies noise and helps carry it we would have heard the noise. Sound travels over water, you of all people know that."

"Yeah," Reece chimed in. "You've yelled at us enough over our lifetime to keep it down when we're out on the water and near other boats or houses because of the amped volume the water makes."

"Besides, I was at the truck when I was…shot." Josh's voice wavered in recollection of that dreadful night. "I would have been much closer to the shooters and would have been able to hear them better."

"All right," Gian said. He powered down the laptop and pocketed the flash drive. "I've got to head out." He stood up as did Jed.

Chapter Twenty-nine

Gian had an idea.

He brought Sergeant Lydia Carlson with him to the Beautella Salon. She was so pretty she wouldn't stand out like a sore thumb like Gian would.

Wavy blonde hair, iridescent eyes that were lustrous with love and empathy for humans and animals alike, and a vivacious personality, she was well known for her passion for the theatre. Relishing plays and musicals, she makes friends with half the talent on the shows.

The word was, no one looked to her for overtime work because she was too busy out there living life to work 24/7. Rumor was, and she sure had the figure for it, that she had been a professional dancer herself before the desire to serve and protect her community enveloped her.

Gian handed her photos of Clyde Collins from one of the CCTVs from the marina and prepped her as to what he wanted her to do.

The police were unable to find a driver's license or a fishing license in Collins' name. All the marine patrol on the ocean, Collins would have been stupid to not have a fishing license in case he was stopped, so he probably stole one from some unsuspecting fisherman.

Facial recognition software also failed. Since he didn't show up on DMV facial rec, the guy probably didn't have a license at all, and that made them suspect he might not be a US citizen.

They couldn't locate an address or phone number for him, and everyone they talked to knew zero about him. Other than Boone, he apparently had no friends and no family and no home.

The fact that he had no paper trail, no past, and he was missing, Gian was betting he was involved in whatever iniquity was going on in Chicory Landing County.

When they went inside the salon, they approached the front counter.

Sergeant Carlson smiled at the young man behind the counter. He was fine looking with pale skin, thin as a Gen X model in tight pants and pointed shoes, and had wispy black hair that flapped when he blinked. And he blinked hot and heavy at the striking Carlson.

"Hi there," Sergeant Carlson greeted him. He smiled at her then tore his gaze away to acknowledge Gian. His white skin paled more when he realized Carlson was a cop and Gian flashed his badge.

"What's your name, sweetie?" Carlson asked him.

"Uh, uh," he stuttered. "I'ma Henry. Henry Roberts. You can call me Henry. Or Hank. Lots of people call me Hank."

He blushed like a new rose. "What uh, can I do for you, sirs, I mean ma'ams, I mean-"

"We have a photo we'd like to show the staff. Is Nectar O'Grady here today?" Sergeant Carlson inquired, although they were already aware Nectar had evaded the police so far and was nowhere to be found.

"N-n-no, sir, ma'am, she- she's well, not here," the attendant stammered, turning whiter yet.

"No prob," Carlson said cheerfully. "Is there a manager on the premises?"

The young man's head swung back and forth and around as if searching for someone to tell him what to do and say.

"Uh, yes, uh, the floor manager, that would be Mrs. Karen Audet. She's, uh," he swirled around frantically searching for Mrs. Audet.

He spotted her. Pointing vigorously, he almost shouted, "There, there, that's her over there. The tall, knockout strawberry blonde near the back of the room."

"Okay, thanks. We'll just-"

The man cut off Carlson, and started blathering, "She was Miss Chicory a few years back, when she was in college, you know. Kind of a town, um, celebrity. A few years back she married her college sweetheart and he was rich! Pete is a philanthropist and the founding pastor of Our Divine Grace Church. He is a popular speaker and lecturer at universities and outreach centers."

"Thanks, we-"

The fellow carried on, "Until she wedded Pete, Karen was chancelloress at Hopedale Florida University. Once married, she didn't have to work, but she did so much charity work, the town just loves her! She said she had too much time on her hands so she came here for a job."

Carlson tried to get a word in. "Do you know-"

But the man kept going. "Between you and me, I think she got bored and wanted to be around folks. She gets a kick out of people, meeting them and she likes activity and problem solving. They say she's always running around doing stuff with her children and adorable puppy Lizzie-"

"Okay, hon, thank you. We'll go speak to her. You've been a real help. We appreciate when civilians are obliging and so friendly." Carlson gave him a huge smile with rows of straight, pearly white teeth, and Henry's mouth dropped and his eyeballs gushed like a lovesick puppy.

Rolling his eyes, Gian started towards Mrs. Audet. When he reached her, she was already facing his direction and realized he was coming for her.

When Carlson joined him and they introduced themselves, Mrs. Audet smiled graciously and held out her hand and shook both of theirs.

"You're here about the shooting," Mrs. Audet said astutely.

"Not exactly," Gian replied. Everyone present that day had already been processed upside down and backwards. "We have a picture to show you and see if you can tell us if you recognize the person." He nodded to Sergeant Carlson.

Lydia held the picture out to Mrs. Audet. She took it and frowned as she examined the photo.

With a slight dip of her head in affirmation, she handed the picture back and said, "Sure. That's Clyde Collins. He partners, or rather used to partner with Koh Boone on his fishing boat, the Fishnet Stalkings. Disgusting name for a boat, isn't it?" Her mouth twisted in distaste. "Comes in here all the time to chinwag with Nectar."

"Do you know anything about him?" Gian asked, while Lydia pulled out a tiny notebook and pen and started jotting down her words.

Karen Audet thought for a moment then shook her head. Tucking a runaway strawberry curl behind her ear, she replied, "No, not really. He never gets more than a haircut and will only see Nectar."

"When's the last time you think you saw him?"

Her eyes tipped up as she tried to recall. Tapping her finger against her chin as she thought back, her mouth crinkled in at a corner. "Well, it's been a couple of weeks, I think. Not since that whole dreadful Koh Boone tragedy." A shiver of horror rolled across her shoulders.

"Do you mind if we ask around to the other staff?" Sergeant Carlson asked.

"Of course not. Please feel free to-"

"I have a little info to share, officers," the woman sitting in the stylist chair beside where Mrs. Audet was standing spoke up. A pink salon cape covered most of her body.

She appeared to be a woman with such a serious countenance, one almost missed the glint of intellect and humor that flickered in her eyes as her riot of dark waves were being highlighted with shimmering streaks of blonde.

Gian and Lydia turned to her with arched brows. "Ma'am? You are?" Gian dipped his head in respect. She had such a dignified persona that her subtle attractiveness took people by surprise.

The woman sniffed, her lips turned up at the corners in a polite smile. "I am Etta Lou Hanken. You may have seen my series on travelogues, 'Under every rock is a civilization' on PBS."

Karen Audet smiled proudly at Ms. Hanken. "Yes, our Etta Lou is our town star. Once an environmental scientist she realized she loves traveling so much and helping people discover their heart's adventures she resigned her job and became a travel agent, podcaster, and of course has her series on TV."

Etta Lou didn't blush at the praise, she just accepted her fame as it came with the territory.

"And how can you help us, Ms. uh…"

"Hanken." A small hand reached out from under the pink cape and shook Gian's large paw. He was careful not to crush the dainty fingers.

"It's my parttime job as a travel agent that I speak of. You asked about Clyde Collins. Clyde and Nectar O'Grady came to my shop. I guess Nectar didn't think I would blab her business, but, all's fair in love and law, right?"

"Uh, sure," Gian mumbled confused. "What does-"

"The pair of them as I was saying," Etta Lou told him, "visited my travel business. As we discussed which destinations they'd like to explore, Nectar asked if I knew anything about countries with no extradition treaties with the U.S."

Gian's brows jumped with the importance of this revelation.

"Oh yeah? Tell us more," he prevailed for her to continue with what she knew.

"Certainly. Nectar claimed she was asking because she was writing a book. Please, it was so lame, the woman can barely spell the word extradition much less write a novel. Heaven knows why she didn't just Google it. I'm thinking pure laziness. Anyway, I gave her the list of countries."

"Interesting. Did they focus on any specific country?" Sergeant Carlson asked the bright woman.

Etta Lou thought about it, then her chin pushed up and she shook her head. "No, not really. Morrocco, maybe, they asked the most about that country. They asked about the Caribbean countries. I told her they had treaties with the U.S. Then Nectar asked if I knew anything about their offshore banking requirements, and which one would be the best one to, ah, hide money in. For ah, information for her book she had quickly added."

Gian said, "And you told her?"

"Well, the Bahamas have very strict banking secrecy laws. That seemed to make them very happy."

Gian's brows daggered down between his dark eyes. "And you didn't think to contact the police with this information?"

Her slender jaw lifted in gravity. A tinge of sarcasm on her tongue, she retorted acerbically, "Young man, if I called the authorities every time someone displayed the least bit of curiosity in unlawful forays into a country, I'd never get off the phone."

The stylist continued working on her hair as Etta Lou spoke.

"Some people just like living on the edge and search for precarious places to venture. Thrill of leaping off the precipice as it were. Some just want to test their nettle, or are adrenalin junkies, or are true life crime fans. Or, they could be writing a novel." One shoulder lifted in impassivity.

Gian and Lydia regarded Etta Lou Hanken with appreciation at her disclosers. Karen Audet just beamed at Etta Lou as if she were a prodigy.

"Okay," Gian drawled coolly. "Is there anything else you can tell us? Did they purchase any tickets or appear to be pinpointed on any one territory?"

Her head swiveled towards him, the cape crinkling as she moved. She fixed it back over her knees when it shifted off to the side. "As I answered the deputy, no, they didn't mention or ask about any particular place. If they'd purchased tickets I would have told you that right away."

Gian couldn't think of any other questions to ask, so they thanked Etta Lou Hanken and Karen Audet and moved on to query other staff.

"So, you're looking at this Collins fellow and maybe Nectar O'Grady also to be involved in, what exactly?" Sergeant Carlson asked Gian.

Glancing around the room, nothing jumped out at Gian that could be considered suspicious in any way. The place had been cleaned up, everyone was going about their business. It was as if a shooting hadn't taken place there recently.

"I don't know. With the large amounts of unverifiable money Nectar is throwing around, Koh Boone's murder, my brothers' shootings, I'm considering it's all tied together and drug smuggling is rising to the top for motive."

"What, like heroin or cocaine?" Carlson walked beside him as he searched out others to question.

Without throwing FBI Agent John Michael's name out there, Gian said, "We're thinking fentanyl."

Her breath caught in her throat. "Oh no. That stuff is deadly. The tiniest amount can cause a quick death. I hate to think that's infecting our beautiful town."

"Not sure about anything yet. But I'll be damned if I let it invade our county and kill our people. We'll get to the bottom of it, of all of it."

When they learned nothing new, Gian and Lydia left the salon. At the car, Gian told Lydia how much he appreciated her assistance.

"You have a way with people, Sergeant Carlson," he told her. "They just open up to you like a trusted friend."

She smiled gaily at the compliment. "Well, I like people. I like to learn about them, their lives, families and so on, and I guess I come across as someone who can be trusted. Some people just want someone to listen, to hear them, to care about them. It's helpful in my job I must say, people open right up to me."

"I'm told you are excellent with your staff as well as the public. I'll keep you in mind if I have further interviewing, is that okay with you?" Gian opened her passenger door.

As she climbed in, Carlson said, "I will be more than happy to do everything I can to help. Just buzz me."

Chapter Thirty

***G**ian headed to the station to discuss with his team what he had learned from his brothers and at the salon. Elation that they were starting to make headway put a spring in his step and a hopeful, yet scant smile on his rugged face.

Hell, he almost felt like whistling. Nah. He called ahead to make sure everyone was there in the conference room.

Before going to the meeting, he checked in with his lieutenant, Huxley McKay.

After Gian told him all the updates so far, McKay sat back in his cushioned chair with wheels and put his feet up on the desk. Ruffling his fingers through his wheat-colored crew cut, he clasped his hands behind his head, elbows winged out. "I hear things are starting to crack open."

Tipping his head back, he peered at Gian through half slit eyes and a tight-lipped critical smirk. "You finally have viable suspects, although at least one is in the wind."

Leaning against the door frame with his arms and ankles crossed, Gian shrugged. "Only a matter of time before we catch up with Clyde Collins. I've got uniforms out rounding up the O'Gradys. It's all coming together."

"Well, that's good to hear, finally a positive note," McKay said.

"Hopefully we pull one thread and that thread will blab and sell out their compatriots and lead us to the biggest fish. We can start making a dent in this drug plague that is killing our citizens and find out who took potshots at my brothers."

"That is excellent news. Except," McKay dropped his feet to the floor and slammed a palm on his desk so hard it sounded like a firecracker going off. "You were supposed to keep your nose out of this. I gave you a direct order. You can't-"

Gian straightened in the doorway, set his hands on his hips and interrupted his lieutenant as he was beginning his tirade. "Yeah, yeah, sorry. Whatever. Listen, LT, you know damned well Cornball Vinci and Simonize Nutcracker weren't throwing their whole weight into this investigation. They had too many other cases pressing at them to allow them to check every I and dot all the T's."

"That's true. You know how busy everyone is." McKay worked to keep his voice low and calm.

"Yeah. They had rookies and admin staff doing most of the legwork that really required good detectives to ferret out information and leads. Although, to give credit where due, Vinci did notice Nectar O'Grady acting suspicious on video and that set us on her trail."

"That's all and good, but-"

"I'm not knocking Vinci and Simon Nucacher, they really are top of the line investigators. They were just limited in resources and time. I closed 3 cases so I had the room to navigate. Besides, not wanting to sound like a broken record, these are my brothers involved, my family. What if someone continued gunning after them, or Deo or Dad or Jessica? You expect me to stand aside with my thumb up my behind and just watch it happen?"

"Well, you have a point, but-"

"I didn't do any of the interviews myself, so the conflict is lessened. Except for this last one at the salon. Yes, I went to the crime scenes, and okay, I did talk with Tex Coltrane, and, well, anyway, we're here. I have the team waiting in the conference room."

McKay held a hand up and his mouth open, but Gian carried on.

“When I called Conny, he said he had a message that they got a result on the blood left on that tree where Koh Boone was found. There was a fake fingernail in the grass there as well that forensics is analyzing, plus a shell casing and a fragment of glass. One or all of them could lead us to defendants and solid convictions.”

“That doesn’t make it okay that you-”

“The forensics team that examined the crime scene sucked. But I met Val Proffer at the scene myself, and I am assured that Val will see to further scrutiny of the area as well as the analyzing of evidence, so I know it will be done properly this time.”

“You can’t-”

Ignoring McKay’s fuming expression, Gian spoke over him, “Not to blow my own horn, but to prove to you I am doing what must be done, these are all great leads and evidence that wouldn’t have spilt if I hadn’t pursued this so doggedly,” his stubborn jaw rose defiantly.

He went on as if McKay wasn’t trying to speak, “We wouldn’t have the blood or this nail to match to a suspect when we have one in custody if I hadn’t gone back out and meticulously re-searched the scene all over again.”

McKay curled one hand into a tight fist on the desk. He glowered reproachfully at Gian. “Stop cutting me off! Let me finish a damned sentence for cryin’ out loud.”

He pointed a fierce finger at Gian, spouting irately, “You see, that there, what if whoever the offender is claims you planted the blood on the tree?”

Gian’s shoulder bumped with lack of concern. “We’ll cross that bridge when we get to it. Besides, how would I get their blood to plant it? That’s absurd. A jury would be laughing the defense right out of town. I have people waiting.” He turned and left the doorway.

At his back, McKay yelled out, “You keep me up to date with every single piece, you hear me, Montanero?”

But Gian was already halfway down the hall. He didn’t see McKay shaking his head with a grimace that turned into a grin.

"Damn rogue cop. If he wasn't so phenomenal, he'd be out on the street handing out parking tickets." His head shifted side-to-side in reluctant admiration, "But he *is* good. Damned good."

In the conference room, Torr, Conny, Simon and several others that were working on the case were seated around the big oval mahogany table.

Conny was whispering to a female deputy he was sitting next to. Obviously flirting, because although the deputy had velvety black skin, her cheeks appeared flamingo pink. Her lashes waggled coyly as she coquettishly twined a curl around her fingers.

"Okay, let's get started," Gian sat at the table. Everyone had a tablet device or lined paper pads with pens waiting. Most had a drink in front of them, coffee, tea, soda and one chocolate milk.

Gian filled them in with his meeting with his brothers and their remarkable recollections that will hopefully blast the case wide open, exposing the reprehensible accomplices and lead to swift arrests.

He advised them as well of the information from the beauty salon regarding Nectar and Clyde Collins' visit to the travel bureau. The questions about countries with no extradition treaties with the U.S. and the speculation that Nectar possibly has secret accounts hidden in the Caribbean islands made everyone's ears perk up.

At his conclusion, there were whoops and hollers and 'Way to go!' around the shiny mahogany. Several clapped enthusiastically or slapped palms on the table.

"Let me add to the good news," Conny crowed with self-satisfaction. He raised his tablet in the air and gave it a little wiggle. All eyes turned eagerly to him. Gian nodded at the detective with the man-bun and goatee to go ahead.

"Yep. Okay, Dr. Audrey Gregg, the chief forensic biologist at the Crime Laboratory Unit gave me her report. Glad she left her job as a veterinarian to come work for the law. She's the leading expert in her field."

"She's the best!" One of the deputies touted.

Giving the deputy a nod of agreement, Conny went on, "Blood came back. The good news is, Dr. Gregg says it matches blood found on the Ruger .454 Casull we located on Koh Boone's boat, which we know was planted."

Conny glanced at Gian to see if he had anything to add. At Gian's silence, he continued with his report.

"It seems that it was as Gian theorized, the recoil was so forceful the scope hit the idiot in the head or nose and splurted his blood and skin cells on the tree. The blood splatter, tiny droplets had a void between them. That would be the perp's head. The blood splatted to either side of his head."

"Makes sense," Simon stated with a nod and smile for his friend.

Vinci lowered his head to the tablet in his hand. "Plus, there's a very slight rounded indentation of where his head slammed into the soft bark and more DNA captured there. The perps cleaned the gun pretty well, except the incompetent dolts skipped the scope and the hammer where the DNA was found. Nectar's gonna wring their stupid necks when she gets her hands on them."

"Unless it was Nectar who wiped the gun," a deputy piped up.

"Not likely," Gian said to her. "Nectar O'Grady doesn't come across as one who doesn't pay attention to every detail, or do the grunge work herself. It was more probable that it was Chip or Oreo. They were the screwballs that stashed the gun on Boone's boat, yet we can presume it was done per her orders. Nectar O'Grady is elevating to the top of the scum list as the ringleader. We don't know yet where Clyde Collins fits in."

"Need to see if any of our suspects have a big bad boo-boo on their face," Simon commented with a derisive laugh.

Conny high-fived his partner. "Yeah! Foil by recoil!" he jested. The rest of the group rolled their eyes.

"What are we, in kindergarten?" one of the deputies twittered. People beside him chuckled.

Giving him a sneer, Conny went on, "The bad news is, Dr. Gregg reported that none of the DNA pulled from the tree, gun and the fake nail found, are in the system. But, when we catch this guy, girl, whomever, it will be very strong evidence we can use to tie them to the case and obtain concrete convictions." His eyes darted down to his tablet.

"Oh, and the glass fragment that was found," he looked at Gian. "Dr. Gregg said it's broken lens from eyeglasses. Probably broke his glasses when the scope hit him in the face. Thus, another nail in the O'Grady coffin. Chip O'Grady who wears the glasses, to be specific."

He got a round of applause. He bowed and grinned like he was accepting an award. "Oh, and the casing of the bullet found in the woods is not from a Casull as that's a revolver and it wouldn't eject a casing."

Gian didn't mention he was the one who found the blood and the nail, and ordered the more recent video surrounding Boone's boat. Conny had relayed the report like he scraped the blood off the tree, nail and gun and hauled it to forensics and analyzed it himself.

Gian said with barely suppressed sarcasm, "We all knew the Ruger was a revolver and there would be no casing, but there may have been more than one gun involved in the shootings."

"Or," Torr said, "it could have been from a hunter or even just people out shooting at cans and stuff. The blood is the most important aspect, as soon as we can find the donor."

"By the way," Gian said placidly, "Chip doesn't wear glasses, Oreo does. And if the scope smacked the shooter in the nose, or face, it would have more likely struck the guy between the eyes, in the middle of the head, not where the lenses were. If that were the case, then we'd have found pieces of the glasses' frame, not the lens."

"Maybe one of the brothers fired at one of the brothers, and the other brother shot the other brother," Simon suggested.

Conny looked at Simon with cross-eyes. "That sounds like a tongue twister, like red rubber baby buggy bumpers or some equally silly nonsense."

Simon cast him an offended glower. "It's not nonsense, it makes sense. One brother fired at one brother and-"

"Enough," Gian snapped. "We'll figure out the evidence of who or what matches whom when the facts are in. Everything else is just conjecture."

Simon cackled, "Yeah, how much wood could a woodchuck chuck if-"

"Stop it!" Torr barked, glaring at the detective who grinned mockingly back at him.

The group shared minor updates then Gian stood up. "All right, if that's all for now," he lifted his chin at Torr.

"Torr and I will head over to that car sales place and see if we can scoop up Bambi Bodine O'Grady. If we put the pressure on her, she may offer up her husband Chip and get us building the heart of the case, and we can start with warrants for arrests and obtain DNA samplings." He motioned to the rest of the people sitting at the table.

"You all have your assignments." He turned to Conny Vinci. "You and Simon are trying to locate Chip and Oreo O'Grady. Start at Mayor O'Grady's office to see if Chip is there. We know Oreo isn't at the beauty salon because the floor manager, Karen Audet has promised to contact us immediately if she sees or hears from any of the O'Gradys."

Gian said to a deputy, "Deputy Kristian, I need you to follow up with all those sightings witnesses have called in about Clyde Collins. See if any of them are worth chasing down. Find out if you can identify any vehicles he may be driving. If we know a make or tag number, we might be able to find him on those traffic cams, what are they called?"

"Automated License Plate Readers, uh, ALPRs," Deputy Nikola supplied.

"Yeah, those things," Gian gave him a curt smile. "Deputy Charles, you and Kristian see what you can work out regarding Collins. And you, Deputy Sills," he said to the flirty girl sitting next to Conny, "I want the mayor brought in. I want all of the O'Gradys brought in even if you find them only one at a time. You and," he glanced down the table to another officer, a young, athletic blonde deputy.

He squinted at her name tag. "Ah, Deputy Stewart, I've heard great things about your meticulous attention to detail and painstaking follow through from Captain Pamela Darling. Keep up the good work. Start a canvass with Sergeant Julijana Henry. She's the top expert in our Special Opts division.

"I want interviews conducted with all of the O'Gradys' friends, relatives and neighbors, and don't forget any business personnel. We've already hit some of the neighbors, but I want every single one of them questioned. I don't care if they've already been interviewed, I want them done again. They might remember something if questioned again."

He inclined his head towards the deputy. "You have exhibited great diligence, Deputy Stewart, I know you will use your exceptional proficient finesse to gain information without angering the citizens."

Deputy Stewart gave Gian a full wattage smile at his compliment. He was normally quite stingy with them so it meant a lot to hear any commendations from him.

"You'll need help, catch up with Deputy Matthews for his aid with bodies to assist you."

Deputy Stewart's expression resolved into a professional plate, her mouth firmed, eyes hardened with her nod.

Conny Vinci scooped up his tablet and cup of coffee and motioned to Simon Nucacher. "Right-o, let's hit it, pardner."

Simon tossed back the last of his chocolate milk and pushed his chair back as everyone filed out.

Chapter Thirty-one

*G*ian and Torr drove to Lantern Lane where the car lot, Ramage's Reruns was located. They parked right out front and strode through the double glass door entrance.

A man scurried right over to them. "Yes, gentlemen, how can I help you on this beautiful day?" He wore a suit, hair neatly styled and heavily moussed. Late thirties, he had a wedding band on his finger and a bright super-friendly smile. He looked from Gian to Torr and his face fell when he saw they both held out badges.

"We need to speak with Bambi O'Grady," Torr announced.

The man's lower lip pushed out ruefully. Shaking his head morosely, he advised, "Bambi isn't here today. Perhaps I can help you. Was there a particular car you were interested in?"

Gian demanded, "Where is she? Where can we find her?" Neither she nor Chip bothered to update their address with the DMV last time they moved. There were many other ways to find it out but this would be the quickest, and they were here now.

"Ah, well, I'm not sure if I can, I mean, is her address confidential under, um, one of the constitutional amendments?" The salesman looked decidedly uncomfortable. He stuck a finger under the knot of his tie and tugged at it.

Gian resisted the urge to reach out and slap him. "You watch too much TV. No, you are not a doctor or lawyer or priest even. There is no confidentiality between co-workers, you can provide this information to the police."

His expression stern, Torr added with iron authority crackling, "We are in a hurry, please don't cause us to have to cite you for obstruction."

The poor man tugged harder at his tie and ran his palm over the top of his thickly moussed hair in agitation, anxiously uttering, "Of course, of course."

"Now, we want it now," Gian tried to keep the annoyance out of his voice.

"Oh, of course, of course," he rattled flustered, and rushed over to a desk with a computer on it and clicked several keys.

Coughing out little grandiose hacks as he typed, he said, "Actually, Bambi has been, uh, quite ill. She has some type of-of disease or whatnot. Uh, called, I forget, it's a virus of some sort." He coughed some more and punched harder at the keys.

While typing, he carried on breathlessly, "Terribly contagious. Our manager Gene Wood sent her home. Shouldn't have been here in the first place. She was so sick, was coughing and sneezing and slobbering nasty germs all over the place. The rest of us were scared we were gonna catch it. Called her Typhoid-Bambi for a while." He looked ill himself with the prospect of getting infected.

"I Mean," he gulped. "Is that why you're here? Do we need to be quarantined? Oh my God," he clutched his tie in panic, his voice rose in a high pitch. "Are we in danger? Do we need to call Hazmat or something?" He squeaked, "Should we-"

"Was it called Respiratory Syncytial Virus?" Torr questioned.

His head rotating all around, at Gian, at Torr, at the back-office door, at the bathroom, the salesman looked about to hurl. "Yes, yes, something like that. Here, here's her address," he jabbered off the data in a shaky voice.

Torr whipped out his phone and texted it to Conny Vinci.

Huffing and puffing, the salesman whined, "You know, I'm not feeling so well myself, I think I need to go home. If you'll excuse me I really need to-" his face white as a snowflake, he started towards the double glass doors.

"Wait," Gian held a palm up stopping his hasty exit. The man's feet screeched to a stop. He appeared frightened, as if he was in imminent danger of being arrested, or exposed to radioactive toxic waste.

"We need to know if you sold or leased any cars to Bambi or any of her friends or relatives in the past month."

Again, they had checked DMV records but neither Bambi's or Chip's known vehicles were spotted on video anywhere near the marina parking lot. Except Bambi's little red Miata was seen on tape at Swabby's Deck the night the crew claimed a woman, a sick woman, had sex with the bunch of them.

"Uh- uh- uh," the salesman panted, eyeballs swirling around his head in hysteria. "Y-yes, uh, a silver SUV, Equinox. Two years old. Sa-" he swallowed hard.

Clearing his throat like it was clogged with a furball, he said quickly, "Said her mother-in-law needed a car and wanted something not flashy, you know, something that didn't easily stand out flamboyantly, like a neon orange Ferrari or something. She- she said because of the mayor and all, she didn't want to attract attention. Now, I gotta go-"

"Need the tag," Gian said calmly, blocking his escape.

The salesman, freaking out, stammered, "But uh- but uh- I don't wanna get-"

"Now."

"OMIGOD, okay, okay, hold on, give me minute." As he furiously typed, he muttered resentfully, "Pain in the neck woman. Never here anyway. Doesn't need to work, has more money than Bezos." He pounded on the keypad.

"Only got the job so she could fool around with Mr. Wood the boss without his wife or her husband suspecting in this small gossipy town, and get cars dirt cheap for her myriad of friends. Only came in once or twice a month, damned wo- here. Now, I need to get to a hospital ASAP!" He thrust the monitor around so the detectives could read it.

Meanwhile, Torr texted Conny and Deputy Kristian the info on the Equinox.

Conny would get out a BOLO on the NCIC.

An electronic clearing house for authorities, the NCIC, National Crime Information Center is where missing persons, stolen property, vehicles, vessels, jewelry, paintings, weapons, etc., crime records and dispositions, as well as active warrants, fugitives and gang information is shared by the FBI and law enforcement agencies across the U.S. as well as connections with Interpol.

"One more question, if not at home, do you know where she might be?" Gian called out to the fleeing salesman.

"Check the hospital!" he hollered as he raced out the door.

At the hospital, Gian and Torr inquired at the visitors' desk about Bambi. They had called ahead, they knew she was there.

"Room 210," the person said after reviewing the computer in front of them. "I believe her husband is with her if I'm not mistaken. He's been here the past several days."

Gian and Torr hoofed to room 210. "Can it be possible that we can grab two birds with one visit?" Torr commented with a comical grin.

As luck would have it, both Bambi and her husband Chip O'Grady were in room 210. Sadly, they might not be able to interrogate Bambi as she was ensconced in an oxygen tent. Naturally, she wasn't wearing any bangles.

When the detectives marched through the door, Chip looked up. He jumped to his feet, his eyes as huge as moons, his mouth fell wide open in fear. Molasses colored curls flopped around his head like it hadn't seen a comb in days.

Torr stated, "Chip O'Grady."

Chip's heaving eyes frantically flit from each detective then to the door.

"Don't make us hurt you," Torr warned as he pulled handcuffs from off the back of his belt and held them out.

"You're under arrest. Turn around and put your hands behind your back."

As Torr cuffed Chip and started escorting him to the door, Gian asked pleasantly, "How'd you get that nasty gash on your nose?"

Chapter Thirty-two

When he was ushered into a room for questioning, Chip fell apart like a house of cards in a windstorm.

They had warrants to take Chip's blood and DNA samples. They stuffed him in a cell to wait while they had the physical evidence rushed through processing.

Normally it would take months to get a return on DNA, but Lieutenant Huxley McKay had the forensics unit sitting on tenterhooks waiting for this material to come through and get tested. It took days rather than weeks or months.

McKay had Chief Forensic Biologist Dr. Audrey Gregg see to the analysis herself. He wanted it done quickly and right. There would be no room for mistakes or questions about slipshod procedures messing up the case at trial.

Chip knew his and his wife's goose was cooked. Not only did the fingernail found at Koh Boone's crime scene match Bambi's DNA, the crew identified her as the woman that had made them sick.

Most importantly, Chip's DNA was identified as the blood stain on the tree as well as on the scope and trigger of the gun planted on Boone's boat. The prints found on the cigarette wrapper were Koh Boone's.

When Gian produced the results of the DNA and blood tests clearly indicating they belonged to Chip, and he threatened to introduce Chip to the electric chair, Chip sobbed out the whole story.

Oreo was already behind bars himself thanks to Conny Vinci and Simon Nucacher, and he was singing like a yellow-bellied canary. Vinci and Nucacher picked him and Gator O'Grady up at Gator's office.

A guard was positioned outside Bambi's door at the hospital in case she took a turn for the better and decided to make a run for it.

Nectar O'Grady was still in the wind as was Clyde Collins.

"You remember your rights as I read them to you?" Gian inquired of the nervous man.

"Yeah," Chip replied glumly.

"How come that wound wasn't visible that day at the clambake?" Gian asked.

Chip shrugged, then winced as he gingerly touched the cut.

"Used heavy duty actor's makeup and huge sunglasses, it wasn't so bad then. But it got infected so it's taking over half my damned face. Plus, it hurts like a bitch."

"Hmm, that's too bad." Gian didn't sound the least bit sorry the fool who shot at his brothers was in physical distress. "Looks like a big ugly scar in the making, if the sepsis doesn't take you out first" He sounded like he was hoping for both to happen.

"Tell us whose idea it was," Torr started the inquisition. He stood poised by the door, hands on his hips, suitcoat pushed back behind his wrists, blue tie dangling loosely around his neck. His dark hair. thicker on the top was neatly combed back, but a lock fell over his forehead. He impatiently shoved it back up.

His wrist cuffed to a bolt on a table in front of him, Chip collapsed in his chair, his exhale gushed out almost in relief to have it all over. He wiped at the sweat that beaded on his forehead and rubbed at the cut on his nose, it was directly between his eyes.

It was quite deep and was clearly festering, all blotchy scarlet with a bit of pus bubbling out. He should have gotten stitches and antibiotics.

Ever since he got smacked with the gun and the wound started really growing, he'd been hiding out in a spare room at his father's office lest someone see the unsightly gash and put two and two together.

"It was all my stepmother's plot," he confessed, freckles jumping out on his ruddy face that turned pale, except for his red nose.

"She bribed my wife with a diamond necklace if she slept with the Seabug's crew. Bambi had gotten sick, you see, real sick." He shook his head with gross chagrin.

"The doctor told her she was highly contagious and her illness could last months. When Nectar heard this, well, we expected sympathy or maybe a new car or something, but no," his head wagged back and forth, anger growing as he recalled his stepmother's orders.

"No, Nectar told her to get up out of bed and go sleep with all those guys. It was so…so perverse and disgusting."

"She was your wife," Torr said.

Chip's head swung towards Torr, humiliation and rage warring over the freckles. "No kidding. However, I had no say in the matter. Nectar controlled all of our purse strings. You think my job as Dad's gofer and Oreo's sweeping up at Beautella paid for our mansions? Hell no," he scowled.

Glaring at Torr, Chip ground out, "We had to earn them by doing whatever Madam Nectar ordered. Half the time, under cover of night we were removing drug boxes from Boone's crappy boat and transporting them all over the place to dealers."

"Of course, we're going to need the names of every dealer and their buyers. Now, what about your father, the mayor? What was his part in all this?" Gian sat across the table from Chip. He'd dropped his dark blue suitcoat on the back of his chair and rolled the white and blue striped shirtsleeves up his forearms.

Chip let out a derisive snort. "Come on, you've met my pops. He's a big oblivious talking head with a cherub body and matching brain. Hasn't a clue. He honestly believes all the money they have came from some inheritance of Nectar's. See, dumb and gullible as a pet rock. No, Nectar runs the show, gives the orders. Gave me the gun and," his mouth drooped and shoulders slumped in dejection.

Torr asked, "Where did she get the weapon?"

"Ah, her gramps, she said. He was a celebrated hunter, bought the gun when he was on some big game safari in Africa."

"Unregistered," Torr stated the obvious.

"Duh," Chip acknowledged ruefully, scratching at his chest over the orange jumpsuit he wore. His nervous fingers left his chest and went back to the gash on his nose.

"We all fly on private jets. Not hard to pick up an illegal weapon on the black market in Africa and bring it back to the States. Enough money will buy you anything you want."

"All right," Gian said. He wondered how all the opulent expenses the O'Gradys enjoyed managed to fly under the radar all this time. You would think being in the limelight of the political office of mayor that prying adversarial eyes would look at everything through a microscope and ferret out every nuance of their wealth.

But then again, most people wanted to sidle up to the mayor hoping for favors, power, celebrity, riches and big careers. The mayor could even approve rezoning for folks trying to turn residential lots into commercial.

"Tell us why the attempted murders. Why did Nectar order my brothers shot?" Loosening his tie, Gian nestled his broad back against his plastic chair and folded his arms over his chest.

His neck bent, Chip's head lolled back. He sucked in a deep inhale, then let it whoosh out long and loud. He sat up straight, clawing at both sides of his head with taut fingers.

The jingling of the chain attached to the cuff reminded Gian of Bambi's bangles tinkling as she giggled while her husband took aim and tried to kill his brothers.

"Um, well," Chip's eyes darted back and forth as if expecting to suddenly get shanked from behind.

Gian slammed his palm on the table and Chip's body jerked like he had been shot himself.

The detective growled through grit teeth, "Enough with the stalling and stuttering, spit it out. All of it. You want us to take the death penalty off the table for Koh Boone's murder you better tell us every single thing, right the hell now."

Gian ignored Torr's side askance glance. He was bluffing with the death penalty, Maine abolished it in the 1800's. But Dimwit chained to the table didn't know that. Gian refolded a shirt sleeve that rolled down and crossed his arms back over his thick chest.

Gian wanted Chip to confess everything before he thought to call a lawyer and then all questioning would immediately halt. They Mirandized him when they brought him in, but he was in such misery and fright he barely heard his rights so he had waved them off.

"Okay, okay, keep your pants on," Chip sneered then jolted back when Gian suddenly uncrossed his arms and made an abrupt move towards him. The threatening glare of warning in Gian's licorice eyes took the spit right back out of him.

"Geesh, back off big guy. Yeah, hell, you probably know it all already anyway. So, Nectar was up to her neck in drug smuggling. Her and Clyde Collins were in cahoots. He and Koh Boone brought in fentanyl on the Fishnet Stalkings under the guise of fishing."

"From Mexico?" Torr asked. "That's a long way to here by boat. Especially the piece of crap boat Boone had."

"Yes, some drugs came from Mexico and also Canada," Chip replied. "Cheaper doing the long haul themselves than paying middlemen to move it. Less mouths to wag if the cops catch them, and fewer greedy thugs to rip you off or demand their percentage." He took a breath and glanced at each detective before going on.

"Boone keeps the boat looking trashy so the feds won't look too close at it. They also drop product off in other states along the way. I understand it starts in China and then the product gets transported by lots of different ways, air, sea, mail."

Gian nodded, they had figured that out. "Go on," he said.

"So, your dad was starting to make comments about the fact that Boone never brought in much of a haul. Jed Montanero's boat, the Seabug was positioned perfectly so that it had a bird's eye view of the Fishnet Stalkings' slip so he could see that although Boone boasted of huge catches, he really brought in very little. We had to do most of our unloading at night or when the Seabug wasn't at the marina.

"Clyde started thinking that Montanero was growing suspicious and might alert the authorities, so, he and Nectar concocted the idea if your brothers were out of the way and the rest of the crew came down with some deadly virus, it would put your dad out of commission.

"If he lost the big lobster festival hoedown, he would also lose customers and, well, money, and that might put him out of business. Or at the least, get his nose out of snooping and look for a cheaper marina to dock at."

Gian clasped his hands together and rested them on the table between them. Torr still stood by the door.

"So," sounding incredulous, Gian said, "your stepmother thought by shooting my brothers all that would happen would be my dad might go out of business or just move? There would be no investigation? That's the stupidest thing I ever heard."

Chip's head tipped to the side with his shrug. "They thought if we killed your father outright it would catch the law's attention right away. Taking pot shots at your brothers could look more like teenaged thugs riding around drunk and shooting at things. Maybe hit them by accident."

Gian and Torr looked at each other then back to Chip. "Go on," Gian said.

"Nectar and Clyde figured if we were careful enough, you cops would never cotton on to us. As a matter of fact, I objected at first because I have more faith in you po-po's and your ability to catch crooks. Apparently, I was right."

He held his cuffed hand up with an ironic crooked grin. "Besides, I'm no good shot with a gun. But Nectar didn't care if they were dead or just wounded, she just wanted them out of commission."

"Nice woman," Torr remarked dryly.

Chip turned towards him. "Wasn't my idea. I'm not the leader of the pack."

"No, you'd need more than half a brain to be that," Torr murmured as he came over and sat at the table next to Chip. He asked in disbelief, "Nectar and Collins didn't think a murder investigation wouldn't expose the smuggling, or point a laser beam of investigation at the marina for that matter?"

Chip shrugged again, he poked at the cut on his nose then wiped his finger on his pants. "Frankly, I don't know what they were thinking. I just follow orders. Like I said, they don't think too highly of the authorities and their ability to think. No offense."

“It didn’t bother you they whored out your wife?” Sitting kitty-corner to Chip, Torr leaned towards the man, incredulous at the idea.

Chip’s face burned to a deep red, he scowled, lips puckered in rage. He suddenly jumped to his feet, yelling, “Of course it bothered me you idiots! But what was I to do? Nectar controlled the purse strings! She gave the orders and we minions merely followed them!”

“Sit down,” Gian said flatly. Chip tugged at the cuff restraining his wrist to the table then thumped back down in his chair with a huff.

“And your wife, Bambi, what did she think?” Torr asked. “How did she feel about being prostituted? Why did she go along with it?”

Slumping back in his chair, Chip gestured with a flippant wave of his unrestrained hand. “Like I said, purse strings. My Bambi likes nice things. Big houses, fancy cars, maids, jewelry. Like the rest of us, she did what she was told.”

“Okay.” Gian continued, “Tell us about the night you shot my brothers.” He twined his fingers together and sat relaxed in his chair opposite to Chip.

Beside Chip, Torr erased the incredulous look from his face that Chip seemed to accept his wife slept with numerous men on at least one occasion and probably more than once since there were a lot of deckhands working the Seabug.

He replaced the incredulous mien with a benign expression. Not his place to judge. But geesh, these people have the morals of a black widow spider. Probably less.

Heaving a heavy sigh, Chip told them, “Well, Nectar gave me the gun. She told Oreo to go with me as she said between us twins we barely had one working brain and we’d be less likely to make any mistakes.” He chuckled mirthlessly at that. He ignored the glance Gian and Torr shared with each other.

“So, Oreo went on his motorcycle and me and Bambi drove in this car, an Equinox Nectar had bought from Ramage’s Reruns where Bambi works. Sometimes. Once in a blue moon. Don’t know why she goes there, doesn’t need the money and she abhors any sort of labor. Work is a four-letter word to her.”

"Why did you go separately?" Torr asked. They now knew what car was driven to the marina that night and the one Nectar was probably currently fleeing in. They can review all the surveillance videos again, and have more evidence when they see that car was present the night of the shootings as well as near Koh Boone's truck where his body was found.

"Dunno. I guess we thought if there were any witnesses having two totally different vehicles would cloud the issue."

Torr asked, "Why did Bambi go? What was her role?"

Chip's shoulders jerked up and down. "She wasn't sick yet. She wanted in on the hunt. In case you haven't noticed, my wife is a bit of an adventure junkie. Trust me, she wasn't all that put out, no pun intended, at having to have sex with all those men." His lips twisted bitterly in repulsion.

"You have no idea how many times she wanted Oreo to join our, um, intimate games. She liked an audience, but she also thought it was way cool to have a threesome with twins. Whatever. She's hot, the sex was hot, I lived with it."

Torr asked, "How come we found a broken eyeglass lens at the scene. You were the one injured by the recoil of the gun, but you don't wear glasses. So, was it Oreo's?"

The corner of his lip pulled in wryly. Chip huffed out a dour scoff, "Huh. We left our damned DNA all over the freakin' place. Great professional hitmen we are. Yeah, it was Oreo's. You'll test it anyway and probably find his skin cells or whatever on it."

Chip's mouth bunching in surrender, he said with derision,

"Yeah, Oreo laughed when the gun smacked me in the face. So I smacked him too, with my fist. Broke his glasses. Ha, served him right. I was forced to do all the dirty work while he stood around playing with his stupid rings." Holding his hand up, he admired the healing cuts on his knuckles.

Won't be wearing any rings now in lockup, Torr thought. Pieces of garbage, all of them, thinking pretty baubles would shine off the tarnish from their ugly souls.

Gian cleared his throat. "Back to the crimes. Why kill Koh Boone?"

"Ah," Chip stretched his neck and yawned. He'd been up half the night with Bambi. "Big mouth. Fool wanted attention. He drank like a fish and started blabbing all this stupid stuff. Hanging out at Swabby's, he'd get trashed and then pretend to get all mysterious and hint that he saw something that night at the marina." He sniffed condescendingly, as if he was smarter than Boone.

"He saw a car, he recognized it, blah blah blah. He just wanted to look important. Thought the other drunks at the bar would think he was a tough dude and the hags at Swabby's would fall all over him to be close to fame, you know, a prize witness. There might be news reporter interviews, or even the tabloids might come calling. Douche." He stuck out his tongue.

"So, he was killed to shut him up," Torr said redundantly. "And that was you, too."

"Nope. That one was Oreo. He wanted in on the fun. Boone was a jerk. Deserved what he got." He rolled his eyes with an irritated sigh. "Although I had to help him hold the big gun steady. My brother's a weakling. Moron, Just stood there staring cross-eyed at us as if he couldn't believe we'd do it."

The detectives didn't need to use a tape recorder as the interview room had both visual and audio recordings. Two cameras in corners blinked red recording everything Chip said.

"Do you know where Nectar and Collins are hiding out? Where can we find them?" Gian asked Chip.

Wiping an eye with another yawn Chip shook his head. "No clue. Right after that ridiculous shot in the salon, yeah," he said reluctantly, "that was me as well. I don't have the best aim, but Oreo is worse. He's blind as a bat without his glasses and not much better with."

"Who was the target?"

Chip bit off a grin. "Why you of course. Nectar wanted you out of the picture. You were asking too many questions, she was worried you were catching onto them. We kept hearing that you guys were asking about scents, apples and crap, so Nectar told me to stop wearing my favorite cologne. When your people came and pulled the CCTV from the salon, at first Nectar thought it was no big deal, standard operating procedures and all that.

"The tapes would reveal nothing except everyone running and screaming, her included. She would look just as innocent as the next guy. She had me stand where she knew the cameras didn't see so I wouldn't be exposed as the assassin." He paused, thinking back.

"She thought with me and Oreo being twins, Oreo was out filming a re-election ad with my dad and that might confuse the issue if I'd been seen. People wouldn't be too sure about who was what where."

"And?" Gian prompted him to keep talking.

His mouth dropping in a ferocious yawn, Chip shook his head like a dog then chewed on a fingertip. "Then she started thinking. What if there was something incriminating the camera caught? Maybe it caught a glimpse of me, or her expression wasn't quite right. Maybe her eyes darted towards me or something. She started getting nervous."

Chip looked from one to the other and shrugged, his words heavy with irony. "She was right. You guys started amping up your investigation into us. Our neighbors were telling us that deputies were coming around asking questions about us. I guess she got scared and took off on the lam."

"You have no idea where she could be? What about Clyde Collins?" Torr questioned.

"Nope. Sorry. Don't really know Clyde all that well. He made himself scarce around the rest of us, smart on his part. Probably not even his real name. They just disappeared. Nectar told Dad she was going to visit some relative he never heard of in Aspen. He hasn't heard from her. He's just a dupe in all this. Nectar married him for his money."

"He doesn't exactly have any," Gian said.

"Huh. No kidding. She soon discovered that mayor doesn't pay all that great, and her needs were extravagant and expensive. She ran through all his savings and inheritance his grandmother left him until they could barely afford a pack of gum. Hence the drugs."

Gian asked, "How did she meet Collins?"

His lips turning down at the corners, Chip shrugged absently. "Dunno. I think they ran into each other at the marina.

She liked to eat at the fancy restaurant and play tennis on the courts of the yacht club. You know, they say you attract what you are. Two folks with greedy, evil black hearts find each other in the dastardly dark playground."

Torr rolled his eyes at Gian.

"All right," Gian shoved his chair back. "We taped your confession but we'll need to have it written down on a probable cause report. Someone will come in and do that. Then you'll go back to a cell until your arraignment."

Chip scooted forward in his chair. "When do you think that'll be? Can I bond out then?"

"Huh," Torr snorted. "Bond for murder and attempted murder, drug smuggling and dealing, and the means for covert unfettered travel out of the country? Don't count on it, bro."

"Oh, bummer." Chip sat back, his face dismal.

Then he perked up. "What about food? Are you gonna feed me? I haven't had a decent meal in a week. They brought Bambi food every day but she'd been too sick to eat. The meatloaf and mashed potatoes at the hospital weren't bad, but they don't really stick to your ribs. Personally, I think the meat is that tofu crap, you know, healthy junk."

"I'm sure someone will feed you at some point, sport," Gian told him.

He and Torr left Chip sitting there, handcuffed to the table, looking forlorn, and hungry.

Chapter Thirty-three

*A*s Gian walked by Huxley McKay's office, the lieutenant called out to him and motioned for him to come in. He held a phone in his hand that he set on his desk.

"Gian, I was just about to call you. Have a seat," McKay gestured to a chair in front of his desk that was messy with papers and files, three more phones and a bunch of other rick rack.

Gian settled in the chair and crossed an ankle over a knee. One brow arched in question.

"Well, I just got off the phone with the CBP," McKay announced then smiled at Gian's quizzical expression.

"And what does the U.S. Customs and Border Protection want with you?"

McKay's smile grew into a grin. "Not me, boyo, you.'

Both brows shot up. Gian parroted, "Me? What the hell do they want with me?"

A woman came in and handed papers to McKay which he accepted with a, "Thank you, Darlene." She smiled and nodded and left the office.

"Here ya go." McKay handed the papers to Gian.

Gian's quizzical brows now drew down between his questioning eyes as he looked at the papers in his hand. "What are-"

"Yep. One for you and one for Torrand. You guys are going on a little trip."

"But-"

"You need to leave right away and get your 'go bag', stop by and pick Torr up on the way. DEA agent Veronica Cleaver will meet you two at the airport." McKay's grin tipped up wider revealing short square teeth, just like his crewcut.

"On the way where?"

Two hours later, Gian, Torr and Agent Cleaver found themselves on a police jet heading north.

"So, we are meeting some border patrol agent at the U.S. and Canadian borders?" Torr ruminated out loud while studying the paperwork Gian had given him.

Agent Veronica Cleaver sat between them. She also was pouring over her paperwork.

"Yeah, the BPA is meeting us at the airstrip with the prisoners," Gian told him.

"Did McKay tell you how they were apprehended?" Veronica inquired, her eyes on the papers, then she looked up at Gian.

"Nope. Said he'd save it all for the agent to disclose."

"Well, it sounds like we're going to wrap this all up, finally." Torr released a long breath. "I can't believe this is over."

"Almost over. Mostly everyone else involved, dealers, Oreo and Bambi are in custody, got the addicts in treatment. We just need to complete this final part and wrap it all up," Gian said.

"Bambi beat the virus, McKay told us, and is no longer contagious so they hauled her off to the pen. Woman was not only sick in the body, her head was crazy warped too." Torr's lips pursed, he shook his head.

"I can't believe the married woman, any woman for that matter would basically pull a 'train'. Having sex with multiple, make that dozens of men at once. Gross, man. I can't imagine the diseases-" he swiped his hand over his eyes to get the grotesque image out of his head.

"Oh well," Gian said, peering out the window at the clouds the jet was streaking past. "To each his or her own. Some people march to the beat of a different drum."

"You can say that again," Veronica said with a laugh. "The men weren't any better, for heaven's sake. The woman was deathly ill with the plague and all those guys slept with her anyway. That's the sick part. It grosses me out. There's going to be a lot of divorces on the horizon I think when all this gets out and wives start getting the virus."

"Gonna be a lot of broken families," Torr agreed. "Damn sad."

Hours later, the jet touched down and the three officers disembarked and trod down the metal pullout staircase to the asphalt.

The jet wasn't commercial so it wasn't parked right up to the terminal. As soon as they started down the stairs the wind struck meanly, slapping their hair and clothes with its icy whips.

Veronica wore her dark blue fleece jacket with the DEA insignia on the breast, and large gold DEA lettering on the back, and matching cargo pants.

Gian and Torr wore dark suits with heavy coats. It was much colder here at the US/Canadian border.

They didn't have to walk far. The party of 8 was standing there waiting for them.

Gian recognized several of the players. He couldn't stop the surprise from flashing on his face at the one person he never would have expected to see there.

The three LEO's strode to the group waiting for them on the tarmac.

Hovering in the biting cold were two prisoners, five armed officers, and a tall slender woman with long dark hair that spun elegantly down her back.

She wore a black suit with gold buttons and an unbuttoned, cobalt blue knee-length coat over it that flapped in the wind. Although she looked serious at the situation, a shade of mirth frolicked in her green eyes.

Nectar O'Grady and Clyde Collins were part of the group. They didn't look happy. In fact, Nectar's prior sweet Doris Day appearance had devolved into someone who looked rode hard and put away wet, more like a fearsome Joan Crawford in Mommy Dearest.

Both were in handcuffs. Besides unhappy, they also looked very angry.

"Hi there, Nectar, long time no see!" Torr greeted the downtrodden felon.

She snarled, "Go fu** yourself, cowboy."

Torr grinned sunnily at her. "Oo, potty mouth. No way for a mother to talk, eh? Listen, Nec, the good news is, it's not quite this cold back home."

Nectar opened her mouth to curse him some more, but the female in uniform holding her jerked her forward. The female wore the olive-green uniform with gold lettering that indicated she was a Border Patrol Agent. She handed an infuriated Nectar over to Veronica.

"Hey there, I've heard so much about you," Veronica said in a cheerful voice as she took control of Nectar.

"Go fu-" Nectar's snarl was cut off as the DEA agent swung her around. Veronica removed her handcuffs and handed them to the female BPA, then secured Nectar's wrists behind her back with her own cuffs.

"Ah," Gian studied the other handcuffed person. "The infamous Clyde Collins. Although we doubt that's your real name. Once we get your prints we'll determine your true identity."

Clyde remained sullenly silent.

The felonious drug smuggler was early forties, lean, slightly above average height with a jutting jaw, beige fly-away hair, pocked skin, long nose and tiny beady eyes that glared around at everyone as if threatening them.

Like he could hurt anyone even if he wasn't cuffed. Gian and Torr would have been on him like hungry fleas on a mangy dog. And they would not have gently restrained him.

Gian copied Veronica and switched out the agent's cuffs, placing his around Collins' wrists.

He turned to a man wearing of all things, a Coast Guard uniform and handed the cuffs to him. "These are yours, I presume, Paul Schmitt?"

Indeed, dressed in a Coast Guard, brown camouflage utility uniform and a brown pea coat with a rank insignia tab indicating lieutenant commander, Paul Schmitt grinned roguishly at Gian. The two men shook hands.

"I knew there was something not quite right with you. And I don't mean your shady behavior. You dressed slovenly and acted that way too, but intelligence gleamed out of those rascally eyes."

The lieutenant commander grinned cheekily at him. "Yah, you flatliner. You were fun to play with."

"Uh huh." Gian examined his insignia. "Coast Guard LCDR? You got a lot of 'splaining to do my devious friend."

Schmitt's head fell back with a clap of laughter. "Yah, ya wiley cunnard fellow you, aye." He turned off the overdone accent.

"Obviously I'm with the Coast Guard. As you know, our duties are to thwart pirates, detect trafficking, drug and human by sea, and additionally to ensure folks are complying with the fishery laws and regs. Our job is to maintain maritime security."

"How did this pair come onto your radar?" Gian nodded to Nectar and Clyde.

Tucking his hands in his coat pockets, Paul told him, "We've been trying to follow the smuggling of drugs that come from China to Canada. We got suspicious of so many large containers, boxes and such that were 'accidentally mislabeled' and sent to the wrong warehouses."

He glanced around at the group as he continued with his story. "We started to watch the warehouses and follow the people who picked up these misaddressed packages. It appeared to be the same goons over and over. The trails led to labs where the chemicals were dropped off for completion before being sent back out to dealers."

Pointing to the ocean, Paul said, "Some of the tracking led to the sea. We started watching the boats that met the people who transported the boxes to the water for travel." Paul indicated Clyde with a motion of his head.

"Lo and behold, a fella name of Koh Boone, and this guy appeared on one of the boats. We've been surveilling them for a while, trying to get the full scope of their involvement and operations. We thought they were unloading the product at the Kifpu Wissei Marina, but we couldn't get close enough on the water without being spotted to scout them. Ergo, I slipped in to observe."

Gian said, "It's too bad everyone isn't on the same connection page. An FBI agent, name of John Michael was in Chicory doing exactly the same thing. Could have worked together, all of us, and maybe wrapped this whole thing up sooner, and without the injuring of my brothers."

"True. But, you know, higher ups and all, want to keep everything cryptic, and on a need-to-know basis. Yada yada."

"Anyway, we're all here now. How did all this happen?" Gian waved his hand at the group waiting patiently in the bitter cold.

Well, Nectar and Clyde didn't look none too patient. They appeared very displeased to be there.

"This is where she comes in." Schmitt gestured to the lady with the long dark hair. She stepped forward. Schmitt said, "May I introduce Canada's current drug czar, Kathryn Roberts."

"How do you do," she said pleasantly with a warm smile. She shook hands with Gian then Torr then Veronica. The attractive woman looked quite feminine, yet clearly had a spine of steel and professional ruthlessness in those green eyes.

Schmitt said, "Canada appoints a drug czar to head the efforts to battle the fentanyl crises. With a law enforcement background, she corroborates with the U.S. and other countries in the fight against drugs." He gestured towards Nectar and Collins.

"She heard on the wires that the U.S. had wants out on these two, that they had skipped out, and since we were already aware that they were familiar with the covert routes to get from America to Canada by sea, she thought they might head here.

"She contacted my people who advised me of her theory. I hightailed it here. The car you States had the bolo out on was found ditched in a mall parking lot. Figuring they went straight to the water, we did a vast search of vessels in the area, and lo and behold, ta da! Here we are!"

He grinned over at the pair who glared viciously back at him. Nectar sniffed and shot her nose up in the air. Her bobbed blonde hair twisted and thrashed in the wind.

"You apprehended them without a fight?" Torr was intrigued at how the take down came about.

Schmitt chuckled. "Well, no. We came upon them with several of our cutters and surrounded them. We made a distraction on one side of their vessel and another agent and I repelled from a helio."

He nodded in Nectar's direction, "The woman," he said, "nasty piece of work, fired at us. My partner Sergio took one in the chest."

"Oh no, is he okay?" Gian asked, concerned for the wellbeing of a fellow law enforcement agent.

"Thank God for body armor, he's okay. I threw a baton at her, knocking the gun out of her hands and another agent boarding the boat took her down."

Gian shook his head and gave Nectar a repugnant frown.

"And this one?" He inclined his head to Collins.

"Oh, he was much more fun," Schmitt said with a droll smirk.

"Not so easy," he stated, grimacing at the felon. "Son of a gun jumped overboard. Naturally, I dove in after him. After a bit of a squabble in the cold as Siberia water, I subdued him and dragged his sorry butt back to our boat." He stuffed his hands in his jacket pockets.

"I told my higher-ups you had a dog in this show, so our people called your people. And, here we are, one big happy family, right Collins?" He grinned spitefully at the man in cuffs.

Clyde spat on the ground.

After a little more chit chat and transferring of paperwork between the detectives and agents, Torr loaded Clyde, and Veronica hauled Nectar onto the plane and cuffed them to their seats then sat down beside them.

The other agents and the czar said their goodbyes and headed off to their vehicles leaving Gian and Schmitt alone.

"You coming back with us?" Gian asked Schmitt.

"Would like to, hear there's a big lobster festival coming up, sounds delish." The Coast Guard officer licked his lips with an avaricious grin.

"Sadly," he said with regret, tugging thick black gloves onto his hands. "Gotta get back to work. My ship is here waiting on me." He pulled out his phone and scrolled through his photos. He showed a picture to Gian.

"When I'm not working, believe it or not I still like being on the water. Nothing better than the sea and the wind chasing you. This is my personal boat," he held the phone up so Gian could see the sleek sailing vessel.

"I can't wait to get back to her, the Golden Fleece, and my fishing rods. Until then, duty calls." He clicked the phone off and stuffed it in his pocket.

They shook hands. "You ever need us, don't hesitate to call," Paul Schmitt told Gian with a pat to his shoulder.

"Ditto," Gian replied.

The trip back was tiring. The prisoners slept but the officers had to remain alert.

Everyone was glad when the jet landed and Nectar O'Grady and Clyde Collins were carted off to jail to await their days in court.

Chapter Thirty-four

When Gian finally arrived home very late to his apartment, he called Nikki as they were to have a date that night that he had to cancel due to his trip. He grabbed a soda before plopping on his couch.

She answered on the second ring. "Hey, Gian, did everything go okay? You're alright?" She sounded anxious yet happy to hear his voice.

"Yeah," he responded warmly. She had waited up for his call and that gave him pleasurable flutters in his belly. He popped the lid on the can. "All the bad guys are safely tucked away."

"So, they're all going to get their due comeuppance?" Relief eased out of her soft voice.

"Well, trials are never a slam dunk and tend to take forever to come to complete closure, but I'm confident all our evidence is airtight. Naturally, the criminal parties are going to get different degrees of jailtime depending on their part in the whole illicit ordeal from the people involved in all aspects of the drug smuggling to my brothers' shootings to Koh Boone's murder."

Loosening his tie, then taking a sip of his soda, Gian said, "We believe Collins will try to save his own skin, cut some time off his likely long prison sentence and start pointing up the ladder to the bigger players in the game. Eventually we, well, the FBI hope to track the chain all the way to China and elsewhere to cut the head off the snake and stall the making and transporting of the fentanyl, start saving lives before they're ever in danger of overdosing."

"I am so glad it's over and that awful Nectar O'Grady will get what's coming to her. What a horrible person, she has no conscience whatsoever. I feel bad for Mayor O'Grady. The papers say he had nothing to do with any of it and was astounded to find out his wife and sons were involved in this vile business."

"Right. Chip, Oreo and Nectar will face the most time due to Boone's killing, Chip and Oreo for pulling the triggers, and Nectar for conspiracy to commit first degree murder for basically hiring him to do it. They're looking at life without parole. Bambi will share in her own punishment for being a co-conspirator."

He smothered a yawn and patted his pocket for his cigarettes. He reached for his soda instead. After a quick guzzle, he said, "Whatever deals he cuts, Clyde Collins will still be going away for a long, long time as well. He and Nectar also face charges of fraud, money laundering, drug trafficking and a variety of other treacherous crimes."

"You must be terribly exhausted, Gian. All that flying and capturing."

Gian reviewed to her the events of the trip to the border and meeting up with Paul Schmitt.

"That weird guy that hung around the marina and all the women complained about that he was peeping at them? *He* was a cop?" She sounded incredulous at the idea. "He was so…so scruffy and, well, creepy."

Gian chuckled. He recalled how he felt about Schmitt the night he ran into him while he was looking for Boone.

"Yeah, my thoughts exactly, guy was a creeper. But he was playing a part being undercover." He chuckled again at the recollection.

"He did a good job," Nikki laughed.

"Oh yeah. However, he truly is a lieutenant commander with the Coast Guard. He's a brave resourceful officer. Glad he uses his powers for good instead of evil and is on our side. Noble fellow all the way around. He caught Nectar and Clyde so I am deeply indebted to him. If they had made it to Canada, who knows where they would have eventually fled to and hidden."

"Just goes to show you," Nikki laughed, "you can never judge a book by its cover. Everyone had him and that John Michael guy pegged completely wrong. So, what's next for you?"

Gian scrubbed his hand down his face in weariness. It'd been a long few weeks with hard work investigating, flying to Canada and turning the prisoners over to the Department of Corrections for incarceration and serving warrants and charges on them. And it was only going to get longer. He sighed tiredly.

"You don't sound glad this is all over?"

Gian heard the note of concern in her voice. "Oh, I am very glad this is done and we can get justice for Josh and Reece. But," he sighed deeply again. "The lobster fest is coming up in a little over a week and I'll have to go out with my dad and Deo."

That close familial word, *Dad*, was getting easier and easier to say, he thought with gladness in his heart.

"We still have more cleaning and repairing to get ready for the big day when we go pull up the lobster traps and net crabs and whatever else he's commissioned to catch."

"It's hard work, I'm sure," Nicolle commiserated with him.

"We've spent the last month cleaning the traps, labeling them, attaching buoys and dropping them in the ocean. The crates sat in solution for around two weeks then we had to scour and clean them, scrape seaweed and barnacles off them. Good times, that. Many needed repairs. It's tedious hard work and there's still so much to do."

"What's the plan? I mean you, Deo and your father are going out to do the fishing by yourselves?"

Lying back on the cushions, Gian yawned hugely, he tried to mask his fatigue behind a hand. He shook his head like a dog to dispel some of the tiredness that threatened to pull him under. He had looked forward to talking with Nicolle all day and didn't want to tank out on her. He yawned again.

"Gian? Are you falling asleep?"

"Huh," he grunted. "About to. I honestly don't know how we're going to swing it, just Dad, Deo and me. He normally has a 12 to 15+ crew for this once a year extra-large haul, and we're down to just us three and I don't have all those years of experience under my belt. I hope I'm more of a help than a hindrance, but seriously, Nicolle, I just don't see how we're going to pull it off."

"It's called, Go with God, Gian. Pray for help."

"Come on, Nicolle, you can't believe in that crap about prayer and higher powers, all that fairytale business. He's never been there for me when I needed him. Not on the streets when my mother abandoned me, or in the gangs or the military or as a cop. Why would I believe in and ask some deity for help that's never come through for me?"

Derision crept in, but really, he'd never accepted belief in God and all that foolishness.

"Hmmm," Nikki hummed. "I see. So the thought doesn't enter your mind that someone somewhere was looking out for you like when your mother left you on the streets and the gang took you in, that you were maybe saved from a gnarly starvation death, or snatched and sold into child prostitution? Run over by a car?"

"Well, I don't-"

"Didn't the gang members feed you, the women and that Rabbi guy gave you schooling. You told me about your miraculous escape that time in the military when you got shot while being pulled up in the helicopter. You survived. Torrand survived. You don't think there might have been some kind of divine intervention in the works then?"

"I don't think-"

"And this whole investigation. Josh and Reece didn't succumb to their injuries and all the bad guys were caught. You weren't hit that day in the salon. I mean, just the whole thing about your family searching for you when you were missing as a child. They never gave up looking for you.

"And when they found you, they wouldn't let you go. They wrapped you up securely in love and compassion. They were patient, never over forceful, just gently nudging you along until you were brought back home to the family."

"Um, you have a point-"

"You have friends and a loving family, a good job that you are great at. Sure, you're talented and skillful, brilliant and persevering, but you don't think in your entire life there wasn't some…presence that guided you, protected you, helped you. Opened your stone-cold heart into accepting all these gifts?" She sucked in a giant breath and let it out with a huff.

"Think about it sometime. But, right now," Nikki said softly, "go get yourself some much needed shuteye and call me when you have time. Okay?"

Gian was quiet. Her words sent feelings and thoughts swirling around in his tired mind. He never thought about the good things that happened in his life.

He figured it was always luck or skill or karma or a combination of the three. He would meditate on her words while he settled down to sleep. In about two minutes.

"Gian? Are you asleep?" she said very quietly in case he was.

"No. Soon. Okay. It's great to hear your voice, Nicolle." He smiled into the phone picturing her in pajamas, her hair mussed, beautiful blue eyes heavy with sleep, and thought about the day they might be sleeping together. Permanently.

The shock of this musing thought no longer surprised, or scared him. His life was changing, and only for the better. For once, he looked forward to the future.

It appeared bright, happy, loving and full with…yeah, a wife and children. And certainly a dog. Yes, they'd definitely need a dog…and maybe a cat. Perhaps they should start out small with a hamster or a turtle until they got the hang of being parents.

"Um, Gian, are you there?"

They said goodnight, happy dreams, and Gian promised to call her tomorrow.

He had some tying up strings to do at work, he needed to get all his reports done, and start on a new case he already got handed.

Because in a week he would be on the high seas before dawn, just him, Deo and their dad.

Oh crap.

Chapter Thirty-five

*E*ven though he had worked long hard hours and saw Nicolle only a handful of times for a quick lunch or late dinner, Gian felt refreshed the day he went to join his father at the marina.

Deo and his dad had brought the supplies to the Seabug last night.

The weather was cool, but not frigid like in Canada. The wind tousled his hair slightly and tugged at his clothes. He wore a midnight blue thermal and dark cargo pants.

The day the lobster festival was planned for was predicted to be dry, sunny and high 60's. It'd be perfect for a day outside with friends and family, music and food.

If he wasn't expected to provide the bulk of the food, AKA lobster, crab, fish, he would be looking forward to spending the day with Nicolle and his family. His hand automatically patted his pocket for his smokes. He wondered how long it would take before he stopped doing that.

But, alas, he had some hard work ahead of him. Fortunately, hard work never scared him. He never shied away from the tough duties, the chasing of rebels or criminals, the long sleepless nights spent protecting the country or getting the bad guys off the streets.

What's a few dozens and dozens of lobster crates to be hauled out of the deep blue ocean to be measured and claws taped, or dragging up the nets teeming with crabs to be bagged and tagged, or reeling in and unhooking the huge bass, bluefish or tuna?

Gian gave himself a pep talk. Last thing he wanted was for his father or Deo to think he was a reluctant whiny participant, that he didn't want to be there helping them. They needed him, and by damn, he'd do his duty. With a damn smile on his face. Dammit.

He parked in the marina lot near the water and traipsed over freshly mown grass to the docks. His boots thunked on the metal docks as he made his way to the slip assigned to the Seabug.

Holding a hand over his eyes to shade them from the sun that was just peeking over the horizon, he gazed out over the water. Thank goodness the water was only a bit choppy, not too bad. The wind was more of a breeze and that held the waves calmer.

He looked down, fat fish swam in circles hoping for a tidbit or tossed bait. Dragonflies still hopped and danced above the water, teasing and tantalizing the hungry fish.

Spotting the Seabug bobbing gently on the sapphire sea, Gian hurried his steps.

Jed had wanted to get started before the sun rose and Gian was running a tad late due to a train that halted traffic for a long time, causing him some agitation in making his father get a late start.

"Yo," he called out as he approached the boat. Expecting to see his dad and Deo only as he hopped on board, Gian's mouth dropped and his eyes popped when he saw they weren't alone. In fact, they had company. Lots of company.

"What the-"

"Hey son, welcome aboard! Look who's come to help us!" Jed shouted joyfully as he greeted Gian with a hug.

Gian stood gaping at the crowd that stood gathered behind his dad.

"But, what on earth-" he spluttered as he took in the group grinning boisterously behind Jed. Some waved, a few giggled, others just grinned broadly.

Not only Deo was there, but so were Torr, Conny Vinci, Simon Nucacher, Lieutenant Huxley McKay, FBI agent John

Michael, Deputies Kristian, Charles, Stewart and Nikola, Agent Veronica Cleaver, Dr. Audrey Gregg, Scientist Val Proffer.

Standing beside Sergeant Lydia Carlson was Nicolle's friend Bobby Brown giving him a little wave. Also present were Etta Lou Hanken, Pat Hooper, Karen and Pete Audet, several other men he didn't know, and the most shocking hunkering amongst the crowd was Tex Coltrane.

"I don't understand," Gian ground out, flabbergasted. "What are all of you doing here?"

"Well duh, G-man." Conny Vinci stepped towards Gian with a sniggering grin. "We're here to help!"

"Help?" Gian repeated with his eyes darting back and forth and all over the crowd, all smiling ear-to-ear at him.

"Yeppers," Conny said. "Your girlie there," he nodded at Nikki Kelly, "she did this."

Stepping from behind Conny, Nikki stood pink-cheeked and with a small unsure smile on her face. She appeared not sure she'd done the right thing and was holding her breath for Gian's reaction.

So dumbfounded at the turn out, "She did this?" Gian could only uselessly repeat what Conny said.

"Yes," Deo came up to his brother. "She was worried for us, so she called Lieutenant McKay and asked if he knew of anyone that could help out." He spread his arms out to showcase the group. "And lucky for us, he did!"

"What do you say, Son?" Jed asked his bemused son.

While Gian gathered his wits, a few others approached him.

Simon Nucacher gestured to the handsome young man beside him with clove-colored skin and blinding white teeth.

"This is my cousin, Thomas, he actually has experience with lobstering and fishing, and he can help captain the boat as well."

A few others moved up and introduced themselves. They were deputies from another division.

Soon, everyone was mingling and talking and laughing as Jed started to give out orders.

Gian found a few of the women surrounding him chattering. "This is hard work, ladies," he said with a frown. "I'm not sure you can do-"

"Oh posh," Etta Lou Hanken snorted. "I was practically born on boats. Deep sea fishing all my life and sailed mostly around the world with friends as crewmates. I can do this, Detective, don't you worry your pretty little head about me," she chided and then left them to join the men who were getting ready to get the ship heading out.

Dr. Audrey Gregg informed Gian, "We women may look frail and useless, but we can help too. Veronica, Bobby and I can measure the lobsters and attach the bands on their claws. We can check for the undersized and the females with roe and let them back into the ocean to have their babies. Plus, we can help the trapped critters like turtles that shouldn't be in the nets and crates run free."

"Pat and I can label and tag the sacks of shrimp and crabs they haul in," Lydia Carlson advised him. "At the 50 per person per day limit on Jonah and Blue crabs, that's a ton of crabs to bag and tag!"

"I obtained the fishing licenses and permits for all the fishers, and Karen Audet and I purchased the food and we'll provide sustenance for everyone," Val Proffer said proudly.

Karen nodded vehemently beside her. "We are women inexperienced with the sea life, but we are not helpless or useless!"

Gian's stepmother Jessica was there as well. She came up and gave Gian a big hug. She stepped back and smiled tenderly up at him.

"You see, Gian, all you had to do was open your heart a teeny tiny bit and let us slink in. You have friends and family that love you, and us, and well, just good people who want to help. All you have to do, is let them."

On her tiptoes, Jessica kissed Gian's cheek then went to help wherever she could.

Gian was left standing with Tex Coltrane. "What the hell are you doing here, you old reprobate?" Gian said with a smile.

Tex hitched up his belt with the king-sized, silver bullhorn buckle and chewed on the ever present half-smoked but currently unlit cigar dangling out of his mouth.

"Well, boy," he said with a jokingly condescending smirk. "I always say, if ya can't beat 'em, join 'em." He huffed and punched Gian not exactly gently in the upper arm.

Tex started to walk away, then turned back and snapped gruffly, "Get a boot on, boy. You ain't here to catch some rays and a lovely tan out on the water, them lobsters ain't gonna haul themselves into the boat. Let's go!" He loped off to join the men already in progress of releasing the boat and readying the tools and equipment for the day's work.

Shaking his head in disbelief, "Will wonders never cease, I can't believe-"

Nikki was standing in front of him with her shy smile. "Is it all right? You're not mad, are you?"

He gazed at the beautiful girl with shimmering eyes and a heart filled with gold staring fondly and uncertainly up at him. Gian recalled the words Jessica had told him that day at the clambake:

Her red brows had knitted together as Jessica said to him, "When you find the one, Gian, the arrow through your heart, you won't think ball and chain, you'll think safety, support, an easing of your heart even as your breath quickens at the sight of her."

Gian realized in that split second, Nicolle Kelly was the whole package. Heart and soul, kindness, smarts, ambitious, compassionate and thoughtful, not to mention so lovely it made his eyes spin to look at her. She was everything a man, him, could want in a woman; a friend, a wife, a mother to his children.

"Yes, Nicolle, you did good, real good. I don't know how to thank you, but I'm gonna try real damned hard to do everything I can to show you how much you mean to me." He held his arms out and his head cocked to the side.

Nikki hesitated all of half a second, then ran into his arms. She wrapped her arms around his neck, his hands spread over her back to hold her tight and their lips found each other, soft, plush, wanting, needing, happy at last.

Gian had finally found home. His home. A fantastic loving family, great friends and the love of his life. It had been a rough ride, but heck, it was sure worth the struggles.

His painful turbulent path led him to a new life filled with wonderment, peace, and joy. Now he just needed the dog. Or cat. Bird? He always thought tortoises were kind of neat. Maybe-

"Hey lovebirds!" Torr called out from the bow. "This ain't no Loveboat cruise you know! Get moving and pull your weight!"

His laugh reverberating off the tossing waters, he ignored the gesture Gian shot him behind Nikki's back and stalked off to get the ball rolling with Jed and his new, albeit temporary yet eager crew.

Epilogue

"Well!" Mayor Gator O'Grady exclaimed. "I must say the festival is a screaming success! Thanks to you and your family and friends, Gian my boy!"

Gator had dropped a few pounds what with all the infamous notoriety of his crooked family, court dates, and negative press and attention.

But he never lost his jolly glow and good-natured smile and friendly laugh. It also helped having the pretty and voluptuous young thing on his arm.

It should have been downright chilly, but the day turned into a beautiful Indian summer afternoon. The sun was bright making it pleasantly warm, overhead the sky blazed blue. A soft breeze spun the smells of seafood roasting and burgers grilling throughout the hodgepodge of merry visitors.

Gian greeted the mayor and inclined his head to the woman. At his arched brow of curiosity towards the lady, Gator chuckled and introduced them.

"This is Skylar Bowman Darling, you know her mother our town councilwoman, Blake Darling Corbett. You've met Blake's sister, Captain Pamela Darling of the Chicory Landing County Sheriff's Office."

"Pleasure to meet you," Gian said to Skylar. "I do know your mother and sister. They both have done great things for our community."

Gator beamed at the praise for his friend. “Sky here is my new campaign manager. She’s gonna help me with my media platform and all the stuff that goes into that! I’m sure she will do a tremendously better job than Chip did, Bless that fool’s soul.”

Gator shook his head in sadness and disgrace at all the evilness his kin had caused during their illegal pursuits. “She has more than half a brain to rub together, doncha honey?”

He squeezed her waist. “Girl has her Master’s in polysci, top 1% in her class, not just a pretty face, eh?”

“Ah, well, I’m sure she will do a fine job for you, Mayor.” Gian was at a loss as to what to say. Gator was just glossing over his son’s involvement in the whole unsavory criminal debacle.

“Oh sure, sure she will. She’s got great stamina, doncha baby?” Gator said to Gian, “She’s won national competitions for track at Uni, she’s a helluva runner, right honey?”

“Well,” Gian glanced around looking for an escape. “I hope you all the best, Mayor. You’re able to put the whole nasty business behind you and move on.”

“Oh yes, my constituents feel sorry for me. I thought they’d turn away because I was duped for so long, but,” he grinned and squeezed Sky. “They are actually rooting for me. I think my chances are good, real good for re-election.”

He wheezed slightly then reached out and shook Gian’s hand.

“Again, thanks to you and yours and the colossal haul you brought in. It totally made this festival! It’ll go down in record books you mark my word! People come from all over to attend this festival and I must repeat, it’s a complete success!”

“It could not have been done without the help of many people, Mayor. So many friends and deputies, many hands pitched in to help us provide the feast for this special day.”

Gian still couldn’t believe the people that showed up on the Seabug to offer their assistance.

He had been shocked to see fellow detectives Conny Vinci and Simon Nucacher, and new friends like FBI Agent John Michael and his LT. Of course, the most surprising aid came from Tex Coltrane the cantankerous ‘ol Texan himself.

"Yeah well, ah, I've got to be, I mean I need to, oh, there's my dad waving for me. I'm sure he needs my help with the grills or you know, whatnot."

"Sure, sure," Gator grinned hugely, squeezing Sky and kissing the tip of her cute nose.

As Gian fled the scene, he saw Nicolle was standing with his father and Jessica.

Deo raised a beer in salute to Gian as he made his way to them.

Josh and Reece were sitting on chairs as they were still a little weak, but there was a bevy of beauties surrounding them bringing them food and drink like they were princes.

His family pulled him in with hugs and pats and kisses on the cheek, that was Jessica's teachings.

"Hey," Deo said when Gian had joined the group. "We're going to take another run at finding our biological mom. It was Jessica's idea. She thinks we need closure. What do you think about that?"

"I think I need a beer." He shook his head in a noncommittal way and looked to where Nicolle was standing.

Nicolle stood shyly as always, to the side, not sure of her place in the clutch of happy kin. Well, soon she'd know her place, right beside him.

Gian stepped over to Nicolle and reached out to her. He took her hand and pulled her to join his family.

Her tea shop was designated to have its grand opening in a few months. He didn't want to take the attention from that thrilling event, so the ring burning a hole in his pocket would have to wait.

The day he slides that ring on her finger and makes Nicolle his in front of family, friends, co-workers and the world will be one of the happiest days of his life.

Tomorrow, it's back to the daily detective grind of chasing down perps and investigating crimes.

But for today, he'd wallow in his family's love, and the adoration shining in Nicolle's lovely eyes when they lit on him. And lobster, lots and lots of delicious red bugs!

"Come on, Son," Jed called to him while waving a spatula in the air. "Join us!"

His family gathered him up, and Jed said, beaming with delight, "Yeah, this is what it's all about, eh? Family."

And lobster.

The End

Dear Reader, thank you for choosing Murder in Maverick Bay!

I know you could have picked any number of books to read, but you chose this novel and for that I am extremely grateful.

I hope you enjoyed this story, and if you did, please leave a review where you acquired it, and look for other exciting titles in my name!

About the Author

Louise Furley loves writing suspense stories and sharing them. Sunny Florida is home where she is a graduate of St. Thomas University with a master's degree, and lives with Bob, her own hero.

Louise is the author of numerous published novels. When not researching or writing, she is dreaming of unique plots, and discovering fresh ventures she hasn't yet experienced in the world. Ride along with her as she travels new and thrilling journeys!

Enjoy life, everyone, and God Bless.

www.ingramcontent.com/pod-product-compliance
Lightning Source LLC
LaVergne TN
LVHW090557110826
845146LV00001B/159

* 9 7 9 8 9 9 5 3 5 8 1 0 7 *